CW01281386

"And mirrors.

She looks at you

from mirrors..."

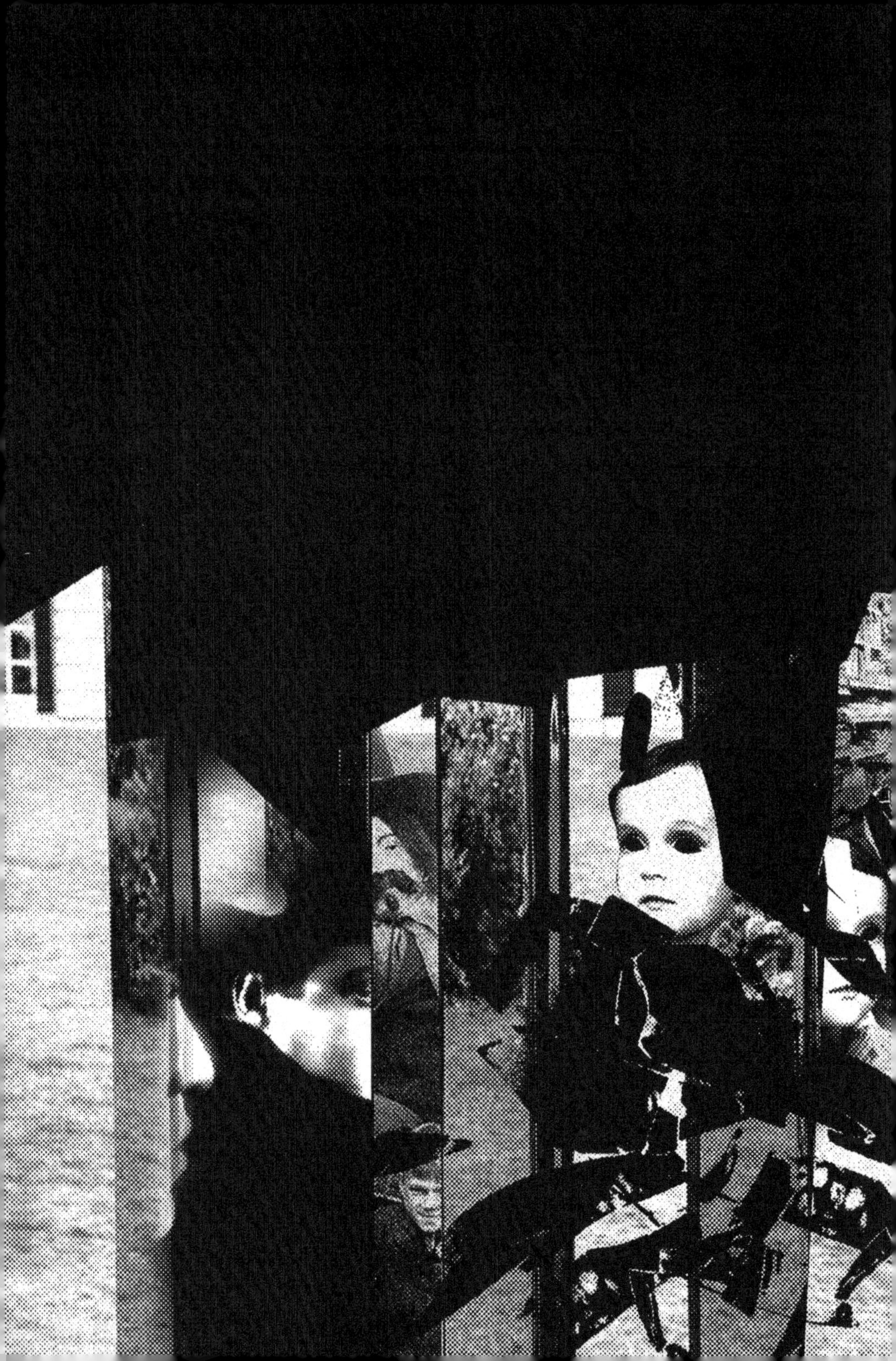

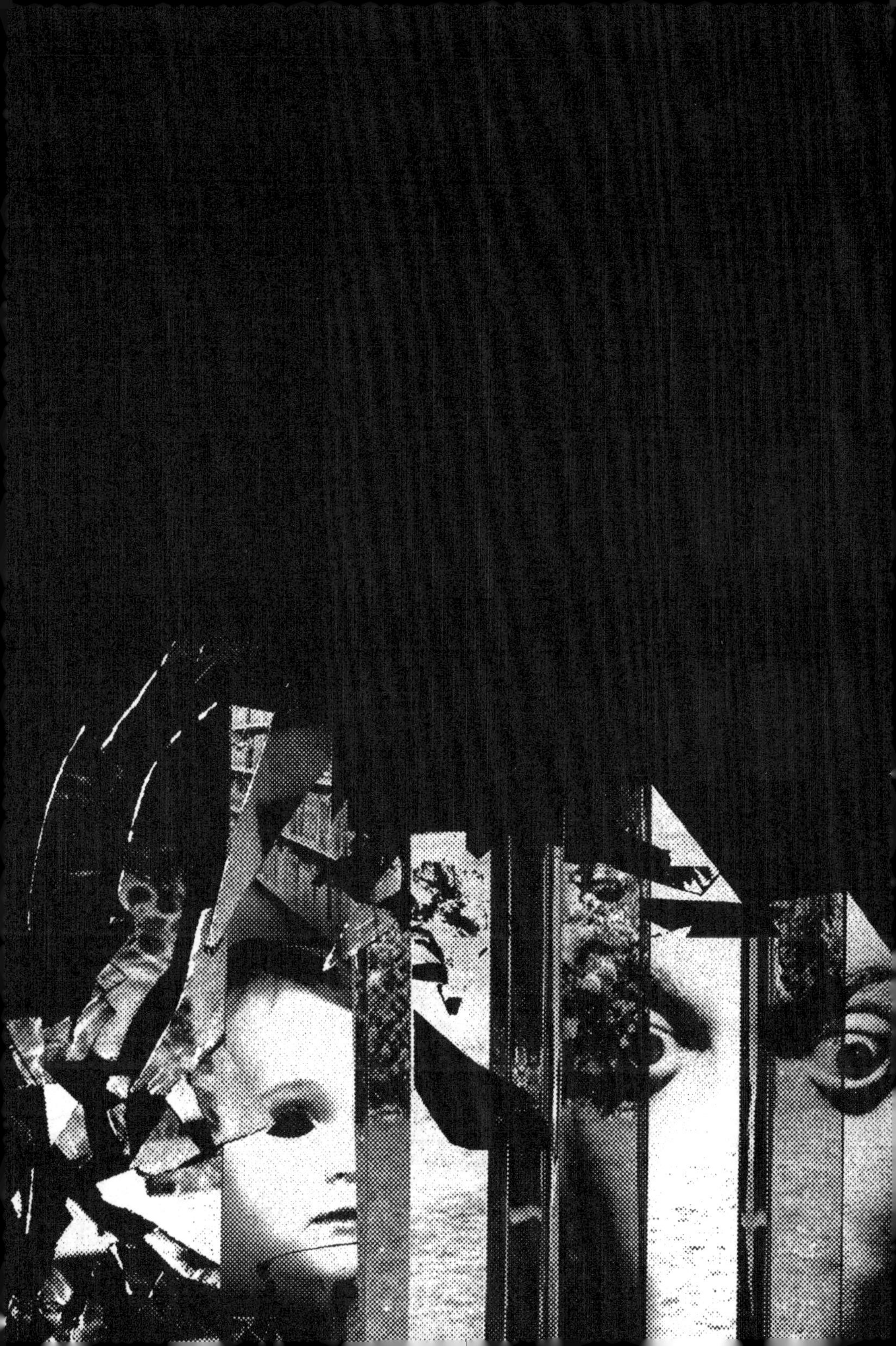

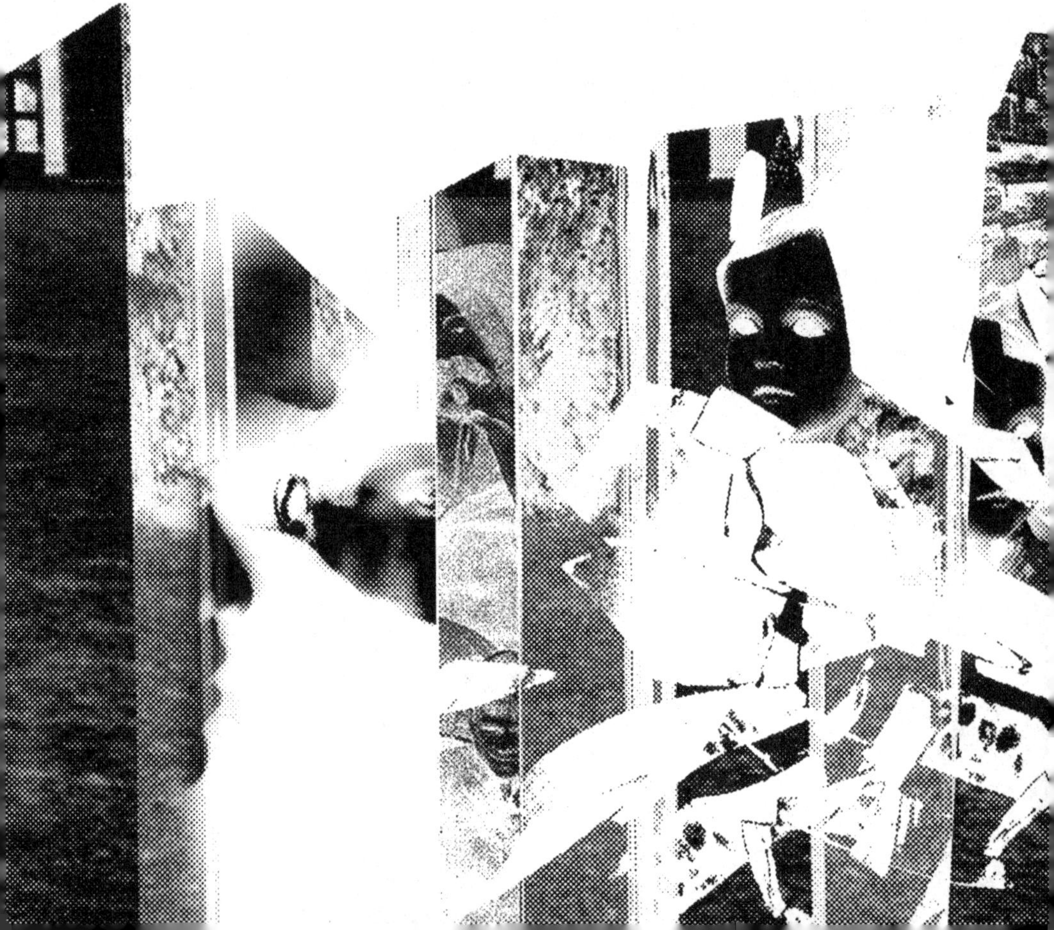

THE PARTS WE PLAY

STEPHEN VOLK

To Pat, Best wishes, SVolk

The Parts We Play
Copyright © 2016 Stephen Volk

The right of Stephen Volk to be identified as Author of this Work has been asserted by him in accordance with the Copyright, Designs and Patents Act 1988.

Published in October 2016 by PS Publishing Ltd by arrangement with the author.
All rights reserved by the author.

FIRST PS EDITION

ISBN
978-1-78636-021-2 (Signed edition)
978-1-78636-020-5 (Unsigned edition)

This book is a work of fiction. Names, characters, places and incidents either are products of the author's imagination or are used fictitiously. Any resemblance to actual events or locales or persons, living or dead, is entirely coincidental.

Author photo by Phil Walters.
Cover and book design by Pedro Marques.
Text set in Sabon. Titles set in Cooper Plate Roman HPLHS and LLRubberGrotesque.

Printed in England by the T.J. International
on Vancouver Cream Bookwove 80 gsm stock.

PS Publishing Ltd
Grosvenor House
1 New Road
Hornsea, HU18 1PG
England
E-mail: editor@pspublishing.co.uk
Visit our website at www.pspublishing.co.uk.

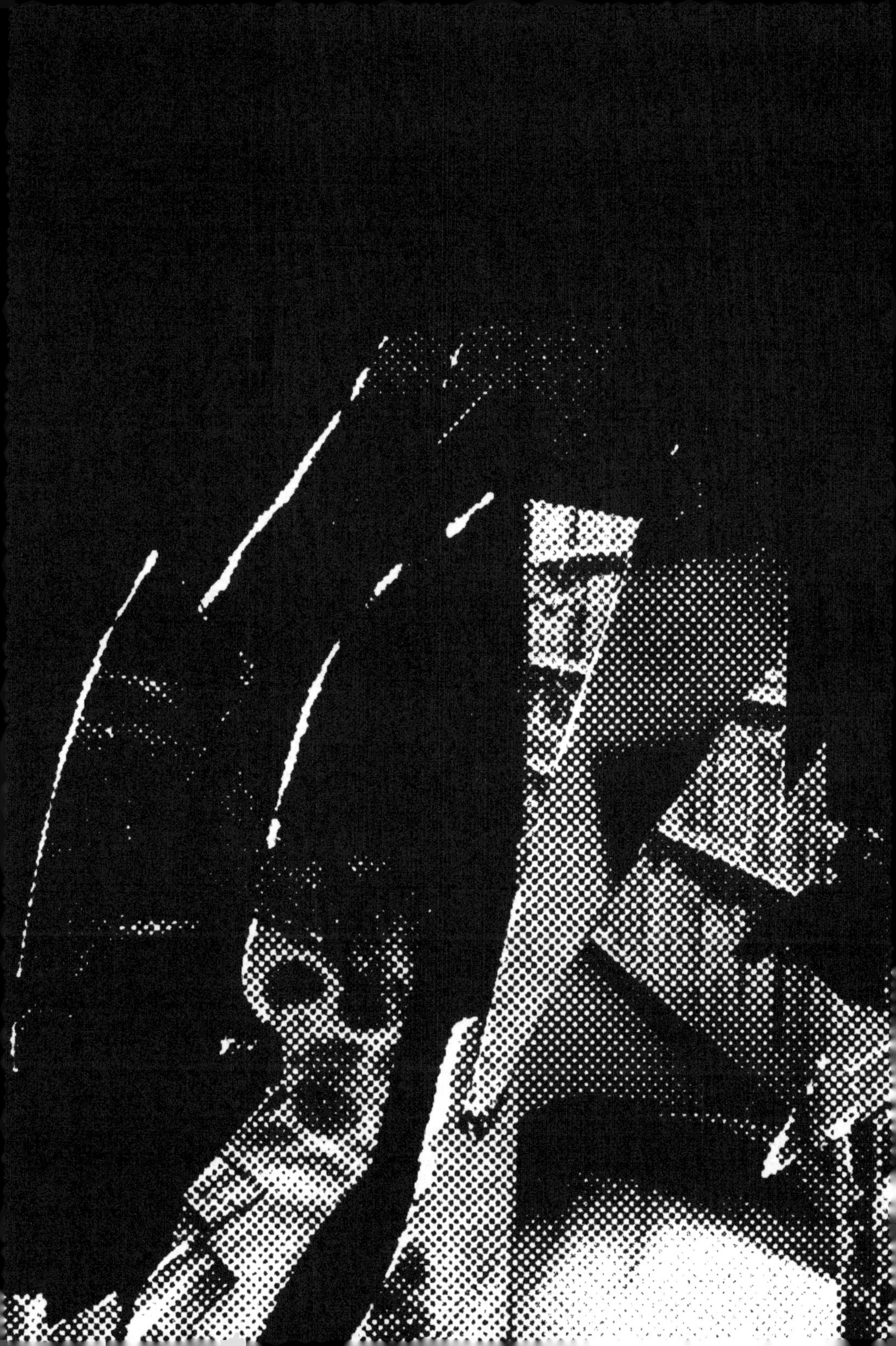

CONTENTS

ACKNOWLEDGEMENTS .... *XIII*

"HORROR AND HEARTBREAK" BY NATHAN BALLINGRUD .... *XV*

CELEBRITY FRANKENSTEIN *1*

BLESS *17*

A WHISPER TO A GREY *45*

THE ARSE-LICKER *69*

THE PETER LORRE FAN CLUB *89*

CERTAIN FACES *111*

WITH ALL MY LOVE ALWAYS ALWAYS FOREVER XXX *149*

MATILDA OF THE NIGHT *153*

THE SHUG MONKEY *199*

WRONG *231*

THE MAGICIAN KELSO DENNETT *253*

NEWSPAPER HEART *281*

STORY NOTES *333*

ACKNOWLEDGEMENTS

Thanks must be exuded to Nathan Ballingrud for his introduction, to Peter and Nicky Crowther and all at PS Publishing for making this book happen, and to Pedro Marques for designing it. I owe a great debt of gratitude also to those individual editors who first helped these stories see the light of day. The works originally appeared as follows:

—"Celebrity Frankenstein" in Exotic Gothic 4/Postscripts 28–29, ed. Danel Olson (PS Publishing, 2012); reprinted in The Mammoth Book of Best New Horror Vol. 24, ed. Stephen Jones (Constable & Robinson, 2013).

—"Bless" in Crimewave 12: Hurts, ed. Andy Cox (TTA Press, 2013).

—"A Whisper to a Grey" in All Hallows 41, ed. Barbara Roden (Ash Tree Press, February 2006).

—"The Arse-Licker" in Anatomy of Death (In Five Sleazy Pieces) ed. Mark West (Hersham Horror Books, 2013); reprinted in Best British Horror 2014, ed. Johnny Mains (Salt Publishing).

—"The Peter Lore Fan Club" in The Burning Circus, ed. Johnny Mains (BFS Publications, 2013).

—"Certain Faces" in Doorways, ed. Steve Lockley (Screaming Dreams, 2008).

—"With All My Love Always Always XXX" as an online Christmas story, ed. Michael Wilson (This Is Horror website).

—"Matilda of the Night" in Terror Tales of Wales, ed. Paul Finch (Gray Friar Press, 2014); reprinted in Best New Horror #26, ed. Stephen Jones (PS Publishing, 2015).

—"The Shug Monkey" in Professor Challenger: New Worlds Lost Places, ed. J. R. Campbell and Charles Prepolec (Edge Science Fiction and Fantasy Publishing, 2015).

—"Wrong" in The 2nd Spectral Book of Horror Stories, ed. Mark Morris (Spectral Press, 2015).

—"The Magician Kelso Dennett" in Terror Tales of the Seaside, ed. Paul Finch (Gray Friar press, 2013); reprinted in Best British Horror 2014, ed. Johnny Mains (Salt Publishing).

—"Newspaper Heart" in The Spectral Book of Horror Stories, ed. Mark Morris (Spectral Press, 2014); short-listed for the Shirley Jackson Award, 2015; winner, British Fantasy Award 2015 for Best Novella.

HORROR AND HEARTBREAK

by NATHAN BALLINGRUD

LET ME GET RIGHT TO THE POINT: Stephen Volk is one of the finest writers of horror fiction working today. Top three, easily. Easily. He's one of a small handful of writers whose books I'll buy on the strength of the author's name alone. A while ago, after reading his majestic novella *Leytonstone*, I contacted Gray Friar Press, his principle publisher to that date, and ordered his entire back catalogue at once. I've never done that with any other writer, and it was a decision that's paid me back tenfold since. In this new collection, *The Parts We Play*, we're presented with a survey of the best of his short fiction published over the last several years, which makes it some of the best horror fiction produced during that span, full stop.

That's really all you need to know, and in the rest of this introduction I'll only be telling you things you're about to discover for yourself anyway. That being said, I never turn down an opportunity to talk about the things that I love, so I'm going to keep going anyway.

Those of you already familiar with Volk will know that he's a highly regarded screenwriter, perhaps most famous for the notorious television show *Ghostwatch*, though he's written much else besides (*Gothic* and the miniseries *Midwinter of the Spirit* being notable examples). So it won't be a surprise to discover that the mystique surrounding movies and television, and those that star in them, is a recurring theme in these stories. In the gruesome satire "Celebrity Frankenstein", Volk examines the strange culture of instant celebrity in the era of reality television, while in "The Peter Lorre Fan Club" he explores the way we relate to the stars we watch on the screen throughout the years. "The Magician Kelso Dennett" gives us a famous magician televising his most dangerous magic trick yet, and the effect it has on the people who wait on the periphery of the camera's eye.

Running more deeply than the influence of cinema, though, is the cultural and geographical identity these stories share. They are fundamentally British, drawing their energy from the folklore and the rich literary heritage of the United Kingdom. Stories like "A Whisper to a Grey" and "The Shug Monkey" call back to the traditonal of supernatural investigators and adventuring champions of science, with the latter story featuring Arthur Conan Doyle's Professor Challenger and his companions staring into an unexpected abyss. British folklore crawls to life in "Matilda of the Night", where a folklorist haunts the bedside of a dying woman convinced she's seen the creature which will carry her soul away; and the devastating "Newspaper Heart," in which a lonely little boy befriends an effigy destined for the bonfires on Guy Fawkes Night.

There are tales which will draw blood, too. Nestled in this book like a razor blade in a piece of Halloween candy is "The Arse-Licker", perhaps the grossest story I've read since Chuck Palahniuk's "Guts". This story about the subjugation of self-respect in service to desperate careerism is the better work, though, defined as it is by its bruised heart and its righteous moral fury. "Bless" is a brutal illustration of the purest expression of love pursued to the point of derangement.

But there's something more to Volk's stories than their elegance, their precision, and their wrathful wit. Something more insubstantial, more difficult to pinpoint. What is it, for me, that separates a Volk story from the pack?

To find it, you have to look closely. You have to let the surge of the plot roll by, you have to wait for the shock of horror and heartbreak to pass. Then you look at the story again, and the details that elevate the work start to become clear.

There's a moment, early on in "Matilda of the Night", in which the protagonist visits an elderly woman in her room at an assisted care facility. She is frail, and she does not expect to live much longer. Part of the reason for that is the engine of horror which drives this story, but mostly it's just because she's very old, and her life is naturally winding down. As the visitor sets up his recording equipment, prepared to interview her in pursuit of his interest in a particular bit of folklore, he notices that she has affixed post-it notes to all of her belongings, color-coded according to whom they are meant for, once she's gone. It's a detail that has no bearing on the story; it's simply a grace note, a pristine little window into this woman's character.

That's one. Now look at this, from "Certain Faces":

The protagonist, a painter this time, is meeting some people in a cafe; she's trying to get a physical sense of them, to suss out their suitability for her project, before committing to paying them to sit for a session. One of the potential models is a young woman named Vicky, whom our protagonist sums up as being particularly unremarkable: "But there was nothing natural there. It was all received wisdom, a Baywatch, Tatler sort of beauty, a copycat creation, something manufactured for men, an advertisement, not a person with anything underneath, and ultimately banal, like someone who works in a building society and everyone tells her she should be a model, and she believes them."

Unlike in the first example, the summation of Vicky's character from a quick study of her face is relevant to the story's theme. But both serve as illustrations of why Stephen Volk is one of my favorite writers of fiction today—horror or otherwise. He writes terrific horror stories, yes—atmospheric, spooky, often heartbreaking, sometimes violent—but a lot of folks are writing terrific horror stories these days. What sets Volk apart is that first and foremost, he writes with meticulous precision about what it feels like to be a human being.

Horror fiction is uniquely suited to address the human condition—the yearning for love, the complicated mechanisms by which we navigate our fear of extinction through every human interaction—but it's surprising to me how rarely it's used toward that end. Most of it succumbs to the temptations of the archetypes, littering itself with characters who exist only to service the culmination of the plot. There are some fine, celebrated horror stories that fit under that umbrella, to be sure. But the ones that most thoroughly satisfy me flip that paradigm: horror is the tool by which character is revealed, not the other way around. You'll find that to be true for much of its best practitioners. Shirley Jackson, in *The Haunting of Hill House* and *We Have Always Lived in the Castle*. Peter Straub, in *Ghost Story* and *Shadowland*. And Stephen Volk, here, and in just about everything else he's written.

My favorite story in this book—and that's saying something—is "Wrong". According to certain narrow definitions, it might not even qualify as a horror story. (It is.) It's about a young man renting a room from an eccentric elderly couple. He builds a kind of relationship with them, as one does when renting in such an intimate setting, and he comes to learn something interesting about them. I won't say any more, of course, because you should discover it along with him. But I will tell you that the story's considerable power does not come from the reveal, satisfying as it is; the power comes from the beautiful denouement, in which the huge, generous heart which informs all of these stories is most clearly and vividly expressed.

Stephen Volk understands that sometimes love is grotesque, and sometimes—maybe even most of the time—horror disguises the most astonishing beauty.

So, yes, these are great horror stories. But more than that, they're great stories about rage, and pain, and loneliness, and love. They tell the human story the way only the best horror fiction can. And no one tells that story better than Stephen Volk.

Nathan Ballingrud
July 4, 2016
Asheville, NC

THE PARTS WE PLAY

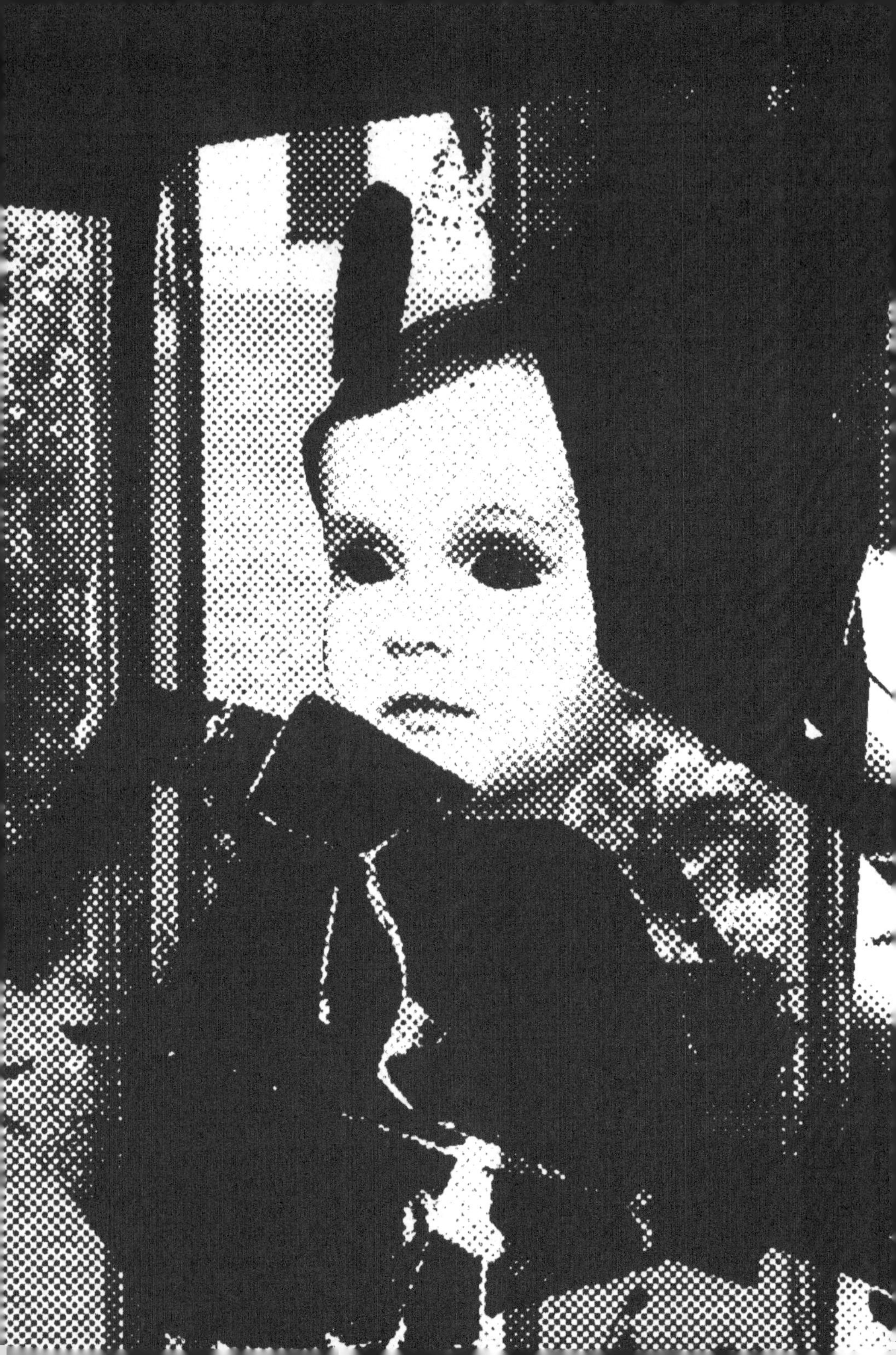

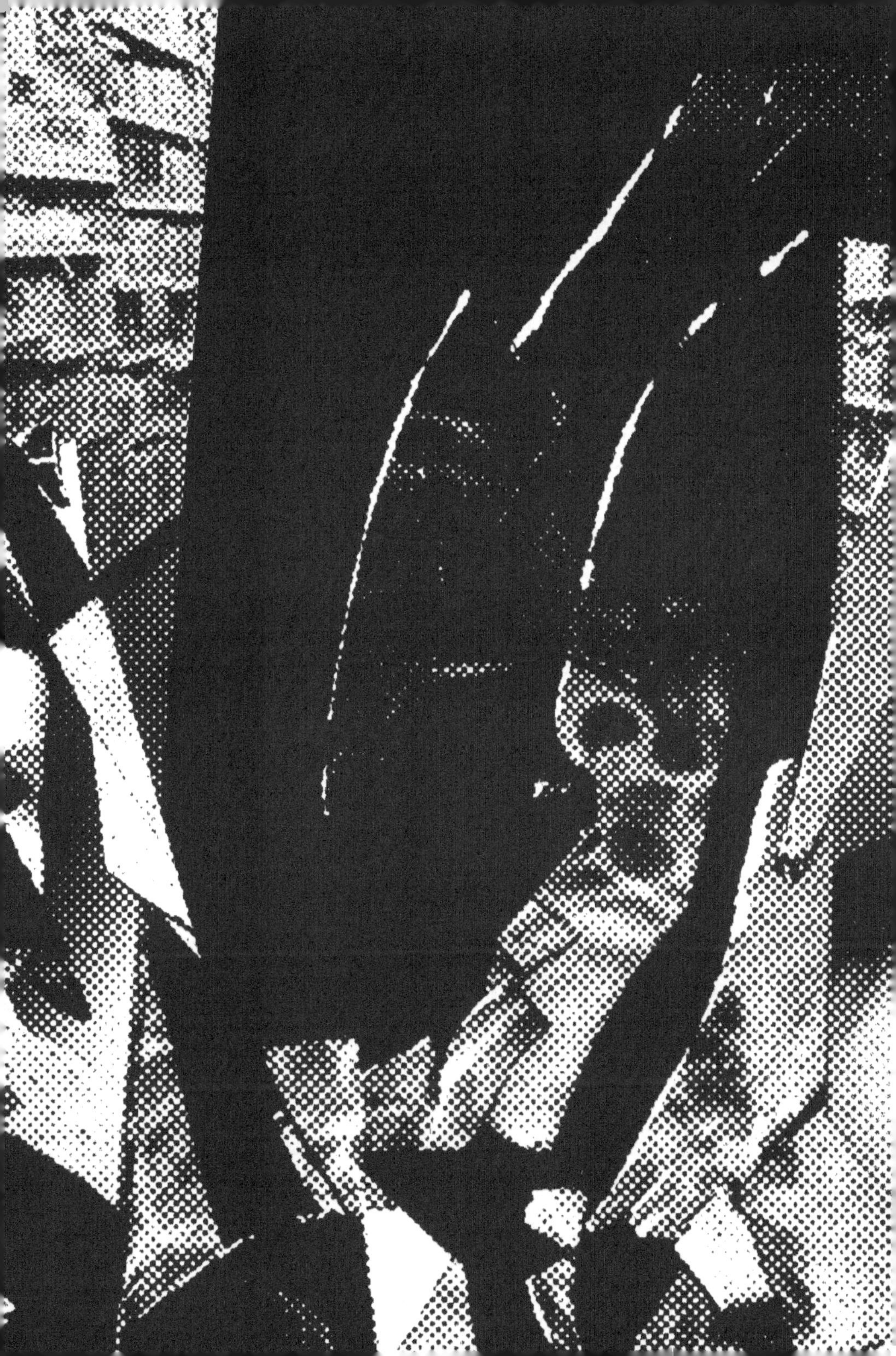

For Pat
. . . who says I'm not a
'horror' writer . . .

And for my grandsons:
George Cartmel and
Henry Cartmel
(when they are old enough)

*I'm not afraid of witches,
hobgoblins, apparitions,
boastful giants, knaves or
varlets, etc., not indeed any
kind of beings except
human beings.*
Goya
(letter to Martin Zapater, 1784)

*What pleases is what
is terrible, gentle, and poetic.*
Georges Franju

*Sometimes it feels like
my shadow's casting me.*
Warren Zevon
("Dirty Life and Times")

Art is always a witness.
Christian Boltanski

CELEBRITY FRANKENSTEIN

IN MY MIND THE GAP WAS NON-EXISTENT between falling asleep and waking up, but of course weeks had gone by. Obviously. There were many procedures to be done and each one had to be recovered from, and stabilized from, groggily, still under, before the next began. I had no idea of the doctors taking over in shifts, or working in tandem, to achieve the program-makers' aims. I was out of it. Meanwhile the video footage of the surgery circled the world. Screen grabs jumping from cell to cell. I learned later that at the moment the titles began running on the final segment of the Results show, we'd already had the highest ratings the network had ever had. *Any* network ever had. This was history, if I but knew it. If I was awake. Then I *was* awake...

Salvator's eyes took a while to focus. Some filmy bits floated in the general opaqueness like rats' tails, which troubled me for a few seconds. That and a certain lack of pain which came from being pumped with 100%-proof Christ-knows-what anaesthetic and various other chemicals swashed together in a cocktail to keep me stable. The *new* me, that is. If you could call it 'me' at all.

I raised a hand to examine it front and back. It was Murphy's hand, unmistakably. I'd know that blunt-ended thumb and slightly twisted pinkie anywhere. The tan ended at the stitches, where it was attached to Vince Pybus's tattooed arm. I revolved it slightly, feeling the pull in my forearm muscles—not that they were mine at all. Except they were. I had this tremendous urge to yell something obscene, but I remembered being counselled not to do that on live TV for legal and other reasons, not least being the show might get instantly pulled. But the word 'Fuck' seemed appropriate, given a new entity had been given life, of a sort, with no actual 'fucking' involved. As befits suitable family entertainment. Primetime.

Anticipating my thoughts, some guardian angel out of my field of vision put an oxygen mask over my mouth—whose mouth? I felt a coldness not on my lips but on Finbar's, wider and more feminine than mine, a Jim Morrison pout—and I drank the air greedily: it stopped the feeling of nausea that was rising up from my guts. Or somebody's, anyway.

I raised my other hand and it was trembling. It also happened to be African American, muscled and smooth. My man Anthony's. I flattened its palm and ran it over my chest, hairless, Hispanic, down to the hard, defined muscles of Rico's stomach. Maybe alarmingly, I didn't have to stifle a scream but a laugh. And almost as if it wanted to drown me out in case I did, up came the Toccata and Fugue, blasting loud enough to make the walls of Jericho crumble, and my hospital table tilted up, thirty, forty-five degrees, and shielding my eyes with Anthony's hand from the army of studio lights, I blinked, trying to make out the sea of the audience beyond.

"Are you ready for the mirror?" said a voice.

It was Doctor Bob and I saw him now, brown eyes twinkling above the paper mask, curly hair neatly tucked under the lime-green medical cap. I nodded. As I had to. It was in my contract, after all.

I looked at Moritz's face as the reflection looked back. Long, lean, pale—not un-handsome, but not Moritz either. Finbar's lips, fat and engorged, maybe enhanced a little cosmetically while we were all under, gave him a sensuality the real Moritz lacked. Moritz, who lay somewhere backstage with his face removed, waiting for a donor. Next to armless Vince and armless Anthony, a fond tear in their eyes no doubt to see a part of them taken away and made famous. I saw, below a brow irrigated with a railway-track of stitches where the skull had been lifted off like a lid and my brain had been put in,

Salvator's darkly Spanish eyes gazing back at me like no eyes in any mirror in Oblong, Illinois. Blind Salvator, now, who was sitting backstage, whose grandfather had been blind also, but had only eked out a rotten existence as a beggar on the streets of Valladolid. Yet here was Salvator his eyeless grandson, rich and American, and about to be richer still from the story he now had to tell, and sell. Salvator could see nothing now—true, but he had seen a future, at least.

"Wow," I said.

Doctor Bob and the other Judges were standing and applauding in front of me now, wearing their surgical scrubs and rubber gloves. Doctor Jude's cut by some fashion house in Rodeo Drive, her hair stacked high and shining. The gloves made a shrill, popping sound. Doctor Bob's facemask hung half off from one ear. I was still in a haze, but I think they each said their bit praising us.

"I always believed in you guys."

"You're the real deal. That was fantastic."

"You know what's great about you? You never complained and you never moaned in this whole process."

It was the Host speaking next. Hand on my shoulder. Sharp charcoal suit, sharp white grin: "Great comments from the Doctors. What do you think of that? Say something to the audience."

With Alfry Linquist's voice, I said: "Awesome."

Soon the clip was on YouTube. Highest number of hits ever.

I got out of the hospital bed and they handed me a microphone. I sang the single that was released that Christmas and went straight to number one: *Idolized*. One of the biggest downloads ever. Global.

As soon as I could record it, my first album came out. Producer worked with Frank Zappa (not that I was real sure who Frank Zappa was). *Born Winner*, it was called. The Doctors decided that. Guess they decided way before I recorded it. Like they decided everything, Doctor Bob and his team, the Judges. Went triple platinum. Grammys. Mercury. You name it. *Rolling Stone* interview. Jets to London. Private jets courtesy of Doctor Bob. Tokyo. Sydney. Wherever. Madness. But good madness.

(The other madness, that came later.)

I wish I could've been me out there watching me become famous. Because from where I sat, there wasn't time to see it at all. Grab a burger and Pepsi, then on to the next gig. I was loving it. So people told me. So I believed.

Big appearance was I guested on the next Emmy Awards, telecast across the nation, giving out a Best Actress (Comedy or Musical) to Natalie Portman, my Justin Bieber fringe covering my scars. The dancers gyrated round me, Voodoo-like. I spoke and the tuxedos listened. I sung alongside Miley Cyrus and got a standing ovation of the most sparkling people in entertainment. Face jobs and chin tucks and jewellery that could pay off the debt of a small African country.

It was weird to have a voice. Somebody else's voice, literally that voice box in your throat not being the one you were born with. Strange to have a talent, a gift, a kind of wish-come-true that you carry round in your body and it's your fortune now. Alfry was my voice but I guess I carried him. Without my brain and my thoughts he couldn't have gotten to the top. Without Anthony and Vince's big old arms and Allan Jake Wells's legs and Rico's perfect abs, without any one of those things neither one of us could've made it. But, this way, we all did.

The Judges gave us a name and it was complete and to say we were happy was an understatement. I just knew Anthony wanted to get those biceps pumped right up fit to explode and I could feel Rico's insides just churning with a mixture of nerves and excitement, and I said, OK buddies, this is here, this is now, this is us, and this is me. No going back. And I could feel every cell of them saying it with me.

And every night after performing I counted the scars on my wrists and shoulders and round my thighs and ankles and neck and said, "Doctor Bob, thank you so much for this opportunity. I won't let you down."

But all dreams got to end, right?

Bigtime.

I appeared on talk shows. Pretty soon got a talk show myself. Letterman eat your heart out. Guests like Lady Gaga. George

Michael. (Outrageous.) Robert Downey Jr. (Phenomenal. Wore a zipper on his head to get a laugh. Gripped my hand like a kindred spirit.) Title sequence, black hand, white hand, fingers adjusting the tie, cheesy grin on Finbar's Jagger lips. Salvator's eyes swing to camera. The cowboy-gun finger going bang.

All this while Doctor Bob and his people looked after me, told me what to sign, what to do, where to show up, which camera to smile at, which covers to appear on, which stories to take to court. Which journalists to spill my heart to. Rico's heart. And I did. I did what I was told. Doctor Bob was like a father to me. No question. He created me. How could I say no?

There were girlfriends. Sure there were girlfriends. How could there not be? I was unique. Everybody wanted to meet me, see me, touch me, and some wanted more of me. Sometimes I'd oblige. Sometimes obliging wasn't enough.

That money-grabbing crackpot named Justine, housemaid in some Best Western I'd never stayed at, hit me with a rape allegation, but truth is I never remembered ever meeting her. It was pretty clear she was a fantasist. We buried her.

Like I say there was a downside, but a hell of an upside. Most times I thought it was the best thing I ever did, kissing my old body goodbye. Didn't even shed a tear when the rest of me in that coffin went into the incinerator, empty in the head. Just felt Doctor Bob's hand squeezing Vince Pybus's shoulder and thought about the camera hovering in my face and the dailies next morning.

But the peasants were always chasing me. The peanut-heads. The flash of their Nikons like flaming torches they held aloft, blinding me, big time. I had nowhere to hide and sometimes I felt chained to my office up on the ninety-ninth floor on the Avenue of the Stars. Felt like a thousand-dollars-a-night dungeon in a castle, the plasma screen my window to the outside world. Doctors checking me, adjusting my medication so that I could go out on the new circuit of nightclubs, appear on the new primetime primary-coloured couch answering the same boring questions I'd answered a hundred thousand times before.

Sometimes I growled. Sometimes I grunted. Sometimes I plucked a sliver of flesh from my knee and said, "I'll deal with you later." And the audience howled like I was Leno, but they didn't know how bad the pain was in my skull. It was hot under the lights and sometimes it felt like it was baking me.

"We can fix that," the Doctors said, Doctor Jude with her legs and Doctor Bob with his nut-brown eyes. And they did that. They kept fixing it. They kept fixing me, right through my second album and third, right through to the 'Best of' and double-download Christmas duets.

The problem was rejection. Balancing the drug cocktail—a whole Santa Claus list of them—so that my constituent body parts didn't rebel against each other. That was the problem. The new pharmaceuticals did it, thanks to up-to-the-minute research, thanks to a scientific breakthrough. All sorts of medical miracles were now possible. The show couldn't have gotten the green light without them. As Doctor Bob said, "It was all about taking rejection. All about coming back fighting."

I told my story in a book. Ghostwriter did a good job. I liked it when I read it. (The part I read, anyway.) Especially the part about Mom. Though Dad wasn't that happy. Tried to stop publication, till the check changed his mind. I did say some parts weren't true, but Doctor Bob said it didn't matter as long as it sold, and it did sell, by the millions. My face grinned out from every bookstore in the country. Scars almost healed on my forehead. Just a line like I wore a hat and the rim cut in, with little pinpricks each side. Signing with Murphy's hand till my fingers went numb. Offering the veins of my arm for Doctor Jude to shoot me up, keep me going, stop me falling apart. I wondered if anybody had told her she was beautiful, and I guess they had. "You nailed it. You've got your mojo back. I'm so proud of you—not just as a performer but as a human being," she said as she took out the syringe.

On to the next job. Getting e-mails from loons saying it was all against nature and my soul was doomed to hell. Well, doomed to hell felt pretty damn good back then, all in all. Except for the headaches.

But pretty soon it wasn't just the headaches I had to worry about.

One day they held a meeting at Doctor Bob's offices and told me that 'in spite of the medical advancements' the new penis hadn't taken. *Necrotis* was the word they used. Bad match. I asked them if they were sure it wasn't because of overuse. They said no, this was a biomedical matter. "We have to cut Mick Donner off, replace him with someone new." So I had to go under again and this time had a johnson from a guy in psychiatric care named Cody Bertwhistle. Denver guy, and a fan. Wrote me a letter. Longhand. Told me it was an honour.

I don't know why, and there's no direct correlation, but from the time Mike Donner's got replaced by Cosmic Cody's, things went on the slide.

Maybe it was chemicals. Maybe the chemicals were different. They say we're nothing but robots made up of chemicals, we human beings, don't they? Well if a tiny tweak here or a tad there can send us crawlin'-the-wall crazy, what does it mean if you get several gallons of the stuff pumped into you? Where are you then?

These thoughts, I'll be honest, they just preyed on me. Ate me up, more and more. Maybe that's the cause of what happened later. Maybe I'm just looking for something to blame. I don't know. Probably I am.

Maybe Doctor Bob knows. Doctor Bob knows everything.

After all, before he made us, he made himself. Out of nothing, into the most powerful man in television. A god who stepped down from Mount Olympus after the opening credits with the light show behind him like *Close Encounters* on acid.

I remember standing under the beating sun with four other guys next to a sparkling swimming pool lined with palm trees outside this huge mansion in Malibu. Servants, girls, models gave us giant fruit drinks with straws and thin Egyptian-looking dogs ran around the lawns biting at the water jerking from the sprinklers.

And Kenny started clapping before I'd seen Doctor Bob in his open-neck Hawaiian shirt walking across the grass towards us, then we all clapped and whooped like a bunch of apes. Poor Devon hyperventilated and had to be given oxygen. I'd felt strangely calm. The whole thing was strangely unreal, like it wasn't really happening, or it was happening to somebody other than me. I couldn't believe that person who was on TV, on that small monitor I was looking at as it replayed, *was* me. Maybe I was already becoming somebody else, even then. We toasted with champagne and he wished us all luck, and I don't know if it was the champagne or the warmth of the Los Angeles evening, or the smell of gasoline and wealth and the sound of insects and police sirens in the air, but I felt excitement and happiness more than I ever had in my life before, and I didn't want it to end.

We were buddies, that was a fact. Through the entire competition he was less of a mentor, more of a friend, Doctor Bob. Then, once I'd won, well, our friendship went stratospheric. And I was grateful for it. Then.

We played golf together. He paid for me to train for my pilot's licence. Took me up into the clouds. Every week we had lunch at The Ivy. Hello Troy. Hello Alex. Hello Sting. Hello Elton. Hello Harrison. Hello Amy. Still at Sony? He wanted me on display. I was his shop window. I knew that. Sure I knew that. But I always thought he was watching me. If I took too long to chew my food. If I scratched the side of my neck. It started to bug me. If I squinted across the room or stammered over my words, I felt he was mentally ringing it up. Cutting his chicken breast like a surgeon, he'd say, "You are OK?" I'd say, "Of course I'm OK. I'm great. I'm perfect." And he'd stare at me really hard, saying, "I know you're perfect, but are you OK?" One day I said, "You know what? Fuck your Chardonnay."

That was the day I took that fateful walk in the Griffith Park, up by the observatory. Just wanted to be on my own—not that I could be on my own anymore, there being at least half a dozen of us in this body, now, that I knew of. Didn't want to even *contemplate* if they'd stuck in a few more organs I didn't know about. The semi-healed scars itched under my Rolex so I took it off and dropped it in a garbage can beside the path. Walked on, hands deep in the pants pockets of my Armani suit.

You know what I'm gonna tell you, but I swear to God I didn't do anything wrong. I wouldn't do that to my mom, I just wouldn't. She raised me with certain values and I still got those values. Other people can believe what they want to believe.

She was making daisy chains.

This little bit of a thing, I'm talking about. Three, maybe four. Just sitting there beside the lake. I watched her plucking them from the grass and casting them into the water, just getting so much enjoyment from the simple joy of it, so I knelt down with her and did it too. Just wanting a tiny bit of that joy she had. And we spoke a little bit. She was nice. She said she wanted to put her toes in the water but she was afraid because her mom said not to go near the water, she might drown. I said, "You won't drown. I'll look after you." She said, "Will you?" I said, "Sure." So that's how come there's this photograph of me lifting her over the rail. I was dangling her down so she could dip her feet in the water, that's all. They made it look crazy, like I was *hurling* her, but I wasn't. The front pages all screamed—*People, Us, National Enquirer*— he's gone too far, he's out of control, he's lost it. Wacko. I hadn't lost it. She wasn't in *danger*. We were just goofing around. And who took the shot anyway? Her mom? Her dad? What kind of *abuse* is that, anyway?

Parents! Jesus! After a fast buck, plastering their kid all over the tabloids? They're the freaks, not me. And that poor girl. That's what made her start crying. Her mom and dad, shouting and calling her away from me. "Honey! Honey! Get away from the man! Honey!" And I'm like . . .

Doctor Bob want ballistic. Brought me in to the Inner Sanctum, Beverly Hills, and ripped me a new one. (Which he could have done literally, given his medical expertise.) I just growled. I snarled. He looked frightened. I said, "See those chains over there?" pointing to his wall of platinum discs. "I'm not in your chains anymore." He shouted as I left, "You're nothing without me!" I turned to him and said, "You know what? I'm everything. You're the one who's nothing. Because if you aren't, why do you need me?" As the elevator doors closed I heard him say, "Fucking genius. Fucking moron."

I could do it without him. I knew I could.

But after Griffith Park, it wasn't easy to get representation. I still got by. Put my name to a series of novels. Thrillers. Sorta semi-sci-fi, I believe. Not read them. Celebrity endorsements. Sports and nutritional products. Failing brands. Except I was a failing brand too, they soon realized.

Then this lowlife cable network pitched me a reality series, à la *The Osbournes*, where a camera crew follow me around day in, day out. Twenty-four seven. Pitched up in my Mulholland Drive home for three months. But the pay check was good. Number one, I still needed my medication, which was legal but expensive, and two, I reckoned I could re-launch my music career off the back of the publicity. So it was a done deal. Found a lawyer on Melrose that James Franco used. The producers sat on my couch fidgeting like junkies, these cheese straws in shades, saying they wanted to call it *American Monster*. I was like, "Whatever." The lights in my own home were too bright for me now, and I had to wear shades too. I'd have these ideas on a weekly basis, like my eyes were out of balance and I'd think a top-up from a hypo would get me back on the highway. It did. Periodically.

More and more I needed those boosts from the needle to keep me level, or make me think I was keeping level. Meanwhile the ideas wouldn't go away. I didn't know if the bright lights were inside or outside my skull. The bright lights are what everybody aspires to, right? The bright lights of Hollywood or Broadway, but when you can't get them out of your head even when you're sleeping they're a nightmare. And rats go crazy, don't they, if you deprive them of sleep? Except the drugs made you feel you didn't need sleep.

One of these ideas was that germs were around me and the germs I might catch would affect my immune system and inhibit the anti-rejection drugs. I was really convinced of this. I took to wearing a paper mask, just like the one Doctor Bob wore when he took my brain out and put it in another person's skull. Wore it to the mall. To the supermarket. To the ball game.

Then I guess I reached a real low patch. The reality show crashed and my new management bailed. Guess it wasn't the cash cow they were expecting. Clerval always was a ruthless scumbag, even as agents go, feet on his desk, giving a masturbatory mime as he schmoozes his other client on the phone, dining out on his asshole stories of Jodie and Mel.

Some reason I also got the idea that germs resided in my hair, and I shaved that off to the scalp. Felt safer that way. Safer with my paper mask and bald head, and the briefcase full of phials and pills, added to now with some that were off-prescription. Marvellous what you can find on the Internet, hey?

Didn't much notice the cameras anymore, trailing me to the parking lot or to the gym, jumping out from bushes, walking backwards in front of me down the sidewalk or pressed to the driver's window of my Hummer. Didn't care. I guess somewhere deep down I thought the photographs and photographers meant somebody wanted to see me. Someone wanted me to exist, so it was worth existing, for them. How wrong can you be?

It felt like it was all over. It felt like I was alone.

Then one day I got a call from Doctor Bob. No secretary. No gatekeeper. Just him. He said, 'Listen, don't hang up on me. You know I'm good for you, you know we made it together and if I made some mistakes, I'm sorry. Let's move on.' I reckoned it took a lot for him to pick up the phone, so the least I could do was listen. 'I'm going in to the network to pitch a follow-up series. And if they don't clap till their hands bleed I'll eat this telephone. It's the same but different: what every network wants to hear. Hot females in front of the camera this time, and you know what, I'm not going to even *attempt* to sell it to them. The pitch is going to be just one word. We're going to walk in and sit down, and we're going to say: *Bride*.

I said: "We?"

He said, "I want you in on this. You're on the judges' panel."

And that's what happened. Contract signed, everything. It was my baby. My comeback. It meant everything to me. I went back to the fold. Doctor Jude kissed my cheek. I *did* have my mojo. I *had* nailed it. I *was* fantastic, as a performer and as a human being . . .

Overnight, I was booked on *The Tonight Show*. I was back up there. I was going on to announce *Bride*. They wanted Doctor Bob to sit beside me on the couch but he said, "No, son. You do it. You'll be fine." And I was fine. I thought I was fine. But when the applause hit me and the lights hit me too I got a little high. I was back on the mountaintop. I wanted to sing—not sing but run, run a million miles. And I loved Doctor Bob so much, I said it. I wasn't ashamed of it. I said it again. I shouted it. I jumped up and down on the couch saying, "I'm in love! I'm in love!" because that's what it felt like, all over again.

And, though it hit the headlines, I thought, what's the big deal? And, when my security pass didn't work at the rehearsal studio, I thought, what the hell? But when Doctor Bob didn't return my calls, then I knew something was turning to shit. Then I got a text from the producer saying my services were no longer required: there was a cancellation clause and they were invoking it. I was out.

I thought: Screw Doctor Bob.

Screw *Bride*.

I did commercials, appearances, while the series ran and the ratings climbed. If the first series knocked it out of the park, series two sent it stratospheric. I tried not to watch it but it was everywhere like a virus—magazine covers, newspapers. I kept to myself. I sunk low. I shaved my head again. I wore my mask. I took my meds.

Sleepless, I wandered Hollywood Boulevard amongst the hookers of both sexes. They looked in better shape than I did.

Scored near Grauman's Chinese. Did hopscotch on the handprints in the cement. Watched the stretches sail by to fame and fortune. Watched pimps at their toil. Sometimes someone wanted to shake my black hand, other times wanted to shake my white.

In McDonald's I picked up a discarded *Enquirer* and saw what I didn't want to see: photographs of Doctor Bob leaving The Ivy with the winner of *Bride* on his arm. Lissom. Tanned. Augmented. A conglomerate of cheerleader from Wichita, swimmer from Oregon, and pole-dancer from Yale. There she was, grinning for the cameras with her California dentition, just like I used to do.

Yes, I sent him texts. The texts that they showed in court: I admit that. Yes, I said I was going to destroy him. Yes, I said I was more powerful than him now and he knew it. In many ways I wanted him to suffer. I hated him, pure and simple.

But I didn't kill her. I swear on my mother's life.

Yes, she came to my house. Obviously, because that's where they found the body. But she came there, drunk and high, saying she wanted to reason with me and persuade me to mend broken bridges with Doctor Bob. When the prosecution claimed I abducted her, that I drugged her, that was all made up. She came to me doped up and in no fit state to drive home. I told her to use the bedroom, drive home with a clear head in the morning. It was raining too, and I wasn't sure this girl—any of her—would know where to find the switch for the windshield wipers. Her pole-dancer arms were flailing all flaky and I saw the scars on her wrists and on the taut, fat-free swimmer muscles of her shoulders.

I put two calls in to Doctor Bob but they went straight to message so I hung up. She had two blocked numbers on her phone and my guess is she called someone to come pick her up while I was out.

I had an appointment with a supplier because my anti-rejection drugs were low. Maybe I shouldn't have left her but I did. Fact is, when the police found my fingerprints all over the carving knife—of course they did, it was in my house. From my kitchen. Anyway, *their* fingerprints were all over the damn thing too.

I didn't break the law. Not even in that slow-mo car chase along the interstate where I kept under the speed limit and so did they.

I know I was found not guilty, but a good portion of the American people still believed I killed her. Thirty-two wounds in her body. Had to be some kind of . . . not human being. And I am. I know I am.

But the public didn't like it that way. They blamed American justice. Blamed money. Yes, I came out free, but was I free? Really free? No way. I was acquitted, but everyone watching the whole thing on TV thought it was justice bought by expensive lawyers and I was guilty as sin. They near as hell wanted to strap me to the chair right there and then, but there wasn't a damn thing they could do about it.

God bless America.

I had to sell my place on Mulholland Drive. Live out of hotel rooms. Pretty soon I was a cartoon on *South Park*. A cheap joke on Jon Stewart. Couldn't get into The Ivy anymore. Looked in at Doctor Bob, eating alone.

Now, where am I?

Plenty of new pitches to sell. Trouble is, I can't even get in the room. Maybe it's true that the saddest thing in Hollywood is not knowing your time is over.

Now the personal appearances are in bars and strip joints smelling of semen and liquor. Not too unlike the anaesthetic, back in the day. I ask in Alfry's voice if this signed photo, book, album is for them. They say, no, it's for their mother. And that's the killer. Nobody wants to say the autograph of the person who used to be something is for them.

Night, I flip channels endlessly on the TV set in some motel, the cocktail in my veins making me heavy-lidded but nothing less than alert. If I see a clip of me I write it in my notebook. Radio stations, the same. Any of my songs, I chase them for royalties. I'm human. Everybody wants a piece of me, but I'm not giving myself away anymore. Not for free, anyway.

I look in the bathroom mirror and I see flab. Scrawn. Bone. Disease. Wrinkles. Puckers. Flaps. I'm wasting away. I'm a grey blob. What they don't say when they build you is that you die like everybody else. Only quicker. Six times quicker. The techniques weren't registered and peer-reviewed, turns out. Nobody looked into the long-term effects of the anti-rejection regime. That's why I've been eating like a horse and my body keeps nothing in but the toxins. When I was passing through Mississippi and collapsed at the wheel, the intern at the hospital said the protein was killing me—the fat, cholesterol, all of it. My body was like a chemical plant making poison. I said, "What? Cut the munchies?" He said, "No more munchies. No more midnight snacks. One more hamburger will kill you."

I'm a nineteen-year-old concoction, hurting like hell. Each part of me wants the other part of it back. It's not a spiritual or mental longing; it's a physical longing and it's pain and it's with me every sleepless second of the goddamned day.

My only crime was, I wanted to be somebody.

Trouble is, I was six people.

At least six, in fact.

To be honest, I lost count after the second penis.

Maybe you can hear the music in the background, in the next room. They're playing 'Teenage Lobotomy' by the Ramones on the tinny radio beside my king-size bed.

While I'm here, sitting on toilet pan, coughing up blood.

Truthful? I'd be writing this the old-fashioned way, paper and pen, except Murph's fingers are feeling like sausages and I'm getting those flashes again in the corner of Salvator's left eye right now. They're like fireworks. Hell, they're like the Fourth of July. That's why I'm talking into this recorder. The one Doctor Bob gave me, way back. The one I needed for interviews, he explained. "They record you, but you record them. You have a record of what you say. They get it wrong, sue their ass." Doctor Bob was full of good advice, till it all went wrong, which is why I guess I'm sitting here, wanting to set it all down, from the beginning. Like it was. Not like folks say it was. Not like the lies they're saying about me out there.

Half an hour ago I rang for a take-out and a mixed-race kid in a hoodie rang the doorbell, gave me a box with a triple bacon cheeseburger and large fries in it. Gave him a fifty. Figured, what the heck?

I've got it in my hand now, the hamburger, Anthony's fingers and Vince's fingers sinking into the bun, the grease dripping onto the bathroom floor between my feet, feet I don't recognise and never did. The smell of the processed cheese and beef thick and stagnant and lovely in its appalling richness—a big fat murderer. The intern was right. One more bite *will* kill me. I know it. The drugs were too much. The side effects, I mean. Like steroids shrink your manhood, this shrinks me. The dairy, the fat. And nobody gave me a twelve-step. Nobody took me in.

I texted Doctor Bob just before I started talking into this thing. He'll be the first to know. He'll come here and he'll find me. Which is how it should be. There's a completeness to that I think he'll understand. For all that came between us—and boy, a lot did—I think we understood each other, deep down.

That's why I know, absolutely, this is what I have to do.

Whether he listens to this story—whether anybody presses 'play' and listens is up to them. Whether they care. Whether anybody cares anymore.

All I know is, I'm taking a big mouthful. God, that tastes good ... A great big mouthful, and I taste that meaty flavour on my tongue, and that juice sliding down my throat ... And the crunch of the iceberg lettuce and the tang of the pickle and the sweetness of the tomato ... God, oh God ... And, you know what?

I'm loving it.

BLESS

I can't believe I started today like any other boring day with the same list of menial tasks and drudgery mapped out in front of me. (That of course is a woman's lot, as we all know.) If I'd known then what I know now, there'd have been a spring in my step. I'd have turned up the radio. I'd have danced. But we don't know what's ahead of us, do we? Any of us. That's the tragedy. That's the joy too. On a day like today, anyway. I didn't wash my hair this morning, which I should have, but it's bitter out in the shower in the utility room and I prefer to stay wrapped up in my duvet till the last possible moment I have to face the day, when the alarm radio has wittered the *Today* programme for an hour then stopped. There were many, many days when that silence didn't rouse me at all, I just slipped away and was gone and wanted to be gone, gone forever. I so wanted that. And so many days I didn't want to step outside the front door, but Lest made me. Till he was sick of making me. Till he was sick of all the effort coming from him, he said. It was like a big rock he couldn't get uphill anymore.

I used to not want to go outside because going outside meant seeing children and that was the one thing I couldn't bear. It was easier to bear my own unhappiness, my own fond and reliable darkness, the treacle in my head and around me slowing me and weighing me down, the bad old good old friend that stopped me feeling the pain.

Sometimes I'd hear them on their way to school. Joking, swearing, playing, shouting. The hope in their souls cutting me like a knife. And I'd weep until my throat was sore. Because I wanted to be there, out there, collecting my child from school or taking her there, and I couldn't be.

I visited her grave every day. Lest didn't like that.

I wanted her photographs out, and he didn't like that either.

I'd ring those psychic phone lines in the paper or on the Internet, and he'd go ballistic over the charges.

He didn't understand. And when I tried to explain, he'd walk away. Leave the room. Slam the door. I think the touch of me, the sight of me, hurt him so much in the end. But I couldn't go away, like he did. I couldn't run off somewhere, run away from me, because I *was* me. I was Kerys's mother. And always would be.

Every night I'd look at her first (and last) school photograph—kindergarten I mean, when she still had her beautiful hair—and gaze into her eyes and dream about her. Having the little whispers and excursions we had in life. But in the waking hours the house was empty, cold, and dead, and I was alone.

Till today.

I do all the shopping I can at the Southville Deli because I like to support the small local retailers, because before you know it they could be gone and it's no good complaining then, is it? So I do my bit, but it's not exactly cheap and more than ever I've got to keep a budget in mind these days, so I go to the Aldi in North Road for the essentials: loo roll, washing powder, that kind of thing. Your main shop-of-the-month type of thing. It can save you a packet, quite frankly. I suppose I'm a hypocrite because I know the small shops are threatened by the big boys. I even went on that march from the Hen and Chicken pub to the Council House, placard in hand, to protest about the new Sainsbury's getting planning permission to rebuild the local store at Ashton Gate increasing it to double its previous size, with consequent air and noise pollution and effect on traffic, not to mention greenhouse gas emissions. It was something I felt very strongly about. I pay attention to those kind of issues about society and the environment. That's why I went. I just hate Sainsbury's with a vengeance. (I can't explain why, I just do). So, sorry, it's Aldi for me, when it's not the Sunday market at the Tobacco Factory, which is just the novelty, really. But nice sausages and cheese, if a bit pricey.

Aldi is really good, I find. This particular one is nice and clean and friendly but not too friendly (I'd hate that) and fairly empty on a Monday morning, which is when the shelves are slightly depleted after the weekend but you do get the all-important reductions. For instance beef burgers, three for the price of one. Or pasta dishes nearing their sell-by date, three for the price of one, also.

I was checking the date on microwave moussaka for one, squinting at the label for calories with my wire basket half full on the crook of my arm when I heard a voice I didn't recognise at first. Weirdly. Silly to think that now, looking back. Really weird.

"Mummy?"

It felt alien and distant, nothing to do with me, then it became ultra-clear and ultra-recognisable as if it suddenly shot into sharp focus in my brain because suddenly I knew it was her.

"Mum-mm-my?"

It had a little sob and plea buried in it that made my heart jump.

Kerys.

I turned and saw her. Oh God. Hair long and gold and shining. It couldn't be anyone else and I couldn't believe it, and I couldn't stop it, the tears just welled into my eyes and I thought I was going to faint and I sank—not to my knees, which were jelly by the way, but to a wobbly sort of crouch—and put the basket with its courgettes and carrots and red and green chillies on the floor beside me.

"Yes," I breathed. "Yes, sweetheart?"

Kerys turned her head and looked at me through her fringe and frown. Puzzled by me. Baffled and wary and afraid, as well she might be, thrust again into the world of the living, from whence I dared not think. I just thought, I'd be terrified too if I'd died and come back, wouldn't you?

Her lower lip protruded. She said nothing but her eyes bulged with tears, the little mite. My baby.

"Here I am," I said softly. "Here's Mummy."

I stood and walked to her. I picked her up in my arms.

"Don't be afraid. Mummy's going to look after you."

I squeezed her tight, feeling the buttons of her coat against my flesh. Flecked the tears from the sides of her eyes with my gloved thumbs. Pressed a kiss to her cheek, which was warm. So much warmer than mine, newly in from the cold.

"Mummy's going to take you home," I said.

When she was inside the car and buckled up she started screaming. Poor darling. I wondered what on earth had happened to her that was so traumatic for her to react like that on her return to earth? Or was it simply the process of passing from death to life again? After all, the passing from life to death was traumatic enough. Who is to say the transition back again is any easier?

Still, she was back now, back with her mother who could look after her and love and care for her. That was the main thing. What was a little bit of shouting when all is said and done?

I put the child lock on. It was the sensible move, I thought.

I started the ignition and drove off singing "There Was an Old Woman Who Swallowed a Fly", the old Burl Ives song. Kerys's absolute favourite. We always used to sing it on long car journeys, if we went to Clevedon or Weston-super-Mare or Cheddar.

Meanwhile I smiled at her in the rear-view mirror but it didn't seem to calm her. She struggled until she was red in the face, and it pained me. I felt awful. But I remembered what the midwife had said to me soon after she was born: not to get upset if they cry, just let them cry themselves to sleep. They will. Main thing, don't show them that you're upset too, or they'll go on doing it, for attention, and that's the slippery slope. So I remembered that advice as I drove home with my daughter, newly back from the dead, in the back seat of my Fiat Punto.

When we came in, she ran away from me straight to the back door and rattled on the handle, but it was bolted and the bolt was too heavy and too tight for her little fingers to pull back. Hanging up my coat in the hall, I said, "Now then, what would you like for tea?" but she just ran into the corner next to the armchair and sat with her arms round her knees, trembling.

"Kerys, love, you poor thing. Come and let Mummy give you a hug."

I stretched out my arms. She didn't move. Shivered like a nervous rabbit in the shadows. I could hardly see her.

"You're safe now. You're home, sweetie."

I poured a tall glass of milk from the fridge, which still had her drawing of me with big, scribbly hair, held on with a Bart Simpson magnet. She didn't emerge and I didn't like to force her or be heavy or horrid in any way.

So I grilled some sausages (grilling always more healthy than frying) and put them on a plate with tomato ketchup and placed it on the table facing the TV. I switched it on and selected CBeebies on the remote. I placed a knife and fork either side of the plate. Took a paper napkin from the drawer, a red one with white spots, folded it in a triangle, and tucked it under the knife.

Outside a police car went by, not in our street but the next one. It was after criminals because the siren was on, going *nee-naw*, *nee-naw*, dropping to another tone, I think they call it the something effect but I forget what. We did it in school but we did a lot of things in school that aren't that useful in actual life. Except I would like to know that word now I've got it in my mind. It's annoying when that happens.

When she still wouldn't eat and still wouldn't come out hours later, I went upstairs and lay on my bed without undressing with my fingers knitted together on my tummy over my cardigan and stayed there until it was dark. I switched the radio on for a while, quiet, with it playing *Just a Minute* with Nicholas Parsons and lay on my side but I didn't sleep. When I went downstairs again the sausages were still on their plate.

"I love you," I said, approaching the armchair and sitting on it, knees first. "I love you so much and I've missed you so much," I whispered. "You'll never know how much I've missed you, Kerys. My baby girl."

I reached down and stroked her hair, wrapping a beautiful yellow curl of it round my finger, her eyes glimmering in the shadows below, looking up at me.

"Who are you?" she said.

It hurt, but I smiled. "I'm your mummy. Don't you remember me?"

She shook her head.

Her lips widened and curled and stiffened and she started to sob again quietly, keeping the sound to herself this time, which made it all the more heart-breaking.

"Don't be sad. You have to be happy, darling. Look. Mummy's happy." I grinned really wide up into my cheekbones. "Mummy's happy because she has you home with her again. See?"

She cried that night. All through that night, poor thing, curled up in the corner downstairs. I hated leaving her there. That first night was awful. The worst, by far. I think because I felt so out of my depth. I didn't know what to do for the best. It was almost that feeling when she was a baby. You think, I can't cope, I really can't do this, then one day it clicks and you think, I can. You know what? I can.

"Mummy! Mummy! Mummy! Mummy!"

I *was* her mummy. Why didn't she understand?

I lay there in agony, praying. Please understand. Please understand! But maybe she couldn't help it that she didn't. It wasn't her fault and I shouldn't blame her for it. If I was in agony, she was too, a million times more than I was, when you think about it. When you think of children who experience bad things like car crashes, or earthquakes, or losing their parents, or seeing their parents die, that's what causes trauma. Well, how much worse is it when the death you witness is your own?

Not the kind of thing you get over in a hurry, that's for sure. I don't think so. On the scale of things, death has to be up there at the top. Your own, I mean.

I realised, no matter what, I had to be there for her. As I had when she was alive. I had to hold her hand, not just physically but mentally also. I had to be her mother like never before.

It was as if God was testing me. Testing my love. He tested me by taking her way, I knew that. But now He was testing me by bringing her back. He was seeing if I was good enough. Strong enough. In my heart.

And I had to show Him I was.

When I got up in the morning I went down in my dressing gown and found that half a sausage had gone and of course I was delighted but decided not to make a big thing of it.

I went back upstairs and washed and dressed and came back down, humming to myself as I did the washing up, sorted the dirty clothes into piles, and put the first wash on, humming all the time. "My Bonnie Lies over the Ocean," I think it was.

Bring back . . . O, bring back . . . O, bring back my Bonnie to me, to me . . .

When I came back from the utility room, Kerys was sitting at the table, a cold sausage in her hand, gnawing the side of it.

"Good morning," I said, looking out of the kitchen window into the back yard. "What a nice morning it is. You know,

I thought it was going to be rainy today, but it isn't. It's really sunny."

Kerys didn't say anything.

She was wary as a pet that didn't know its place yet, unfamiliar with its territory. When she finished one sausage she set to work on the other. She must've been hungry. It was nice to see her enjoying her food. I poured a glass of milk and she drank that too. She made a big gasp when she finished it and had a white moustache on her upper lip, which made me laugh.

I leaned across to wipe it off with my hankie, but she didn't want me to and slid down her chair a bit, so I didn't.

I said, "Let's go upstairs and brush your teeth and comb your hair."

She didn't nod.

So I stood up, walked to the door, and held out a hand, making a fist then splaying out my fingers.

She got off the chair and put her little hand in mine.

After we'd done both those tasks, I looked at her reflection in the bathroom mirror. "There. That's pretty. You don't want to cry, do you? It's a shame to cry with a pretty face like you've got."

On the way back down she stopped at the top step and gazed into her bedroom. Catching sight of some familiar toys, I could tell. Elephant and Monkey-Monk. That was good, for bringing back nice memories, I thought. She padded a few steps to the door and pushed it tentatively open.

"See? Nothing's changed. It's just like it was. Exactly as it was. As you left it. I made sure of that. Other people wanted me to change things, but I wasn't having it. No way, I said. This is Kerys's room."

She looked back at me.

I smiled. "I knew, see. I didn't *know*. But I knew you wouldn't leave me. Not forever. And I was right, wasn't I? Here you are." I dropped to my knees. "Oh, my baby girl. My chubby-chops. Give us a cuddle." I thrust out my hands, Al Jolson fashion.

She walked back towards me and I wrapped my arms around her. I pressed my lips to her cheek and I enveloped her and the feel of her hit my brain in a heady rush like an amphetamine, I imagine. I felt giddy. High on sheer happiness, you could say. The unbelievable happiness of a dream come true, and all the privilege and pride and amazement that comes with that. I wanted my warmth to become her warmth and I never wanted to let her go. And I really, really don't think she did either. Deep down. How could she?

"There, that feels nice doesn't it? Isn't that the best feeling in the world?"

She didn't say anything, but I didn't expect her to. The important thing was I saw it in her eyes. It was definitely in her eyes. Sparkling, shimmering there. I don't know what you'd call it exactly. But I know what I'd call it. I'd call it love.

Kerys was four years and two months old when she passed over with her perfect little hand in mine, and she hadn't aged a single day. It was remarkable. Three years had gone by in earth-years, human years of torment and agony for me, of the sleeplessness, of the nights walking aimlessly, skinny, wrapped in my dressing gown in the cold, cheeks sunken, pills, the uptake-inhibitor blockers, whatever they were called, not washing, not caring about anything forever, it seemed like . . . yet for her it was as if time had stood still.

She'd been in suspended animation somewhere. I didn't mind where. I didn't *care* where. I didn't want to think about it. The idea of it was almost like a bubble, and if I thought of it too much, it might go pop. I was terrified I might do something and it would all be over, so I didn't.

Still. Three years. And instead of this gaping hole in my stomach and soul, it was suddenly like I'd looked away for half a second and looked back, and there she was. Oh God, I thought, I'm such a lucky person. I've had my bad luck in my life, I know, but I've had good luck too, and the good luck, Kerys, my sweetheart, my darling, is you. You lost your lovely hair. You lost your lovely smile, remember? But you never lost me. Never.

"What would you like for lunch today? Fish fingers? You always liked fish fingers. They were your favourite."

She shook her head.

"Pizza?"

She shook her head.

"Toast? Cheese on toast? Egg and soldiers?"

She shook her head.

"You always were a fussy eater."

I cooked fish fingers in the end. Put a great big farty dollop of ketchup at the side of the plate. Cut them in three pieces each, mouthful-sized, and blew on them hard before holding out the fork. She chewed, swallowed, then opened her mouth wide for more. She ate three of them and was beginning the fourth.

"Your favourite," I said, laughing. "Didn't I say they were?"

That evening we sat bunched up together watching TV. Kerys had her Winnie the Pooh dressing gown on. I had my arm round her. I'd bathed her so she was radiant and tingly and smelled of that mild, milky bath oil. It was a joy seeing her get reacquainted with Bob again. We called him Bob because when you pushed him underwater he bobbed back up again. I think it'd been Lest's idea, which made me a little bit sad that he wasn't here to be with his daughter anymore. But that was his decision and he had to live by that now. Nobody asked him to walk out and abandon me. If you abandon someone when they're at their lowest ebb, I think that tells you what kind of a person that is, at the end of the day, and that's an eye-opener to the kind of person you made your marriage vows to and vowed to spend the rest of your life with. Anyway, my personal feelings to one side, Bob was quite a good name for a plastic duck.

I'd wrapped Kerys up in my biggest, fluffiest bath towel—fluffy duck, fluffy duck—then when we got downstairs immediately put the electric fire on to cosy up the room.

Points West announced itself with swirling planets and rousing drums, and amongst the headlines at the top of the programme I glimpsed the blurry image of a CCTV camera in a supermarket, of a hooded figure in an anorak and a smaller figure, legs dangling.

I switched it off.

Kerys was still singing "Fluffy duck, fluffy duck . . . " to a Monkey-Monk dancing on her knees and her eyes were not on the screen.

I didn't like the idea of her seeing the bad things they always showed on the news: death, crime, and nastiness. I didn't want her to have nightmares thinking there were bad people out there, that the world was only full of nasty people, because it isn't. It's mostly full of the vast majority of good people who do nice things and not the minority who don't.

"Up the wooden hill to Bedfordshire."

It's well known that negative things can affect the mind of young people. Psychologists and sociologists, all sorts of scientists, have done numerous studies over the years, so they know it's true. Well, I don't want my daughter growing up influenced by such images. I want to be a responsible mother.

It was quite emotional to see her back there in her own bed, snuggling with the blankets under her chin, in her powder-blue pyjamas with raspberry spots, newly washed and ironed. Monkey-Monk on one side of her, Elephant on the other, and Big, Little and Tiny

Ted all watching from the foot of the bed under the shadow of the bookshelf, protecting her from whatever bad beasties her dreams might bring. She had a little army of soft toys: Roo and Raggy, Red Cushion, Seb the Zebra . . . To think, I was seriously considering placing Seb the Zebra on her grave next to all the lovely flowers people brought, toys and dolls and even a pair of twinkly ballet shoes to see her to the next word. As I tucked her in, I wondered what gifts she'd been given to accompany her on the journey back, what the angels in their wisdom had given her. Or maybe they'd just given her something abstract, like joy. Like hope.

"I used to read you this in the hospital . . . " I said, closing *The Gruffalo* as I finished reading it, though I hardly needed to, I almost knew it word for word.

"Hospital?"

"Yes. Do you remember?"

She shook her head. "Why was I in the hospital? I forget."

"Because the blood you had was bad, darling." I lifted a curl from her forehead. "It was nasty to the rest of your body . . . It was going round like a monster in the woods, eating things up . . . Like The Gruffalo, it was . . . but we weren't afraid of it, were we? We were like the mouse. We weren't afraid of its knobbly knees and turned in toes, and the wart at the end of its terrible nose, were we?"

"Was I brave?"

"You were. You were the bravest mouse in the deep, dark wood."

"Did I get better?

"No, darling, you didn't." I touched her cheek. "You tried. Nobody could try harder. You were a fighter, but it was no good."

She pondered. "Was I sick?"

"Very."

"What happened after I was very sick?"

"Darling, you died and went to heaven. But that doesn't matter now, because you're back."

"Were you sad when I died?"

"Of course I was sad. I'd lost my little girl."
She frowned. "What was her name?"
I couldn't resist tweaking her nose.
"Her name's Kerys, silly."
"That's a nice name."
"It *is* a nice name. That's why I gave it you."

She said nothing. She looked round the room anxiously. I bent over and kissed her cheek.

"Night night. Sleep tight. Don't let the bedbugs bite. And if they do, bite the bad, bad bedbugs back!"

That was a routine I hadn't said for a long time, and when I heard it come out, and remembered how Kerys used to chuckle so loudly and join in, my throat tightened. This time, though, she didn't join in. But she was tired. There were blue crescents like bruises under her eyes. She was exhausted.

I switched out the bedside light and sat on the floor as I always did, holding her hand until she went off, perhaps for ten or fifteen minutes but sometimes for half an hour or an hour but I never minded because it was our time together, just us, mother and daughter, not even speaking, just being, me sitting listening to her breathing, the breathing of the life I'd brought into this world, my heart completely full of love, love for life and love for God for giving me this remarkable thing, feeling the little twitching of dream-sleep in her palm . . . then having to, but not wanting to, let go . . .

Returning downstairs, the real excitement of what had happened started to sink in. I wondered if I was right to keep such a momentous, amazing thing to myself. Struggling with my own personal feelings, I felt it my duty to share the news with Kerys's father. We were separated, but it was his right to know that his daughter had come back to the world of the living. Some things were undeniably bigger than two adults breaking up who couldn't see eye to eye anymore. Much bigger.

The first time I rang his mobile it went dead. I tried a few minutes later and the same thing happened. The third time he answered. He must've recognised the phone I was ringing from, because he said, without any preamble, "How did you get my number?"

"Lest? Are you in a pub?" I could hear the background noise clearly. *Don't You Want Me Bay-bee, Ohhhhh* . . . and a lot of people shouting to be heard over it.

"What does it matter to you where I am?" I could hear women laughing too. Wittering in these ugly, loud voices like animals.

"I . . . I was just thinking on your behalf," I stammered. "If . . . If it's not convenient to talk, I can call you back some other time."

"Yeah. Never. How's *never*? *Never*'s a convenient time, Esmée." Perhaps his nastiness dawned on him because he sighed, and a sigh can be a sign of regret, can't it? I remembered the look on his face so many times. The look he probably had right now that wanted me to not be there. "Fucking hell, whatever you have to say, say it. Get it over with and leave me alone."

"Don't be angry. It's a nice thing."

"Really? Since when is anything to do with you a nice thing?"

"It is. Honestly." I could hear the quaver in my own voice. Feel it in my lower lip.

"Esmée . . . "

"She's back. She's really back. Kerys is back, Lest."

"You know what? Fuck you."

"I know it's unbelievable. But you've got to come round and see her. I've just tucked her in and . . . " But all there was in my ear was the burr of the dead line. "She's beautiful. She's perfect . . . " The burr didn't stop. I wanted his voice to come back on, but it didn't. "Hello? Lest? Hello? Lester?"

I thought, of course, that kind of news, it's gargantuan. He's probably leaving the pub right now. He's probably hailing a cab. Getting in the cab right now, giving the driver the address. This address. Coming straight here. Why waste time with conversation? He wanted to see Kerys. See her for himself. See me. See what I was telling him was true. And when he arrived he might be suffering from shock. He might want to calm down a bit before going upstairs. I should make him a cup of tea. I should put on the kettle. I should make a pot. One tea bag of Darjeeling and one of English Breakfast, just the way he liked it.

The kettle boiled.

The red light came on. Ping.

It switched itself off, the steam rising up the net curtain beside the draining board. I filled the teapot, warming it first as my grandmother in Cardiff used to do, then giving it a stir with a spoon. The heat almost burned my fingers as I did it.

In half an hour it was stewed.

In half an hour I realised he wasn't coming.

I thought of him sitting there that time in the caff when I burst into tears and I didn't know why. It was just something insignificant. And he said, really harshly, "What is it now?" And I said that wasn't fair, to say that when I was upset. How would he like it? He said, "Jesus Christ, just tell me what's wrong." I said, "Nothing." And I was wiping the tears from my eyes with this tatty cheap bit of serviette or kitchen roll. He said, "Tell me before I go. I've got to go in five minutes and I don't want to leave you like this." I said, "You don't give a shit about me." He said, "You shouldn't get upset like this over nothing. That's all I'm saying." I said, "I can't help it."

He wasn't coming.

Perhaps he was afraid. He was always afraid of things, Lest. I was always the strongest one. Perhaps he didn't believe me. Well, that was his business. His prerogative. I wouldn't ring again. One day he'd regret it. I knew that. One day he'd know what he'd missed out on. So, so much. But for now all I could think was, you fool, you bloody fool. How could I have married such an ignorant fool?

Sitting there in my kitchen, I wondered if there was somebody out there who'd understand. And the person who obviously sprang to mind was Amos, the vicar who talked to us before the funeral and was nice. If anyone would be sympathetic about Kerys coming back, it would be Amos. That kind of thing happened in the Bible, so it wouldn't come as that much of a shock to him. Not as much as it would to ordinary people anyway.

He'd said to me in his deep Congolese accent, "Do you believe in the Resurrection to Eternal Life through Jesus Christ Our Lord?"

"I do," I'd said.

"Well, good. Good. Everybody must," he'd said, sitting on my sofa with a sherry in his hand, wearing red socks. "Because without that belief, what do you have? You have nothing. Nothing." He held my hand. Dark, black hands, black as tarmac. "And I can reassure you as an absolute fact that you will meet your daughter again, of that I have no *fragment* of a doubt. No *fragment* at all."

It was late now. Nearly midnight, but I decided to ring him anyway. He'd left his number and he'd said at the time of the funeral not to hesitate, if I felt I needed to talk at any time. Any time at all. I'd been to church every Sunday and listened to his sermons, some of which I understood, and I'd shaken his hand as I'd left, and looked into his big brown African eyes as he'd asked how I was feeling, but I'd never taken him up on the offer of a phone call. So now I did. The number was in my book. Whether it was his home or office number I didn't know.

It rang about five times and was then picked up by a messaging machine, which played a synthesiser version of the Hallelujah chorus. I listened to it, then listened to his deep, syrupy voice asking me to speak clearly after the tone. I hung up before the beep.

Because during the music I realised I didn't want anyone else to know. Why did anyone need to know?

I knew, and God knew, and that was all that mattered.

It wasn't anybody's business, the two of us, and now I'd thought about it I didn't want anybody to know what had happened, to be honest. People can say vile things about stuff they know nothing about. People are always eager to do that. Whispering behind their hands when they think you're not looking. Broadcasting it, on the quiet. Spreading lies about you that you don't even know about. Petty, malicious gossip. You didn't have to have a miracle happen or someone return from the dead for them to start rumours flying round here and in this instance it *was* a miracle and it *was* someone returning from the dead and I didn't want any Christians having their say either, or some other fundamentalist Muslim or whatnot saying it was Their God did it either. That didn't interest me. What interested me was looking after my daughter. So the best policy from then on was keeping her indoors and out of sight and out of the public gaze. Like they used to say on the football pools: "Tick this box for No Publicity". Well, I ticked that box for No Publicity. Too right I did.

The next morning Kerys set up a game of Connect 4 on the coffee table in the sitting room with the curtains drawn and the sunlight outside. We played best of thee and she won two, so I said, best of five. When she won five I said I gave up, she was the champ. The undisputed champion of the world.

She went quiet.

I sorted the tablet-type counters into two piles: red and yellow.

She said, "Can I go now?"

"No, darling," I said, placing my first yellow, *kerplunk*, in the centre row. "Of course not. This is where you belong. You know that, don't you?"

That night she cried again. She was like a little fallen angel, fallen into my arms. But she'd get over it. She'd learn to love me, I knew, just like she used to. Once she'd stopped being so muddled up.

From my bedroom I sang "My Baby Has Gone Down the Plug Hole". A song my father always sang to me when I was a baby, according to my mum. When he'd come back from the club "tight" (as she put it) after playing snooker with his mates, he'd stand in his vest and underpants singing that song at the top of his voice, rocking me in his arms.

When I'd finished there was no sound from Kerys's bedroom next door. I crept in and saw that she'd gone peacefully to sleep.

I bent over and put my ear to her lips and I could hear her breathing. I could feel her warm breath warming my ear and it was lovely. It was glorious. Glory, glory, glorious, my baby. My little girl.

She opened her eyes, sniffing awake.

"I want my mummy."

"But I am your mummy. Look."

"I had another mummy . . . Didn't I?" She looked up at me. "Her name was Julie."

"No, darling." I poked the blankets in around her. "You're just confused because you went to heaven and now you're back."

"Where's Julie?"

"Julie isn't here."

She became more upset. "I want Julie."

"Julie isn't anywhere, sweetheart. You imagined her."

"Was she an angel?"

"That's right. She's not here but she looked after you once when you were somewhere else."

"In heaven?" She sniffed.

"Yes."

"What was heaven like?"

"I expect it was nice. I didn't go there, so I don't know, silly. *You* tell *me* what it was like."

"I don't remember."

"I expect it was wonderful. I expect the people loved you there."

"I think I remember a house. My house."

"Well . . ."

"My house. A house with a red door and a cat."

"Heaven has lots of cats. But in the end the cats wave goodbye to the little children and the little children come home. And the angels say goodbye to them too. With a kiss. And sometimes you don't remember that goodbye kiss because you're asleep."

She said, "I think I don't remember that."

"But that doesn't mean it didn't happen, does it?"

My daughter shook her head. I lay next to her with her hand in mine. I lay there beside her and we slept.

The next day we played hide and seek. She always used to love that. I counted to twenty but I jumped over some of the numbers, going straight from twelve to fourteen, from fifteen to eighteen, because I knew she'd already found a hiding place under the table, and she always loved me eking out every ounce of the suspense before coming to find her. And she always knew that she'd get a scare and a great big tickle when I did catch her, so there was the anticipation of that in addition.

"Again!" she laughed. "Again!"

After about ten goes I was exhausted but she was still raring to go. It had lost none of its novelty, and she none of her energy. Until I found her sitting on the floor of the utility room staring at the cat flap in the back door. Her laughter trailed into silence.

"Was there a cat in this house?"

"Yes there was."

"Where is he?"

I tried to get my puff back. "He went away, sweetheart. Do you want some orange juice and a fruity bar?"

"Where did he go?"

"He went the same place you did. He went to heaven."

She stared at the cat flap again, then up at me. "Was he the cat I met in heaven, then?"

"Yes he was."

"What was his name?"

"His name was Oliver."

"Was it?" Her little face looked bewildered. " . . . I forget."

"That's because you're back home now, precious." I crouched. "And God takes those memories away, little by little. To give to other boys and girls. Because you don't need them anymore."

I heard a sudden loud knocking at the front door. Not a normal knocking, but the knock of someone who knocks doors all day. It's their profession.

I could just see into the hall and I could just see two dark shapes through the opaque glass.

Uniforms.

I could hear the squawking radio of one of them.

I put a finger to my lips and went "Shshsh" to Kerys, and Kerys immediately got the message. Let's pretend we're not here. It was like a game. It was like hide and seek. She was excited by it. For a second I thought she was going to laugh out loud but she didn't. I tugged her slightly towards the back door, holding her cheek against my hip.

The police officers knocked a second time.

I listened hard in case they spoke to each other, but they didn't. I stayed where I was without moving until I heard the police radio fade away and the knocking moved to next door. I heard the voice of the Asian woman whose name I didn't know talking to them.

"That was a good game," I said.

"That was a good game, Mummy," Kerys said.

Mummy.

I had butterflies in my tummy because it was the first time since she came back she'd used that word.

"That was a good game, Mummy," I said too.

I didn't like lying at the best of times, and not answering the door to the police felt like lying. It preyed on my mind all day. Let me declare I've always been completely law-abiding and respectful of the law my entire life. But I couldn't risk what the authorities of any kind might do. The police are forces of might and punishment, and they preserve the status quo. And what I had wasn't the status quo, was it? It could get me into trouble, I knew, but that wasn't uppermost in my mind. What was uppermost in my mind was I had to think about my daughter, not myself.

"Did I play with this?"

I looked up and saw that Kerys had taken a European doll with coffee-coloured skin from her toy box. It had long black hair and long legs and a red dress.

"Was this my favourite dolly?"

I nodded.

"I like her," she said.

"I know you do, darling."

Kerys was upstairs in the bath when you knocked the second time like some kind of knell. Knocked and rang the doorbell, this time. It was seven thirty. I know because *EastEnders* has just started with its swirly aerial view of the River Thames. I wondered if you could hear the theme music, so turned it down quickly on the remote. Probably closing the barn door after the proverbial horse had bolted, I thought, but I couldn't be certain.

Peeking into the hall I saw the two shapes had returned. Black shapes, seeming to be chatting on my front doorstep through the glass. But I couldn't hear the words.

I slipped into the sitting room, edged along the wall behind the sofa, and parted the drapes no more than an inch to peep out. I saw you in your black body armour and starched white shirt, big radio on your lapel. I caught the other constable turning in my direction and he must've seen the curtain twitch, or me, or both, because he said something and you rapped the knocker harder and I knew this time I had to answer the door. You weren't about to go away, and what's more, ignoring you would look suspicious.

After quickly plucking at my hair in the hall mirror I opened the front door.

"Mrs Bentley?"

"Yes. I'm Esmée Bentley."

My first thought on seeing you was, here's a good-looking chap with a cleft chin, slightly swarthy looking, I wouldn't mind betting he had some foreign blood in there, possibly Greek or Italian, but not Middle Eastern or anything. The one standing beside you, so fresh-faced he could have come straight from sixth form, still had his helmet on, making him look surprisingly military. But you did the talking.

"Mrs Bentley, we'd like to ask you a few questions, if we may. It's concerning the disappearance of a little girl in the area."

"Oh?" I checked the buttons of my cardigan.

"You've probably heard."

"No, I haven't heard." It was surprisingly chilly, but then I'd been sitting in front of the fire.

"Oh . . . It's been common knowledge round here. It's been on *The News*."

"I haven't heard. I don't watch *The News*."

I think it was the other one who said, "None of the neighbours told you?"

"I don't talk to the neighbours. I haven't been out very much, as a matter of fact." I realised I was smoothing my wet hands in my woollen top. "Bath time," I explained.

"There's been a lot of police activity," you said. "I'm surprised you haven't noticed. The little girl's name is Sophie Markham. She's four years old. Long blonde hair. This is her photograph." You held it out to me. Not a photograph as such but a printout like a wanted poster with a little girl in the middle of it. I don't know why, but you were trying to fool me, giving her that strange name. You were being cunning. I had to think on my feet if I wasn't going to fall into your trap, that was clear. I held it carefully, not wanting to get it damp with my thumbprints, and though my heart was pounding, it didn't even tremble. "Have you seen her at all, in the last few days? Or at any time? Anything might be useful to our enquiries."

I looked at it, then shook my head.

"Like I say, I haven't been out and about, last few days. Sorry." I held it out but you didn't take it back. I wanted you to take it back.

"She was last seen in Aldi's in North Road," said the younger one. "Do you shop in Aldi's?"

"Yes." I thought I'd be honest, because I knew he was trying to catch me out, and you can't catch someone out if they tell the truth. I handed him the poster instead and he took it.

"We're in the process of enhancing the CCTV footage," you said, giving the impression of being senior in some way. "At the moment it's Mr or Mrs Blobby."

"It's quite upsetting." I said.

"It is."

"That's why I don't watch *The News*, you see."

"Her mother's extremely anxious, as you can imagine."

"Well it makes you anxious. *The News*," I said. "Can I have another look, please?" Daring, you could say. Bold. The young policeman hesitated then gave the printout back to me, but I didn't gaze at it for very long, this Sophie Markham as you called her who I knew was Kerys Bentley. Just long enough. "No. Never. I'm sorry. It's awful. I hope she turns up safe and sound."

I could tell the two of you found that last expression I'd used inadequate. You were staring at me. Perhaps not staring exactly. But you shifted from foot to foot and looked at each other. I wondered what you were conveying. What you were up to, in your minds, generally, in your deviousness.

"Well, if you have any information that might be of use, please contact us at this number. Would you like to keep this flier, by the way? Put it in your front window perhaps? It has the Crimestoppers number on it."

"No. I don't think so."

I thrust the little poster back towards you.

You took it and put it in your briefcase, inside which I

glimpsed a whole batch of others, identical. You were looking over my shoulder.

"Could we talk to your husband please? See if he . . . "

"My husband doesn't live here anymore. He moved back to Fishponds a long time ago." I tugged at my collar where I felt my skin going a bit red. "It's just the two of us now. Me and my daughter." My eyes must have moved slightly because your eyes tilted upwards. Clearly you could hear the splashing noises and Kerys heartily singing "Mud, Mud, Glorious Mud" at the top of her little voice. I laughed, and you laughed too. "She's in the bath," I said.

"Happy soul."

"Can't shut her up."

"Tell me about it," said the young one.

"Soppy sod." You muttered, putting on your helmet.

"What?" complained the other one.

"Nothing wrong with a dad being besotted by his child," I said. It was obvious your friend had one of his own at home. I could see it in his eyes, and he wanted to be back there and cuddling her, not on a cold doorstep talking to me. "I think it's lovely."

"Well," you said, adjusting your chinstrap. "Sorry about your husband."

"I'm not."

The corner of your mouth twitched up in sympathy. A sparkle in your eye. Little crinkle of crow's feet.

"Anything . . . let us know."

I nodded as you moved down the path, out of the spill of light from the hall. You were almost at the gate when I said, "God help what that poor mother is going through. I'm sure she's getting a lot of prayers tonight."

"I'm sure she is. For all the good prayers do." You were in shadow now. "I doubt she'll sleep, I know that. Goodnight, Mrs Bentley."

"Goodnight."

From upstairs you could hear Kerys calling for her mummy.

"Goodnight," I said again, seeing your smile out there fade into the dark with a faint sparkle of buttons.

Your swarthy smile was nice. For a moment or two it made me feel safe and I wished I'd felt safe in my life before that day, that evening during *EastEnders*, a long time before, but I hadn't, and it's no good crying over spilt milk.

I didn't close the door too quickly. I didn't want to do anything to attract undue attention. I heard the click of the latch of the gate before I pressed the Chubb lock shut and flipped the snib. Then bent down to bolt the door at the bottom.

"Mu-u-ummm?"

"Coming."

I thought (quite clearly, as it happens), you obviously have access to council records, the electoral register for voting purposes and so on. Why did you not know my husband had moved out? I'd put it on my census form. Maybe you hadn't looked there yet in your inquiries. People imagine the police are super-efficient, thanks to *Inspector Morse* and so on (I blame TV for a lot of erroneous presumptions), but very often they aren't. You only have to read the papers occasionally to know that. Who was that murderer up North, and they'd gone to his house and talked to him and hadn't realised he'd killed all those women, and ruled him out of the investigation? Like them, you'd simply got your facts wrong . . . made a mistake . . . and that was good. For now.

Of course it was.

But you'd double check. Eventually.

That's what policemen do. That's their job. Checking.

And you'd realise sooner or later. Realise that, according to the most up-to-date information on your database or whatever, Mrs Esmée Bentley lived alone.

Sooner or later, sooner rather than later, definitely, you were going to piece it all together.

I knew that now.

And strangely, or perhaps not so strangely, I thought of those Roman soldiers who ganged up and stormed into the last supper and arrested Jesus. How they never gave a damn about His powers or the miracles that had happened. How they never believed that Jesus had brought a man back from the dead. Or that Jesus Himself came back on the third day after being crucified. They were disbelievers. They were blasphemers. They were murderers. Well, this was the same. This was similar.

You weren't going to believe me. I knew that. You weren't even going to *listen* to me. I knew that too. I wouldn't be able to get a word in sideways when you next came through that door. When you next knocked on that door for me to answer it.

Mud . . . Mud . . . Glorious Mud . . .

I switched off the hall light with a crushing, numbing certainty that when you came back you would take Kerys away from me. You wouldn't let me speak to her, even touch her, ever again. And that thought was too much to bear. That thought, I knew, would destroy me, if I let it. But like a revelation, like an epiphany, I had an idea, an idea so clear it shone down on me like a light breaking through the clouds. But it wasn't so much an idea; it was more of a message. Because an idea is just an idea, but a message is a message and you have to obey it, you have no choice.

Mud . . . Mud . . .

And the message had a perfection and the reason it had perfection was it must be coming from God, and it was an escape and it was an answer, all wrapped together in one big, big thing inside me.

Glorious . . .

And I set my foot on the bottom step and set my sights on the landing high above, knowing with total conviction and certainty what I had to do. What I *must* do. However hard it might be, because this was God willing me to do it as he willed me to do all things and all the good things in this world of evil. It was the logical thing. It was the right thing. It was the good thing to do. I just had to have the strength in my heart to do it . . .

You see that, don't you?

Now? Now that I've explained everything?

What was being asked of me? What was so, so clear?

That God in His heaven was opening His arms once more in his vast embrace.

And I had to send her. Send her back to heaven.

Not for long. Not for ever.

Sleep, my baby, sleep, my darling, sleep.

Just for a little while . . .

A WHISPER TO A GREY

Here's to the horse with the four white feet,
The chestnut tail and mane,
A star on his face and a spot on his breast,
And his master's name was Cain.
   —Children's skipping rhyme

OF COURSE YOU HAVE NO INHERENT REASON to believe what follows, and may dismiss any conclusion that may be drawn from it, but it behoves me to say that, though in my travels and studies I have catalogued many stories of the Supernatural which come from anecdotal rather than personal experience—this is not one of them.

The area where all took place is now much the same sleepy Wiltshire idyll it was then. You may have passed through it if you have taken a particularly circuitous route from Warminster to Devizes, though it is not easily seen from the train. If you *had* seen it, you would have remarked, I am sure, upon a fine equestrian monument depicting Sir Christopher Beath, parliamentarian and judge, whose family, together with the abbey of St Augustine, gave the town a name almost longer than its high street—Beath St August.

I arrived at the station to investigate a perplexing apparition known as the Steeplejack, which had been perceived intermittently scaling the church spire of Newich (pronounced Newch) five miles away.

The date was August 1st, and I was surprised to find Beath's market square decked in bunting, thronging with people, and hopping to the sound of a sprightly band consisting of fiddle, pipes, and drum. I had walked into, I soon discovered, the traditional Lammas-tide Horse Fair.[1] The incidence of such a fair, as opposed to a sheep fair, cattle fair, or common-or-garden market, I later learned, dated back to the time of Henry II. The noble animal was certainly in evidence, in the shape of every breed from Percherons and Shires to Connemara ponies, with some as fine as ever graced the turf at Ascot in between. The creature was also present symbolically, for instance in the mummingplay being acted out beneath the old oak by gaily painted Obby-Osses. There were also 'horseshoe cakes'—a crescent-shaped variant of black pudding made with salt, meal, and pigs' blood, which were selling furiously from a stall nearby. Interestingly, did the townsfolk but know it, those unsavoury crescents betrayed a direct lineage to the horse as a lunar symbol, leading back to the Hathor of the ancient Egyptians. Everything around me seemed folklore come alive, all I had read in dusty books suddenly vibrant and meaningful, and I was eager not to let the event go unattended.

I quickly deposited my bags at the Busheller's Arms in Wren Street, and returned.

The Rigbold Morris had attracted a large, enthusiastic crowd, and I wandered past the jangling of bells and the jolly wail of the accordion through to the square proper, where play turned

---

1. I knew from my studies that such a festival derives from the Celtic calendar: Samhain (November 1st) celebrating the start of a new year, Imbolc (February 1st) the start of lambing, Beltane (May 1st or May Day), the return of summer, and so Lugnasad (August 1st), the beginning of harvest. This was the day when the first corn was ground and made into loaves as offerings to God. The Saxons called it *half-maesse* (loaf mass) and thence comes the word 'Lammas'.

to hard business, with a little hard drinking thrown in to clinch the deal. The scrupulous purchaser lifted tails and examined teeth, sealing the sale with a spit in the handshake. Purveyors advertised their horses in the manner of evangelical preachers, taking bids here, then there, then reminding the future owner he had invested in no less a steed than Alexander's Bucephalus. The gavel struck, and so it went on, with intoxicating speed and bewildering expertise. Then occurred a bizarre incident which set in train the even stranger events which followed.

I noticed a Clydesdale led out by a stoop-backed farmer, who trailed it around the ring to increasing howls of derisory laughter. True, it was not an impressive specimen. It limped, snorted, and coughed like an old miner. Its nostrils dripped cobwebby saliva, and its eyes were sad and dull. It had not been looked after with care and, ultimate ignominy, was now only worthy of mockery—and the attention of the buyer from the knacker's yard. Thus, it seemed, its fate was sealed. But then the extraordinary happened.

A man fought through the crowd past me. I saw only the blur of red neckerchief and moustache. He stepped squarely between the farmer and the abattoir man and must have quickly made a better bid, because the first man moved away, shaking his head in disbelief. The money that changed hands made the laughter ring even louder—directed now not at the horse but at its new owner.

The man paid no notice, and led the tired old nag out of the market place into a nearby field.

A crowd, largely of children, followed. It was not long before my own rapt attention was no less captivated than theirs by an uncanny sight.

The man knelt beside the horse he surely had never seen before in his life, tore away its harness like shackles, put his cheek to its own, and spoke to it as gently as a mother might to a babe in arms. Within minutes the old nag was transformed, and sprang up, strutting, snorting, and tossing its head like a spry young pacer. The crowd applauded unreservedly—and I joined them.

I looked at the fellow standing next to me, hoping to share my astonishment, but he, who had been the most spirited in the mocking laughter stakes, simply stared through cigar smoke at the scene before him. Here was a chap to whom joy did not come easily. The broken cheek-veins and the glazed, fishy eyes told their own miserable story; all the more miserable because his hand rested on the shoulder of a small girl with pink ribbons in her hair, and with all the brightness of eye her father lacked.

The man in the field was now circling the horse quite calmly, with only the merest gestures of his hands like a mesmerist. The horse would first lie down, then stand, then walk around him clockwise, then anti-clockwise. He used no perceptible word of command, no instrument such as a stick, and yet it was completely under his control, as if man and beast *understood* each other, implicitly, without the benefit—or perhaps the hindrance—of language.

He was a Gypsyman, with the cherry-wood complexion and dark curls that typify that race, and a physical bearing that makes a mere city-dweller like me feel like an over-powdered poodle. Under that gentle poise was a calmness of spirit, an affinity not only with the animal, who seemed powerless and besotted, but with the very soil and trees around him. I admit that, watching him, spellbound, I realised my long incarceration in libraries had denied me something. I had pulled no ploughs, seeded no land, brought no creature into the world, or seen any out of it. I looked at my pale, un-calloused hands and envied him.

By evening, the noises of the fair had abated to the crackle of bonfires and the sound of stalls being dismantled.

I came down into the public bar with the intention of enjoying a drink before an early night, to prepare me for the trip to Newich the following day. Who should be poised in the comfort of the inglenook seat, amongst the horse brasses and shoes that decorated the chimneybreast, but the Gypsyman.

With him sat a young woman and her son, whom I would have estimated to be no more than twelve years old. The woman was turning down the boy's collar and showing in plain view an unpleasant growth, a wart or wen the size of a penny, under his right ear. I watched with growing curiosity as the Gypsyman reached into his knapsack and took out a large jar, from which he extracted (this is not for the squeamish) a large garden snail. The snail was placed on the growth, held there for a minute or so, neither child nor mother repulsed by the idea, then removed. The woman rose, bowed, placed a few coins in the gypsy's palm, and took her son's hand in her own. When they were gone, the Gypsyman carefully took a twelve-inch length of rose-thorn from his bag, and proceeded to impale the mollusc on one of its hooks, then set it, still squirming, propped on the mantelshelf of the open fire.

He looked up, as if sensing my gaze, and raised a finger to the wide black brim of the hat he still wore. I returned a raise of my glass. I walked over and said I had admired his show of skill that afternoon, and asked if I could replenish his pot. He nodded, and when I returned with it so done, he murmured *"Dordy roy"*—something I later learned to mean, "You're a gentleman." He was not uncomfortable with the silence that loomed—one that I, however, felt obliged to fill.

Settling in the seat opposite him, I asked from whence he had travelled.

He gave a wry smile. "Egypt."

I laughed and said I had read about the Forest of Dean, where, for certain folk, the name had been coined: 'Dukes of Little Egypt' or 'gypsies'. He seemed impressed—a little. I observed that he had no caravan. Was he alone? Wasn't that unusual for a gypsy?

He replied, "No *vardo*, no *rawnie*, no *rackli*." His accent seemed rural English yet strangely foreign.

Conversation flowed, or rather trickled, in this fashion. He asked me my profession.

I said I dealt with old books, old stories, history, tales, legends.

"You want to know legends?" he said. "You know the legend of The First Horseman?"

I said I didn't, but would like to hear it very much.

Once his whistle was suitably wetted, he began to tell me that the gypsies had many myths about the origin of their kind. One was that they were descendants of the Biblical Cain; alternatively, their progenitors were those who had refused a bed to the Virgin Mary; or then again, that it was the first gypsy who had forged the three nails used in the crucifixion. "Whichever be true," he said, "gypsies be doomed to wander the earth as punishment ever since."

"And which do you believe?"

"One on Sunday, one on Monday, and one the rest of the week." He grinned as he supped. "The more you believe in, the less chance of being wrong."

The door banged open and a hush fell as a barrel-chested man in great coat and top hat, flanked by a trio of pugilistic-looking ruffians in cloth caps, strode in as if he owned the place—which I was later to learn he did, along with large chunks of the county. A beetle-browed stare was cast round the bar, which held upon the two of us. When his knuckles hit our table top, shadow no longer concealed the unpleasant visage of the cigar-chomping man I had stood beside earlier.

"They seek him here, they seek him there . . . " He threw his gloves and hat to one of his cronies while another commandeered for his master a schooner of port. "You've led me a merry chase round every ale house in town, my man!"

It was clear at the outset that the Gypsyman thought of himself as nobody's 'man' but his own. He consequently did not look up.

"I shan't beat around the bush," the visitor barked. "I saw your exploits earlier at the Horse Fair, and I won't indulge in idle flattery. Suffice it to say I'm prepared to offer you employment on my estate. Forthwith. As of now. Full board and lodgings and a stable boy's wage, starting tomorrow. What do you say to that? Eh?"

The Gypsyman said absolutely nothing.

"I'm offering you a job, you idiot! Don't you understand plain English? You know who I am, don't you?"

"Yer." The Gypsyman gazed lugubriously down at the beer in his pot. "You the *gorgio* who's innerruptin' my pint."

The room exploded into laughter.

Instantly the Gypsyman's hat was snatched off his head by one of the heavies. "This is the Marquess of Beath giving you the time of day, heathen! Act respectful!"

"I've a good mind to horsewhip you for that sort of insolence." The Marquess was becoming puce. "But I won't. I won't because you're a disgusting, filthy vagrant who doesn't know any better. Goodness knows why but out of the goodness of my heart I'm giving you the chance to improve yourself. I'll bet you've never had a proper paid job in your entire life. Who would trust you? Why, you're near as spitting to a *darkie*!"

I saw no pang of hurt in the Gypsyman's eyes. He simply turned to me calmly, refilling his pipe. "That reminds me of a story, *diddikai*," he said, a smile toying with his lips. "O Del—that's our word for God—he made the first man out of chalk and put him in the oven to bring him to life. But he left in too long, brought out too burnt— he was the first *negro*. So O Del, he try again. This time he take out too soon. Pale as flour. He was the first the white man. Third time, God get it not too brown not too white—just perfect colour—and that was the first gypsy."

The Marquess bristled. "Three square meals and a roof over your head, every night. Guaranteed."

"I have a roof over my head every night. It's called the sky."

"Very clever. Very amusing. I can play poker too, sir, if that's your game. I'll see you, then, Sundays off, to do as you please."

"Now I have every day to do as I please."

"You drive a hard bargain, wretch. Very well. I'll give you a *foreman's* pay, but that's my final offer. Take it or leave it!"

"Who says I want foreman's pay?"

"Then for pity's sake, man, what *do* you want?"

The Gypsyman shrugged loosely, much as a scarecrow might shrug. "*Want* is a word always used by a man who has too much."

Lord Beath was broiling under his skin now, his neck the colour of sliced raw beef. "I'm not bandying words with you anymore, clown. My patience is wearing *extremely* thin. Name your price. Now. It's the chance of your lifetime, damn it."

"No sir." The Gypsyman's smile dropped. "It's the chance of *your* lifetime." He spoke very slowly. "You want to buy me. But I don't wish to be bought," he said, and rose.

"What do you mean?" Beath was taken aback. "Damn you, I haven't finished with you yet! Don't you dare turn your back on me! Hear me out!" His outpourings meant nothing to the Gypsyman, who kept on walking. Then the aristocrat was forced to grasp at a straw, and it happened to be the right straw: "If you care about these poor dumb animals, you'll listen!"

The Gypsyman stopped at the door but did not turn.

"I own an Arab stallion recently shipped in from Tangiers," said the Marquess. "It cost me—well, it doesn't matter to you what the thing cost me. The point is, it was meant as a birthday gift to my daughter, but it's completely wild, like a mad thing. It has kicked holes in the stable walls, bitten fingers off, refused food, foaming at the mouth—the vets don't know why. No-one can go near it. I've had the best trainers in England up here, and the Continent, but none of them can break it."

"Shame," murmured the Gypsyman. "All that money down the drain." He reached for the door handle.

Lord Beath's voice rose. "Before you go, my friend, I tell you this. If my daughter is not riding that horse within a month, thoroughbred and beauty it may be, I promise you it will be shot and sold for dog meat."

I saw the muscles in the Gypsyman's back clench. He rolled his skull on his neck before turning and walking back until he and the landowner stood face to face.

He held out his grimy hand.

Beath hesitated, then reached out to shake it. Before he had, the Gypsyman had spat in his own palm and clasped the Lord's firmly. "I shall."

"Shall? Shall what?"

"Name my price," whispered the Gypsyman, before the other's hand was extracted, with effort, from his grip.

After a pause, the Marquess told him to be at the stables, six o'clock sharp the next morning, and in the same bombastic flurry with which they arrived, he and his hangers-on left. The Gypsyman did not return to his seat beside me, but instead sat alone in the shadows across the room, silent in the hubbub around him, playing with a loose thread on one of his coat buttons. Sensing that he did not wish further conversation, I went to the bar to ask the landlord to give me a morning call, no later than seven. He ensured me he would do so. I wished him goodnight and turned to wish the same to the Gypsyman—only to find that the chair was empty and he was gone.

Next morning a knocking snapped me awake and I arrived in a bewildered demeanour at the breakfast table set for me. The landlord's wife, a merry soul, tried to seduce me towards the bacon fry-up ("Put some meat on you") but my delicacy and reason steered me to the kippers.

I was immersed in writing in my journal an account of the curious day before, when a voice said, "Your kippers, sir."

I looked up and, to my surprise, the twelve-year-old boy I had seen with the Gypsyman stood before me. He wore his shirt unbuttoned, and as he turned to go, of the unsightly growth I had seen on his neck there was no sign whatever.

After breakfast, before setting on my journey, I went into the empty bar and found the thorny twig still leaning on the mantelpiece—and that the snail was dead.

The rest of that day was spent in Newich, and nothing of note concerning the present narrative occurred until the following morning, when I set out for the same location.

Outside the inn stood a magnificent dray, to which were harnessed two equally magnificent Suffolk Punches, enjoying well-earned water from the trough. My usual disinterest in animals lapsed, and I could not resist stroking the fine fellows' enormous necks. The drayman and I were chatting idly—he amused at the city fool, I don't doubt. I then chanced a question, idly, as to whether he'd seen the extraordinary exhibition by the Romany chap at the Horse Fair; did he know of any way to control a horse to the extent of dancing, prancing, stopping, or starting with no apparent reward or punishment? The drayman suddenly went very quiet, and regarded me now with deep suspicion. He then climbed onto the dray with his colleague. His parting gesture was to knock on the wooden seat beside him, three times.

The incident preoccupying my mind, that evening I explained to my landlord what had happened. He shrugged and said, "He's probably one of them too."

"One of whom?"

"You never heard of the Horse Whisperers? The Brotherhood of the Horseman's Word?"

I shook my head.

"I don't know much," he said. "But I'll tell you what I *do* know."

He said his first knowledge of the Horse Whisperers came when, as a young boy thirty years before, he saw gypsies attending the Horse Fair at his home town in Lincolnshire. His mother called them the *Yan Tan Tethera*.[2] He went on to tell me that the 'Word' they whisper is secret to this day, and they are duty bound not to reveal it to anyone but a blacksmith or a military farrier, on pain of death. That was where their Order originated from, it seems; the only horses native to the British Isles are Connemara,

---

2. This expression I have only been able to trace to Cumberland shepherds' dialect for 'one, two, three'; but perhaps a shepherd's relationship with his beasts is not so far removed from the Horseman's with his.

New Forest, or Shetland ponies, so inevitably any secret society based on horsemanship must have its roots in the Roman cavalry and the mediaeval farriers who inherited their expertise. Perhaps the Gypsyman's art did, then, come from Egypt, one of the many mysteries of that ancient civilisation.

But that art was not confined to equine skills. The landlord of the Busheller's said his uncle went to the *Yan Tan* for a cure for rheumatism, was given a garter of eelskin to wear, and had never had a bit of trouble since. He himself remembered being given a potion made out of powdered horsehair and mouldy bread to banish worms. This made me surmise that the Horse Whisperers were akin, perhaps, to the 'Cunning Men,' or white wizards, of Essex and East Anglia—an agricultural sect created at a time when tradition, legend, and magic were as trusted as the fact that season followed season.

The rest of that day, the rest of that week, was spent largely at Newich Church.

Finally the explanation for the ghostly phenomenon was forthcoming: a colony of rats in the belfry was scaling the spire for windfall nuts and fruit embedded in the covering of moss. At dusk, in a certain light, the swarm gave the appearance of a climbing figure. My recommendation to the rector was not bell, book, and candle, but the rather more prosaic cure of rat poison.

On my final visit, however, the priest, when pressed, confirmed my suspicion that the Marquess of Beath was a most disreputable individual, who blamed his excessive drinking upon the death of his wife, though rumour had it that cause and effect were exactly the reverse. He was merely a brute with a bank account, and a terrible employer given to violent rages, thrashing his servants to the point that their nerves were shredded, or they simply walked out. "He spent a fortune on a stallion that no-one can tame," I said. "Perhaps it is a match made in heaven. It sounds as if they deserve each other's vile temperament."

That evening, as a bleary August sun rested on Heyman's Hill, I strolled back to town along the line of the river with a sense of accomplishment that a natural explanation had been deduced and all was accountable in the world. The cobalt flash of a kingfisher was explicable, and even the balmy crackle of ferns against my shins the mere science of a summer's day.

Before I had emerged from the woods overlooking Beath Chase, I began to hear the most lovely, natural laughter. I parted some branches, and in the field not two hundred yards from me saw a purebred black stallion with a girl of eleven on its back, circling a man who held neither lunge nor whip, but stood with hands in pockets, chewing a frond of grass. It was the Gypsyman. The horse was trotting gaily, and the girl, whom I clearly recognised as Lady Romela Beath, was laughing with unbridled (no pun intended) joy. Her white skirts shimmered and a dainty hat sat tilted on her head, and she was riding, with what horse-people call a good seat, the mount I knew must be the 'crazed' Arab—yet it was as docile as a seaside donkey. I questioned the evidence of my eyes. Was it *possible* this could be the same creature that had been described as unbreakable? The Gyspyman was laughing too, as if there were nothing more perfect in the world than a man, a little girl, and a horse, under God's sky.

I felt immediately like a spy, and so retreated into the shade of the undergrowth, peering out with my binoculars. They focused on the rugged yet kind features of the Romany as he lifted the girl from the horse's back, his strong hands looking huge against her tiny waist. It was a moment of great intimacy, but total innocence.

Nevertheless, my guilt overcame me. I returned my glasses to their case and hurried back through the woods to find the well-beaten path to town. Suddenly I heard a loud snap, and a cry was torn involuntarily from my lungs. I fell, but did not fall—for my ankle was gripped in the vicious jaws of a trap. I tried to extract my foot, but the trap's metal teeth were relentless and, shocked by the sight of seeping blood, I lost my balance and toppled backwards into a bush, scattering a cacophony of starlings and thrushes asunder.

Thereafter I lapsed in and out of consciousness. My eyelids fluttered at the sun lancing out of the canopy above, and what followed took on the semblance of a morphine dream. Alerted by my shout, the Gypsyman's face floated into my field of vision. I found his touch as calming as if he had administered a sleeping draught. If he uttered a prayer it was in a language far beyond my knowledge or comprehension. Lady Romela stood at his shoulder, until she backed away and ran to fetch help on his instruction. He made a shrill whistle, as if imitating a bird call, then prised open the trap and released my foot, exposing a long, ugly bite mark. He assured me that no bones were broken, then he took off his red neckerchief and tied a knot in it—this, by the logic of sympathetic magic, to inhibit loss of blood. Next, he proceeded to clean the wound with hog's fat, then bind it with cheese rind, strips of old harness leather, and strands of spider web, while I watched and tried to memorise his actions through a semi-anaesthetised haze.

Some minutes later I saw a chestnut mare without reins or saddle approaching through the trees, and the Gypsyman helped me onto it. My body protested that I had never ridden in my life, but he told me to hang on tightly. He then went and whispered into the horse's ear. It nodded—I swear it *nodded*—and was away. I am convinced it galloped, for it seemed to cover the distance in so short a time, and yet it felt as smooth as being carried on a hammock.

The next thing I knew, we had arrived outside the Busheller's Arms. I slid off the horse's bare back, but almost before I could turn, the mare was galloping back the way it had come. It had vanished by the time the landlord came out, alarmed by the sound of hoofbeats, and caught me in his arms as I finally succumbed to oblivion.

I woke the next morning lying in my bed, fully dressed and bathed in sunlight, thinking it *had* been a dream. That comfort was soon dispelled. My host arranged a visit by Dr Cass, the local general practitioner, who despite the rips in my trouser leg could find no corresponding wounds, or marks of any kind, on my skin. I began to tell him what had transpired, but gave up when I saw he was already packing his black bag. "You may say that, but it's simply impossible," he opined. I was tempted to quote *Alice in Wonderland*, who said that one should believe at least one impossible thing before breakfast. That morning, I did.

My business in Newich completed, I returned to Oxford, where several cases of Supernatural interest awaited my attention—namely the haunting of Box Tunnel, and my future involvement with the strange affair surrounding the Coptic Liturgy. I admit I quickly forgot the curious incidents that had occurred in Wiltshire, thinking them of passing folkloric interest, but inconsequential. As things turned out, they were anything but. The consequence was to greet me, horrifyingly, from the pages of the *Times*, less than a month later:

LADY BEATH MURDERED
GYPSY STABLE-WORKER CHARGED

A travelling Romany Gypsy and horse trader, of no fixed abode, was charged yesterday at Salisbury Assizes with the wilful murder of Lady Romela Beath, aged eleven, on 29 August.

Inspector Hart of Wiltshire Constabulary said that he saw the gypsy at Newich police station, where he charged him with having murdered Lady Beath. The man said nothing except that he understood the charge.

Lady Beath, the only child of Sir Anthony Egerton, Marquess of Beath and the late Marchioness, Isabel, Baroness Conant, was found in a hayloft at her father's stables ...

What the *Times* passed over was dwelt upon by other publications. She had been killed by a pitchfork, the spikes of which had punctured her lungs and heart.

I was shocked to the core. This very man I had spoken with, laughed with, and bought a drink for—was this a man who could *kill*? Did the secrecy in those eyes that held the oath of the Horseman's Word also disguise darker inner motives? Was that fellow, that plain fellow, who seemed so at one with the beasts of the field, no more than a beast himself?

My mind was in turmoil. I had no answers.

Over the next days and weeks I scanned the newspapers, all the newspapers, begging for the news that this was all a dreadful mistake. No such news appeared. Instead, I travelled to Wiltshire, and had to endure the awful accumulation of evidence from the public gallery of the courtroom.

The Marquess broke down in tears when asked to relive the moment he found his daughter's body in the blood-drenched hay. He said he had dismissed the Romany the previous day, without remuneration, because of what he saw as the 'unhealthy interest' he showed in his daughter. He said he never dreamed that the man would be so base as to return and wreak his revenge upon such an innocent.

Throughout this testimony the Gypsyman stared at Lord Anthony, saying nothing.

He himself had no defence. He could not account for where he was at the time of the murder—the act of sleeping alone in a field rarely has witnesses.

The Prosecutor asked him to explain how a horseshoe was found under Lady Romela's pillow. He merely said she was "feeling sick of heart".

This raised the whole question of charms and talismans, which both the Defence and Prosecution bandied about for days. The Prosecution's case intended to stitch together its evidence with the implication of a secret sect, and thereby a suggestion of witchcraft which the jury would inevitably link to the ritualistic quality of the murder. The Defence, on the other hand, wanted to avoid this line of assumption by a simple statement from the accused that he was not a witch, and have him state what he was.

This, of course, the Gypsyman would not do. He simple said, "Hele, conceal, never reveal, neither write nor dite, nor recite, nor cut, nor carve, nor write in sand," and at a later point: "Not to any save a blacksmith or a farrier." But I knew that even if the court could find one, he too would be bound by the same oath. He would not break his vow for the sake of his neck, and that, to me, is courage more than any so-called hero who shot his enemy with a rifle at a hundred yards.

He was asked outright how he had made the old nag at the Beath Horse Fair sprint like a gelding. He merely said that the learned gentleman would do so himself with a chunk of raw ginger under his tail. The courtroom responded with laughter. Similarly, he countered every other question of black magic with tired, if futile, ease.

But a pitchfork is a pitchfork, and the evidence was conclusive that he belonged to a secret society that had evolved from a mediaeval craftsman's guild, rather like the Freemasons, and with its own oaths, passwords, salutes, and handshakes.

The Prosecution finally put in the witness box a man from Scotland who had some knowledge of the Aberdeen Brotherhood of the Horseman's Word. He was asked to describe what he had seen one night in his home town, in an isolated barn at Martinmas, whereupon he described a group of thirteen people who initiated a blindfolded youngster, the 'Orra Loon', with a crown (which as it happened was a hat designed to look as if it had horse's ears), robe, sword belt, horse blanket, and a leather girth. At the end of the ceremony, the lad was led into the 'cauf-hoose' for a 'shak O' Auld Hornie'—to shake hands with the Devil (whose cloven hoof, surely, when one is blindfold, must feel strangely like a calf's).

The Prosecutor went on, from this curiously irrelevant statement, to submit for the jury's information that the Inner Circle of a Horse Whisperer's coven (his word, not mine) was known by the Greek word for ring, *kuklos*. It is interesting, he said, that in 1865 a group of young cavalry officers in Pulaski, Tennessee, took this word *kuklos* for their club or clan, spelled clan with a K for the sake of alliteration, and called itself the *kuklos* klan, or Ku Klux Klan.

This association with murderous evil was, in my opinion, unforgivable, but before the judge's gavel had fallen to quell the hubbub, it was out. The seed had been sown in the minds of the jury, and once planted it could not be undone. The Gypsyman, in his only show of emotion, gently shook his head.

The next day he was pronounced guilty of murder and sentenced to death. Before being taken from the dock for the last time, he gave one glance towards Sir Anthony, and slowly and deliberately knocked on the wooden rail, three times. A murmur of perplexity rose from the court, and the poor man was taken below.

You may recall that the British Romanies united to present a substantial petition of appeal against the verdict to Downing Street, to no avail. The Gypsyman, whose name I never knew, and which never appeared in the newspapers, was hanged.

He must have been aware of my presence in the public gallery, because to my astonishment he left, addressed to my care, his knapsack, the contents of which intrigued me more, even, than Pandora's mythic box. Opening it the day after his execution, I found a horsehair necklace, a phial that to my delicate nose seemed to contain urine, and another substance that a chemist friend of mine found to be a mixture of quicksilver, sulphur, saltpeter, and East Indian resin. There was also a lump of lead the shape of a quail's egg, a pot of animal grease, some feathers, and a wire 'twitch' for pinching a horse's upper lip when working on the hindquarters.

Most interesting of all, I found two talismans. The first was in a leather pouch, and was a small thing, like a wishbone wrapped in raw, rotting flesh. It smelled foul. This, I discovered from research, was called the *frog*. A frog or natterjack toad is killed and laid out until the flesh has rotted off it; the bones are then scattered in a stream, and the bone which goes against the current is selected. This is invariably the ilium, or main bone in the frog's pelvic girdle. It resembles the 'frog' or V shape on the underside of a horse's hoof, thus making both a verbal and visual pun so important to magic. The second amulet was a spongy pad of tissue which had a pleasant odour—a mixture of sorrel, bryony, cinnamon, rosemary, and tansy. This is called the *milt*, and is a small pad of tissue found in a foal's mouth when it is born. The Horseman has to be very skilful to get it out before it is swallowed. He then dries it, and impregnates it with aromatic substances. These two were, then, the 'drawing' and 'jading' amulets used by the Horse Whisperer: the frog to repel, the milt to attract. These were not the implements or fascinations of a murderer.

A horse whinnied in the street outside my window and, struck by an irrational feeling of deep remorse, I resolved then and there to return the knapsack to Beath St August. What to do with it when I got there, I had no idea.

I arrived on the morning train and renewed acquaintance with the landlord of the Busheller's. I am not certain whether he shared my misgivings about the trial, but our mutual knowledge of the case prevented us sharing light conversation. I took my pint and could not help but sit in the same seat near the fireplace that I had occupied when I talked to my Romany friend. I sat the knapsack next to me, and though a book was open on my knee I did not read a word.

The bar-room was empty, so when a man in hunting pinks entered, I noticed him.

He ordered a double, and no sooner was it down his throat than he ordered another.

"Steady on, lad," said the landlord.

"Steady on nothing," said the young man. "You try and steady on after what I've seen." He closed his eyes and the second glass was banged down empty. His boyish face was pale as parchment.

The landlord leaned forward. "You know what a publican is here for, lad? To pull pints? No. To lend his ear if it's needed. To share troubles if troubles need to be shared."

The huntsman laughed. "You don't want to share mine!" He suddenly noticed a brown stain on his white trousers and rubbed it furiously, beginning to sob. I walked over, put one arm round his shoulders, and guided him to a chair by the hearth. The chap's teeth were chattering and his eyes as fixed and shiny as buttons. In the light from the window, the brown stain was now clearly as scarlet as his tunic.

"What on earth has happened?" I implored.

"The Beath is dead. Sir Anthony. The Marquess, that's what has happened—*dead!*"

"What?"

"Don't—it's a fact," he said. "Less than an hour ago. I've just come back with Dr Cass. Give it a second and he'll be in too, you see if he isn't. The others just shot off their separate ways, but I needed a stiffener before I can . . . anything."

"Good God!" I said.

"God, good or otherwise. He's dead. And I saw it happen. Damnedest thing. *Damnedest* thing in the world."

"Was it his heart?" asked the landlord.

"What heart?"

"Then how?" I asked. 'An accident of some kind?"

"Aye. Some kind!" The man nodded and took several deep breaths. "We gathered at the Chase early this morning. The Marquess had some foxes caught and was ready to release them soon after breakfast. It was a trick he liked, to ensure the day wasn't wasted. Champagne ran like water, of course. He was sozzled by the time most of us were awake. We had to fit in with his plans, naturally. We had to join his toast; he insisted we all raised our glasses: 'To English justice!' So we did, and smashed our glasses in the fireplace. He roared with laughter like a madman.

"Most of us had come with our own mounts, and stood waiting while Beath went to get his hunter from the stables. It was a longer wait than we expected. The hounds were baying incessantly and becoming restless; they wanted to get going. There was still no sign of Beath.

"In the end, I was elected to fetch him. I found him at the stable doors, wrestling with his hunter's reins, tugging with every ounce of his strength to try to pull the beast from the barn. It would not move an inch. It refused point-blank to emerge, and so did every other horse in the stocks—every single one, even when Beath lashed at them with his whip.

"Finally, in an absolute rage, he stormed back to the courtyard, and demanded Featherley get off his horse and give him the reins. Featherley hesitated, and Beath, taking it as refusal, swiped him across the face with his crop and dragged him from his saddle. Ignoring the man's bleeding cheeks, he mounted Featherley's grey and ordered the hunt to begin.

"We moved off into the fields, walking and then trotting behind the pack of hounds, eagerly awaiting the first sign of a scent. At last they found one, and were off over Mellish Hill towards the old Saxon hill fort. We followed down into the dale and through Aldice Wood past Colm Leigh Farm. I was keeping pace with Beath at the head of the running, and now we were separate from the rest, tracing the scent up a steep incline to the grassy plateau of The Hob. All this time, the Marquess was cursing the fox, the horse, the weather, the land, the hounds, and everything else in sight.

"It was back in Aldice Wood that he and I trotted through a clearing, our heads low to avoid the branches. I slowly discerned the scene up ahead through the crisscrossing of foliage, and I'll swear to what I saw to my dying day, and it was this: the hounds sat obediently and calmly, heads turned back as if waiting for us to follow them. Some fifteen or twenty yards ahead, on a log, sat the fox, similarly looking back and waiting for us—he and the dogs seemed in that moment peculiarly united in some inexplicable conspiracy—but before I could call Lord Beath's attention to it, they were away in a blur of the red brush and brown-and-white pursuers.

"I was certain by now, with that and the incident at the stables, that something very strange was in the air. This feeling was never more acute than when Lord Beath's horse stopped dead in a stretch of open countryside, absolutely rigid in spite of the digging of the spurs. Lord Beath suddenly turned, with a look of sheer terror.

"'Did you hear that?'"

"I said I hadn't. 'Listen!' he hissed. There was nothing but silence.

"Then I heard, quite distinctly, a brisk *knock-knock-knock* on wood. 'There!' cried the Marquess, in a mixture of rage and fear. 'Don't say you can't hear it now!' I said of course I could—and there was the woodpecker at that far tree making it!

"Beath grunted and began whipping his horse, or rather Featherley's grey, mercilessly.

"I was on the point of voicing an objection, at the risk of getting the same treatment as Featherley, when the grey's head twitched, her ears flickered, she snorted; and suddenly she rocketed from stock-still into a gallop. Totally unprepared, Lord Beath almost flew from the saddle there and then, but cling on he did, and I stood frozen as horse and rider shot up across the hill.

"It must have been only moments later, perhaps even a fraction of a second, before my own horse was after them, but they had gained a remarkable distance.

"What more is there to say that I haven't already said to the doctor? Featherly's grey was going full gallop at the hedge, and at the last moment refused it. Lord Beath was thrown, then the horse flew into a gallop again, as if a sudden order had been given it. When we found him, a quarter-mile on, he was quite dead—of a broken neck, Dr Cass said. A freak accident. Act of God, if you like. The Marquess had become ensnared in the loop of his own reins; they had twisted like a noose around his throat, and he had been throttled as the horse ran mindlessly on.

"Now, barman, one more for the road, please, and I'll be away. And not on horseback. You'll never catch me on one of those things again as long as I live."

There is very little to add.

The next day I took the Gypsy's knapsack, along with his milt and frog amulets, to the nearest blacksmith. He gave me the same strange eye of suspicion as the drayman, but took them without asking for an explanation—not that I could have given him one, apart from the feeling of blasphemy I experienced with them in my possession. I have since learned that it was a Horseman's trick, if he was not paid, to smear the jading substance over the threshold of a stable to make the horses refuse to come out. More importantly, I wondered what the Horseman's price *was*, and whether he had been denied it, in the manner of the Pied Piper of Hamelin.

It may be of interest, as an addendum, that I have also learned that three brisk knocks are known as the Horseman's knock, and are probably used in their secret initiation, or as some sort of salute or identification. I am also told that, to this day, horses shy at the gates of Beath Chase and refuse to enter. The house itself, and the stables, fell quickly into disrepair, and were demolished. A landscaped parkland took its place, but you will still find the name on a good map.

Last of all, with regard to the combination of substances— cheese rind, rotten leather, etc.—which the Gypsyman applied to my wound: ten years later, in 1928, the discovery of penicillin in mould cultures was made by Alexander Flemyng.

So science merely rediscovers the knowledge of the past, which stares us in the face through folklore, legend, and the Supernatural. Perhaps, ten years from now, we shall similarly unveil a scientific explanation for communication, albeit a whisper, from beyond the grave.

Perhaps; perhaps.

THE ARSE-LICKER

I HAVE TO SAY I'M NOT REALLY temperamentally suited to business, as such. It's never been a particular interest of mine. To succeed, to really succeed, you have to have a ruthless streak and a selfish, ambitious bent. I have neither of those attributes. I don't think of them as being particularly desirable attributes to have, to be honest with you. But you have to fit in, obviously. You have to pretend you're one of them. It's a dog-eat-dog world out there. So I've learnt to look like a dog and bark like a dog, but I'm not really a dog at all. I'm probably a worm.

Not that it worries me unduly. You have to come to terms with who you are in life and I realised fairly early on I wasn't exactly a go-getter. I wasn't somebody who others looked up to or were impressed by in any way. I was physically unprepossessing and intellectually average. My parents never deluded themselves I was special, because I wasn't. In school I always envied the children in class whose arms always shot in the air when they had answers to the teacher's questions. The ones who got gold stars. The ones who got the school prizes or won cups on sports days. I never acquired any of those noble achievements for effort, probably because I never really applied any effort to anything. Though I did pick plums from the tree in our garden once and leave them in a paper bag for our English teacher, and I'm sure that was instrumental in getting me get a B+ at the end of term. After that she definitely looked over at me with a smile on her face, Miss Hexham, so that had to mean something, I thought. She had a nice smile, Miss Hexham.

This is the crucial thing, you see. From an early age I learnt how to get what I wanted by ingratiating myself.

I found that if my mum said she loved me as she tucked me up in bed, it was politic to say "I love you too" back. Experience showed things worked in your favour that way. If you said to your grandparents "I miss you" when they visited, as often as not it meant they'd buy you more Lego. Basically, if you show people you like them they'll find it very difficult not to like you back. All the more so in the workplace. If you treat the right people—always the big cheese, never the breadsticks—with innate reverence and pander enthusiastically to their every whim, however ill-founded or undeserved, there's a good chance you might prosper, while others who have been less conspicuous in their admiration go to the wall.

My behaviour was simply a strategy for survival in life. I didn't plan it. It just fell into a pattern that way. I didn't know I was doing it, half the time. It was just—well—*me*.

Telling X that they'd saved the company. Telling Y that the way they dealt with a situation was impeccable. Telling Z that I envied their resolve and business acumen beyond measure. That I thought their wife was great fun and their children were gorgeous enough to be photographic models—though neither was even remotely the case.

Frankly, it was my default position. It was also, frankly, the one thing I was good at.

For instance, I would offer to cast my eye over one of Innox's internal reports in my spare time, saying the next morning I thought it was brilliant. Sometimes, as a way of nuancing my effluent praise, I'd offer spurious notes—" . . . not that one can really improve on *perfection* . . . "

I'd get him a tea or coffee. "Milk, no sugar, isn't it?" (I'd long since made it my business to know it was.)

Staying late. Making sure not only was I last in the office but that he *saw* I was the last in the office.

"Don't work too hard!"

"I won't, Brian! Love to Margaret and the boys!"

Careful to leave a spare jacket on the back of my chair, so it looked like I was first in the next day.

Opening doors before he got to them.

Calling the lift.

Calling a cab. Paying the taxi driver before he could delve into his pocket for change.

Getting flowers for his wife on their anniversary. "No worries. There's a florist right next to where I get my baguette at lunchtime. No trouble at all. What does she like? Roses, d'you think? How much do you want to spend? No, don't give it me now. We can worry about that later."

Brushing crumbs from a seat before he sat down. Wiping the table under his coffee cup with a paper napkin. Offering him my expensive retractable ballpoint pen across the boardroom table when his had run out.

"Keep it."

"No . . ."

"Don't be silly. Really."

"Are you sure? Well, that's . . ."

Bingo.

More brownie points.

"Nice tie. Beautiful colour. Brian, I'm not being rude, but do you mind me asking where you get your male grooming products? Do you use moisturizer? Because lately you look ten years younger. No, you really do."

Birthday cards. Naturally.

Christmas cards. Vital. Quality ones. None of your cheap charity rubbish. The message written inside carefully composed for the occasion. Not too long. Not too obsequious. Not too crawling or obvious. Just striking the right balance between formal and friendly. Just implying, slightly, that his friendship as a colleague and mentor was so important that without it you might take your own life. That kind of thing.

It was an art.

An art I'd perfected over years of diligent application. It put me in a special position. Close to the throne. It gave me the ear of the King. It made me secure and unassailable.

Or so I thought.

His name was Terry Kotwika, and from the moment he said "Hi" I decided I didn't like him. I don't like "Hi" at the best of times. I don't see what's so wrong with a good, old-fashioned, Anglo-Saxon "Hello". But mainly I disliked him because he wore his suit like a best man at a wedding who wanted to sneak out at the earliest opportunity for a Silk Cut. He also had a haircut like Paul Weller. Never a good idea. Not even if you're Paul Weller.

We were all called into the boardroom and change was announced. I don't like change. Innox was rubbing his hands with glee—never a pretty sight—and we were introduced to two thrusting new executives joining the company with the specific brief of bringing in new clients. Oh, goodie.

There was another chap, Rashid Parker, who seemed pudgy and ineffectual, incessantly hoisting his belt up over his draught-excluder of a midriff bulge. Even his moss-like beard was apologetic. I could handle him. He was invisible even as you looked at him. This other one—this *Kotwika*—that was another story.

As soon as the meeting dispersed, I hurried up and shook him enthusiastically by the hand—old habits die hard—impressing on him how eager I was to work together. He didn't reply, simply staring me out with a fixed, oily grin and crow's feet entrenched at the sides of his face in an expression somewhere between indifference and contempt.

I was the one who should have been contemptuous, if anything. I was the Financial Director and this was the first I knew about us taking on new blood. The other board members wandered off, silently peeved at being cut out of the loop. I merely knocked on Innox's door, poked my head round, gave him a staunch thumb-up and whispered that I thought his decision had been "really exciting".

I lied.

The duo were good at their job, no doubt about it, but they looked down their nose at us in accounts. We were the bean counters, while they were the alpha males of the pack. They even sat in their chairs differently. They *lolled*.

Even so, it didn't bother me at first. Live and let live is my motto. I never rock the boat. Then something did rock it. My boat, anyway.

We were in a meeting. Kotwika had his little take-out cardboard cup of latte from Starbucks because it was just after lunch, but I didn't have a coffee and, as I was going to the kitchen, I asked Innox if he'd like me to get him one too. "Milk, no sugar?"

"Three bags full, sir," muttered Kotwika. And *sniggered*.

I pretended not to notice, but there was a definite smirk on his face. And when I came back from the coffee machine, the smirk was still there.

I think it was the smirk that did it.

After that, whenever I opened a door for Innox, or pushed the lift call button, or brushed his chair with my hand before he sat down—I knew Kotwika was watching. I knew Kotwika was at his desk, yards away, *lolling*. Not saying anything. He didn't need to *say* anything. It was enough just to *loll*.

Pretty soon I didn't need to look at him to get a cold chill on the back of my neck. And when we'd go to the Cittie of Yorke in High Holborn after work, that's where it would happen again. I was always first to the bar, ordering the first bottle of red wine. Knowing the Shiraz Innox liked best. And when the others drifted off after the first bottle to catch their little trains home to suburbia from Farrington or Waterloo East, I'd habitually keep my beloved M.D. company over the second bottle, and third. Listen to his tiresome tales of woe, however boring. Laugh at his long-winded jokes and stories I'd heard a hundred times before. Endure yet again why his wife didn't understand him and his spoilt children made his life a nightmare. And if he got too paralytic, I'd make sure he got a cab to the station. Sometimes be there to mop the dribble from his tie and make sure he got on the right train to Dorking.

"Colin. What a surprise, mate." It was Kotwika, already with a bottle of Shiraz and three glasses. "Are you going to hang up Brian's coat? There's the rack over there. Go on, old son. Chop, chop."

When I turned back from the coat hooks, there he was, laughing. Innox sitting beside him, laughing too.

Which was the moment I knew it could all be taken away from me in an instant. Everything I'd worked for. Everything I'd put my heart and soul into all those years.

I felt inadequate. I felt pathetic. Most of all, I felt threatened. But I didn't know what to do about it. I suppose I waited for an opportunity to land in my lap. And land in my lap, eventually, it did.

I was presenting the annual figures for the company and they weren't good. They weren't optimistic at all. I couldn't sugar-coat it. Budget restraints had to be made. The question of redundancies came up, as I knew it would. The directors had gathered in the conference room—we all knew the writing was on the wall, quite frankly—and I'd been up all night working on the only rescue strategy I had to offer, but really it was a strategy to do what I wanted and had waited for patiently for the previous three months.

"Last in, first out." I lifted my eyes nervously. "Sorry, but it's the only practical solution. The blunt fact is it's far too expensive to get rid of people who've been with the company for years—twenty, thirty years, some of them. The pay-offs, pensions. Look at the bottom line . . . " I could see Innox's normally florid complexion turn the colour of Milk of Magnesia. "Horrid, I know—but we can't think with our heart, we have to think with our heads, if we want this company to survive. It's rotten, but..." A pall of gloom descended like a slab of concrete as they silently perused my single, brutally concise, final page of A4. "I like Parker and Kotwika as much as anybody, I really do, but..."

For a long while nobody spoke, and neither did I.

Innox said, "Bugger." He leaned back and exhaled air at the ceiling, looking like a *putto* misplaced from the ceiling of the Sistine Chapel. "Hell." He threw down my spreadsheet, which skidded across the surface of the boardroom table and ended up, almost magically, in front of me. "Fuck."

"I wouldn't like to be in your shoes, telling them," murmured the ash-blonde stick insect from Human Resources. "Do you want me to do it?"

"Fuck off, Christine," said Innox.

"Brian's fantastically good at giving people bad news," I said. "I've seen him in action first-hand. He really is exceptional. Even inspirational."

Innox didn't look at me. Maybe he didn't even hear me, and for a short, unpleasant frisson of time I thought I might have overstepped the mark.

"Fuck off, the lot of you," he said. "And Chubb, tell the two of them to step in here and let's get it over with. Bollocks," he added, like punctuation.

Most of the staff had gone home. They tended to drift away early on a Friday. I never did, of course. I think I was arranging a BACS payment to a freelancer who'd chased me twice by e-mail and three times with a phone call, virtually claiming he was living a hand-to-mouth existence and his house was about to be repossessed and his children sold into slavery, no doubt. The usual sob story. Water off a duck's back to me. I always tried to avoid payments in the month they're invoiced, delaying them into the next quarter by subterfuge or obfuscation, preferably. That was my job.

Innox was working late too. Seeing a tweak of an opportunity, I rapped the glass separating our two offices and mimed the drinking of a hot beverage. He nodded as if I'd read his mind.

"Coffee or tea?" I mimed.

He lip-read, calling back: "Coffee. Thanks. You're a life saver!"

I smiled, at the time absolutely convinced we were the last ones in the office. Most of the overhead lighting panels over the desks were off and the black lady was circumnavigating with her ridiculously large vacuum cleaner, a machine roughly contemporaneous with Stevenson's Rocket. So when I saw Terry Kotwika standing at the coffee machine, it stopped me in my tracks.

I hadn't spoken to him since the fateful day. Not surprisingly, I had kept my distance. This was the first time I had seen him close to, and it shocked me to see that he was a shadow of his former self, monochromatic under the fluorescent tube.

"Hi. What did you want? Coffee?"

"Yes," I said. The wind taken out of his sails, he seemed almost human.

"I'll make you one."

"No, it's all right. Actually I'm getting one for Brian."

"That's OK. I'll get one for him too."

"Sure?"

"How does he like it?"

"Milk, no sugar. I'm the same. Are you sure about this?"

"Yeah. Why not?"

"OK. Well. That's really kind of you. Thanks. Thanks a lot."

If it was a parting gesture, it was a nice one. I felt my cheeks reddening, so turned away and returned to my monk's cell.

On the way I passed his desk and could see now that it was starkly denuded of personal possessions. Everything—the robot pencil sharpener, crayon drawing to "Daddy", pictures of his wife and kids making faces on a rollercoaster ride—all had been piled into a cardboard box.

I sat at my own, dumbly staring at my screen saver until he brought me my mug. As he turned to go I said: "There are cuts across the board these days, everywhere. You can't be certain of anything these days. It's terrible."

He shrugged philosophically.

"Terry, you know it was pure logistics. Nothing personal."

"No. Of course not."

"You know what they say. One door closes another one opens. Got to stay positive, eh?"

"Sure."

"Everyone's suffering in the current economic climate."

"Absolutely."

Then, to my astonishment, he turned around, came back in and, smiling, took my hand in both of his, smiling as he shook it, but he didn't meet my eyes and I thought he looked—*diminished*. After he shut the office door gently after him, I sat there drinking my coffee, draining it to the dregs.

When I woke up on the floor of the conference room, the first thing I realised was that the cleaner's contraption was no longer thrumming in my head. The panic question of how I'd got there kicked me fully awake and I jolted involuntarily, eyes popping open, legs flailing in all directions as I discovered a gag in my mouth and wire or some kind of plastic flex tying my wrists together behind my back.

I crabbed, spidered, Catherine-wheeled with my left buttock as a pivot until my shoulder blades hit the wall.

Kotwika sat opposite me, semi-slumped, legs out straight on the carpet tiles, the tread of his shoes facing me. As I squirmed wildly and fought for breath, he merely picked up a greasy bundle of paper smeared with chilli sauce and devoured what remained of a half-eaten doner kebab, remaining nonplussed as I writhed, wiggling as best as I could towards the door, struggling to hoist myself to my knees and attempting whilst keeping my balance to head-butt the door handle and effect my escape.

The most he did was to lick the chilli sauce from his fingertips and squint slightly in irritation at my gyrations. He knew of course—as I was soon to discover—that escape was impossible. It only took a few bangs with my chin and nudges with my cheekbone to deduce the door was locked. I could see through feverishly blinking and de-focused eyes that the open-plan office beyond was swathed in darkness, and I was trapped with—for want of a better word—a fucking madman.

Needless to say, my futile attempts at screams for help and miserably stifled howls of anguish fell on deaf ears. Kotwika let them pass like a wind through the trees, with a degree of patience that, under different circumstances, I might have found laudable. Not that my exertions got me anywhere, geographically or psychologically. They resulted only in a drastic lack of breath within minutes and I concluded the very minimum I needed to stay alive was to keep breathing. Easier said than done, when you're trussed up like a Christmas turkey in the company of an insane person. Then I saw the legs.

As my shoulder slid down the door, the sound of a moan that wasn't mine made me twist awkwardly. From this position I could see a man's lower limbs under the boardroom table on the far side. He was standing up but leaning over, the upper part of his body—which I couldn't see from that angle—outstretched on top of it. Flanked by an avenue of chairs, the legs were bare and pale and sparsely hairy, pinstriped trousers and white boxer shorts bunched at the ankles over lime-green spotted Happy Socks and slip-ons. Even without the moan, which was distinctively bovine behind its gag, the Happy Socks were a clear identifier that the person was Brian Innox.

I yelped in a voice shrill as a woman's, straightened my spine in a snap, scuttling away from the sight, bringing my knees up sharply when I reached the corner to stop myself from keeling over on my side.

"I'll open the door for you, sir. I'll carry your lunch, sir. Warm your seat sir? Third floor, sir? Like the taste of your Kiwi, sir. Open your zip sir? Shake it for you now, sir?" Kotwika crouched to look me in the face. "Do you know *irritating* that was? How *sick* it made me feel—*Every, Single, Day*?" I felt the cold O of the barrel of the pistol—later identified by the police as a Glock 9mm—against the centre of my forehead: from my eye-view it looked like a silver Boeing 757 had embedded itself into my pineal gland. "But don't worry, *everyone's suffering in this economic climate*." The pupils of his eyes shone like nail heads. "No. *You*'re going to suffer, arse-licker!"

I felt my scalp give a little as he dragged me on all fours to the far end of the conference table, the gun to my skull the whole time. Then he hoisted me by the hair so that I was forced to a kneeling position and slapped me lightly on the cheeks as if to ensure my fullest attention. Only when he moved aside, clearing my line of sight did I truly understand what was happening. Only then did I grasp the full extent of his lunacy.

What faced me was Innox's naked arse, in all its pallid glory, its flesh textured with gooseflesh now it was exposed to the elements, albeit warmed by the hot breath of the fan heaters overhead. I was facing two dunes separated by a tight-lipped crack, each puckered and dimpled by the herniation of subcutaneous fat and age-old blackhead craters as well as fresher eruptions, a few in the constellation turning acid yellow at their tips. Below and between, where his underwear must have gathered too tightly, I could detect a blush of chaffing not unlike nappy rash.

I felt sick. I heard the fridge open and close behind me and a bottle top hush as it unscrewed and Kotwika emptied a bottle of orange juice over my boss's exposed behind with the panache of a chef adding olive oil liberally to a salad.

I had to fight to stop my gorge rising in my throat because I didn't want to suffocate, but I emitted strange strangulated sounds of protest.

The liquid ran into the V-shaped cleft at the coccyx and followed the down-guttering to stripe the legs, dripping onto the floor, chased by a generous squirt of the soda siphon that was always on the drinks table, delivered with a painterly flourish.

Innox's buttocks clenched and shuddered as the force of air and water hit them. After the tsunami the skin shone like Michelangelo marble. I half expected the next phase to be a swift buffing by Polish windscreen-cleaners with chamois leathers. But no . . .

Kotwika yanked the gag off me and presented to the tip of my nose a thin slice of lemon held in small metal pincers kept beside the ice bucket.

"No . . ."

"Yes. Oh yes . . ."

Turning away from me, he slid it into the crack of Innox's behind, where it hung precariously, half-in, half-out.

"Do it, *Arse-Licker*. Do what you're best at. Go on! *Do it* and I might just let you *live!*"

He stood behind me and shoved the gun barrel against the back of my head.

For a second I wondered if having my brains blown out might be preferable to the obscene act he was asking me to perform—and perhaps others would have made a different decision—but I realised instantly, or pretty instantly, I had no choice. My mind was racing but I couldn't afford it to be racing. Racing wasn't going to help me. I had to concentrate. No, I had to *stop* concentrating, stop thinking, and just do it. *Just do it*, I thought. *Just stop becoming dead.* That was my priority. Anything else can wait. What you feel about it can wait. What you feel afterwards can wait. Don't even go there. Make my mind blank. Blank.

For Christ's sake—just do it!

I shuffled forward on my knees, level with Innox's arse. It grew closer. It loomed. I could see his back buckling, the tails of his shirt and jacket rolled back. I saw the back of his bald head and the fact that his arms were tied down by rope from the blinds, but as I hobbled closer I lost sight of that and his rear end became my sole focus, as it had to be. The arse with the soda water dripping off it was all. All I dared think about. All I dared consume in my brain. I couldn't allow in anything else. Any sliver of guilt, regret, reluctance, repugnance, revulsion . . .

My stomach heaved. I made noises like a crow. Like I'd swallowed a crow. I couldn't help it.

My nose inches away, its contours hypnotised me. Then became uncannily sharp and vivid. My mouth and lips became desert-dry. My eyes fixed and dilated. I felt I they were exploring the foul landscape like an ant on the face of God. Or God roaming the cold, shivering flesh of a plucked chicken at Tesco's. I was almost touching it . . .

I tried to empty my mind as my face approached the white, hairy, pimply, surface. I licked it, tentatively at first. My tongue retracted involuntarily. My body buckled and spew shot out.

I regained my composure, telling myself it was just water, water and orange juice, water. Nothing, nothing at all.

My insides were having none of it. Coiled like a cobra, my cheeks filled up and I vomited a second time, spraying my knees and forming a puddle on the carpet before me. It came out like a stop-valve had been released. I felt light-headed as colourful spittle hung from the chair-backs.

I forced my tongue out a second time, extending it fully. It was unbearable. The very idea was repulsive. Appalling. Obscene. But what could I do? I was at the mercy of a total maniac. How did I know what he might do if I refused? People got abducted, tortured, kept prisoner, for weeks sometimes. Awful things happened to them. Unspeakable things. How did I know what he would do if I didn't do this?

This was the least of evils, the very least of all possible evils. I knew that. I definitely knew that. And I had to embrace it.

And so, I went in. Feverishly now, to get it over with. Like a dog at its bowl. I ignored the grunts and whimpers coming from the figure bent over the table, quivering as he was, shuddering with impotent rage. I simply stuck to the task in hand, went over every inch of that arse with my tongue extended, rasping against the whiskery flesh like sandpaper. Ignoring the vile stabs that spiked at my taste buds. Ignoring the fact that everything in my biology was telling my stomach to retch yet again—but I couldn't let that stop me. I had to go on. And soon it would be over. The stink of fear expelling from his bowels would be over. The stale nitrogenous urea on my tongue would be over. The heady intoxication of terror as I rubbed the tongue against the full, mythic power of the *glutei maximi* to lick the last droplets of liquid would be over . . .

And finally—it was.

"Arse-Licker!"

I fell back on my knees, gasping, my chest lurching. I think I may also have been sobbing like a baby when he pulled me up by the hair again.

"You think you're done, Arse-Licker? We're not done. We're not even *started* yet. That was just an aperitif, an *amuse bouche*. Now we have the main course."

Which was when he opened the tin of baked beans.

I whimpered.

"Go on. Go for it, Arse-Licker. You know you want to. You know you love it. Licking the old arse . . . "

The sweet sugar of the tomato sauce hit the air and I refused to even think about it this time. I went right in, with a certain sort of defiance. I didn't even look at him. I got my nose right in, starting at the top of the left leg where the beans were running down as if chasing each other, and flicked my tongue at them individually, chameleon-like, working it in long, lingering diagonals, then figures of eight, finally diverting in the latter strokes into short dinky lapping like a cat. All the while thinking of the beauty, because if you thought of the ugliness you were lost. Ugliness would destroy you. Only the beauty would help. Only the beauty would keep you strong.

Gradually the artificial sweetness from the can was displaced by the all-too-human odour of putridity, sweat, and stale urine of my colleague's nether regions. Gradually my roaming pink protrusion delved down to the wrinkles behind his testicles, wiggling at the tufts and warts and dangleberries ensconced there, his gelatinous backside pushing against the orbit of my eyes.

When it was done I keeled back then buckled, hunching forward, exhausted, mentally and physically drained. And wept.

"No, please. No more. Please."

"What do you mean, Arse-Licker?" He was grinning. "You don't want to miss out on *dessert*."

I swayed on my knees and heard the hiss of the aerosol, and tilted my body forward to lick the squirty cream off Innox where the baked beans had been. Truth is, I never liked spray cream. But it wasn't a question of liking, it was a question of surviving.

And I realised then, as my retching subsided, that nothing was too far for me anymore. I could do anything. Be anyone. Do anything. And that, as I closed my eyes and licked my lips, frightened me.

I had no idea what time it was now. It might have been midnight. It might have been the early hours of the morning.

"Can I go home now, please?"

"You *are* home, Arse-Licker. Don't you know it yet?"

I think I did. I really think I did.

Then I heard the ping of the microwave, and the smell hit me as its door opened.

Over the next half-hour he spoon-fed Innox a hefty supply of instant curry mixed with laxative, leaving the Vesta and Ex-Lax packaging in my eye-line as an act of sadism. I didn't give him the satisfaction of being horrified. In fact, perhaps surprisingly, a pleasing numbness descended on me as I contemplated the inevitable.

Trying to keep it in, Innox contorted, belly down, in agony, his suffering made all the more poignant by the fact that the gag stopped any full expression of his feeling being vented as his digestive system protested against the onslaught. What *was* vented in the fullness of time was his unrestrained bowels, in a stuttering explosion of loose, khaki-coloured shit.

The "hung for a sheep/lamb" analogy sprang to mind. When you had licked baked beans and squirty cream from a grown man's arse, it was but a small step to lick shit from it too. It was an extreme to which I'd never dreamt I'd go, an action to which I never in a million year imagined I'd descend. But such is life. Full of little surprises. And sometimes we have no real idea of our true potential, but we find it.

I waddled forward and stuck out my tongue once more.

A line was crossed. I crossed it.

I subsumed myself in the task. The awfulness overwhelmed me. I was sickened, yes, but I went beyond the sickening. Beyond the foul and the fetid and forbidden. Beyond what society and civilisation labels with words like *obscene* and *repellent*—reaching, in that heightened moment at the bum-hole of my Managing Director, a kind of epiphany.

As I visited and revisited it, like a shrine, like an icon, I began to see the arse—that arse and any arse—as something not to be loathed and rejected, just as Christ himself was loathed and rejected by those who misunderstood him, but as the holiest thing in creation. It was *complete* in its arse-holiness. It was the lowest thing in creation, the very mechanism of poison and detritus, not to mention sinfulness and sodomy—but could it not be *exalted*? Like the sinner who is embraced in heaven?

After all, as I often now say, does not the word '*anus*' contain '*us*'?

It began there in that conference room with a gun at my head. That's when I saw the light. The light of that dark, dark passage that is part of every one of us.

There were no rules. There was just the doing, the doing of the unknowable. And what came next didn't even matter. All that mattered was the moment. Savouring the moment. Because you knew, you really did know, it meant freedom.

I licked it off. Taking my time now. What time was it? There was no time.

Kotwika placed an After Eight between the bum-cheeks. I teased it from side to side with the tip of my tongue and snaffled it up, rewarding Innox with two large, parenthesis-shaped licks either side of his rectum.

I was saying it along with Kotwika now:

"Arse-Licker! Arse-Licker! Arse-Licker!"

"Almost done."

He put down the Glock and picked up a drill, which looked

like a gun, but bigger and chunkier. It was in the rucksack he brought to work every day. He fitted it with the largest in a set of drill bits and tested it in the air. It whirred noisily as it spun. Standing with his legs apart with his back to me he inserted it into Innox's exposed rectum and switched it on. The sound muffled Innox's death rattle as his back passage split and blood splattered out as if from a plumbing leak on all sides of the figure blocking my view.

"Arse-Licker." Kotwika said it like an invitation, turning to me, scarlet from the waist down.

"Arse-Licker," I replied. It was like a language now. We didn't need any more words. We were beyond that. We understood each other. Perfectly.

This time I didn't just lick, I immersed myself.

The arse closed on me, like a communion. The blood from a hundred abrasions filled my mouth. The cup of my tongue did runneth over. The ravaged anus was a cavity. I buried myself in it gladly, bloody-buttocked-blind and at one with the universe.

Which was how they found me, twelve hours later.

My face pressed to the rear end of my dead boss.

The police, that is. They had to prise me out. Literally. I didn't want to leave. When the gun had gone off, I metaphorically buried myself in the dark. In the shit. In the blood. It was a safe place to hide.

When I came out I hardly noticed the body on the floor with not much of its head left, Kotwika's suicidal brains splashed over the wall. Not in a neat pattern but as if someone had thrown a pizza at it and some of the bits of pepperoni still clung there. I was almost sad when the paramedics wiped the shit from my cheeks and nose with their antibacterial wipes, but I could hardly protest.

At the hospital I was given a clean bill of health. The police officer in charge asked me what had happened in some detail. I think he expected me to break down in tears, but I was quite good at describing the events fairly dispassionately. He and his sidekick, who wrote down everything, became increasingly pale as I gave them chapter and verse on what I'd been through. They said it must have been hell. I wasn't about to tell them it was quite the reverse.

In time a young counsellor asked if I thought about my ordeal much. I said I didn't, but I lied. I thought about it all the time. He said I must be relieved that the judge imposed reporting restrictions regarding details of the crime. In fact, as he talked to me, I could think only of the arse secreted in his black slacks and what his buttocks might feel like under my tongue.

I've moved on to a bigger and better company now. I have a bigger salary, a more commensurate pension plan, a hefty bonus structure, and a far larger house, but the truth is, I've moved on from such petty concerns.

My mission in life now is much more basic, and much more difficult.

To find the ultimate experience of the kind that excites me.

Luckily, my job takes me many places. Amsterdam. Copenhagen. New York. Hong Kong. Shanghai. Sydney. I go to high-powered meetings and trade conferences. Stay in four-star hotels.

Fortunately, all over the world there are places that you go to do what I do, well known to the *cognoscenti*. I sniff them out, if that isn't too vulgar a metaphor. Sometimes I don't have to. Sometimes your eyes just meet across a crowded bar in Bangkok or Bolton, and you know without exchanging a word. You just read the signals. It's pretty obvious, really.

By day, I sit in meetings about corporate finances, fantasising about enormous rumps pressed to the plate-glass windows of the skyscraper, their glorious, bulbous musculature offering itself to my tongue, and I give thanks to the undiagnosed sociopath Terry Kotwika for imparting his wisdom, for introducing me to a new world of kaleidoscopic sensation previously merely black and white.

My search is a personal one, and, dare I venture, a profound one, for all its apparent simplicity.

It is, you see—for all the impossibility of the quest—to find, and lick, the absolute apogee of bare buttocks. To explore the A-list of A-holes and discern the perfect pair, the *Anus Mirabilis*—"rump of wonders". The Premier Cru of arses. End of all ends. Absolute perfection.

I've become something of a connoisseur. The German butt tends to be either athletically taut, or overly flabby. Americans are ill-defined. The English, loath to reveal themselves. Antipodeans, surprisingly eager. The Chinese invariably giggle at the roughness of my tongue. Scandinavians grunt. Welshmen grip the floor covering. The Spanish buck like bulls. The Japanese treat the whole thing with the decorum of a tea ceremony. Some behinds are suffocating Montgolfiers. Some are like two peaches in a bag. Some have slack or overused tunnels. Others, bruised anuses the colour spectrum of a baboon's face. Some bum-flesh is cold as Arctic Roll, others hot as molten lava. But I love them all. I want to have them all. Lick them all. Every sun bed-orange or Miami-tanned inch of them. And every pale, pimpled pouch that seems never to have seen the light of day.

And there you have it . . .

There's little more to say except, here. Here's the two hundred dollars. Can I have a glass of water? My throat gets rather dry after all that talking.

Thank you. It's important for my tongue to be moist. It's important to have enough saliva.

Is here all right? Are you warm enough? I'll kneel on the carpet. You face that way. That's right. Legs slightly apart. That's perfect.

Thank you for listening. You've been a good listener.

Now, please bend over.

THE PETER LORRE FAN CLUB

COME IN! KICK THE SNOW OFF YOUR BOOTS! Take off your gloves and warm your hands by the stove. It gives a good heat, this wood-burner. Thank God. This morning when I woke up there was ice on the inside of the windows. Imagine. On the inside!
—It's . . .
What?
—I was going to say, "It's cosy . . . "
It is! Appearances are deceptive, eh? You might think from the outside, you probably *did* think, it's a derelict old farmhouse, about to fall down at any minute.
—Perfect . . .
Yet inside, a palace! A veritable . . .
—Yes . . .
How are you, Dieter?
—You're enjoying yourself here.
I am.
—Plenty of logs. Plenty of food, by the look of it. All the home comforts you could wish for.
Oh, I think I could wish for more. Yes. One can always wish for more, don't you think? Unbutton your coat. Take off your hat. You look uncomfortable.
—I'm not uncomfortable at all.
You'll roast.

—I'm not uncomfortable at all.

So be it.

—I'll sit here. Wood-burners are extremely efficient, I've heard. More so than an open fire.

So they say. It's logical, when you think about it. The iron walls absorb the heat and let it out slowly rather than it all being lost up the chimney. I do like the smell of wood smoke, don't you?

—I never really think about it.

It doesn't bring back memories?

—No.

Of childhood? Of winter?

—Not really.

Ah. Oh. Well. I'm making coffee. Would you like a cup?

—No, thank you.

It's really no trouble. It's already made, look. The pan is just coming to the boil. I got out two cups when I heard the car trundling up the road. Nothing fancy, I'm afraid. Just cheap tin mugs.

—I'm not sure I . . .

For old time's sake.

—Perhaps, then . . .

You must. I insist!

—Well . . .

How long has it been? Don't tell me! I don't even want to think about it. We were children. Well, if not children—youngsters. Now the razor scrapes roughly on our cheeks. Then it used to slide over the skin as if it were glass. And we thought we were so grown-up, didn't we? We thought we could teach the world a thing or two.

—The world still needs teaching.

Do you remember? Seriously? One week we would go to your grandmother, the next week to mine. They were only two streets away, but we'd always alternative it. Always for *Blechkuchen* and coffee, to talk about the film we'd seen that afternoon. And my granny would go, "Stop! Stop!" She didn't understand movies. She thought they were the work of the Devil. Or the gypsies from the fairground who steal children. She didn't understand when we talked about cameras and lighting and storylines. She would waddle off to the kitchen with her hands over her ears.

—She made good cake, Vogel.

She did. She did. Is your grandmother still alive?

—No. She died in the bombing.

Oh, I'm sorry to hear that.

—Are you really?

Yes, of course I am. I liked your grandmother very much. I liked the way her knitting needles would stop clacking and she'd squint through her spectacles as if to say, "You think that? Well, don't be so sure of yourself."

—And she was right. We were cocky so-and-sos. Just because we knew movies we thought we knew everything.

Do you take milk?

—No.

It's fresh from the cows. You always took milk in coffee. Warm milk, I remember.

—I don't anymore.

Your taste has changed.

—I'm a grown-up. Now I find hot milk makes it sickly.

Impure.

—Excuse me?

Nothing.

—You were lucky you had your uncle and aunt to put you up here.

They are good people.

—You call them *good*?

Wouldn't you?

—Perhaps I would if I were in your position. But I am not in your position.

That's true. You're not. You'll have it black, then. Like me. We'll both have our black coffee together.

—You know why I'm here?

Of course.

—How did you know it would be me?

I had a feeling. Take it by the handle. It's hot.

—Thank you.

It'll warm you up. You'll need warming up. The weather's turned nasty and it isn't going to stop in a hurry.

—We'll do what we need to do and then we'll be gone. Before the roads ice over.

I don't blame you. You don't want to get stuck here. In the middle of nowhere.

—No, we don't.

You know, coffee reminds me of those Saturdays, and those Saturdays remind me of the movies.

—Hmm . . .

What was your favourite? Come on. What was the one that sticks in your mind?

—I don't know.

I think for me it will always be *M*—Fritz Lang, of course. Some kind of genius, no?

—No. Not to me anyway.

Oh, don't think of it through the eyes of the person you are now, think of it through the eyes of the person you were then. Was it the first horror we saw? I mean the first *real* horror? Yes, we'd seen *Nosferatu* with its vampire-puppet Count Orlock. Murnau at his best! Fantastic! We must have seen *Caligari* too, with its twisted, crazy sets. But this was different. Don't say you don't remember. This was set in a grey, normal city like our own. The monster didn't go after beautiful women; he went after children like us. Someone or something ghastly is prowling the streets—a creature. But when we see it, it isn't a creature at all, it is like a child—a frightened child itself. Yes, he cuts them with the pocketknife he uses to cut up oranges. Yes, he lures them with candy and toys. But he's at the mercy of an awful compulsion. Then the order goes out to mark the child-killer with an "M"—on his back, like this! He runs. They give chase. He's terrified. Now we're less frightened of him and more frightened of the mob out to get him. The angry mob that wants to tear him limb from limb. He committed what he did because of love, but they do what they do because of hate.

—They loved the law. They loved the law that protected the city they loved.

Those greasy, fat individuals with sausages down their trousers? They didn't seem like defenders of the civic good to me. Were they the heroes? Really? Or did they just like dishing out the punishment to someone weaker than them? Someone who couldn't fight back?

—A story is open to many interpretations, Vogel. The more flimsy the story, the greater number of possible interpretations.

You think so?

—Anyway, too many stories obscure too many facts these days. We depend on stories instead of actions. Facts and actions are what is important in life, not a load of make-believe.

You've forgotten the thrill of seeing those images?

—No, not at all. But I've put them in their place. We were young. We were easily led. Certain stories appeal to certain urges. Some types of tale have to be resisted. You know that when you become a more mature adult.

And so, what happens next?

—What do you mean?

In the story.

—In the movie, you mean? I don't know.

Come on. They drag him down underground to carve out his stomach—to do to him what he did to his victims. Hideous little creep! He screams shrilly, bleating with fear, cowering in the corner. He hides his faces in babyishly soft, squirming hands. When the hands come away they reveal these big, round eyes. "Don't let them *hurt* me!" he screams. What big eyes he has. Like the fairy tale. Perhaps he *is* from a fairytale, this creature. This child-man. He pleads with them. He can't help it. The voices told him to do it. He'd black out. He'd wake up and see the horror of what he'd done. "Help! They're going to kill me!"

—That voice...

Unmistakable.

—You do it well, still. You sound just like him.

He's not difficult to imitate, in a superficial way. But do you remember the impact of that moment? The shrillness? Demented but searing. Guilty but defiant. Full of pain, but with a harsh, guttural, beautiful musicality. Like the rasp of a broken violin. With a truth in it that can only be the sound of a man pleading for his life. And the face of what? A clown? Certainly a flat, round face, almost like a mask, with soft-boiled egg eyes staring out. A comical face, somehow? A face to laugh at—and yet... No. Not at all. You remember? Tell me you remember!

—It was a film. A thriller. A potboiler. He was an actor.

But *what* an actor!

—When I told my father I'd seen that film he gave me the stick, I remember that.

Our parents didn't want us to see such filth.

—Maybe they were right.

That's why it was so exciting!

—*What* was exciting?

To see through another person's eyes. To see a world like no other, that you couldn't even imagine.

—I just remember being afraid.

That's why we talked about it for days! Why we went back and saw it again and again! Why we wrote down a list of every scene from memory. Wrote a story of our own, even. Acted it out in the woods. Went like this with our fingers, pretending to look through the camera. We shouted "Action!" and "Cut!" Came home with a film inside our heads.

—I just remember having nightmares.

So did I! There's nothing wrong with nightmares, Dieter. Sometimes they remind us what it is to be truly alive.

—Now you've lost me.

Sorry.

—You always were the intellectual one.

Was I? No. I don't think so. I always talked a lot, that doesn't mean the same thing at all. You were thoughtful. I was mouthy. I could easily boss you around.

—Did you?

Do this. Do that. Yes. I regret that now.

—As far as I was concerned, I did exactly what I wanted. Nobody told me to do anything.

You were taller than anybody in class. Taller than most of the teachers. I hung around with you because there was no chance of louts like Anton Albers picking on me with you standing next to me.

—I never had a fight in school.

You didn't have to. They'd take one look at you and run a mile. You never had to lift a finger. You frightened them off, thank God. Didn't you wonder why we didn't have any other friends? Not real friends. It was always just you and me. Dieter and Florian.

—Didn't bother me.

Didn't bother me either.

—We had a good time, you and I, in those days.

We did. Oh, we definitely did. No doubt about it. All our plans about leaving Cologne. You becoming an actor. Me becoming a writer.

—Dreams.

Did you ever go to stage school like you wanted?

—I realised it was a waste of time. And you? The writing?

Only for newspapers.

—Something, at least.

Stories. It put bread on the table. But I could never forget it.

—What?

His face. That frightened yet come-hither face on the screen, inviting us in. Those bottomless, sallow eyes under heavy lids. Our favourite actor!

—What fools we were.

Why do you say that?

—Why do you think? Cutting photographs from movie magazines. Making that stupid scrapbook with his name in big letters on the front. Typing our own biography of him, each taking our turn at your father's typewriter.

I remember asking him who Brecht was.

—Such wasted time, all of it.

Why?

—Well, the pointless information about, who? Nobody important. A film star. Finding out about his family. All the meaningless details . .

Born 1904.

—I don't believe it.

In the Austrian-Hungarian town of Rózsahegy.

—You still remember?

His mother died when he was four. And he hated his stepmother.

—Who cares?

We cared! Then his family moved to Vienna. His father Alajos, Jewish, middle-class, bookkeeper at a textile mill. Originally wanted him to go into banking.

—Big surprise.

His real name: Lásló Löwenstein. How he changed it . . .

—I wonder why?

What makes a person a favourite actor, d'you think, Dieter?

—I have no idea.

Not a *good* actor. That involves skill, talent, intelligence, photographic presence, all the rest. But—*favourite* actor?

—I'm sure you're about to tell me.

One that *touches* you. That's all. It's really that simple. They touch your heart with their humanity. It doesn't matter if they're fat, thin, good-looking, built like a Greek god, or look like the boy next door. They have to have *humanity*. And when they do and it communicates to you, it doesn't let you go.

—I see. I get it now. Is this a kind of plea of mitigation?

Not at all.

—What is it then?

It's a conversation between two friends over cups of coffee.

—If you say so. But if you think you're impressing me or intimidating me, you're wrong.

Why would I try to intimidate you?

—Because you always did. You said so yourself. Like I say, always the intellectual. You haven't stopped talking since I arrived here.

Forgive me a little indulgence. For old time's sake.

—You keep saying for old time's sake. You don't seem to be aware of the severity of the situation.

Oh, I know the severity of the situation very well. I just want to talk, a little.

—What about?

About movies.

—So let me say what *I* think, Vogel, shall I?

Please.

—Your favourite actor. Your heart-rending darling. This . . . this *Hungarian* who grew up in Vienna. Berlin was good enough to come to for a leg-up in his career, joining those theatre groups, I remember that. Germany was his *home*. He made perfectly good films here until he decided to abandon it.

Yes. When Hitler came to power.

—Then he ran off to Paris and hopped over to London to play slimy villains in Hitchcock films—a white streak in his hair and a duelling scar on his cheek, smoking a cigarette—the absolute and utter picture of Germanic putrid elegance. Speaking English in that breathy, nasal accent for the audiences in London to laugh themselves silly at.

I don't know if they laughed.

—What the hell did they do then?

Perhaps they loved him. Like we did.
—Only because we knew no better. He buggered off to the West. You can't deny it. Instead of making good German films like *F.P. 1 Antwortet Nicht* or *Was Frauen Träumen*, he chooses to star in, what was it called, that abomination? *Mad Love?*
The Hands of Orlac! Ah!
—Please! A psychosexual melodrama where he is reduced to . . . to some sort of insane egghead with rolling eyes?
"I, a poor peasant, have conquered science! Why can I not conquer love?"
—Don't laugh! It was disgusting. He was like some bleached-white larva, force-fed and covered in sweaty grease.
Professor Gogol, one of his most outstanding creations!
—A maniac. A *German* maniac!
Made by a German director. Karl Freund.
—Another traitor welcomed by America's open arms!
Toland, too! Fantastic lightning. We lost them all. The masters of light and darkness!
—Good riddance.
You think so? . . . You *do* think so, don't you? . . . Oh. How times change.
—For the better. Yes . . .
And you've changed with them. I notice you've even lost your regional accent. How did that happen?
—It happened because I wanted it to. Sometimes to get on in this world you have to put behind you where you came from.
Apparently when Peter acted in *The Man Who Knew Too Much*, his English was so bad he learnt his part phonetically. That's quite an achievement, isn't it, when you think about it? You'd never know to watch him, though. His portrayal is so full of . . . nuance and exquisite expression. No wonder Hitchcock used him again in *Secret Agent* . . .
—And after that, what? Off to Hollywood to play more sinister foreigners. That ridiculous series where he plays the Japanese detective . . .

Mr Moto!

—An Austrian-Hungarian German playing a slit-eyed Jap. What could be more laughable? There he was in the California sun, taking the Jewish dollar, while people were fighting and dying in Europe. *We* were fighting and dying. For our Fatherland! Did he care? Striding around that fake Devil's Island in a white linen suit?

You saw it then?

—What?

Strange Cargo? Oh, and did you see him as Polo, the oh-so-gentle kleptomaniac in *I was an Adventuress*? It's the all-time favourite of his female fans. My wife adored him in that picture. They all want to be Vera Zorina as the con artist turned society lady. He's so puppydog-like. So endearing.

—No, strangely enough, that is one I haven't seen.

That's a shame. Stroheim and Peter are magical together.

—In fact, I've made a point of avoiding all his American films. I can't say they interest me in the slightest.

I suppose you have a strong opinion on the matter. That's why you're here.

—I don't have a strong opinion on the matter. And the reason I'm here is that I was given orders.

By whom? I'm just curious.

—By my superiors. They had a list of certain people.

Certain people.

—That's right.

And these certain people . . .

—It was decided that certain actions needed to be taken. I happened to see that your name was on the list.

And did you think that was good luck on your part, or unfortunate? . . . That you saw my name on the list, I mean?

—I didn't think of it either way. I thought of it as a job to be done.

Do you want a top-up of coffee? It's still on the stove.
—No.
Here. I'll have to pour it away if you don't.
—Just a little. That's enough. Have some yourself.
You're the one who needs warming up.
—No. Really.
I insist. Let me be a decent host.
—Very well.
No cake, I'm afraid.
—No.
No cake. No grandmothers.
—No. That's true. It's very quiet here. No noise. No bombardment.
Just nature . . . Does it make you anxious?
—Just a little. It's strange. You become accustomed. To the strangest . . .
I'm sure. I'm sure . . . The coffee's not stewed?
—No, it's perfect.
It doesn't taste like bat's piss?
—I don't know. I haven't tasted bat's piss. It's good bat's piss.
Ha. Mm. I don't know. Pretty average bat's piss if you ask me. The piss of a fairly average bat.
—I don't understand.
What don't you understand?
—Any of it.

—Even you . . . Surely the final straw was when Lorre became an American citizen. Did you not feel affronted? Hurt? A German actor—*our* actor—becoming American?

I think an actor, if he is special, Dieter, has to belong to the world.

—But did you not feel it in your *heart*? When you thought of our devotion to him. The scrapbook. The conversations in our tent in the forest, into the dead of night. The fact that we wrote to him at the studio in Berlin, asked him for a signed photograph? Waited every day for weeks for the postman to arrive with his reply? Then we shared that photograph. Two weeks at your house, two weeks at mine. That was the kind of devotion we gave him. Didn't it feel like he'd spat in our faces to you?

No.

—Why not?

It was up to us to love him, not the other way around.

—Why?

Why? Because that's the movies, my friend.

He was never going to be your beloved *Aryan* type. He was never going to look heroic and Siegfried-like in a Nazi uniform with a huge swastika flag and a sunset behind him like in the posters. Let's face it—he would never get through a casting call with Leni Riefenstahl, would he?

—So instead, what? The fidgeting fairy in *The Maltese Falcon*?

Joel Cairo! I thought you never saw any of his American films.

—Sometimes it is necessary. In order to know the enemy.

Yes, of course . . .

—And *you* saw it, I know. You and your friends. In the Society. Your fellow fanatics.

Admirers. Yes. We did.

—How did you get the print? How did you get the projector? How did you let the others know when there was going to be a film show? Was it always in the same place?

—My name is on your list yet you don't know the answers to those questions? We met each other. It's as simple as that. We talked about films, to begin with. We found out the films we had in common. It was like finding—in coded terms at first—another addict to the same illegal drug. And perhaps it was coincidence but we found out the actor we all loved. We breathed his name to each other laden with excitement, just as you and I did, way back when, in prehistory. *Peter Lorre*. The outside world was horrible and we needed a friend we could trust. *Peter Lorre*. Somebody suggested a place. A film. We held hands in the dark. Our first—let me think—was *I'll Give A Million*. Bit of a disappointing Depression farce, but he lifted our spirits as Raskolnikov in *Crime and Punishment*. We must have watched it a dozen times—and never tired of it for an instant! Extraordinary how von Sternberg lit Marian Marsh to look just like Dietrich. Then we smuggled in *Stranger on the Third Floor*. Have you heard of it? Wonderful low-budget crime story. Really. And there's a glorious scene with Margaret Tallichet! We gave him a standing ovation in the basement of the *bierkeller*. But then, we always did.

—And yet you are surprised I am here?

No. Not at all. I'd heard gossip from back home that my old school chum had found his vocation. I knew it was only a matter of time before we came face to face.

—You always were superstitious.

Well, in this case, it came to pass.

—So, why didn't you run? The rest of your family has. Why didn't you?

Excuse me. I'll adjust the stove. Warm those embers before they go out altogether. I doubt it's worth putting on more logs.

Where were we?

—Your little club.

Ah, yes. It was our duty, you see. To watch all the American ones he starred in. *You'll Find Out*—that was another, with Karloff and Lugosi, really just a spoof on *The Cat and the Canary*. But Peter is so fragile, so elegant and slender, like a mentally disturbed Chihuahua. I can see the luminous bone structure of his face right now as he slides his cigarette holder into a mouth full of rotting teeth . . .

—Complete and utter decadence. Like the *nancy* he plays opposite Bogart, the great he-man, in *The Maltese Falcon*. A poodle newly returned from the shampoo parlour. Vile, like every performance he commits to celluloid these days. I hope he chokes on the fact that we put scenes from *M* to good use in the Propaganda Department since he's gone.

So I've heard. I suppose it was inevitable. Correct me if I'm wrong, but I understand your illustrious leaders lifted scenes out and edited them into an entirely different film. What was it called? Oh yes—*The Eternal Jew*. Catchy title.

—We leave catchy titles to the Americans. Like *All Through The Night*. Blatant anti-Nazi propaganda that your screen idol starred in.

And *Casablanca*.

—More American tommyrot. Gum-chewing rubbish for the compliant masses.

Hard to get hold of in this country . . .

—But you did. Enjoy it?

Enormously. Like all forbidden fruit, it was delicious. To begin with, we could barely play the soundtrack louder than a whisper, out of fear. As the film continued, we crawled closer in a huddle and pressed our ears to the speakers. The specks of dust danced in the air above our heads, but when the projector was turned off, we clapped till our hands were sore. We didn't care anymore if the whole of the Gestapo and Joseph Goebbels himself heard us. That immortal double-act with Sydney Greenstreet again. Perfection. A small part, but as ever Peter made it his own.

—Latest in a long line of whining, bug-eyed monstrosities.

I daresay, to you, he can only be the ugly little Jew.

—He was an ugly little Jew in Germany, so I would hazard a guess he is an ugly little Jew in America.

The ugly little Jew who once said, "There isn't room for two murderers in Germany, Hitler and me." That's quite good, isn't it? Doesn't that amuse you?

—Do we have to talk much more? I'm sick of reminiscing about this man who made a fortune out of playing the snivelling German—always the sweating, grubby degenerate.

But there cannot only be heroes, Dieter, with their golden hair and perfect physiques. Supermen and superwomen. Sometimes we have to see the worst of us. Or just . . . *us*.

—So, who are *your* heroes? Out of curiosity.

People who never have their names carved in stone, but sometimes, perhaps only once, do the right thing.

—Not actors, then?

Sometimes actors. Actors are brave in their way. Portraying our flaws. Our fears. Our terror. Our essential pathetic nakedness and vulnerability. Being our mirror sometimes. Do you ever look in the mirror, Dieter?

—I have better things to do. Work to do.

I was forgetting.

—You're living in the past. In a dream world. Those were innocent days, our childhood. We didn't see those films for what they truly were.

Which is what?

—Unwholesome. Corrupting. Subversive.

Degenerate.

—Yes! For God's sake, Vogel. You knew you were breaking the law by watching them. All of you did. Your mad Society dedicated to this . . . this *imbecile* performer. What were you thinking? That you could get away with it? Or didn't you care? You knew it was *verboten*. These things are banned—everybody knows that. *Why?*

Why?

—Why did you *betray* us?

Ah . . .

—Before I saw your name on the communiqué, I thought often about what might have happened to you. What you might have become. Would he have signed up to be one of us? I doubted it. Would he keep his head low? Perhaps. Sometimes I thought you might have become one of the fucking Edelweiss Pirates, those *Bundische Jugend* who managed to wriggle out of joining the Hitler Youth. I've been in pitch battles with that lot. They sing popular songs—the sort you like—not the traditional music the Party approves of. They wear their hair long and have knives hidden in their socks. They paint slogans on walls, distribute leaflets, throw bricks through munitions factory windows, put sugar into Nazi staff cars' engines. Derail trains. I thought you might be involved in that. In the *serious* resistance, at least. But *this!*

I know.

—You did none of that. You just wanted to watch stupid films starring a stupid actor. Why?

Because I'm a coward, my friend. Because I don't believe in much, but I believe in this. It may seem like a small thing to you, but it is the one small, silly thing I realised I would be prepared to die for.

—Now you've lost me again.

Yes . . . I expect I have.

I wondered about you as well, as a matter of fact. All the time. After we went our separate ways, after school was finished and we looked around like startled birds for something to do with our lives. It's funny we never kept in touch. No letters, nothing. It's like we both knew we were tramping off into different worlds, leaving our childhood Paradise behind. Did we have any idea *how* different? I'm disappointed you never became an actor, though.

—I'm not. After three months the tutor said I would only ever make a mediocre one. So, I thought, what is the point in trying?

If being the best was the main thing you were aiming for, perhaps you were in the wrong place anyway.

—Perhaps I was. I don't really care anymore. It all seems unbearably trivial, in fact, the very idea of it.

Well at least you get to wear a costume every day now. And you play that part well, I must say. You almost convince even me. But, you see, I can remember when you fell off that swing we made over that dry riverbed behind Gustav's house and broke your leg, and I carried you home. And your mother put you to bed with hot milk and didn't call the doctor because she thought you were play-acting. She didn't call him for three days and three nights, and every time I called round for you to come with me to the movies I walked home with tears running down my cheeks because I could hear you sobbing in pain.

—Your memory is better than mine.

You've turned off the stove.

—It's time to stop reminiscing, Vogel. Come on.

All right. I thought you said I was the bossy one. Where's my scarf? Oh, I see it.

—Here.

You know . . . The thing is, the key is, I think he has such melancholy eyes. I don't mean the man, the real person—I mean the black-and-white ghost we saw up on the screen. I think he mesmerised me from the first moment I set eyes on him. I think I saw my father ten, twenty feet tall. Gigantic, but insubstantial. Chubby, yet slim. Anxious, yet frightening. Trembling. Stupid. Funny. Ridiculous.

—Ridiculous?

I saw me. I saw you.

The eighteen-year-old boy came in from outside after briskly knocking. Flakes of snow fluttered from the shoulders of his uniform. His gloves and black boots shone wetly but the blue eyes under the helmet did not meet those of the bearded man, Florian Vogel, only those of his clean-shaven commanding officer.

"Sir, we couldn't find any more rope, but we found a decent length of wire attached to the fence-posts. We're ready now."

Should I wear my coat?
—You should. It's cold outside.

Florian Vogel blinked as the freezing air hit his eyes. He always thought that snow had the effect of dampening sound—it was one reason he found winter contemplative and serene, like the blank page of a manuscript waiting to be filled with words—but today it seemed to muffle everything, to erase, to deaden, to hold a finger to its lips and say *hush*, demanding the landscape to keep a secret.

The smell of burning pine needles was strong in the wind and he was grateful for that. He knew that, impervious to his fate, blue smoke was rising from the chimney-stack behind him as he walked, and he wanted to hold that aroma in his nostrils for as long as he could, breathing it deeply into his lungs. Mixed with the coffee flavour still fresh on his tongue it had the strange intoxication of Mother Nature imbued in it, and he absurdly imagined if he continued to think of it he might stop shivering as he followed *SS-Obersturmbannführer* Deiter Grau towards the small copse of leafless trees a hundred yards or so from his uncle's farmhouse.

Over to his left, near the semi-collapsed barn, he saw a squat, bow-legged man in the uniform of an *Oberscharführer* kicking something. It seemed to be a sack, but as his stomach lurched Vogel soon made out that the soldier was holding something by its hair. The thing was a child, a girl, the five-year-old daughter of his cousin. Her name was Hannah. Her misshapen head hung from the hair and was covered in blood. The shape below her head did not resemble anything living or human. The man continued kicking.

Vogel did not close his eyes, but he did tilt his head forward so that he did not see the things hanging in the trees.

He had seen another soldier, his prick semi-stiff in his hand, pissing a crater in the snow with a stallion-spray of red-brown urine. He could also hear two dogs barking. One was the mongrel farm dog chained to a post by the woodshed, its cry abruptly cut short by three rounds of pistol fire, a blasphemous curse and the sting of cordite in the air. The other sound, which continued unabated, was the incessant bark of a slathering German Shepherd tethered in the back of a camouflage-rendered Opel-Blitz truck which sat on the pitted, ice-laden driveway to the farm, a Kubelwagen parked at a skewed angle next to it. The dog's claws scratched madly at the metal slats, not in desperation to escape, but aroused to fever pitch by the salt scent of blood.

Dieter?

—Don't talk.

Did you know that he was originally up for the Basil Rathbone part in *Son of Frankenstein*?

—Quiet, now.

That would be a movie worth the price of admission, no? Can you imagine? Just picture for a moment what our Peter would have done with that role. Just imagine that *double-take* face of his—those quick changes he does, gliding so swiftly and brilliantly from manic laughter to pity, from absolute hatred to absolute joy. Imagine! Can't you hear him? "It's alive! It's *alive!*"

—Shut up. I've had enough. It's over.

The gangly eighteen-year-old gave the hangman's knot a twist with the stick for good measure to tighten it under the man's ear. Barely a second later Vogel was hoisted into the branches to join the inert effigies that had been his uncle, aunt, and cousin. His legs kicked spasmodically. One boot flew off in a parabolic arc which nobody cared about. Even the ghastly had become tiresome to them. The wire cut in, right to the bone, as they knew it would. Tongue and liquid emerged. All Dieter Grau cared about was that it was done.

He took out a silver case. It was an implicit signal for the others to light up as well. He was too tired to give orders, and they were too tired to take them. In the dark void of the valley they all cupped matches in their hands, traded the glowing tips of their cigarettes, raised their jaws, and blew acrid smoke, unbuttoned their collars and scratched their flea-ridden armpits. One came back from the farmhouse with a bottle of schnapps and they passed it round singing a song popular in the barracks. The figure in the air above them was now no more than an obscene, jerking chandelier.

Dieter Grau wished he would get on with it and die. He wished the light would go out of Vogel's eyes quickly so that he could get on with his life. There were others to track down and exterminate. Other enemies of Hitler, the glorious Reich, and the German spirit.

One of the men climbed on the shoulders of another and pulled down Vogel's trousers. The others laughed uproariously. Dieter Grau didn't even turn away anymore. He'd long discovered it was wrong to depend of these loyal chaps' bravery and patriotism, day in day out, and not allow them a little buffoonery to let off steam when the occasion arose. What did it matter anyway? The man was dead. Or near as, damn it. Another in the unit took a bayonet from his belt and stuck it in Vogel's belly and groin several times in quick succession. The body revolved, and when it came back to face them the blade was tossed to another infantryman who stabbed it more vigorously, until pus and intestines spilled out. The first man took his knife back and sawed off the genitals, which they flung at each other in an impromptu game until it bored them, then fed them to the dog. The strings of tendons flicked against its muzzle as it chewed.

Dieter Grau sat in the Kubelwagen with his hip flask, the contents numbing his lips, until it was time to go. His men washed their hands in the snow and rubbed ruddy stains into their uniforms. It was always his task to inspect the corpse. He found nothing of interest in terms of military or intelligence information. Just, in Vogel's inside jacket pocket, next to his heart, an old back-and-white photograph of a movie star. Without thinking for an instant, he tore it up in small pieces and stuffed it into the dead man's mouth.

Standing erect, he looked at his watch. It was night and he didn't like travelling in the dark, but if it needed to be done, he did it. Without question.

For Adam Nevill

CERTAIN FACES

I WAKE FEELING LOST AND SCARED, not scissoring upright like in a cheap horror film, but filled with the dull, heavy dread that another day has begun, a day no different and no easier than the one that went before. I wake more tired than when my head hit the pillow. I feel like a lump of lead and someone will drop me in a pool of water, and that's the day, and that's me going through the day, till I hit the bottom. Then it happens all over again. I twist to see the clock radio on the floor, which reads a red 6.30, and I pick up my Annie Proulx and start to read. Except I don't read, I go over the same page three, four times without taking it in. I'm not awake and I'm not asleep. I'm buzzing. My husband opens an eye, the other sunk deep in the pillow. His grunt is warm, groggy, inquisitorial. Eventually I drop the book beside the bed and turn onto my side and try to sleep again. I'm staring at his back and waiting for the alarm while a figure of eight of predictable thoughts knot my stomach like food poisoning. I wish that's what it was. And this part lasts forever, the thinking, tell him, tell him, tell him. The thinking, which is worse? Not telling my husband, or not telling the police?

As per usual, I'm just falling deep asleep when the alarm drills into me. It makes me ratty. Gavin wakes now, well slept and fresh and I'm angry at him, envious. He knows I've been awake, I always have. I can't help it. It's my body clock. I can take a nap in the afternoon, no problem. He never can. He says there are too many things to worry about in the daytime.

We're all legs and arms on the sofa bed in the main room, like unwanted stopovers in our own home. He's been decorating the bedroom—orange, scarlet, navy blue, my idea—and the closed door doesn't keep out the smell of turps. He sits at the end of the bed with his long, curved white back and grabs the remote control and an ashtray and switches on breakfast TV. I find my nose with my specs and see one of those big-mouthed presenters with microscopic tits and a tight lime green shirt.

"I hate that bloody woman," he says, the cigarette waggling between his lips.

I say, "What's she done to you?"

The lighter clicks. He puffs. "Nothing. Look at the state of her. Jesus."

I say, "Eamonn Holmes is no oil painting."

"Those lips," he says. "They're abnormal."

"Switch it fucking off then," I say.

I don't expect him to, but he does, his back still to me. It's like someone pulls the plug on the room.

I say, "Joking."

In the silence, he acts like he hasn't heard me.

His weight lifts from the bed and he heads for the bathroom and I cross the bed on all fours and pick up the remote control and turn it back on.

"Gavin. Don't be an idiot. Christ."

I hear him close the bathroom door. "I'm having a shit. Is that all right?

I turn up the volume. The girl on TV is wearing more lipstick than I put on in a week. I pull the sheets up over my knees. If my gran in Aberdeen didn't like someone on TV, she wouldn't switch off, she'd talk to them. She'd tell them to bugger off, silly sods. Or she'd cover her head with a tea cloth so she wouldn't have to see them. When I got my A-level results and got into art college, she ran down the hall to hug me, waddling like an oversized hair-netted baby.

As I open my knicker drawer, I wonder if Vicki Hartwell had a Gran who hugged her when she got into college, who had tears running down her cheeks over her A-levels, as if that was the last thing she had to worry about in the world, her granddaughter's life would be fine.

I sometimes wonder how it happened between Gavin and me. How does it happen between anyone, I suppose? All I remember is needing a fireplace taking out because I was desperate to flog it for the money, and someone recommended this guy who was a builder who'd been to art college, like me. We got on, but we didn't say that much. He was what my mum called quiet spoken. There wasn't any roughness about him. One night we shared a bottle of wine and I got weepy. It was a hard time in my life. We went to bed and before I knew it he was spending two, three nights a week with me. It was just natural. He didn't seem bothered I had a grown-up daughter. Then when I said I wanted to move away from Edinburgh he said, "Aye, why not?" and before I knew it, we were buying a flat together down south. After a bit he said he wanted to get married, which was nice to hear. I laughed, but it was really nice. Maybe he felt it was time to eradicate my past, give it a new coat of paint. I don't know.

I'm always first up, first dressed and watered, first to rummage in the bread bin. The toaster's chirruping like a time bomb and Gavin hasn't emerged from the bathroom. When he does, I slam the cutlery drawer and say, "I'm sick of making the *fucking* breakfast every morning. Why is it me that has to do everything around here?" Now he sulks, like a little boy who's had his legs slapped. He thinks things like this bother me, but they don't, not really.

I want him to answer back, but he doesn't. I want him to yell at me, but he doesn't. He comes up behind me and rubs my arms and plants a kiss on my neck. I don't move. I empty a carton of three-day-old milk down the sink.

I realise I have my hand over my stomach. I don't know why. It's like someone else put it there.

Gavin dresses, in the tartan lumberjack shirt I bought him for his birthday but is now only worth working in. Says he'll be in The Fox at seven. That's a novelty.

I say, "Let's not make it The Fox."

He says, "Where do you want to make it?"

"Anywhere. Nowhere. I don't care."

"OK. Forget it."

He knows I want a slanging match. I want him to suffer today. I want him to suffer instead of me.

But he doesn't play the game. He doesn't even slam the door. His Silk Cut lies recumbent in the ashtray on the corner of the bath and I prod it till the smoke stops rising. There's an anorexic girl from Marie Claire on the floor, advertising shoes. I sit on the broken loo seat, forearms strapping my ribs, feeling them ache and heave and the desert-dry saltiness spreads out from my sinuses, and I'm crying, and it doesn't surprise me anymore.

Vicki Hartwell was completely forgettable. I would have forgotten her in five minutes, I think, if things had been different. She wouldn't have stuck in my mind, visually or any other way, really.

She was one of these people who's never had a problem, probably, getting a boyfriend, because she has a pretty face. But she's never stood out either, because there's nothing unusual about her face either. She was completely conventional and completely boring.

Having said that, she was very confident with the way she looked. She knew she looked all right, and maybe that's what put me off her. I wish I had her confidence. I actually like people who are slightly nervy, insecure; I don't know why. It might be because I want to feel in a stronger position because I'm the one that's having to paint them, and I don't want to feel like the shy one. So it could be to do with that, but it's more than that. I think I like people with flaws, it reassures me. People who don't show flaws, who are all front, I find that frightening, people with no self-doubt. I don't think anybody's really without doubts and fears. Some people cover it up, that's all. Cover it up well, that's the thing. I can't relate to someone who's really confident, 100% confident, 100% of the time.

What attracts me? Usually, it's an interestingly shaped head. Usually that's the connection with the short hair. Also, I do like men who have a sensitive, feminine look about them. It can be very well hidden, but it is there. And I like women again who have a boyish masculine side to them as well. I like people to have a bit of both. I think that's probably why I didn't like Vicki Hartwell, because she was too 'girly'. It was too one-dimensional. There was no more to find out. There was too much oestrogen there, just like with some guys there's too much testosterone flying around.

I suppose what I'm looking for is a nice combination. That's why you'll find pictures all over my studio of Michael Clark, DV8, k.d. lang. Because I think we all have both, and if you can get both, it's probably one of the strongest requirements.

At the beginning I was naive. I used to ask people to come round and I'd struggle to paint them, and it wasn't right, and I'd have to pay them, which was mad. So I got in the habit of meeting them first in some neutral zone, and I always said beforehand, "Please don't be offended if I can't use you, because it's nothing to do with prettiness or attractiveness, it's just that I personally can't use you." And, apart from what happened with Vicki, that usually works out fine.

The one who phoned me was this guy Emyr Winter. I remember because he had to spell it because I thought he said Emma, a girl's name. I said, "Sorry. I was still flustered from rushing to catch the answerphone from cutting in." I said, "Yes, this is the real me. This is not a machine."

There was pub noise in the background. The sound of the smell of sticky floors. Then this kangarooing Welsh accent, quite high, quite nervous. "I'm—er, ringing about the card you put in the Metro Cafe? Sitter stroke model required by professional female artist?"

"That's right. That's me."

"We were—my friend and me, were wondering like, what's *involved* exactly?"

He made *involved* sound like some long drawn-out gynaecological word. I wondered if he was going to be one of those ones who thought the word *model* was some euphemism for blowjob, but then I thought, you can't go by a voice, he might have a brilliant head, and that's what I'm after. So I leaned against the wall, looking back at Gavin slumped in front of *Parkinson* with a San Miguel balanced on one knee, and said what I usually say: "Well, you sit, in a chair—clothed, by the way—and I paint you. Heads. Heads and shoulders, that's all I'm interested in. Don't worry. I'm not after your body." That was my usual line, to put people at ease.

The penny dropped, literally. Two gobbits of change gulped up by the payphone, and the pub ambience cut back in, laughter, but not from him. Had he heard what I'd said? "That sounds all right, then. Nothing too drastic."

"Nothing drastic at all."

A voice muttered impatiently in the background amongst the chinked glasses.

He asked about the pay.

"Well, it isn't a fortune. Four pounds an hour. You'd get more babysitting." I heard him cover the mouthpiece and relay it. I imagined facial expressions.

"That's orright. There are three of us interested, actually..."

"Great. Well, I'll have to have a look at you."

He said his flatmate's name was Paul Rolt, who had a girlfriend called Vicki. He said they were all students at the university up on Coombe Down. At that point I took it all three of them shared. It was only afterwards, from the *Chronicle*, I found out that Vicki lived with her parents in Colerne. But that was the impression

I got, that they were students and they all lived together in Bath.

"I'll have to have a look at you. You might not all be—you know, suitable . . . "

"Suitable?"

"Well, you know. I have certain requirements, certain types I'm looking for. They're not strictly portraits, they're more imaginative. They represent me, what's going on in my head, as much as anything." I realised I was sounding pretentious, so I shut up.

"Oh, yes. Well you're the artist, you know what you're doing," he said. "So when would you want us to come round and pose, exactly?" I remember he used the word *pose*, which I hate, but I suppose it's a word normal people use.

"Well," I said. "What if we meet up first?"

"Only, like I say, we're all at the university. Would it be in the evenings? Only, the day might be awkward like."

"Let's talk about that when we meet up, shall we?"

"Oh, oh. OK. Right. Fine."

I suggested the Metro Cafe, since they knew it, at 11.30 the following morning, a Sunday. I said they did a good all-day breakfast, and he said they'd have to give that a test drive, he looked forward to that.

The last thing he said was, "You'll know us because we'll all be sitting together, there'll be three of us. And Paul and I have got short hair."

So I thought, that means nothing. I said, "You'll know me because I'll be covered in paint."

This bloke Emyr laughed, like it was a joke.

When I walked into the Metro Cafe on the Sunday morning I walked right past them. I didn't even notice them, they were that interesting.

I don't know what I was expecting. I used to live in a gay area of Edinburgh and I had terrific models from a semi-gay cafe called Fat Tuesday: three, four different models a week. The Metro, with its Parisian *Eurotrash* cum bombed-out barbershop look, maroon woodwork and fake marble effect walls, freaky found objects, and Gwen Stefani blaring out of the speakers, or Kaiser Chiefs, or Moby, had the same mix of clientele: young, gay poseurs. Even the layabouts looked like Rufus Wainwright. It attracted the type I liked. Shaven heads, nose rings, tattoos, a certain beatnik, punkish, retro, androgynous, that *Blade Runner*, Björk, Michael Stipe, Calvin Klein junkie-chic. It was perfect. The perfect trawling ground, the perfect watering hole. So when they said students, I expected the same, only more so: hip, wacky, slight offbeat, slightly sexy in whatever way, I don't care.

One of them must have seen I was wearing this baggy shirt splattered in paint, because a man's voice behind me singsonged, "Be-hind yoo!" And I turned and thought—as soon as I set eyes on them—shit, you're not right, oh no, none of you are right at all. They were dead boring looking.

"Oh. Hi there," I heard myself saying. "Nice to meet you." I couldn't believe there was this great big grin on my face as I shook hands with the three of them and pulled a chair under me as I was introduced to them. Hi, hi, hi. At that stage I was thinking, I just want to get out of here, I just want to terminate it here and now and go. I wanted to say look, thank you, sorry, but goodbye.

They were all smoking, especially this Vicky girl, who I suppose was pretty in a very conventional, conservative, *Bride & Home* kind of way. I could see her walking down the aisle, that's what she was made for, I thought, that's all she wants in life. I'm not saying you couldn't tick all the boxes, sure. Round face, pointed chin, a child-like smile which seemed to nudge her cheekbones higher, waves of Barbie-doll ginger hair which you could see were her crowning glory, shampooed twice a day and dried for three hours, groomed to oblivion. Even the occasional shy, girly toss of the head. But there was nothing natural there. It was all received wisdom, a *Baywatch*, *Tatler* sort of beauty, a copy-cat creation, something manufactured for men, an advertisement, not a person with anything underneath, and ultimately *banal*, like someone who works in a building society and everyone tells her she should be a model, and she believes them.

She took off her dark glasses and said, "Sorry we're a bit . . . " and poked out her tongue and rolled her dull eyes. "There was this party over in Larkhall and they got into the tequilas. I have got *such* a hangover it's not true. I don't even remember walking home. I remember this water pistol fight, but that's about all. We're all a weeny bit . . . " She gritted her teeth sheepishly in place of a word and fluttered her eyelids. I don't know if I was supposed to be impressed or something. I thought she sounded like an idiot.

"Delicate," said the Welsh one. "Green around the gills."

"*How Green Were My Gills*," said the other guy, her boyfriend, Paul, standing up, taking off his own shades. "Have you ordered anything?" I said yes, a cappuccino, and he did some semaphore to the waiter pointing down at my head giving the thumbs-up. He had a South African accent and tree trunk legs in shorts, like an overgrown little boy, with a greasy Beatles cut like you get on Lego people.

I just felt instantly this was a waste of time. Two of them weren't physically right, and the third one, this Emyr, who might have been physically a possibility, wasn't right personality wise. He was like Tintin. Fifteen layers of clothes on, all too big for him. The shirt label on the back of his neck stuck up like a flag. I could have painted him, but he kept staring at his shoes. He just seemed incredibly bashful. I don't actually think he could have managed a sitting. I think he would have had a panic attack.

Vicky sat with her back to the brightly sunlit street. They had a *Sunday Times* pulled limb from limb all over the table top, and their ashtray was already a grey, spilling crematorium. She said, "I suppose one day we'll be able to say to our grandkids, there we were in that cafe chatting to that famous artist. And see that picture on the wall? That's your gran, that is."

The others chuckled.

"In the National Gallery, aye," I said. "I don't think so.

"You don't think you'll be famous?"

I shrugged. "I don't think this is exactly the Deux Magots, is it?"

Emyr looked up from his trainers. "What's that when it's at home?"

"It's a skin disease," said Paul. "Like dermatitis."

"It's that cafe in Paris where Picasso hung out," I said. "And Albert Camus. And Sartre, I think. You know. That existentialist lot."

"No," said Emyr with an uninflected honesty. "Not really," and looked back at his shoes.

"Emyr's studying Oceanography," said Paul.

"Floating little boat-shaped things in tanks of water and looking at screens going blip, blip, blip."

"And what are you studying?" I asked Vicky.

"Beauty Technology," she said without any visible irony, leaning forward to allow some ash to be rolled off her cigarette tip. "Part-time."

"Political Science," said Paul.

"You come from the right country for it," I said.

"I do," he said. "Where did you study? You did study, I presume."

"Aberdeen."

He raised both eyebrows.

"And then the Royal College."

He blew smoke.

"Of Art."

He nodded and brushed non-existent ash from his knee. My cappuccino came, with a Virgin Mary for Vicky. She blinked a lot, I noticed, like the cigarette fug she chimneyed irritated her own eyes, or she needed glasses and was too vain to wear them. She never seemed to completely focus. It may have been that she was suffering from some allergenic pollution due to the mascara she wore. All three were equal possibilities.

"It must be really, really difficult, and that." *And that.* She had a Wiltshire accent, but probably thought she sounded like a

BBC newsreader. "I mean finding the motivation. You must be incredibly self-disciplined. I mean, without a boss, without clocking on, without a wage packet, getting up and getting down to painting away every day."

"Not really. I have to earn a living. I've got a mortgage to pay like everybody else. It's not a hobby, it's not for fun—it's a job."

"But you must love what you do, though."

I made a face. "Sometimes. Not all the time. Not when it's not going well. When it's going like shit, it can be hell, I hate it."

I could see she didn't understand that at all. "But at least you're expressing yourself. You're lucky. Most people don't get a chance to do that."

"Everyone can make marks on paper, to a certain extent, if they want to enough. Everyone can draw. I don't believe in this bollocks that you're born with it, like some gift. You don't talk about a plumber having a gift, or a doctor. You work at it. I work at it bloody hard. Through the night, sometimes, seven days a week. It makes me laugh. It doesn't flow effortlessly from your fingertips and there's a masterpiece, like people seem to think."

"That's not what I meant."

"No, sorry, I'm just saying that's what a lot of people think."

"Well, most people are ignorant, aren't they?"

I was waiting for it, and true enough, she said she'd always been artistic. Her dad said she was drawing all the time, as a kid.

"Oh," I said. "You weren't tempted to take it further?"

She curled up her nose, tilted her head. I thought: *you really are a very thick person.*

Paul said, "At least you don't work for anybody, you don't have anybody breathing down your neck."

I laughed. "Tell my gallery that."

"So do you rate Picasso then?" said Vicky. "I mean, what they say, do you think he's a proper painter? I mean, to some people he just splashes it all over, all this abstract what-not."

"Well, it's an acquired taste, I suppose. I'm not sure I got into it before art college. If you start to work with problems on canvas you start to see what it's all about, but you shouldn't feel inadequate if you don't appreciate it."

"I don't feel inadequate," Vicky said. "I just think it's taking the piss. It's as simple as that. You know, squiggling something and selling it for ten thousand quid, it's ridiculous that is. You can buy a car for that."

"You're probably right," I said. Thinking, hey, I didn't do five years of art school to go fifteen rounds on Picasso's Blue Period with a beauty therapist.

"What about opera?" said Paul. "What do you think of that?" Like they were all in the same airy-fairy bag.

I didn't know what to say. "I don't know much about opera, to be honest."

"You can still give an opinion," he said. "Can't you?" He was looking at me. Not staring, but looking.

"I don't know, to be honest." I tried to say something funny. "Load of fattish women singing about dying of consumption most of the time."

He didn't laugh. "She doesn't know," he said slowly, still looking at me, his eyes not moving from me.

Then Vicky Hartwell said, "How much money do you make? Not being rude or anything. Just curious."

I thought, put it like this, I'm not jetting off to the South of France. I'm not jetting off anywhere unless I get another exhibition or Gavin builds an extension pretty sharpish. I fidgeted and licked the froth off of the back of my spoon and said, "It varies."

"Enough to make a living, though?" said Emyr.

"Occasionally." I laughed again. I don't know why.

Vicky said, "Look, I expect you'll want to see these. I brought them along anyway." She lifted up these hefty WHSmith albums with tissue paper out of a Threshers carrier bag, and stacked them on the table. "They'll give you some ideas. Won't they, Paul?"

I leafed through the photograph albums, delicately, as if they were aged Bibles that might crumble to the touch. "That's from a holiday me and Paul went on to the Seychelles. Have you been to the Seychelles?" I shook my head like a dunce. "Love-ly," she said dreamily. "*Love*-ly . . . "

My eyes flickered back down to bikini shots with a thong tight up the crack of her behind. Topless ones showing off the off-white breasts against a gravy-coloured tan. Backlit shots, with her legs apart in the waves. The tossed hair of a Page 3 girl.

She arched back her head and blew smoke.

"She's not shocked." Vicky nudged Emyr's arm. "She's seen a lot more than that in art college. A *heck* of a lot more."

"I bet," said Emyr, his head level with his chest.

I leafed through the rest, robotic now, playing the game but not really looking. There was something dirty about them, vaguely sleazy and intrusive. Private. A bathroom shot, after the suntan oil. The white rim above boxer shorts lowered an inch. Naked in the pool, floating strawberries of nipples under the scummy aquamarine. I could see she thought that was somehow artistic and that I would understand, that there was common ground. Legs apart, bent over. 18-30 meets Readers Wives. I could see the pale, soft line of her bikini wax. I couldn't wait to hand them back.

"Good photographs."

What else could I say?

She looked at me and gave a little shrug, like she knew that already. "My boyfriend's a good photographer. He's got talent. He did my friend Stacy's wedding, everybody said his pictures were better than the professional's." She leaned across and kissed Paul on the cheek, and ran her hand down his thigh. He grinned like a petted Labrador.

"There you go," I said.

"David Bailey," said her boyfriend, miming a camera and clicking the shutter.

"There was this little bar run by English people, they were ever so nice. They said it was a change not to talk about the Royal Family or British beef. They opened this big bottle of Calvados. We got *such* a hangover that night, it's not true. I felt like somebody hit me over the head. I couldn't lift my head out of the pillow for two days."

I was thinking to myself, she's very proud of her breasts. She is very proud of the fact that men like her breasts.

Then Vicki Hartwell asked me, "What kind of painting do you do?"

I never know how to answer that, so I mumbled about the BP Award and they nodded as if they'd heard of it, which they obviously hadn't. If I said I'm influenced by Egon Shiele or John Kirby or Ken Currie they'd be thinking I'm this bighead artist showing off, so I said, "Figures and heads," embarrassed-sounding and annoyed at myself for being like that. (Then I thought, who are these people, anyway? Why should I worry what they think? I just want to get out of here. I just want to see the bottom of this cappuccino cup.)

I put another spoonful of sugar in, and I could tell Vicki was thinking, Oh yeah, she could afford to shed a couple of pounds around the hips, in those leggings.

"The card is one of mine," I said, and went and fetched the old Private View invite still blue-tacked to the imitation Louis Whatever mirror with my number written on it. I passed it round. They obviously hadn't looked at it that closely.

Vicky said, "Is it a good likeness?"

"Not really."

Emyr said, "Has he really got a neck that long?"

"Artistic license, isn't it?" said the smug boyfriend. "Does he really have a dappled, blotchy face with red and green bits all over it?"

I said, "Not really."

"Do you know what it looks like?" he said, holding it. "A penis. The long neck, look. The head at the top with the red cheeks and the shiny head like a glans. It's like an *engorged* penis. Is that intentional?" He had a little cut under one eye, as if someone had bashed him. He had whiskers breaking through an erupting splatter of pimples. "Or is that my dirty mind?"

I didn't say anything.

"It's your dirty mind," said Vicky.

He said, "She's heard worse than that at art college. A *lot* worse."

Emyr was peering closely at the card. "He's got an interesting-shaped head."

"It's like that joke that bald people tell," I said, taking it back. "About God creating human beings, and those heads that weren't perfect, He covered in hair."

"I don't know about that," said Vicky, laughing a little bit.

I said, "What is it about gay men? I don't know."

"Don't look at me," said Paul.

"They seem to keep all the best ones to themselves," I said to Vicky.

"Oh I don't know," she said. "Mine's not a bad catch. I'm not going to throw this one back, am I?" She stroked the downy hairs on her boyfriend's forearm.

"They all look the same these days," said Emyr, all bony shoulders, coffee froth making dirty brackets around his mouth. "Like clones, like robots. Have you noticed? So they can recognise each other, I expect. There was a time not so long ago, they were trying to cover up how they looked, make it not so much a giveaway, like. Pansies, my mam used to call um. Then it was queers, wasn't it? Then it was gay."

"Now it's back to queers," I said. "Queer is OK. They like to be called queer."

"*Nev-er*," said Emyr.

"Haven't you heard of Queer Power?" I said.

"Emyr hasn't even heard of Power Rangers," said Paul, with his hand on his girlfriend's bare knee, and they laughed.

"Hilarious, Paul," said Emyr. "You're such a wit, I'm not kidding, you ought to be on *Newsnight Review*."

"Yeah, there's a fair few shaved barnets on that," said Vicky. "They're all over the place nowadays, aren't they? You can't get away from them."

I looked at George Polish Name, on the card in my fingers. I don't know what attracts me to gay men, or gay women for that matter. Maybe I just feel safe with them. Maybe I don't feel threatened. With the shutters back and light falling on him, George is a beautiful object, his red ears sticking out, his bluish chin, his bony shoulders, the dot of white on his nipple ring, the three horizontal lines that segment his fat-free abdomen. The cupped, entwined fingers in his lap. I noticed as I painted him for the first time that his hands seem much older than the rest of his body. They could be his father's hands.

"How do you find them? Models?" Emyr asked. He shot a glance at Paul. "Shut up. It's interesting, this."

Paul held up his hands, tucked in his chin.

I said, "I first saw George in The Fox. I thought, there's a really physical guy, but vulnerable, with shaved head and tattoos and who's done everything to himself to look mean, but with these warm eyes like a puppy. I felt like a man eyeing up some leggy blonde in a miniskirt. I couldn't take my eyes off of him. I wanted to know his name, where he lived, what he did for a living. Then I went up and said, Hi, my name's Stella Beatty, I'm a painter, will you sit for me please? Not quite those words, but something equally embarrassing, and George blushed. And from then on, I knew he was perfect. Pubs are great for models."

"You just went up to him? Just like that? And asked him?" said Emyr, astonished. "In a pub?"

"Yeah. Where else? I always used pubs and cafes in Edinburgh. I'm always looking for faces. Faces at bars, faces across a cafe, faces at a disco, anywhere."

"Isn't it embarrassing?"

I shook my head. "Not anymore. I've gone past that point of thinking, oh shit. I pretend it's not me, it's this confident person I'm not. I just go up to them. I used to be shy, I'm quite a shy person really, but you can't afford to be. You have to say to yourself, you're a painter. It's your job. You have to find people to paint. It's as simple as that. You've got to earn a living. You see people. They attract you, for whatever reason . . .

"*Inspiration,*" Emyr said, hunched over even more, eager beaver body language, hugging himself and grinning like there was something absurd and wonderful about the word.

"Are they real? The tattoos?" he said.

Paul was directing the packet of Silk Cut Extra Mild at his girlfriend's mouth, like a microphone.

"People ask me if I make them up, if I just add them on. 'Course I don't, I mean, what's the point of that? I mean, the point is, that's the person, that's a part of them, that's why it's there."

She plucked a cigarette with her lips.

"And do you know a lot about the people you paint?" asked Emyr. "Do you know them really well, mostly?"

"When I'm painting I don't really want to know anything about them. They're an object. I'm not looking for information, or a story, like a *Laughing Cavalier* sort of thing, because that's too sentimental, too crass. Not that I'm not interested in them as people. I am, in the sense that I'm really interested in what makes people tick. I've always been interested in that. At school for instance, and always, even now, I always really notice hands—hands and heads. I can still picture exactly what my French teacher's hands looked like, more than I can remember anything she actually taught me: I could draw them now, the thick blue veins like paint from a tube, the big bulbs of these knuckles with arthritis."

Emyr said, "It must be amazing to have that kind of *observation.*" It was another word he made a big dipper out of.

"I always used to watch, to stare, even on the bus down Princes Street, and wonder all these things about all these people. My mother would tell me off for being rude and showing her up. I could never understand why looking was such a crime. You know?"

Paul Rolt dragged the colour supplement onto his knee and resumed reading an article about Billie Piper.

"This is probably boring," I said.

"No," said Emyr. "It isn't. Not to me."

The others didn't say anything.

"At art college, of course, they employed people for you to stare at," I said. "I don't know what my mother would have thought of that. But the models were terrible. Once I said to one of the tutors, I don't see why I should have to paint this Big Fat Old Man anymore, I'm sick of it. And he said, Well, we can't get anybody else. As if, think yourself lucky for this Big Fat Old Git to draw. Then I read this thing in a book on David Hockey and he said that when he was at the Royal College he could not believe how *repulsive* some of the models were, and he complained, and they said, What's your problem? So I felt, right—there's David Hockney saying it, it's not just me."

Vicky was looking at her watch.

"Sorry," I said.

"Do you have any idea what a one-bedroom flat is going for in Bath?" she said. "Roughly?"

"No, not really."

Nobody said anything for a while.

"We've got our heart set on a honeymoon in Yucatan. I'm not quite sure where it is, but it's supposed to be beautiful."

"Mexico," said Paul, drawing a map of the Caribbean Sea in the air, livening up again.

"They have these little huts right on the beach," said Vicky. "Just like Robinson Crusoe. And these bars that serve cocktails and fruit, it just sounds like Paradise. It's expensive, but my attitude is, bugger it, you only go on honeymoon once, don't you?"

"Hopefully," I said.

"She made a mistake in the Seychelles," said Paul. "Tell her about your mistake in the Seychelles, Vic." Vicky looked blank. "You know." He made circles on his chest with his thumbs.

"Oh yeah," she said, covering her mouth. "I bought this beautiful bikini from Jolly's, in white, right? It looked beautiful on the beach, sunbathing, perfect."

"Then she went in the water."

"Then I went in the water and . . . " She made a startled face which was intended to convey everything, horror, embarrassment. She shook her head at the memory. "You know."

"She . . . "

"Don't!"

"Put it like this. There was not a lot left to the . . . "

"Paul, shut up!"

"Imagination, shall we say?"

She elbowed him. Her breasts shuddered slightly when she did. I noticed for the first time she was round-shouldered and not as petite as I first thought. She crossed her arms, but she wasn't embarrassed, not really. She was enjoying it. Her bloke kissed her and I watched moisture pass between their lips in the brief suction sound as stubble met freckles.

"Ah! What about that feller who puts half a dead cow in a tank then," said Vicky suddenly. "What do you think of *that*?"

"I think it's beautifully made," I said.

She groaned and so did her boyfriend.

"I'm serious," I said. "Have you seen it?"

"No. Why would I want to see it?"

"Besides, what else would you do with a dead cow?"

"Eat it," she said. "That's what human beings are supposed to do with cows, isn't it? Eat them."

"McDonald's?" I said. "Burger King. Wimpy's."

"It's disgusting. A cow with a baby inside it. That's not art, please don't tell me you think that's art. What's so clever about sticking something like that in a glass tank?"

"Who says it has to be clever?"

Emyr said, "My dad always said he'd never pay more than fifty quid for any work of art in the whole history of the world. Not a Rembrandt, not the *Mona Lisa*. Nothing."

"He'd pay fifty quid for a ticket to Cardiff Arms Park though, probably, wouldn't he?" said Paul.

"He didn't see the use," said Emyr.

The conversation seemed to last forever because they kept

talking. Vicki kept tossing her hair from the back of her neck with both hands. She had these immaculate nails, these painted nails. She must have looked at the state of mine. You can't get it off, not even with Swarfega. She looked at me like I was a different species. Not exotic or interesting, just alien, like a vegetable on your plate you haven't encountered before.

So I tuned out quite a lot, and when I tuned back in, she was saying, "Of course I won't be available on Saturday and Sunday, but the best day for me is probably Wednesday when we have a half-day, or Thursday between . . . " And the boyfriend had his Filofax out and he was full of, I'm doing this and I'm doing that too. And the third one, I kept thinking, he's a possibility, but he was the one looking at his shoes, he was going, I will be available, sort of like twittering, and I thought: *No. No, none of you. None of you is any good.*

But I kept smiling like an idiot. I think it was to cover up my real feelings, in case they showed through. I was such a coward. It was my fault. I should have said. Maybe I'd feel different now, if I'd just *said* there and then. Not that it would have made any difference to what happened. How could it?

And while they were going on about their availability, I wanted to stand up and say, stop, listen, none of you are any good to me, you're boring, you are all tedious shites and I can't bear sitting here anymore. And it was so *pathetic* because what I ended up saying as I got up was, "Right, well, must dash. I didn't realise the time and, um—I'll give you all a ring next week." And I started to walk to the door.

"But you haven't got our phone numbers," Vicki piped up, a little startled but too dim to get it.

"Oh God. Have I not? Oh right!" I said, thinking I didn't want their poxy phone numbers, and before I know it there I am, writing it on the back of my hand, reading it back to them, checking it's correct.

"She looked like somebody who should have been at home behind the counter at the Stroud and Swindon."

Gavin laughed at his forkful of lasagne. "That bad, eh?"

"Jesus! Worse," I said, knocking back the wine. "I'm not kidding. They were *so* boring, I don't know—I just glazed over, it was like *aeons*. I couldn't wait to get away and I had to sit there, sit there with the geek looking at his shoes and listen while she rattled on about her holidays and she'd say *what do you think of Picasso then?* Like, what the fuck? And, I'm not kidding, when she looked up and said *But you haven't got our phone number!* Jesus fucking Christ!"

We laughed, tears bulging in our eyes, fanning the hot pasta in our mouths with our hands.

"You've got to phone them," Gavin said later. He'd seen the number written on my hand while we were in the kitchen cooking. He asked me if it was important. I'd started to rub it out with a wet finger and he'd stopped me. He said it again, now, as he crisscrossed his knife and fork on the empty plate. "Come on. You've got to phone them."

"Why?" I said, light-headed from the second bottle of Andes Peak. "Bollocks."

"Go on, bollocks. It's not fair."

"It's not bloody fair being bloody boring-looking and wasting a morning of my time!"

"Go on." He got up and turned down the Morcheeba.

"Hey . . . " I said. "I was enjoying that."

"Go on. Do it now. Get it over with. You know if you don't, they're going to be ringing you up sooner or later."

I moaned. "I can't. Not now, I'm too pissed."

"Good." He took hold of both my hands and lifted me from my chair. "Do it, come on . . . "

"She was so boring."

"I know."

"She was so full of herself."

"I know. You said."

"They all were. So fucking *boring* . . . "

I started to laugh uncontrollably. Gavin laughed too. He hung loosely against the wall, his face falling against mine, lips to lips. I held his face. It was nice.

"I love you."

"You appreciate me now then, eh?"

"No."

He read the number off my hand and dialled it, and held the receiver to the side of my head.

As the ringing tone burred, he slid his hand down the front of my trousers, behind my belt. I felt his fingertips in my pubic hair. I slapped his wrist. He kissed my ear, tugged it between his teeth. I smelled wine. We laughed. Vicki Hartwell answered the phone. There was music in the background.

I said, "Hello. This is Stella."

She said, "Stella! Great."

My heart dropped, so I said quickly, "Look, I'm awful sorry and everything, but I need a certain type. I'm doing this painting, and it's nothing to do with you, all of you—but I'm only looking for certain faces. Sorry." The more I tried to embellish the thought, the worse it sounded. To me, anyway.

Her reaction was just an "Oh," as if she was completely surprised and didn't understand.

"It's not like you aren't pretty or anything," I added hastily, giggling. I had a headache now—a clash between sobering up and wanting to get hammered. I frowned.

She said, "I understand." And by now she sounded shirty a little bit.

I said, "I am sorry."

There was a gap. Somebody turned down the music. "Oh, well. It can't be helped." A tremor in the back of her throat now.

I started to get embarrassed. "I've got to go now," waiting for her reply, giving her a gap to speak in.

"Well thanks for ringing," she said. "Thanks for the coffee."

I hung up, and a moment later remembered that the coffees

had been bought by her. It made me feel bad. I don't think she said it on purpose. I think that kind of guile was beyond her. She was upset. Perhaps.

Gavin had taken the plates into the kitchen and was dumping them in soapy water. I picked up the salt and pepper from the table, and refuelled the two wine glasses.

She'd get over it. So would I.

Gavin came back and rubbed off the phone number on the back of my hand with a J-cloth.

"She loved herself," I said. "She loved herself too much."

"You're feeling guilty now," Gavin said.

"No."

"You're worried you hurt her feelings."

"No. She's too full of herself for that."

"Is that why you didn't like her then?"

"She was thick," I said. "She was thick as a plank and she was confident, with it. She thought she was the bee's knees. I like people with a bit of self-doubt."

He puts his arms around me. "Is that why you like me?"

I said, "Who says I like you?"

We exchanged the wine breath in our mouths. He uncoiled my belt and unzipped my trousers. He stood behind me and pulled down my knickers and positioned his prick under my buttocks. It felt warm and gentle. His hands began massaging my shoulders as he stiffened harder and got bigger. I rubbed my cheek against his knuckles and whispered, "I like being naughty."

"You're my wife. I'm your husband. We can do what we like in our own home. Can't we?"

I said, "That's true." I took off my clothes, and then his, and we made love on the carpet, which felt uncomfortable, and great, and somehow criminal, and somehow good. He felt like what he was: a nice, good man. "I love you."

"Why's that?"

"Because you're big, fat and ugly," I said.

Vicki Hartwell. Vicki Hartwell.

I didn't even know her second name until I read the newspaper. The story first appeared on the Wednesday. The Wednesday after the Saturday.

Gavin came in with a *Chronicle* like he usually does on the way home from work. He'd been painting a Georgian ceiling up in the Circus and he went to lie in the bath. I was worried he'd done his back in again. He said he was in agony. I didn't see the early evening news, the ITV West news, it was probably on that. I just saw her face in the paper, on the front page, that blow up of her from her eighteenth birthday party, with a little bit of red-eye from the camera flash, and the teeth and the low cut blouse and a weeny bit squiffy, letting her hair down a bit and enjoying it.

I felt that woozy feeling you get when you stand on a cliff and lean over the edge and for a second it feels like nothing is holding you there. My first instinct was to call Gavin, but I just sat there, and didn't.

I said to myself, calm down, it's not so bad. It says MISSING. It doesn't say what's happened to her. It's not like they've found her body or anything, all chopped up. That's all it says, just MISSING.

I had to tell Gavin. I picked up the paper and went and tried the bathroom door.

It was locked. He always locks it. It always irritates me.

He said, "What?" Shirty.

"How long are you going to be?"

"Why?"

"Dinner's on the table in five minutes, that's why."

"All right. I'll be out in five minutes. OK?"

I went back to the table and sat with the paper spread out in front of me like a map. I closed it when I heard the bath plug pulled. Gavin prowled the room wrapped in a towel. "Where's the number for that chiropractor Jill was talking about?" I turned the paper over, face down. *Her* face down.

I looked in from the kitchen at him as I dished up the meal. He had a little wet curl on the back of his neck, as dark as Indian ink, head bent over the paper. We sat and ate. He didn't say I looked like I'd just seen a car accident or anything. He started at the back page, with the sports, flapping the paper in occasionally extravagant folds. Every mouthful of my food was forced in like a gag, stuffing words back down into me. I was waiting, and I knew what was coming, but I didn't know when. Then he said in a mumble: "Jesus. Did you read this?"

"What?" I said, butterflies inside.

"This girl . . . "

I said, "I know."

"Unbelievable . . . Right around the corner."

"Yes."

I thought, *I'll tell him. I will tell him. How will I tell him? How?*

"That nightclub, Manhattan's . . . "

"What do you think of the noodles?" I said. "I know it costs a bit more but you get better quality with the Marks stuff, don't you? That's what you pay for."

"She was born in Nailsea, where Roger comes from," said Gavin, surprised, and started to read it out: "Police worries intensified when they learned from Vicky's parents that the red-haired student at Bath University always let them know her plans in advance. She never went anywhere without picking up the phone, Mr Hartwell said. She knows what worriers we are and she's very responsible." He flickered a look at me, a shrug. "It seems to be entirely out of character, said DI Rob Kernow of Avon Constabulary, which gives us great cause for concern. If anybody has any clues as to Vicky's whereabouts please contact the nearest police station, where all information will be treated in complete confidence." Another look. "In the early hours on Sunday morning a story of tragic misunderstandings quickly emerged. Vicky Hartwell had gone to the nightclub in Tilley Street on Saturday night in the company of her boyfriend Paul Rolt and his flatmate Emyr

Winter. During the course of the evening Mr Rolt became annoyed that Vicky was spending time with some old school friends, and at 11.30 went home in a minicab from Ab Cabs in King's Square. Not knowing that Mr Rolt had gone home, Mr Winter also left Manhattan's to go to Skorpio's Kebab House in Millet Street with some student friends. Her schoolmates last saw Vicky at approximately 12.15, when she left the dance floor to look for her boyfriend. She has not been seen since.

"Vicky's photograph has been printed on a poster by the *Chronicle* and appears all along Tilley Street in the hope that it will jog somebody's memory. Police are asking for anyone with any information on Vicky to contact this Crimestoppers number, blah, blah . . ." Gavin's voice trailed off. He looked at his plate as if he'd forgotten that he'd eaten. He bent the paper in half and pushed it to me.

"I read it before. I told you." I got up. "Do you want a beer?"

"Have you got a cold one?"

"Think so."

He pulled the paper back, turned it back to him, picking his teeth. "Pretty girl, look, too . . ."

"Awful," I said in a small voice. "Awful . . . " I opened and closed drawers looking for a bottle opener.

"She'll turn up, Stell," Gavin said. "Don't get upset. She'll probably turn up. They always do—one way or another."

I brought him the beer.

"You're not having one?"

"No, I'm fine."

But I'm not thinking, I'm thinking of his words: *They always do—one way or another . . .*

One way or another . . .

By the end of the week, the same picture was appearing in the nationals, bigger now, and it is saying things like POLICE FEAR FOR

SAFETY OF VICKI. The police were still pleading for the public to come forward. It was all over the local TV news, Manhattan's in its tired neon scrawl, blinking, un-hip, corny, the police with their clipboards, talking to youngsters as they went into the disco the following Saturday night. Amish-tight WPCs contrasting with half-cut girlies, glittering-midriffed *Pop Idol* wannabes, biting their lips, arms crossed round their ribs as if trying to keep in their anorexic vital organs. Boyfriends loitering with their shirttails out, tongues of their trainers lolling and cool and quietly hungry, thinking of their hair gel and not of the police's result that night, but theirs.

The mother was at the press conference, again, a repeat, looking like a ghost. I wondered, how can she go to the hairdresser's? How can she put on lipstick? How can she fill up the car with petrol? She looked frightened by the cameras, Delia Smith facing a firing squad. Her husband fussed over her hand like it was a precious object he had just found in the snow.

"What do you want for dinner?" I left the sofa-bed to Gavin with his long legs taking it over. "I've got the liver and bacon or the beef."

"I'm not fussed."

"They're both 'not suitable for home freezing,' so we can have one tonight and the other one tomorrow night. What do you fancy?"

"They released the boyfriend, then."

"You're not listening to me."

"I'm watching the television."

"Bugger the television," I said. "Hello. I'm here, this is me. I'm real." It came out louder than I meant it to.

I went to the kitchen and he sloped after me. He hovered by the door while I unloaded the dishwasher.

"I keep thinking about her," he said, by way of explanation, opening and closing random cabinets. "Thinking she's out there somewhere, in a cellar. Some fucking nutter . . . Horrible, horrible . . ."

I looked at him hard. "You think I don't think about that?"

He looks hurt. Hurt that I look hurt. He doesn't understand anything. He takes the knife from me. "I'm cooking. I'll do it."

I take it back and puncture the film over the packets of liver and bacon. "I've started now. I'll do it." He goes back in and sits down.

I was at a dinner party when somebody said, "Is there any news about that girl who went missing? What was it? Four weeks ago?"

"You think they'd turn up something," said the Welsh woman who'd already been racist about the Scots. "Fingertip search. Divers in the weir. Dogs. Helicopters, the lot. I mean, for someone to vanish without a trace, into thin air, virtually."

"Don't be stupid," said her husband. "It happens all the time." She looked momentarily crestfallen and her neck reddened as I watched her chasing some rocket and radicchio round the smear of balsamic vinegar on her plate.

"Dreadful," said the woman who came without a bottle. "Dreadful."

"What do you think happened?"

"Well it's obvious, isn't it?" said her boyfriend, topping up his glass of red.

"Is it?" I said.

He looked mystified by my comment. He said, "Well. Some bloke, obviously."

Anna cleared the starter plates and told us that the main course would be a while, so we could feel free to pollute our lungs. We did. She was good like that, even though she'd given up for two years herself. She empathised with the addiction in others.

"What's her name?"

I listened to some wine pouring.

I said, "Vicky Hartwell." I wasn't sure if I said it out loud, so I heard myself say it a second time. "Vicky Hartwell."

"There are some nasty people in the world," said the woman who didn't bring a bottle.

"Her poor mother, that's what I keep thinking," said Gavin, clearing something from between his teeth with a fingernail. "What's the worst? Believing your daughter's dead or believing she's still alive?"

Anna came back into the room and announced, "Five minutes." She took off her apron and her husband rubbed her back and told her to relax.

"Alive," said the woman from the health food shop, stroking a roll-up. "Alive is worse. If it was me, if it was my daughter, I'd rather she was dead, anything, I'd rather they found the body. The idea of her *suffering* . . . you know?" She shivered under her hippy mane like she'd touched a snake. "God, I couldn't bear it. Not knowing. God. What you imagine is ten times worse."

I excused myself and went to the loo. I didn't need to go. I sat there in the minimal bathroom, no frilly toilet roll holder, no odd socks spilling from the laundry bin, no toothpaste stains around the sink. I considered if I could cry, and wash my face, and not look red-eyed when I returned to the table, or arouse attention, when there was a tap at the door. Gavin, asking if I was all right. Me, saying I am.

In the car driving home, Gavin said, "I don't know what's wrong with you. I was worried. It was embarrassing."

"Oh, it was embarrassing. Sorry." I turned down the heater. "Concentrate on the road. How much wine have you had?"

"One glass. Not even a glass, actually." He flipped the wipers to smear away specks of drizzle. "Is it something I've done? Tell me. Stella, is it me? What?"

I laughed through tight lips. It was supposed to mean, don't be ridiculous, but Gavin looked as though I'd mocked him, injured him. "No. It's not you." I rubbed my eyes. They felt like sandpaper.

By the time we got in, it was half past one. Still standing in my wet raincoat as he pulled out the sofa-bed, I said I was going to sleep in the bedroom. I said he had to be up early and my tossing and turning with my bad back kept him awake. I made it sound like I was thinking of him. He shrugged, plucking at the corners of the sheets. He said if I cared about him sleeping badly, I knew he always sleeps badly on his own. I said let's give it a crack. Just tonight. He said, "You're the boss."

I said, "No I'm not. Don't say that."

"What do you want me to say?"

That night I lay awake for ages, my eyes in a jetlagged daytime alertness out of synch with the sleeping world outside. Some time later I heard Gavin padding nakedly to the bathroom, I listened to the string-pull light swinging and tapping against the wall, the extractor fan, the steady stream of piss, the flush kicking in finally on the third try. I heard him pause at the door, as the flush went into hissing mode, and he came into the darkened room and looked down at me. He stood beside the bed and whispered, "Stella? Are you all right?" I didn't move. I visualised his tall, naked body in the gloom, his square shoulders and collarbone catching a spill of light, his tousled pillow hair, his baby bewildered eyes. I listened to him breathing, half expecting him to get into bed beside me, or touch me with his warm workman's hands. My heart was beating hard. I kept my eyes tight shut, I played dead, and after a few more minutes, I heard the creaky boards counting his footsteps back to the sofa-bed.

The next morning he brought me breakfast in bed. He pampered me. Poached eggs on toast, done to perfection, runny, pot of tea, little milk jug, and a little chocolate valentine heart he must have got from the corner shop when he got the milk. He sat on the bed and kissed my cheek and said, "I've decided. I'm going to start decorating today. We're going to move back in here by the weekend. I'm sick of that bloody put-you-up. I'm going to chuck it out."

I don't know what it is with tea, whether it always tastes nicer when somebody else makes it. That tea was particularly nice.

By the time I'd got up he'd left, and I found another heart in red shiny paper Sellotaped to the corner of one of my canvases. I wanted to put it in a box, in cotton wool, in silk, like a diamond ring. I looked at the portrait I did of Gavin six months before, with the primary colours, the light bulb and the hula-hoop, propped against the wall. It caught something about him: the quizzical, cartoony optimism, the openness, the strength, the safety. He was a nicer person than I was. Than I could ever be.

I felt the pot and the tea was still warm enough to drink.

It's been twelve weeks now. Three months.

The face that I had no interest in is everywhere now, a mocking population explosion of clones, all shouting: VICKI HARTWELL—MISSING. Posters on walls, that grainy snapshot, billposted amongst the vivid pastels of the jungle and techno venues. In waiting rooms, at the doctor's surgery, in the pub. The lipstick, the hair, the tipsy smile. I pass a shop window and I see it. I nip in a newsagents and I see it. I buy a stamp at the post office and there it is: VICKI HARTWELL—MISSING.

She smiles at me in the hairdresser's salon from the poster with backward letters in my mirror.

"That girl. All this time. God. I wonder what's happened to her?" says my hairdresser, John. "Such an ordinary, attractive young girl too..."

I say, "Do you think she's attractive?"

He shrugs and lowers his voice. "Well, I'd have got rid of that frizz for a start off. That went out with Pan's People, that did."

"She was to somebody," I say. "Attractive, I mean."

"Oh yeah. Somebody must've fancied her, mustn't they? Somebody must've liked her face." He teases up some more random spikes. "You always think that stalkers are always after your

Jill Dandos or your Jodie Fosters, but who knows what they fasten on to, really? Who knows what they're looking for? The hair, the eyes?" As he talks I look at *Glamour* and *Elle* on the coffee table with their panther-faced cover girls, ash-black faces and lilac, succulent lips, and waif-junkie child-bride fashion spreads, and think of the furious masturbators who use Freeman's catalogues, the baby clothes sections. Nothing is sacred, safe, anymore. There's nothing that cannot be used. "Do you know why you fancy someone? I don't It's a total mystery to me," he said, snipping.

Six months later, and she still hasn't been found.

"How did you do that? It's a humdinger." Gavin takes off his socks and boxer shorts and sits naked on the toilet seat. I look down into the Body Shop formaldehyde and see the dark cloud of a bruise on my thigh.

"I don't remember." I cup water over my breasts. "I didn't even notice I'd done it." I raise my knee out of the scum and examine it. It has a green penumbra and pointillist pricks of red in the centre. I sink it back under and consider the rest of me, like a pathologist might do. A gash on my forefinger from a pencil-sharpening scalpel. Dotted claw marks on the back of my hand from next-door's cat. A scar from falling from a swing, aged six. Scabs, grazes with explanations lost in time. If I were dead, if they slid me out of a metal cabinet, what clues would there be?

Vicki Hartwell. Vicki Hartwell.

Repeat anything long enough and it becomes abstract, losing its meaning. It's no longer a name, just a mnemonic for a feeling, a feeling of dread. A dread of what's happened to her, of what might happen to us, any of us. Our bodies. What people might do to us. Can do to us. Cut us, bruise us, burn us, make us afraid, make us think we're going to die. How vulnerable we are. How easy it is for someone to do us pain if they want to.

"Can I get in after you? Is it still warm?"

He makes circles in the water with his hand.

I sit up. Put on my specs. "I'm getting out."

"You don't have to."

"No, I've finished. You get in."

I stand up dripping, our naked bodies—one wet, one dry—passing each other without touching. I feel like, if he gets too close, he will know, by osmosis or something. It will seep out of my skin. I can see he thinks I'm being cold. He is right. I brush my teeth. I spit into the spiralling water, the minty froth flecked with blood from my gums. If I close my eyes I see her, her immaculate lipstick, playing with her shimmering hair, her manicured, slightly chubby hand stroking her boyfriend's inner thigh.

"You've shaved your legs. Thanks for telling me." Gavin sinks into the formaldehyde.

There's a nasty cut on my shin from the razor and I hope to God it'll heal.

It is nine months now since she went missing, and the police are scaling down the investigation. The conclusion is that she either doesn't want to be found or something very bad has happened to her. The TV news shows the same footage of Manhattan's, a litany now, the shots as familiar as those of an endlessly repeated Tesco commercial. The detective in charge, DI Rob Kernow, looks older, as respectful as an undertaker, with the sound turned down on his life.

There isn't a day I don't think about her. I don't think there'll ever be a day now when I don't think about Vicki Hartwell.

Gavin comes in from the pub. He's been drinking. I know what's coming and I dread the predictability. When we're in bed he presses his excruciatingly hot, erect penis against the side of my thigh and kisses my shoulder. I say, "Gavin." I feel him wilt and he turns away, and after a moment I turn and face his back. I try to detect some reaction in his breathing, but I can't.

He says, "We've got to do something about this, Stella. If we don't it's the end. If sex goes out of a marriage it's the beginning of the end. We may as well say it's over, that's it."

I say, "Is that what you feel, is that what you want?" I manage to sound as if I'm accusing him. He just sighs. Later that night I hear him lying on his back and I know he's wide awake and so am I. I can't bear to touch him. I daren't.

I think, it could be me in a ditch, in a coffin, in pieces, because I'm frightened, and it's killing me, it's killing us, if I let it.

The next morning I make him scrambled eggs on soda bread toast. He wakes groggy, still asleep when I put the tray on his knees and say, "I want to tell you something tonight. Something I should've told you a while ago and I have to tell you now.

He looks up, like I've told him he has six months to live. "Is it somebody else?"

"No, not in the way you think. Nothing like that."

"What is it then?"

"I'll meet you in The Fox."

"Is it bad?"

"It's nothing. Not really."

"It is something.

"It is something, to me, yes."

That lunchtime I get a phone call from my daughter up in Edinburgh. It's the usual voice that still sounds about twelve on the answerphone with a singsong "Hi, Mum. Only me. Just wonderin' how you're doin'. I'm fine . . ."

There's a reason for this call. I pick up. One of the paintings I did of her is propped against the wall. It turns out she's jacked it in with the creep she was besotted by. She got sick of handing him out her hard-earned cash from the clothes shop and she's going to share a flat with Marje, who makes sandwiches in a deli off Princes Street.

I say, "That's good news."

She says, "Well . . . " It turns out she needs two hundred quid deposit. I can see it a mile off. I say I haven't got it, but by the end of the conversation she's saying, "Thanks, Mum. How are things with you by the way?"

I say, "Oh, the usual. Working hard."

"And how's Gavin?"

"He's working hard too."

"Good, good."

I walk down Tilley Street past the police posters of Vicki Hartwell, past the burger take-away and Manhattan's, both gearing up for the Friday night throng, bouncers squeezed into bomber jackets like toothpaste in a tube, miming tai chi to each other.

The Fox is a builders hangout. I can never tell if the walls are tobacco-coloured paint or if it's the years of exhaled ale breath and tar. A blue cloud clings around the ceiling and the floor's already sticky. Gavin has commandeered a small table and a vodka has my name on it.

"Cheers."

The smoke is already biting the back of my throat, so I think I might as well light up. He pushes a packet of cigarettes towards me. I look into his eyes. I light the last one in my old pack. "Thought I'd save you fighting your way to the cigarette machine," he says. "It's hootchin'."

I scan the bar. Old habits die hard. An arm like a tree trunk is wrapped in tattoos like a malignant vine. A shaven-headed Vin Diesel lookalike kisses a girl on the cheek. An earring, a kit bag, straight from the gym. George Polish Name would fancy him. I like his head—soft, round like a baby's. My type. I remember first seeing Gavin here, not loud like his mates, nothing to prove, no prejudice, no preconceptions, and admiring the Dennis the Menace badge on my leather jacket, asking where he can get one.

I say, "What did you do today?"

He wobbles his head unenthusiastically. "More shifting fireplaces. They're taking all those nice Victorian fireplaces out. God knows what they're doing with them. They're worth a fortune."

"Don't knock it. It's bringing in the money."

"I hate it."

"It'll be over at the end of the month."

"I still hate it."

"That's right," I say. "Make me feel guilty."

"How?" he says, pained. "Make you feel guilty? What have I said now? Christ's sake. I can't open my mouth anymore."

I say, "Ask me about my day."

"Let me read your mind."

"Correct."

"Shitty."

"No. Productive."

"Oh. I never was good at reading minds." He doesn't ask me outright. Maybe doesn't want to know, maybe thinks whatever it is will go away. Is he making me suffer, or has he genuinely forgotten why we're here?

"I met that girl." I take a sip of vodka. "Vicki Hartwell."

I look up now. Gavin is colourless, as if someone has pulled the plug.

"She was that girl I told you about in the Metro Cafe. The one full of herself." My eyes wander off his face to the beer glass rings on the table. "I'm sorry, I'm really sorry. I know how you must feel, that I've been lying, deceiving, keeping something from you, but look, I was afraid. I thought you'd say go to the police. I couldn't face it. Then I felt a coward. Then it just got out of hand, it was like if I kept it inside I could pretend it never happened, that I was never a part of it. But it felt worse and worse. It felt easier to forget about it than to face telling you. I know it was wrong.

I just . . . " His eyes are focusing on arbitrary objects around the room, like he doesn't know where he is anymore.

When I run out of words and he focuses on me, finally, it's like I'm a person who beat him as a child.

"Say something."

"What?"

"Anything. Please."

He stares at me, like he's seeing a person he's never seen before. "A girl's gone missing, Stella."

"I know, I *know*. What was I supposed to do? Tell the police? Tell them what? What could the police do? They've done everything. What difference would it make?"

"It doesn't *matter*, don't you see?"

I said, "I didn't do anything wrong. I didn't do anything to feel guilty about." The ashtray rattles as I poke the cigarette to death. Roy Orbison thunders from the juke box and a bunch of students throw up a cheer from a nearby table—whether for Roy or not, I don't know.

Gavin says, "I'm going home." He's halfway to the door when he turns back. "Are you coming? I don't move. He walks back to the table. "You're not walking home on your own. Are you coming?"

I go to the bathroom. It all pours out. There's no way he can't hear me, but he doesn't come to see what's wrong. I pull out yards of orange toilet roll and I'm sobbing and sniffling, and by the time I look in the mirror my eyes and nostrils are red and raw and it feels like I've been pummelled in the stomach. I ache.

When I come back in, the TV is off and his clothes are folded on the armchair and he's in bed, naked, with his back to me. I undress and switch off the overhead light and get in, naked, ice cold.

It's impossible for me to sleep and neither can he. He isn't moving, but I can feel him, he's shifting around inside, unsettled and confused and raging but with nowhere to go. He's afraid even to move, that it'll betray something, or let something explode. I know how he feels. I kiss him on the chest, breathing out alcohol warmth onto his prickly hairs. I see a gulp go down his throat. He doesn't blink. I hear a couple of drunks outside singing the theme from *The Godfather*. The bedsprings twang as I move closer and wrap one arm and one leg over him.

He says firmly, "For Christ's sake, Stella . . . "

A stone ball forms in my throat. I peel myself away from his body and lie rigidly on my back. His breathing breaks in little fits and starts, but he's trying to hide it. He's like a board lying next to me.

After an hour, perhaps two, I'm still wide awake. My eyes have got accustomed to the dark. It's hard even to shut them now, they're so dry and swollen and fixed. The room is grey, just monotone, colourless shapes with no people, no humanity, no life, no sound. I start to think I am the only person in this drowned, undreaming world, when I hear his disembodied voice, his croak say, "Why the fuck did you tell me?" It sounds like a stranger. It sounds like someone who despises me. "I didn't have to know this," it says, angry and lost, with his back still to me. "I didn't have to know."

In memory of Melanie Hall

WITH ALL MY LOVE ALWAYS ALWAYS FOREVER XXX

FLEET SERVICES WAS PACKED. It always was, on the run up to the holidays. They'd learnt to be patient over the years. They knew they might not see the right candidate for a while. But there always was one.

Cars circled like vultures, looking for a parking space. The tension had already set in as people ventured out on their yearly obligatory trek to stay with relatives: a sure recipe for the onset of strife, stress, ulcers, and arguments.

Iestyn and Michaela had no family as such, no children, and they didn't envy the unhappy throng they observed with detachment from behind the windscreen of their Mini. They were happy—more than happy—with each other. They were soul mates.

Iestyn turned the dial to direct the heat to the windscreen, which had begun to fog up. He asked Michaela if her feet were all right. "Lovely. Toasty," she said, giving a little wriggle. Iestyn smiled.

An unconvincing Father Christmas stood outside the entrance, shaking a bucket aloft, collecting for charity, no doubt. As if people weren't cash-strapped enough. A lot out there having trouble making ends meet, and here, look at them, loaded with gifts that most of their friends and family don't need and don't want. Futile gestures that go straight in the attic or straight in the bin, some of them. The extravagance was disgusting.

To Iestyn and Michaela it was. It was a world of Haves and Have-Nots. And they were not prepared to bow down to the dominance of Capitalism. That's what Iestyn said, years ago—and Michaela agreed with him. They simply refused to give in to this orgy of spending. The mass-marketisation of a Christian festival that was supposed to be about love, and giving.

But giving wasn't everything. Sometimes, to make a point, you had to take.

"Here we go."

They got out of the car. Iestyn blew into his gloves, cocked his head.

Following his gaze she spotted it. A blue Audi packed to the gunnels with presents. Boxes of all shape sand sizes decorated in their bright festive wrapping paper—holly, robin redbreasts, reindeer, Santa on his sleigh. Tied up with big red bows, carefully labelled to Mum, Dad, Sis, Granny, Grandpa.

Irresistible.

They'd seen the family scamper off to get a meal, children in spotted wellies and earmuffs, baby in a polar beat hat with ears. Michaela kept an eye on the services while Iestyn disabled the alarm and jacked the boot.

Two minutes and forty seconds later everything was in the back of the Mini covered in a blanket and Iestyn was putting the car in reverse. They'd got it down to a fine art.

They didn't believe in Christmas being ostentatious. They'd usually open their stockings in bed—invariably stockings from their latest plunder, if there were any. Otherwise, they gave it a miss.

Then it was time to open the presents, which had been carefully arranged all round the Christmas tree (the one they'd got from that Ford Mondeo five years ago).

They took it in turns, as usual. The first one ("To Nan, All Our Love") was a garlic crusher. Iestyn's ("To Eric XXX") was a diary with Rudyard Kipling on the cover. Michaela tore the paper off one to "The Best Mum In The World" and found a Nigella cookbook. Iestyn opened one to "Uncle Tim" and got a book of science fiction stories. "Great!" said Michaela, "You like those!" He also got a Nick Cave CD, a box set of Ealing classics, and the obligatory chocolate orange. She got a dressing gown, slippers, and a Marks & Spencer voucher worth £50.

"Well I don't know about you, but I'm happy with mine!" he said, as he said every year.

"I'm happy with mine too!" Michaela echoed, and they kissed.

"Wait a minute, we haven't finished yet. Look, there's one more under the tree." Iestyn retrieved a box about eight inches square but only about an inch deep. He read out what was on the label: "With All My Love Always Always Forever XXX."

Michaela giggled. "Open it."

He did.

Her jawed dropped. "I think I might swear in a minute. Iestyn, it's beautiful."

And it was.

A necklace with gold segments linked together like small vertebrae, but there was nothing sinister about it—it was gorgeous.

"Blimey," Iestyn said.

Grinning, Michaela turned her back to him and he put it round her neck, from which she lifted her hair.

In the mirror facing her she could see the gold and silver pendant the size of a watch face, intricately carved in microscopic detail. It now rested between her breasts and shone in winking of the Christmas lights. She groaned in orgasmic pleasure as he fastened the clasp at the back.

Which was when the mechanism started. So like a clock that Iestyn didn't realise at first the sound was coming from the necklace—and when he did, realised that it was *tightening*.

Perhaps five seconds of shock passed before he tried with fumbling fingers to undo the clasp and possibly another five seconds before Michaela asked him what was wrong and then almost immediately knew what was wrong, and her own fingers grasped at, then pulled at, the necklace. Five second later it was already hard to squeeze them between the metal and her flesh.

Iestyn knew there had to be a wire in the mechanism, somewhere inside those vertebrae, being coiled into the clockwork motor of the pendant—a pendant now rising and pushing in under Michaela's Adam's apple—but he could do nothing as the necklace cut like a razor into her skin, as the seconds and then minutes passed, nothing but scuttle away, stuffing his mouth with his fist to stop his own screaming, hers long throttled as her feet kicked at the discarded wrapping paper and toppling Christmas tree. All he could do was watch as it whirred and clicked and whirred and clicked without stopping until it reached bone.

MATILDA
OF THE NIGHT

ONLY A LITTLE dwt, *I was. Four or five, see. Remember it like it was yesterday. Anyway, this day I run into our front room—the posh room, playin' like—not allowed to but I did sort of thing, and these three people looked round, all in a row on the settee, they were. All looking identical. Like a family. Man, woman, child. Just looking at me. All dressed all in black. All tight and polite, like, with their knees together. Give me the creeps, they did. Duw, aye! I was out of there like a blummin' shot . . .*

The quarter-inch tape ran through the Revox. The machine sat so that its turning reels faced the rows of semi-lit young faces.

Well, I told my mam after, and she said, "Don't be daft. There's nobody like that been in here. Nobody's been in that room for a twelvemonth!" And I said, "Mam, I saw them!" But she wasn't 'aving it. Marched me in and showed me. Wasn't nobody there, course there wasn't. But, true as I'm sittin' here, this is it—a week later my father dropped dead of a heart attack. Bang! Out like a light. Down by the Co-op. Out like a light! . . .

Ivan Rees switched it off with a twist of his hand, killing the old man's rasping, heavily- accented voice.

"Phantom funeral guests." The illumination stuttered into being. The ranks of students blinked as if awakened from slumber, which possibly they had been. "I got that from a retired collier in Pontypridd. Variation of the typical 'spectral funeral', also known as *toili*, or *teulu* in north Cardigan, probably from the dialectical pronunciations of the word for 'family'; or *anghladd*, unburied; in Montgomeryshire, *Drychiolaeth*."

Rees jabbed a button on the keyboard of his MacBook Air linked up to the overhead projector. An old woodcut of a house with a bird sitting on the roof appeared on the screen behind him.

"Other Welsh omens of death include the Corpse Candle or *Canwyll Corph*—lights appearing over the house of the soon-to-be deceased, or predicting the route of the funeral procession—and the *Deryn Corph*, or 'Death Bird', as you see here flapping its wings against the window of a sick person, often in the form of a screech owl . . . "

He brought up an engraving of witches with those birds, in one of Goya's *Caprichos*.

"The word *strega* in Italy refers to both 'owl' and 'witch'—an association that goes back to the mythology surrounding Lilith, Adam's first wife, who became a creature of darkness and child-stealer in Hebrew folklore, basically for answering back her husband. Interestingly, in China they call the owl 'the bird who snatches the soul'. The cross-cultural connections are fascinating."

The Edvard Munch woodcut fell over him now—a vampiric owl-death-woman.

"Then there's the *Cyhyraeth* or 'death sound'. A dismal, mournful groaning said to be made by a crying spirit. Which is nothing in comparison to the dread prediction of the banshee in Ireland. Here in Wales we have effectively her sister, the *Gwrach-y-Rhibyn* . . . "

To the audience's surprise, Marilyn Monroe appeared on the screen in titillating close-up, from *Some Like It Hot*.

"No, she doesn't look like Marilyn Monroe." Chuckles. "In fact there's still a saying in parts of Wales if somebody's—aesthetically challenged: '*Y mae mor salw a Gwrach-y-Rhibyn*'—'She's as ugly as the *Gwrach-y-Rhibyn*'."

More chuckles. His PowerPoint threw up another Goya print—a ghastly crone with monstrous visage and bat-like appendages.

"For the record, she's a hideous hag with long, matted hair, long black teeth, one grey eye and one black eye, a nose so hooked it meets her chin, withered arms, a crooked back, and leathery wings. In other words, the sort of female that doesn't even get a shag after closing time on a Friday night in Newport city centre . . . Oh, I don't know."

Laughter, more full-bodied this time.

"Anyway you wouldn't want to see what she *really* looks like, since anyone who sees her face or hears her blood-curdling cry, dies. There's an etymological similarity here with a witch called *Yr Hen Wrach*, who lived on an island in a large bog inland from Borth, Cardigan, described as seven feet tall, thin, with yellow skin and a huge head covered in jet black hair. This fearsome harridan was said to creep into houses and blow sickness into people's faces, thus causing illness. So another portent of death, of sorts, in another guise . . . "

Hans Baldung Grien's *The Bewitched Groom* showed a witch leering through a window at a dead man.

"Literally, for the non-Welsh-speakers amongst you, *Gwrach-y-Rhibyn* means 'Hag of the Dribble' or 'Hag of the Mist'—connecting her to all sorts of stories of the lamia/swan maiden type we looked at on the Gower and Glamorgan coast. Sometimes she's called *Mallt-y-Nos* or 'Matilda of the Night', who rides the night sky alongside the Devil himself and his hell hounds . . . "

Bottom and Titania in a scene from *A Midsummer Night's Dream* superimposed themselves over Rees, rendering his plain denim jacket and jeans exotic, melodramatic. As he walked to and fro they decorated his skin like multi-coloured, shifting tattoos.

"Marie Trevellyan groups her in the category of the *Tylwyth Teg* or Fairy Folk also known as *Bendith y Mamau*, Mother's Blessing. In times past they've been spotted at local markets in Haverfordwest, Milford, Laugharne, and Fishguard. Some sources say that, come mid-Victorian times, they were driven out by Nonconformists and temperance, but the truth is belief in them persisted until only a generation or so ago. I clearly remember my own grandmother blaming them for things going missing round the house. Neither goblin nor ghost, they supposedly had human midwives and feared iron, hence the lucky horseshoe—which as we know is always the right way up because if you hang it upside down, all the good luck runs out. According to John Rhys in *Celtic Folklore*, the *Gwrach* may have been a goddess of the pagan Celts, like the quasi-divine hag of Ireland. Indeed, in *The Golden Bough*, Fraser says the *Gwrach-y-Rhibyn* is the name given to the last sheaf of corn cut at the culmination of the harvest ritual. Yes? At the back? Lad in the Cardiff City shirt?"

A hand was in the air.

"Isn't there a theory that what we call the Fairy Folk might have been real?" The speaker was undeterred by sniggers. "Several writers suggest there was once a pygmy race on these islands, called the Cor—as in Korrigan, 'she-dwarf'—driven underground by invaders. What I mean is, bones have been found in caves, haven't they? Of short people. Ugly compared to human beings. With magical beliefs. Certain evidence they buried their dead, worshipped the moon, had rituals and some kind of social life . . . "

"Unlike most people in this room," said Rees.

Groans.

"No, yeah. I mean, seriously," said the boy. "We just call them Neanderthals."

"Oh, I know what you *mean*. I *do* know what you mean. Stan Gooch, eat your heart out. And the ginger-haired amongst you, beware of your large big toe. They walk amongst us!"

More laughter. The boy blushed slightly and shuffled in his seat.

"Yes, there's the theory that these imaginary creatures might be the faint memories of another, long-lost indigenous species—the Bronze Age replaced by iron," said Rees. "But as I've said before, it's not the folklorist's job to explain the inexplicable. That's not our business—our job is to record, analyse, and classify. The reality or not of what we examine is irrelevant." He took the spool from the Revox and held it up. "Our work—your mission, if you choose to accept it—is ecology. It's incumbent on us to save this rich resource from being lost. Our stories are ourselves. We mustn't let them die."

He hoped what he said was going in. He tried to discern a glimmer of interest in their dull, placid faces, in their *incuriosity*, but was sure all they cared about was passing the module. Level one (CQFW level four): ten credits.

He killed the PowerPoint, closed the laptop. "OK, go home. Start thinking about your essays. Next week we'll be talking about the Devil's hoofprints and changelings."

He saw Glyn at the foot of the steps, leaning back against a stone plinth outside the university building, flicking through a copy of *GQ*. Rees could not see for the life of him, and never could, why a perfectly intelligent man would buy such superficial drivel, but he knew better than to let it turn into an argument. Glyn had his childish, boorish side, which for some inexplicable reason he liked to cultivate. Rees supposed it was that macho aspect of gayness that had become all too blatant since he himself was growing up. Men beefing themselves up in the gym in an attempt to contradict the cliché of mincing effeminacy. Glyn certainly fitted into that category, biceps and pecs bulging ridiculously in a T-shirt several sizes too tight—but had just become another cliché altogether. He'd been immensely more attractive twelve years ago when they'd met, before all this nonsense, before the steroids, but Rees had given up on telling him that. How could he tell his partner that looking like a He-Man doll bordered on the disgusting? Once, Glyn had said he wanted that: wanted to look disgusting, wanted people to stop in the street and point at him and say he looked monstrous, grotesque. Rees found he couldn't battle such absence of logic, so had long since given up trying.

"Doctor Rees? Doctor Rees?"

The voice came from behind him. Young. Breathless. Female.

Glyn stood up straight and put the *GQ* under one arm.

"You've got a groupie."

Rees turned.

"Can I have a quick word, please?" The girl facing him was about nineteen. He knew exactly what Glyn was thinking. *Scarf. Anorak. Bless. Mouse woman. And that hair. Poor thing. Why doesn't she do something about herself?* "My name's Katrina." *Scottish accent. Sexy. But would a little makeup kill you, love?* "I'm doing your class as part of my M.A. in Welsh and Celtic Studies. I'm hoping to go into teaching."

"I'm, er . . . running rather late, as a matter of fact."

"It's—It's about the *Gwrach-y-Rhibyn*."

"Oh. As I say, if you want to discuss it in more detail we can do that in the next session . . ."

"No, no. You don't understand. You see, it's quite a, well, coincidence. Do you believe in coincidences? I'd heard the name before. I thought 'God'. I didn't think it was real. I thought it was a made-up word."

"It's not. It's really quite well documented." Rees looked at his watch.

"No, this isn't documented. This is from an old lady. An old lady who's dying."

Dying.

Rees's turned to face her.

Dying?

"You can talk about it next week, love," said Glyn. "I'm sure he'll be all ears." He tugged Rees's arm but Rees wasn't budging.

"Hold on, hold on. What old woman? Where?"

"In the nursing home where I work. Shifts. Bit of extra income to support me through college, while I'm doing my—"

"Yes, yes. I get that. What did she say, exactly?"

"She kept talking about her, this *Gwrach-y-Rhibyn* thing. Well, I didn't know what it was. I just thought it was gibberish. A lot of them are in a world of their own. They just ramble and the best thing is to let them get on with it, sort of thing. But she kept saying it. 'She's coming, she's coming!' and getting really, really upset about it. Inconsolable, at times. And one night I heard her crying, and I went upstairs to her bedroom, and she said to me, 'She's been. She's *been!*' All mad-looking. And that night an old man had died—Captain Birdseye we used to call him, lovely old bloke. And the thing is, there's *no way* she could have known. She couldn't have heard. She lives in a completely different part of the building. And nobody else knew until they found him the next morning. But *she* knew. She knew that this *Gwrach-y-Rhibyn* thing had come to get him. And she was right."

It was called *Morfa*, which even his rudimentary knowledge of his native tongue told him meant "marsh" or "fen". The building was one of those vast Victorian piles on the way out of Porthcawl, formerly a grand hotel, now, with sad inevitability, a residential home for the elderly, overlooking the sweep of the appropriately named Rest Bay. Rees had been on several holidays to the resort as a child, and remembered being confused between the local funfair, Coney Beach, and the Coney Island mentioned in American movies, in the same way he thought Dirk Bogarde and Humphrey Bogart were the same person. Strange how the embarrassment of those things came back to him now, along with memories of freezing sea and damp sand.

As he got out of his Citroën and hoisted the Nagra out of the back, he could hear the dim strains of a karaoke version of "I Could

Be So Lucky" increasing in volume as he stepped into the reception area. In the Day Room he could glimpse a middle-aged woman in a sequinned dress singing into a hefty microphone with the verve of a cruise ship entertainer. A podgy, greasy-haired boy sat manning the playback machine with his back to her while she belted it out. Geriatrics in armchairs watched with loose jaws and gummy, bewildered mouths. One old dear was doing the twist in decrepit slow motion.

"Hello. My name is Doctor Ivan Rees," he said to the pretty if overweight girl behind the desk. "I'm from Cardiff University." He didn't usually have recourse to the title doctor, but in this instance he thought it might be helpful to oil the wheels of accessibility. Luckily, he didn't need to explain in laborious detail that he was Associate Lecturer in the School of Celtic Studies, M. Litt (Oxford), Ph.D. (Columbia University, Bethesda, Maryland), M.A. University of Wales (Aberystwyth), or why he was there, because she was already saying she'd had a conversation with the Staff Nurse, who'd told Rees on the phone she had no objection to his visit as long as the resident in question didn't. Which was a hurdle far simpler to cross than Rees had imagined.

The pretty if overweight girl, whose name was Tina Griffiths, led him straight upstairs. "Katrina told me about you."

"Did she? Good. I hope."

"I don't know that you'll get what you want, though. They get very confused. They can't remember the word for 'telephone' or what they said five minutes ago, but they can remember years ago like it was yesterday."

"That's what I'm interested in."

He had a sense of anticipation he hadn't felt in a long time, and it had been as if Glyn resented it. Rees hadn't been able to concentrate much on the French film about persecuted monks they went to see immediately after meeting Katrina, and when Glyn tried to discuss the movie afterwards, Rees could hardly focus on what he was saying. When they got home he hadn't thought he was doing anything wrong by going straight to his bookshelves and taking down Giraldus Cambrensis' *Itinerary Through Wales*,

Nennius's *History of the Britons*, Walter Map's *De nugis curialium*, Rev. J. Ceredig Davies's *Folk-Lore of West and Mid-Wales* and T. Gwynn Jones's *Welsh Folklore and Folk-Custom* of 1930. Glyn hadn't seemed in the least bit interested that in the next half hour he'd had it confirmed that there was no record of the *Gwrach-y-Rhibyn* that wasn't at least a hundred years old, and even then quoted from the usual suspects. No doubt about it. This was the first genuine first-hand experience of a death portent in over a century. This was gold dust.

At 2:00 a.m., after tossing and turning, Glyn had stood naked at the bedroom door and asked him to come to bed. By the time Rees had registered what he had said, and turned from his computer screen, there was nobody there.

"She'll tire very easily."

"Of course."

"Mrs Llewellyn gives the illusion she's strong as an ox. She isn't." Tina escorted Rees along a corridor and through a fire door. "She has so much cancer in her, you could virtually scratch her skin and see it. Like one of those lottery cards." The girl rapped the door they came to, and Rees asked if she'd heard the woman talk about the *Gwrach-y-Rhibyn* as Katrina had. "All that morphine, if you ask me. Or whatever it is in the pills they're giving her to stop the pain." She raised her voice. "Bronwen? It's only me, love. Tina. Orright if we come in? Are you decent?" She turned to Rees with a wink and a whisper. "Scares easily, see. Lot of them do. Got to be careful."

Entering the room, Rees's first impression was the heat belting out of the four-bar electric fire. It hit him like a wave, then he remembered how old people felt the cold. The second thing was the smell, a sickly perfume odour used to cover something worse. Third was the sight of Bronwen Llewellyn lifting her body from the armchair facing the window. A small woman with thinning ginger hair, extraordinarily piercing blue eyes—had she had her cataracts done or did she need to?—and rounded nostrils that put Rees in mind of a bullock. A frail bullock.

He extended his hand. She walked straight between them and shut the door, evidently to keep the heat in. She pressed it. Opened it. Shut it again. Opened. Shut. Walked back between them to the sash window overlooking the grounds. Checked the catch. Locked. Unlocked. Locked. Unlocked. Rees could tell that Tina knew unless they broke the cycle this could go on all day.

"Bronwen, sweetheart. This is Doctor Rees from the university. D'you remember? The one who wrote you that nice letter?"

"I'm not dull."

"Bronwen likes to make sure the doors and windows are shut tight, don't you, Bronwen, love?"

"Because that's how she gets in. Through *cracks*."

Tina looked at Rees. The music downstairs had changed to a spirited rendition of "Stand By Your Man."

"OK. I'll leave you to it, then."

The girl was barely gone before Bronwen picked up a quilted draught-excluder in the form of a snake and rammed it against the bottom of the door with the toe of her slippers.

"And mirrors. She looks at you from *mirrors*."

Rees looked around and saw that the mirrors in the room were hooded by supermarket carrier bags or tea cloths held in place with drawing pins. He forced a friendly smile.

"Your room looks nice."

"This isn't my room. The things are mine, but it's not my room." Bronwen Llewellyn had an unmistakable Valleys lilt, sing-songy but not unintelligible. She'd record well. That was important, and a relief.

"Well, the things are nice. What are the labels for?" He'd noticed there were coloured Post-It notes on most of the objects. Royal Doulton figurines, a glass swan, an oval frame with a Pre-Raphaelite print in it—*The Lady of Shalott*. Even the bedside lamp and chest of drawers.

"That's who they go to when I pop off. No arguments. Organized, I am, see. Red is Jean. Green is Dilys. Blue is Mavis. Yellow is Oxfam."

She lifted her swollen ankles onto the footstool as Rees sat on the bed, the Nagra beside him, setting up the microphone on the small table at her elbow. He could have used his iPhone to record her, as his students now did, but he'd become accustomed to recording on quarter-inch. Not so much that he resisted new technology, but this was the technology he'd known and relied upon for over twenty years. Perhaps he himself was superstitious in that regard. Old habits being only one step removed, perhaps, from magical thinking. Soon this tape would join the others, hundreds, meticulously labelled by subject and location on his study shelves, dated, indexed and cross-referenced—the sound files themselves copied and saved as MP3 files in that ether tantamount to a supernatural realm called Dropbox. He'd considered her use of the Post-It notes absurd and morbid, but it occurred to him now that he himself was guilty of labelling objects for people who might look at the artefacts long after his demise, just as much as she was.

"Here, am I going to sound Welshy? Last time I heard myself on one of them things, Crikey Moses! Welsh, be damned? I used to think I sounded like Princess Margaret!"

"It's painless, I promise." He blew into the mic. "One, two, one, two." The red needle wagged like a warning finger.

"Rees? That's a Welsh name, that is. You don't sound Welsh. English, you sound."

"Lost a bit of it going to uni, I expect."

"Glad to get rid of it, I expect," she said, with no apparent disdain.

He laughed. Truth is, she was right. He couldn't wait to get away and talk like normal people. To lose his past in RP and anonymity. To reinvent himself.

"You want to read this first." She produced something hidden down the side of the chair. An exercise book, pink for a little girl, with cartoon horses and fairies and bunnies on the cover. She thrust it at him forcefully. He felt obliged to take it, opening it to find the first page full of a list of names and dates written in a terribly shaky copperplate hand. Old-school education never goes away, he thought. Even if the faculty to hold a pen does.

"You know what that is?" Bronwen was confident he could not answer. "That's the name of everybody who's died. Here, I mean. In this place." She pointed to the floor with a finger bulging at the joints with arthritis. "Since I come here, anyway. Everybody who's heard her and seen her."

"You mean—I'm sorry. They *told* you they'd seen her? The Gwrach-y-Rhibyn?"

"Don't be *soft!* How can they tell me when they're dead? Nobody can *tell* you. Not once they've seen her."

"No, of course not."

"Once they *see* her, that's it. You can't get away from it. You can't get out of it. That's that. And I'll be *oocht* when she comes for me, too. And that'll be soon. Don't you worry."

He saw a cloudiness come over her eyes and thought it a kind of bewilderment. He thought of her cataracts again. Then saw the shudder of her lower lip with its aura of downy hairs, and a tremor in the hand that gripped the rim of the arm of the chair, and realised that it was fear.

"Can you—Can you say that again, please? For the tape?"

He switched it on, and before he could ident the recording with his own voice, stating the day, time, and full name of the subject, she spoke again, staring at a space above the fireplace as if she was alone in the room.

"They're dead. Just like I'll be dead, once I've seen the Gwrach-y-Rhibyn. Once she comes calling for me." She blinked and with an unstable, jerky movement turned to look at him, almost as if seeing him for the first time. Then he saw a little girl eager to please. "Was that all right?"

He nodded. It was. It was perfect.

The spool turned, a stray thread curling a corkscrew admonition in the air.

The cold of the wind from the sea did not infiltrate the room but he could hear the slow fingertips of rain tapping the windowpanes.

"Fifteen kids, my mam had. Can't remember them all. Names. Some of them didn't live, see. They didn't in them days."

"Where was this?"

"Troedyrhiw. She always believed in them. Put a saucer of milk out for them every Sunday, the *Tylwyth Teg*. 'Don't you aggravate them,' she'd say, 'or they'll have your guts for garters.'"

"Which one is Mary?"

Rees had the old photograph album on his lap. It felt like an alien artefact. Nobody had photograph albums these days. They just uploaded their jpegs and selfies onto Instagram, Facebook or Twitter.

"This one, bless her. Like a little doll, she was. Bronwen and May, it was. May and Bronwen . . . " The old woman began fiddling with the locket on a chain round her neck. "I used to torment her terrible. S'pose I was jealous, her being younger and getting all the fuss, like. We used to share a bed, and I used to tickle her till she wet herself. Wicked, I was." She opened it and showed it to Rees, but in her trembling hands the face he could make out was blurred and indistinct. "I used to tell her I could make her hair fall out by just staring at her, and she'd scream blue murder. Then one night I started telling her about the *Gwrach-y-Rhibyn*." She snapped the locket shut and let it drop onto her wrinkled, puckered chest. "I told her there was this witch outside the window who was so ugly that if anyone set eyes on her they'd die of fright, just like that."

Rees eased forward, elbows on knees, knitting his fingers together, but said nothing. He wanted this pure. Unspoiled.

"And she said, 'No there isn't, Bron. Don't be 'orrible. It's just the branches in the wind. I know it is!' And I said, 'Are you *sure*? Are you *sure* that's all it is?' And she said, 'Yes!' And I said, 'What if it's *not* branches, though? What if it's her long, long *fingernails* tapping the window—tap, tap, tap . . . "

The old woman gulped and sniffed.

"Well. She screamed the house down. I had to go and sleep in my mam's bed, and my dad slept with May. I was awful. Even before that night I was a handful. And after that, well . . . "

"What do you mean?"

Her face seemed to sag. Her hands made little folds in the knees of her dress and a frown of resistance, of conflict, of hurt, cut into her face.

"If you . . . "

"No, I'll tell you. You came here to ask and I'll tell you. The next morning, I rushed in to wake her, see. I jumped in bed and cuddled up to her and tickled her like I always did, havin' a bit of fun. But she didn't move. She was cold and white like one of them enamel plates we had in the kitchen. I said, "Come on, May! Play! Play with me!' I tried to wake her but I couldn't. Nobody could." Her eyes fixed on the bars of the electric fire. They bulged and shone glassily, each reflecting a dot of light.

Rees found his throat dry as he listened.

"And I knew, sure as eggs, Matilda of the Night had got her. She came for my little sister all those years ago. And now she's coming for me . . . "

Rees felt a faint draught on his cheek and knew that the door had opened behind him. He hadn't heard it doing so but was now certain that somebody was occupying the space directly behind his left shoulder. He turned round.

He saw the tray with the microwave plate cover sheltering a meal, and holding it in both hands, the overweight but pretty Tina Griffiths.

"There you are. Meat and mash. It's time Doctor Rees was making tracks."

Rees looked at his watch and saw that it was 06:00 p.m.—he'd lost all track of time. As the girl placed down the tray he also saw a plastic container with around fifteen assorted pills inside it. Her daily dose. For what? Angina? Heart? Diabetes? Anxiety? Cholesterol? Or all of the above?

"Did I order meat and mash?"

"Yes you did, love."

"I don't like meat and mash. I like fish."

"No, you ordered meat and mash. It's beef. Beef and gravy."

"Oh, I like beef. I just don't like meat." Bronwen noticed Rees unplugging his recording equipment, coiling a cable round his hand. "He—He doesn't want to go. Does he?" Her lip shuddered with agitation. "Do you? Hmm?"

"I think I have to," said Rees. "She's in charge here, I'm afraid."

"But what—what if she *comes*? The *Gwrach-y-Rhibyn*? What if she comes *tonight*? And you're not here? What *then*?" She was becoming tearful, and this upset Rees but did not seem to bother Tina spectacularly. In fact she became clipped. Firm.

"Bronwen. Now. Doctor Rees can't stay, can he? He has to go home. He's just a visitor. You know the rules, my love."

"Why? You've broken the rules before. You know you have. When Cliff was bad, you let his wife stay. Well now *I'm* bad. What about me? I'm *dying!* And I want him to *stay!*" Her voice stuttered into sobs. "I want someone with me. I'm frightened, can't you see? None of you buggers care! Nobody does!" Tears glistened on her cheeks. "Only him! He's the only one who listens to me!"

"She's upset, look," said Rees, taking the strap from his shoulder. "I'll stay. It's no problem. I don't mind staying. Honestly."

He sat down and watched Tina sigh and mop the old woman's tears with a few sheets from the box of tissues on the coffee table. Then a few sheets more. And a few sheets after that, till the childlike sniffling had subsided.

Just after midnight a thin young man of African ethnicity popped his head round the door and asked Rees a second time if he wanted a filter coffee. This time he said yes, thank you. He was tired but he had no intention of sleeping. At 02:00 a.m., quiet settling on the house with an almost physical presence, he paced up and down for a few minutes to stretch his back, then sat on the stool next to Bronwen Llewellyn's flowery and be-cushioned armchair.

Tap. Tap. Tap.

All being recorded. Night. Branches on the far side of the curtains.

Tap. Tap. Tap.

He thought of Bronwen's sister, Mary. May.

Eyelids heavy, he thought of the May Bride and May tree cults mentioned in Graves's *The White Goddess* . . . the mythic significance of the horse and the hare . . .

May. Maybe. Might. Perhaps.

The old woman's lips were moving slightly and he could see her eyeballs revolving under her lids. She'd been like that for five hours but he hadn't switched off the tape except for putting on a new one. She was dreaming and he wondered what she dreamed. She was almost forming words, and he stood for almost an hour with the microphone an inch from her mouth in case she did.

Arriving home in Penarth, he found he was famished. He put on a slice of toast, booting up his computer as the toaster chirruped, and ate it standing up as he typed the details into his archive list, not sure if it was excitement, caffeine, or tiredness that made his hands visibly shake. Too exhausted to edit, he calculated he could get six or seven hours' sleep before heading back to the nursing home. As it turned out, it was five o'clock in the afternoon when he woke inexplicably anxious about where he was for several seconds, and was helping himself to some brie and slices of apple with his leather jacket already on when Glyn arrived home from the Wetherspoon's in Cardiff Bay where he worked, the old Harry Ramsden's.

Glyn saw that Rees was dressed to leave and his face dropped. "Jesus Christ, you could've waited. I've got pasta. I was going to make meatballs." He dumped his carrier bag of shopping on the kitchen surface. "I don't know why I bother."

"The ingredients will keep till tomorrow."

"Oh, you'll be around tomorrow?"

"I don't know."

"Well, thanks."

"Look, I had no idea you were cooking. I'm going out. I have to go out. How could I know?"

"You'd know if you picked up the phone. You'd know if you spoke to me."

Rees looked at the ceiling and rolled his eyes. Glyn hated when he made him feel like a child. Rees was a year older than his father, but he didn't want him to *be* his father—far fucking from it, thank you very much.

"You still don't get it, do you?" Glyn threw a bag of tomatoes into the chiller compartment of the refrigerator. "Where were you last night—*all* night? Did it cross your mind I might like to know? No. Did it even cross your mind I might be worried? No. Your mobile was switched off . . ."

"Yes. I was working."

"Why?"

"I had to be."

"Why?"

"Because I have to get this story. The whole story."

"Why?"

"For God's sake, because time is running out, if you must know. Because if I don't get it now, I'll never get it." Rees didn't want the food anymore and left the chunk of cheese and apple core on the plate. He zipped up the case of the Nagra as Glyn made great theatrics of stocking the kitchen cabinets, banging doors ludicrously. "Look, I apologise if I didn't explain, but this is ridiculous, it really is. Why are you so angry?" Rees walked to the door, picking up his headphones en route.

"I'm angry," said Glyn, "because it never entered your head, did it? Well, did it?"

The overcooked lamb chops defeated her. She sawed at them with a knife then gave up, exhausted, chest heaving. He made weak tea from the jug kettle. As she sipped it he thought of those thin, sipping sounds appearing on his tape.

"Bronwen, when did you first hear about Matilda of the Night?"

"When did you first hear about Father Christmas?"

"I mean, was it from a relative? Do you have relations I could go and talk to?"

"All gone," she said. "You get old. Nobody left, see. Not much of you left either, in the brain box. You don't want to get old, I'm telling you."

Rees sniffed a laugh. "I am old."

"How old are you then?"

"Fifty-three."

"That's no age."

"Say that to my twenty-year-old students." He remembered Glyn was that age at the start of it. Teacher and pupil. The old, old story.

"Then they need their bloody heads examined. Parents still alive?"

"My dad died when I was seven."

"What about your mother?"

Rees shook his head. "Ten years ago. I was in America."

"You weren't there."

"Working. Studying. Same thing. Conference. Talking to complete strangers." He felt the warmth of the bars of the electric fire. He blinked his eyes. They were unaccountably dry. "I got a phone call in this dreadful hotel room. This Holiday Inn—you know, where all the rooms across the world are identical? There was no time to do anything. It had already happened. She was gone. The worst thing was hearing all that emotion in my sister's voice and being so far away." He realised he was playing with one of the DayGlo Post-It notes and stuck it back where it was meant to be. "Do you want me to close the curtains?" Bronwen said nothing. He walked over and tugged them shut, then sat back down.

"Sometimes it's easier to be on your own," she said. "Then the people you love can't be taken away. And sometimes you keep yourself in a box, try to pretend it'll never hurt you again. But it does."

Rees told himself he didn't understand what she meant. But even as he tried to dismiss it, it made him feel raw, exposed, uncomfortable. He needed to get out for a minute.

"I'm just—just going to get some water. Is that all right? Do you—do you want some?"

Bronwen didn't nod. She stared glassy-eyed. Her hands supported her cup and saucer and thoughts and words seemed to have deserted her, or she had absconded to memory. He left the room with the tape spools turning and gently closed the door after him.

He walked to the water cooler at the end of the landing. The floorboards did not creak under his footsteps. He yanked a paper cup from the dispenser, half-filled it and took a gulp. He poured the residue into his cupped left hand and rubbed it over his face and the back of his neck, then rubbed his eyes too.

In a nearby room he could hear an elderly person moaning in their sleep. It almost sounded like weeping. He hoped they were dreaming and this wasn't the sound of their waking despair. When he was a child he had wondered long and hard why old people did not rage screaming and gnashing at the prospect of death, and he still could not completely understand why they didn't. The fact they might settle into a kind of numb acceptance only struck him as even more horrifying.

A large window overlooked the garden. The wind from the bay was considerable and in the semi-dark he could make out hydrangea bushes undulating and the branches of trees gesticulating mutely in pools of artificial light. He untied the ornate tassels of the curtains and dragged them tightly across to overlap each other.

"Is that the one with George Clooney?"

The nurses down in the reception area were talking about what movie they fancied seeing. He walked back, leaned over the banister, and saw them eating jaffa cakes below.

"Oh, is that with that comic off the telly? I can't stand him. He really does my head in, that bloke. I'm not kidding."

Rees opened the door to see her on her feet, swaying unsteadily, shoulders heaving.

"No, you can't! I'm not ready! Skin off! *Skin off, you bloody*—" She was facing the window with an outstretched hand. Saw him now. "She's there! She's *out* there! I can *hear* her! I can hear her bloody *whassnames* flapping!"

"Sit down. Please sit down, Mrs Llewellyn. Just sit down and I'll take a look for you." He managed to settle her into her armchair, then opened the drapes to see what she had seen—except he didn't. "It's just the canvas come loose from one of those parasol-type things in the garden . . . "

"No! It's her *wharracalls*—wings! It's Matilda! Matilda of the Night! She's out there with her long hair and, and long fingers and she's after me. She was perched on the windowsill. I *know* she was!"

"Shshsh. Honestly now. It's nothing." Rees bent down to pick up the cup and saucer, fallen from the arm of her chair but miraculously unbroken. As he stood up he felt Bronwen clinging to his sleeve, sobbing.

"You'll be there, won't you? When she comes back?"

"I don't know if I . . . "

"When she does come for the last time, please! I promise I'll tell you everything. You'll have everything on your tape like you want it. I'll tell you everything I hear and everything I see, I promise. Just say you'll be with me." Fear shone in the old woman's eyes and Rees didn't feel able to look at it.

As gently as possible he peeled her fingers off him. He sat her down and knelt and placed his hands over hers, which were ice cold. He looked at her and could feel the warmth emanating from his skin but he couldn't feel hers getting any warmer, at all. This is the way it will go, he thought. The cold. The cold that cannot be warmed. Is this the way we all go? Grey and cold and separated and lost?

"I will. I promise," he said.

"She *wants* me to do it."

"But *you* want to do it, that's the point. You want her to die, don't you? You can't bloody wait."

"Rubbish."

"How is it rubbish? When she dies you'll have exactly what you want. You said so yourself. A recording of someone experiencing this—this 'death visitation', whatever the fuck that is."

"She's going to die, Glyn. Whether I'm there sat beside her or not. I can't stop it happening."

"No, but you can use it. For yourself. For your precious collection."

Rees sighed in exasperation. "This isn't for my *collection*. Christ. It's more than that. How do I get through to you? Nobody has catalogued something like this—ever. This isn't some piddling article in *Folklore*. This could be my—my *Man Who Mistook His Wife for a Hat*. Something that gets me noticed, finally."

"Me. Exactly. You're a bloody vulture, Ivan. Haven't you got any feelings of—"

"Why should I not have feelings? Of course I have feelings. It doesn't mean I shouldn't do my job."

"And what's your job? To prey off this demented old biddy who—"

"So what do you want me to do? Abandon her? She's all I've got." Rees corrected himself. "*I'm* all *she's* got."

"Freudian slip."

"That's not true."

"It is true. It's more important than I am."

"Don't be preposterous."

"Preposterous, am I? If I'm preposterous, why are you with me? I'm serious, Ivan? Why? Because you don't seem to want to be with me or listen to me half the time. Do you actually *want* to be loved?"

That made Rees laugh out loud, and it shouldn't have, because it chilled him to the bone. "What's that supposed to mean?"

Glyn stared at him across the dining table. "What *do* you want, Ivan, eh? Because I'll be honest, I don't have a bloody clue."

Rees stood and scraped the residue of his tuna salad into the waste disposal. He could feel Glyn smouldering but didn't turn to face him and waited for him to leave the table. The chair rasped.

"Go. Go and watch her die, Ivan. Be there, if that's what matters to you so much. But if I matter to you, stay with me tonight instead of her."

She opened her eyes blearily, tortoise head sunk deep in the propped-up pillows.

"Thank you."

"For what?"

Still half in sleep, the truth comes easier than in wakefulness or daylight. But hesitant. "I'm not scared when you're here."

He pulled up the fold of the blanket under her mottled, stringy chin. "Go to sleep."

She already was.

A shadow hand crept across the wall and rested on his shoulder.

Rees shook awake with a gasp, the dream already doused. The Holiday Inn banished. The hare run to ground. Was it time to get up? Was he late for school? Mum?

"The Manager wants a word with you," said Katrina close to his ear.

"Now?"

"Now."

What time was it? How long had he slept? He remembered looking at his watch when it was 05:00 a.m. What time was it now? Five past seven.

Nack-nack-nack-nack

The tape spool was spinning, its tail flapping with a metronomic tic. He switched the machine off and lifted his coat from the back of a chair.

Blinking, he felt like a little boy summoned to the headmaster's study as he descended the stairs past a wizened monkey of an old gent hung on the elbow of an obese carer as if to cruelly emphasise the difference. But Penny Greatorex, revealed after a knock on the office door, did not look like a headmaster. She wore the hard superiority of an MBA, contrasting noxiously with a chunky cardigan depicting a timber wolf. The pleasantries were minimal. Katrina left them alone and soon he realised why.

"Dr Rees, I'm sure you're a very bright man but do you seriously think that talking about 'omens of death' is really appropriate to this kind of establishment?"

Instantly on the back foot, Rees told her how he'd explained fully to the Staff Nurse and she'd given permission for him to visit.

"She had no business to. Sara is only an RSN."

"Well, I'm sorry, but Mrs Llewellyn seems more than happy to . . ."

"That's as may be, but we are the ones legally responsible for her care. And I'm afraid the feedback from some of my staff is that her mental wellbeing has deteriorated since you began coming."

Rees stiffened. "It might seem like that, but truly, I'm not the cause of her increased anxiety at all. I'm merely listening to her."

"Well, perhaps indulging her in her dementia and paranoia isn't doing her a great deal of good, let me put it like that. I'm sure you'd put it differently, but that really isn't my concern. Our resident's welfare is. And in her current state she's a very emotionally vulnerable lady who doesn't require any additional stress in her life. So I'd appreciate if you would leave the premises, please."

"What?"

"Oh, come on. Apart from health and safety concerns and insurance concerns, can you imagine what her relatives—or her relatives' *lawyers*—would say about a complete stranger staying in her room overnight? Can you *imagine* how embarrassing that would be if some accident happened?"

"She *has* no relatives." He laughed. "If you knew anything about her, you'd know that." He tried to stop his anger from rising.

"I'm not prepared to debate this, Dr Rees. I think you can see that."

"Yes, I can." Afraid of adding something he might regret, he turned on his heel.

"Where are you going?"

He thought that was obvious. "Upstairs, to say goodbye to her."

"I'm sorry. I don't think that's a good idea in the slightest."

"For God's sake. She'll be upset if she sees I'm gone without saying something." He looked at her in her timber wolf cardigan. "But you really don't give a shit, do you?"

"Yes," Penny Greatorex said, her face showing a glimmer of hurt. "As a matter of fact I do. Very much so." But this was her domain—alpha of the pack—and she wanted him out of it. "Jérôme will bring down your equipment to your car. There's no point in waking her, is there? God knows, the day is long enough when you're their age." She didn't look up from the year planner, which was now getting her undivided attention.

Having loaded the Nagra, his shoulder bag and laptop into the back seat, Rees sat with his hands gripping the steering wheel for several minutes before finally turning the ignition key. The engine gave its tinny French snarl. He looked up at the landing window and half-saw a face with a crayon-squiggle of hair.

He turned the Citroën in a tight three-point turn and crawled to the automatic gates, which opened as if hauled by ghostly hands. Pausing where the driveway met the road which would take him home through Nottage, via the A48 and Culverhouse Cross, a route he infinitely preferred to the motorway, he adjusted the rear-view mirror and saw his own eyes, sandpaper-dry from the kind of conflict he loathed and usually avoided, then sharply turned from their accusations.

He realised he didn't want to arrive back at the house while Glyn was there, and Glyn didn't normally leave for work till about eleven. Instead he drove to the Museum of Welsh Life at Saint Fagan's, his old stomping ground once upon a time, but he wasn't thinking. He should have known they weren't open until ten. He turned around in the car park and drove to the coast. He didn't really care where he was driving. He found himself at Llantwit Major, walking along the rocky beach where he and his father had caught crabs in a plastic bucket, the smell of bladderwrack and crushed limpets in his nostrils. Distant figures crouched and splashed. The cries of children easily entertained. Wind nice as a razor. Familiar wind, mind. He thought of rolled up sleeves and varicose veins.

His cheeks burned.

Glyn's Doc Martens were not by the front door. Rees slid off his trainers. The smell of burnt filter coffee stung his nostrils. He dropped the paper cone and its contents in the waste bin under the sink, swilling the black residue in the glass jug under the tap, and poured it away, something he always did because his boyfriend didn't. It wasn't even an annoyance to Rees anymore. He accepted it, in the way he hoped Glyn accepted the million and one ways his own habits were no doubt irritating. Tolerance. Habit. Acceptance. Wasn't that what having a relationship was about?

Openness?

He almost heard Glyn's voice saying it, and tightened. What if he didn't want to be open? What then? Why was he being forced into being something he wasn't? Why couldn't he just be who he was?

For the next few hours he sat immobile at the kitchen table and listened to the erratic rhythms of her breathing.

He listened to her lips smacking, her occasional snort and snore and deep, long silences. His pen hovered over paper as she turned over in her slumber. As she wheezed and fretted and stretched under the starched nursing home sheets. (How many had died in those sheets?) His eyes closed as she coughed and mumbled and grunted. He was the sole and private audience to a symphony of moans. The aural hieroglyphics of her inner life.

Tap tap tap . . .

Branches. Trees.

He frowned, leaned forward. A thin, plaintive sobbing. Hardly audible. Reaching out to him, for comfort. Last night, yesterday, the past caught on tape.

Memory. Fear.

Rees paused it and sipped his glass of water. Glyn was normally home at five in the evening if he wasn't working evenings. Now it was six. Rees rang The Fig Tree to book a table for dinner. Their favourite place in Cardiff, and walking distance. *How many people, sir?*

"Two," he said.

Staring him in the face from the notice board was the old snapshot of Glyn and himself in Rhodes, uncannily tanned and exceptionally happy. There he was, in that rough old taverna, making a fool of himself. Deludedly happy for a passing, photographic instant. Drunk. Silly. Wasting his time. He never even liked the sun. What was he doing there? What was he pretending?

He suddenly felt completely exhausted, and remembered he'd only slept for an hour or two at the most. He went into the bedroom.

Fully dressed, he unbuttoned his collar and lay on one side of the double bed and curled up, wrapping one arm under his knees. His eyes remained open because he was so overtired his stupid body was fighting it, churning up too many random and unwelcome thoughts. Like Bronwen in her room, crying, not knowing why that nice young man (young?) didn't come back when he said he would. *When he promised!* He imagined her ball-jointed paws feeling the empty place on the corner of her bed where the Nagra had sat, her devastated expression—lost, lonely, discarded—as below at the desk two overweight nurses ate biscuits from a tin and discussed the latest Peter Andre programme. His throat felt blocked. He thought he was going to choke.

He sat up and took off his clothes. The heat was making him restless and adding to his woes. He dropped his socks and underpants on the carpet, picked up a wire coat hanger for his shirt and trousers, and opened the cupboard door.

They were all gone. Glyn's jeans. Glyn's workman's jacket he got in Amsterdam. The linen shirt, the one Rees always told him to wear to dinner parties. The harem pants that had seen better days. *Only good enough for the bin.*

Rees stood back three faltering steps and could see that the suitcase on top of the wardrobe was gone too, and his stomach lurched.

The drawers with the folded T-shirts and sweaters he knew without looking would be empty. He wondered about the toothbrush. The shampoo that gave that orange and lemon scent to

Glyn's hair he'd get a whiff of when he kissed his neck. The odour vividly came back to him. Smell. Sound. Touch.

He'd checked the landline for calls when he'd come in, always, but checked again. *You have no messages.* (That voice. Whose voice? Who was she? Was she alive? How did we know for sure?) Back in the bedroom he snatched up his iPhone from the bedside table where it was plugged in to recharge, tapped in his four-digit password, but could see instantly that the speech-bubble logo showed nothing. He scrolled sideways with his finger, pressed *Contacts*, then *All Contacts*. Thumbed down to "G". Tapped the name. Glyn's mobile number flashed up.

Rees stared at it. He could ring it. He knew he could. So what was stopping him? His innards felt like lead. An ache incapacitated him, physical and real. It was in control of him and he was at its mercy. He didn't know why.

He pressed the exit button, letting it die and placing it back down where his wristwatch lay.

The wall was bereft of wallpaper, plain concrete, with thin lines of water running down it. He was puzzled why nobody was panicking and thought he should tell them there was a leak somewhere above them before a disaster happened. He might get into serious trouble if he didn't mention it, and it worried him. Tina wore makeup. Her mascara was running, her head tilted slightly down. She was sobbing pitifully and he wanted to put his arms around her but before he could reach her she drew back the starched white sheet from the body on the slab. He was wondering why somebody didn't answer that bloody telephone as he saw it was Bronwen Llewellyn, mouth caved in without the benefit of teeth, eyes sky blue and dead as buttons, redness pooling and sticky at the back of her skull.

He woke, stabbed by reality. Not a gasp in him. The dark still had work to do. The sheet twined round one naked leg, he was alone, still.

"Hello." The throbbing iPhone now illuminating his cheek. "Yes?"

We leave the lights on. I don't know what she was doing up and about, but a lot of them go wandering, it's not that unusual. You can't lock them in like prisoners, can you? She must've had a hell of a bump. Tina said she was just lying there at the bottom of the stairs, groaning. Couple of minutes she had this massive bruise all up her thigh, turning purple, you could see it. God knows what she thought she was doing. She must've been out looking. Looking for someone . . .

He saw a branch. He saw its knuckles. Its mossy fingernails.

Yes. The Royal Glam in Llantrisant. Aye, I just came on and they told me. Hell of a crack, they said. Going all in and out of consciousness, really confused and in pain. They didnae try moving her till the paramedics got here. Sirens and everything. Yes, Penny went with them. She just rang with the latest. Said they'd checked for fractures and were putting her in for an MRI-type effort . . .

Rees threw on clothes, grabbed his jacket and patted his pockets, checking for his car keys. He reached the front door and swirled back. Cursed at his jelly-mind, foggy from sleep, the urgency of Katrina's voice having thrown him. He'd forgotten his priority completely. He lifted the Nagra strap. Snatched a few boxes of pristine quarter-inch still in their cellophane wrapper. Hit the light switch.

It was what she wanted, he told himself. He was doing what she'd asked for.

Drizzle barely more than a mist made his view of the night semi-opaque through the thinly speckled windscreen. He flipped the wipers.

On. Off. On. Off. On. Off.

His headlight beams picked up the wraith of a shaggy pony limping across the road through Llantristant Common, emerging from fog and disappearing into it again like a heavy-hoofed intoxication, a pagan acid flashback.

He blinked from the *GIG Cymru/NHS Wales* logo—BWRDD LECHYD CWM TAF HEALTH BOARD—following the arrow to the car park and snatching a ticket at the barrier, before running through the emptiness to the footbridge.

MAIN ENTRANCE/PRIF FYNEDFA

A congregation of wheelchair-users lurked under the portico, backlit by the bilious strip lighting of the interior, the side of them facing him in shadow. The figures seemed to have gathered as if in ritual formation around an ashtray on a stainless steel plinth. He saw their dappled skin and heard their damaged lungs crackling as they gnawed at their cigarettes.

To his left a grille covered the shop. A little boy was crying and plucking at the slats, and Rees imagined the mother was in the nearby toilet with the occupant of the empty buggy he now passed. The information desk to the left was unmanned—no-one in sight—so he kept walking, lured towards a central atrium. The floors were colour-coded, he now saw—lines painted in red, blue and green running through the building like arteries, directing people obediently to their shuffling appointments with Surgical Assessment, with Anaesthesia, with Supported Recovery, with death. This was where it happened. This was where it always ended. This was the building built for it. The shininess and disinfectant not so much fighting E.coli or MRSA but fragility, despair, and the fucking inevitable.

He looked at the overhanging signage and found CRITICAL CARE (ICU)—the arrow pointed right.

SOUTH WING/ADAIN Y DE

He took to the stairs three at a time because the lift was taking an age. He didn't strictly know she was in Intensive Care. She might be in a general ward, or A&E. She might even be on her way home with cuts and bruises for all he knew, but somehow he believed his instinct was right. He felt bad when he saw that the reason the lift was delayed was a gurney with an old man lying on it fighting for breath.

Ahead of him down the corridor he saw Penny Greatorex with her mobile to her ear, and he paused, nose to a window while she passed. Not that he needed to—she was far too involved in her call to notice him. Who was she ringing? *The* home, or *her* home? *Darling, sorry I'm late, but one of the old ladies is very inconveniently dying.* Outside the window a coarse expanse of green plastic flapped like a sail, tethered to scaffolding poles. Once she'd got in the lift, he hurried down the corridor through the double doors from which she'd emerged.

"Bronwen Llewellyn. A patient called Bronwen Llewellyn?"

The dark-haired nurse baulked. "You'll have to ask on the ward."

"Which ward?"

"I'm sorry, I can't tell you that."

"Oh, for God's sake."

Seeing his obvious agitation, she pointed. "That one. Sixteen."

His palm shoved the heavy door. It didn't give. He looked through the glass, shielding his eyes. Pressed the intercom next to the entry phone. It squawked. He asked if he could see a patient, please, giving Bronwen's name. The intercom went dead, cut off like the last crackling message of a Spitfire pilot.

Through the window a nurse with fat arms approached the door, opened it halfway but blocked his entry with her bulk. He tried to read in her eyes what she knew, but it was impossible.

"The nursing home informed me. I know this is . . . but I came here as . . . "

"Are you a relative, sir?"

He could not think of an alternative. "Yes."

"Siân? *Diolch yn fawr i chi.*" The voice came from behind her. She stepped back, letting the door open, and Rees saw a skinny, blond man with a stethoscope curling out of his pocket finish writing something on a clipboard. The chap was in his twenties and not conventionally handsome (usually a euphemism, but in this case true). "Mr Llewellyn?"

"Yes."

"Your mam's been in the wars, poor thing. Have you come far?"

"Quite a way."

"Well, you're here now. That's what matters, eh? We put her in a room to herself. To give her a bit of peace."

In a way he was prepared for it, in a way it hit him like a ton of bricks. He expected the hospital bed, the clouding oxygen mask, the drip, the white patches on her chest connected to the ECG flickering its digital data. What he didn't except was to see that vital bundle, that sprightly calf, looking like a punctured bag. Nostrils flaring under the plastic, hissing cone. Wrinkled lips pouting and twitching. Eyelids struggling to so much as flicker. Eyes—black eyes from the fall—themselves hooded, failing, pooped. The massive lump at her temple, hideously discoloured and embossed with a dozen stitches like the work of some brutal staple-gun. Worst of all, the cruel harshness of the Venflon needle rammed into that snappable forearm with its sagging skin lined like bark, the cotton wool absorbing an ooze of dark blood. He wondered how many times they'd gone for a vein and missed. He thought of her yelp and recoil and tears, and the platitudes that would have come back at her. It made him shudder.

"I know," said the doctor, or registrar as he called himself, whose name was Sand. (*Dr Sand*—it sounded like a comic book hero, or villain.) "She's getting her sleep, and that's a good thing after what she's been through. The fact she hasn't broken anything is a miracle, but a bash on the skull isn't funny for anybody— especially at her age. It looks worse than it is, with all the inflammation, but that will go down. Our worry is the impact on her system, something like this. We have to keep an eye on a head injury, in case there's any sort of bleeding in the skull, any haemorrhaging, any swelling. So far so good, but the next twenty-four hours is the crucial time. We can't take anything for granted. I'm sure you understand."

Rees looked at the blue-black bruising muddied around the crook of her elbow. His mouth was desert dry. He clacked as he swallowed.

"Is she going to die?"

"I've told you all I can. So far she's been a brave old thing, love her."

"Just tell me the truth. Please. What are the chances of her pulling through?"

"I really can't give you chances, Mr Llewellyn. All we can do is keep an eye on her and hope for the best. I'm sorry."

"How long have I got?"

Dr Sand paused at the door. "You can stay as long as you like."

———

He sat beside the bed. Did not pick up her hand as he felt, peculiarly, he might break her. Or that his gesture might be some kind of imposition, one she didn't want or need. Old people tended to have very clear boundaries of privacy and didn't like them abused. This is what he told himself.

Wach, the breathing in the oxygen mask said. *Wachch . . . Waaccchhh . . . Waacher . . . Wachch-ur . . .*

"Wrach-y-wribyn . . . nuh . . . wraaach . . . "

Her eyes, stuck with a rheumy, Galapagos glue, opened. A leaden cloud having moved across the sky of them.

"Tilda . . . Muh . . . Muh . . . "

Rees didn't need to struggle to make out the words.

She turned a groggy inch to him, struggling to focus.

"Put it on . . . " Throat caked with suffering. "Put it on."

Her arm lifted, bone, skin. He followed the line of her quavering finger. It led to the Nagra he'd placed on the chair next to the door.

The lick of leader made a rhythmic tick and tock. In a quite mesmerising way if you let it be, one spool blossomed with tape as the other slowly diminished. Luckily he had a collection of little plastic clamps and one of these held the microphone to a metal rib of the bed head, coiled with gaffer tape. It was important to position it as close to her mouth as possible to get a clean recording.

"Uh . . . Matilda . . . I . . . Aye . . . shush . . . shush . . . "

"Brownwen? Bronwen? I'm here. I'm here, look. What do you want to tell me?"

"I want to tell you . . . " Her feather-light fingers tugged the oxygen mask to one side, the elastic cutting a scar-line into her cheek. Its hissing became louder. "I want to tell you you're a good boy."

Where was that coming from? Was that the painkillers talking? He fought a smile.

"Bronwen, do you remember our arrangement?" He reached between his legs and brought his chair round, closer.

"Arr—Arrange . . . ?" The mask, skew-whiff, twisted, added to her look of helpless puzzlement. Resembling a dislodged red nose, it made her stray hair look like a clownish wig.

"Yes, our arrangement. What you'd tell me? If I came? D'you remember?"

She lost all her strength at that point and her arm fell from the oxygen mask to the bed. Something about the brown paw of it frightened him, but he reached out to hold it.

The door opened. He retracted his hand like a thief.

"How's she going? Is she sleeping, still?" The camp voice and bleached hair betrayed the ICU nurse's sexuality. The plucked eyebrows and sun-bed tan added to Rees's impression he must be a drag queen on the quiet. "I've come to change her dressing." What dressing? Of course—her thigh. Katrina had said. The rainbow bruising. Maybe other damage he didn't know about. "Why don't you go and get a bite to eat for ten minutes? A coffee or something? But it's bloody dreadful, I warn you."

"Thanks," said Rees, easing himself to his feet.

"What's this palaver?" Drag Queen said as he peeled down the sheet, thumbing at the mic. Slim hips and slip-ons. "It's not interfering with our equipment, is it?"

"No, I cleared it with Dr Sand," Rees lied. "He said it's fine."

The ICU nurse looked at the Nagra, then at him. Rees wondered what he was thinking, but didn't really care. One thing he did know—if this was going to be a long night, he did need that coffee, and better to do it now whilst Bronwen was being properly supervised.

"Ten minutes," Rees said to her, imagining she could hear.

GROUND FLOOR/LLAWR GWAELOD

The hospital cafe was trying hard to be a Costa, but towers of plates full of chips and rejected pasties destroyed any illusion. The server clearly spent more on piercings than on personal hygiene, and the wipe of a ubiquitous cloth saturated with toxic spray only moved around the grease on the Formica tabletops.

Rees tried to concentrate on the sounds around him while his Americano cooled: the squidge of doors swinging open and closed, the squeak of nurses' rubber soles and trolley wheels on highly polished floors. The sounds alone gave him a sense of place. Other than that, he could have been anywhere: an airport, a shopping mall. They anchored him.

He'd left the spools turning. Let it record everything, just in case. The odd word, the odd sound—it might mean everything later, when he played the reels back in the hermetic comfort of his own home. *Home.* He wondered what that meant now, and thought of the house in darkness, empty.

He dug out his phone. Messages? None. He looked at the back of his hand, the blue rivers running under the pink surface. He remembered an old trick a friend used to do, plucking the skin on the back of your hand and counting to ten. The longer your skin stayed pinched before becoming soft again, the older your skin was. He remembered when he did it, in his twenties, he was only fractionally a one. The last time he did it he reached four.

He looked up, aware of being watched even before doing so. The gaze came from three people seated on a lime green sofa. Man, woman, child. Dressed formally, in black, as if they'd come from a funeral. They weren't looking at each other. They were looking at him.

Through the corridor window, the sheeting that straitjacketed the scaffolding outside sucked in and breathed out like the building's lungs. Its green glistened with rain.

Rees pressed the ICU intercom again and waited, rubbing the mysterious but nonetheless physical tension in his neck. He heard some whispering and light, conspiratorial chuckling behind him—his first thought being that he was being laughed at, ridiculed, humiliated. Memories of the schoolyard. He turned, and through an open door into the ward opposite he could see two nurses stripping a bed. They stopped laughing abruptly when they saw him, frozen until the door reopened.

He hadn't registered the notice board before. This time he did. The thumbtacked greeting cards written by young hands, thanking the nurses for being lovely to Nanny or Grampa. Saying, praying, these votive offerings, that they were glad to have them back. That they didn't want their last memory to be of them sitting in that terrible bed, yellowing and shrinking, accursed by medical bafflement. Young, unblemished faces, smooth cheeks. It seemed an act of abuse to expose them to it. And there they were—the trite pictures of dogs, cats, cuddly bunnies. Or was it a hare?

He stopped dead. Katrina stood with a semi-wet raincoat over her arm, nodding to a nurse. He felt his stomach knot at the thought of what she was being told, but when he caught her eyes and she gave the flicker of a smile by way of greeting he knew it wasn't what he feared. As the nurse hung up her coat, Katrina took a tissue and wiped the rain from her hair and face.

He sat with elbows on knees staring at the old woman, tube trailing from the oxygen mask clamped like a vicious sucker over her puckered maw, lips forming invisible syllables, the occasional fearful gulp or gasp as if to remind them, or herself, that she was still there.

He could not hear the rain on the roof. They were isolated from it. The bastion of medicine and pharmaceuticals protected him here, he was not sure from what—he supposed, from nature. From night.

Muh . . . tild . . .

"I remember when I was about seven," said Katrina, "or maybe six, asking my mum, 'Mum, what's death?' And she said— she'd answer anything, my mum—'Och, you get a wee taste of it every time you go to sleep, hen. That's all it is. A big, long sleep.' I didn't close my eyes for a month."

Katrina wanted him to smile but Rees didn't respond, so she filled the silence.

"Hey. She's had a good innings. When it comes, it comes, eh?" She saw him look at the floor and misinterpreted his lack of communication. "It wasn't me who went to Penny, by the way."

"It doesn't matter."

"You didn't think . . . ?"

"I didn't think anything. I don't think anything. Let's just leave it, can we?"

"You know all that stuff about the *Gwrach-y-Rhibyn*? I think she was just lonely. I think she'd say anything for a bit of company."

"And in the end," said Rees, "who's she got in the world? Just you and me."

"And her son." Katrina saw Rees's features jolt as he tried to make sense of what she'd said. "She never mentioned him? Kai?"

"No. What the hell? Why didn't *you* mention it?"

"I didn't think it was important. To you, I mean. Anyway, he lives in Spain. According to her, they couldn't wait to put her in a nursing home and they were off. 'Course, old people can be very one-sided about things like that. Maybe the guy had no choice. Maybe he lost his job, ran out of cash. Had to downsize. He had a family. Kids."

"She has grandchildren?"

"Oh, yeah. Four. She gets photos, letters. I tried to get her to do a Skype but she wasn't having it. It was always: 'It's up to him.' She's proud, our Bronwen—and a bit pig-headed and a bit of a well, pain in the arse too at times. They get like that. You can't tell fact from fiction."

"In your vast experience," murmured Rees, pretending it was not for her ears.

"Well. Sorry. I'm sorry you didn't know. Anyway, what time is it?" Katrina looked at her watch. "They phoned and e-mailed him as soon as it happened. The fall, I mean. His contact numbers were on file in case of emergencies. Obviously. He should be landing at Heathrow soon, if his flight isn't delayed. I hope to Christ he makes it in time."

"In time?"

His spoken thought didn't need elaboration. He voiced it only to be cruel to her, because she was being cruel to him by saying this. He didn't really know why. Katrina stood, and he was only dimly listening now.

"Penny's gone off to collect him. I think it's all the old girl has ever wanted, really, deep down. For him to be with her at the end. Isn't that all any of us want in the end? To not be alone?"

Rees's eyes were fixed on the old woman. He heard a sharp intake of breath, saw her jaw glove-puppetting behind the plastic hiss, the tendons stretching in her neck. "What can you hear, Bronwen, love? What can you see?" He circled the bed and lifted the microphone from the sheet to rest on her undulating chest. Held it there with the flat of his hand. "Bronwen?"

"Nnn . . . She'll be here, now just . . . Buh, above, above us, she is, sh, she is, now just . . . Blummy toes scratchin' the flamin' roof, can you *hear* them? Scra-scratchity scratch-scratch . . . Flamin' . . . nggghff . . . puh." The vowels drifted— consonants becoming stutters and starts and mute spits, lips contorting in some dream-life, eyes only briefly alert and cognisant, and he could tell it was burdensome, a torture. She sagged, thorax lifting the black bar of the mic with the each mucus-filled rattle.

"What did she say?" He looked over at Katrina but a shrug was the most the girl could offer.

Now Bronwen's mouth flexed like a sphincter. A newborn mute and writhing for first breath. Until which, pain. Just pain.

Rees felt a wave of nausea, a scent-memory of grease and acidic coffee courtesy of the cafeteria.

Chu-kak! Chu-kak! Chu-kak! Chu-kak!

The sound—a sudden feathery slashing—startled him, tugged his chin to see the tape on the Nagra had run out and the loose tail was flailing, whipping circles, ablur. He'd seen this a thousand times before. Stupid that it had made him jump, something so innocuous and banal.

He walked to the machine.

"I better ring her," said Katrina, getting up. "See if he's touched down. They don't allow you to make phone calls in here. I better go outside. I'll be back in a minute."

Rees said nothing. She probably thought she'd got on his nerves and needed to give him a bit of space. She hadn't. Not really. It was all petty. Pointless. She was a decent sort. There was nothing wrong with her. He didn't like putting down people the way Glyn did. She was ordinary. She was not a deep thinker, or snappy dresser, but that wasn't a crime. She cared. That was why she'd come, after all. And that said a lot. And for some strange reason, now, he wanted to acknowledge this to her in some way that wasn't condescending or trite, but she was gone.

He turned the recorder off, took the delicate stray end of tape between his thumb and forefinger of one hand and pulled out a length of it, enough to insert it carefully into the gap between the heads, then curled the free end back round the empty spool. He switched to "Rewind" for a few seconds and put on his headphones. He wanted to know what she had said—or tried to say.

He pressed "Stop" then "Play".

"... *can you hear, Bronwen, love? What can you see?*"

The sharp intake. Disembodied now, though he knew it was from the person lying behind him. Not clearer in meaning but more ambiguous. Fright? Surprise? Discomfort?

"*Bronwen?*"

Rees listened to the muffled, shuffling sound as, a ghost on tape, some audio doppelganger, he had lifted the microphone from the surface of the hospital bed and placed it—pop, *numb*—on her hollow chest.

"Nnn . . . She'll be here, now just . . . "

A laugh somewhere. Why had he not heard it? Faint. Several walls away. A cackle at a dirty joke, it sounded like, then stifled in a snigger by the hand of a nurse realising ICU was no place for such hilarity—or was it a patient's relative attacked by a short, savage burst of hysteria?

"Buh, above, above us, she is, sh, she is, now just . . . "

Then—the other noise . . . Something. What was it? Even fainter . . .

"*Blummy toes scratchin' the flamin' roof, can you hear them? Scra-scratchity scratch-scratch . . . Flamin' . . . nggghff . . . puh.*"

For once he wished Bronwen would shut up. It was a background drone, lifting high then dropping low . . .

He stopped the tape and rewound it again. Turned up the volume.

Pressed "Play" again.

"*. . . scratchin' the flamin' roof, can you hear them? Scra-scratchity scratch-scratch . . . Flamin' . . . nggghff . . . puh.*"

Of course . . . An ambulance. *Ambiwlans*. The siren and its Doppler effect, growing louder as it pulls in to A&E on the far side of the building. Not a cry at all. Not a *bird-like cry* or screech. Not a *drawn-out* screech at all . . .

He saw it, bright green and luminous yellow, flapping? Why did he think, *flapping?*

"*What did she say?*"

His own voice in the Sennheisers, hooking him.

He wound it back. Rewind. Stop. Play.

Ambulance/Ambiwlans

Too far. Earlier than the first time. Katrina's voice.

"*. . . should be landing at Heathrow soon, if his flight isn't delayed. I hope to Christ he makes it in time.*"

"*In time?*"

His own voice. Bitter. Old. Cruel. More like his father's.

In the pause it rose again. The siren. *But it wasn't there before*—it most definitely wasn't *there* before, the wailing. The shift from high pitch to low—almost musical. The cawing ululation... How could it be *earlier* this time? How could it be *growing*? Getting *louder* even now, as he listened?

"... all the old girl has ever wanted, really, deep down. For him to be with her at the end. Isn't that all any of us want in the end? To not be alone?"

His back to Bronwen Llewellyn, Rees switched off the Nagra and tugged away his headset as if it was on fire, her words—in reality now—suddenly sharp in his ears, as sharp as was possible from behind the oxygen mask:

"*Gutter* she's hanging from now... *cowing* looking in at us... knows, see, she does... it's her job, see... *swining* thing, she is..."

Without turning he grabbed another tape box and let it fall to his feet, sprung open on the floor, clear plastic fluttering after it. He tried with feverish fingers to lace up a new reel, yanking out a yard of the white leader. He fed it past the recording heads and made a loop, knotting it onto the empty spool before pressing "Record" and "Play" simultaneously. He realised he was panting and held his breath.

"Bronwen Llewellyn. Royal Glamorgan Hospital. Tape four. Time... Time..." It became a question—"Time?"—not even for the tape anymore, and it was always for the tape. *Always*. Because the tape would outlast him—wouldn't it? Though now he seemed its servant. The tape asked him for more but he couldn't give it. Not a fact, not a confessional, nothing. The most he could give in the abject silence was his fear.

Knowing he must, he turned to face the bed.

Katrina sat with her back to him. She was facing the old woman, slightly bent forward, forearms on thighs, wearing her Dorothy Perkins raincoat. He could see in harrowing clarity dark, mercury rivulets beading down it, lines chasing each other.

"You were quick," he said, forcing a lightness into it that stuck in his throat.

Katrina did not reply. Nor did she turn.

She extended a hand to rest gently on Bronwen's and it was not the hand he last remembered as Katrina's. Of course he had not examined it, not had occasion or need to, but Katrina's had been soft and white, and now the skin was—what?—brown, if not grey, and he was sure if anything her fingers had been rather dainty, but these? These were too long, surely—far too long, and the knuckles too many... The most appalling thing of all was he now saw that the figure's back was hunched quite notably, the head sinking low to its chest as the hand with palpable urgency squeezed and shook the old woman's.

Almost paralysed, yet feeling the sac of his testes prickle and tighten, Rees knew that the object was to wake her and that Bronwen knew this with unique and horrible certainty. He could see that she had her eyes so tightly shut that her entire face was a route map of wrinkles pointing at a central point. Her lower lip shook in her non-babble, shining with rogue spittle as the oxygen mask misted in bursts. She resisted. She *resisted*. Weak as she was, enfeebled as she was, mute as she was, she was defying the night with every ounce of her embattled being. But the night was relentless. It persisted. It was waiting, predator at the water hole, with its filthy, lank, coal-black hair, for her to give in, as it knew she must.

It was waiting with immoral, sickening patience for her to open her eyes.

"No," Rees said, voice his own again, not his father's, not on tape, not artificial or an electromagnetic reproduction but alarmingly real. Knowing that more than almost anything he'd had in life, or wanted in life, he wanted Bronwen's eyes to stay closed.

"Not her," he breathed. "Not yet."

In bemusement or arrogance the hunched figure did not respond, and Rees knew what he had to do. Seeing past it the flickering eyelids that tried so hard to keep shut, he grabbed its shoulder and yanked it round to face him, tearing its gaze from its victim.

Two swishing curtains of long, thickly matted hair fell either side of its Geronimo cheeks, the face framed by them hard to reconcile as human. It filled his vision, riddled with warts, Neanderthal brow sloping above a bony ridge overhanging holes dug into putty. In the same instant the lips of a jutting jaw, ancient and simian, pulled back from a mouth with frightening elasticity to display gums blackened and rotten as it emitted a sound he failed to define even as it consumed him.

Strangely, he remembered seeing a programme about the making of a monster movie of the 1950s which showed the roar of a dinosaur ravaging New York created by the amalgamation of recordings of a bear, an elephant and a howler monkey. His brain tried to deduce, to codify, oddly, some similar recipe for what was assaulting his ears, but the task defeated him. Even in that grasping moment of lucidity, on another level, he understood completely that he was lost in the all-encompassing trap of it. There was no escape but to succumb, and the burden of resistance was shockingly easy to divest. He let it bathe him, that strange manufacture of the vast, insouciant yawn of a lion, the manic glee of a chimpanzee and the plaintive top C of a mezzo-soprano singing La Cieca's aria from *La Gioconda*—the first opera he had seen that had made him weep. It—all of it—rose, transporting and yet holding him like a claw.

Perhaps he found beauty in that sound because he knew that if he was hearing it, Bronwen was not.

And even as the noise coursed through him, he knew that the only scream they'd hear on the tape would be his own, torn from him now as a crippling fire exploded in his chest, fissures of agony snaking down one arm. Pain choked him as he tried to blot out the inhuman howl of the *Gwrach-y-Rhibyn* with his own. But he was doubled, quartered, falling, fallen, as the polished floor raced to hit his splayed hand then, as it twisted, his forehead.

Hiroshima whited him back to the world. Faces? Faces he didn't know. Demons. Saviours. Making him afraid. Fishermen hauling him back from drowning. But drowning felt best.

Two hundred joules. Stand back please!

The kick again. Cold. Shirt ripped open. Paddles descending.

Not responding. Nothing happening. One more time. Stand back please! Stand back!

"She's coming for me," he could hear somewhere in the room. "She came for him, and next she'll come for me." And he knew Katrina, upside-down Katrina, returning now from outside, would comfort the old woman in her madness.

He didn't care. What mattered was that she was safe. That she had time. Time enough to see her son. Time to make a difference. And the light was bright. And he didn't mind that either. He didn't mind anything very much at all.

And the last thing he listened to was his own voice in his own head.

"To the folklorist, nothing must die. There is life every time a mouth opens to tell a story."

Now I am a story, he thought.

Tell me.

THE SHUG MONKEY

1. A PERFECTLY IMPOSSIBLE PERSON

Professor George Edward Challenger contemplated sausages. The construction thereof, the manufacture thereof, the biology thereof, and not least, the taste thereof, as he sliced the end off one specimen, examined it closely through eyes narrowed to slits, sniffed at it with cavernous, dilating nostrils, inserted it into his mouth, and chewed. Even at this early hour he could not desist from being a man of Science.

Knowledge had always been as much the ex-president of the Palaentological Society's sustenance as anything physical. Not that he was indifferent to the consumption of food. Far from it. His appetite, in keeping with his appetite for brain fodder, was voracious, some might say gargantuan, as the proportion of his girth and the evident stress upon his waistcoat buttons amply testified. The night before, the landlady of the Three Horse Shoes had raised an eyebrow when he had said that four sausages and four fried eggs would suffice for his breakfast, thank you very much, with perhaps a moderate portion of local mushrooms, and yes, some bubble and squeak since it was offered, and devilled kidneys, if it isn't too much trouble, with tea and toast and marmalade to follow, if you please, since breakfast is hardly breakfast without toast and marmalade, don't you agree? Even hearing, let alone consuming, such a list had made the small woman feel slightly giddy as she'd toddled back to the kitchen of the public house, shaking her head to herself. However to Challenger this was but a light snack to keep him going until luncheon.

"Begin," he said to the young man sitting across the table. "I cannot speak while I masticate, but I can listen. Tell me why I am here." The professor shook out a folded gingham napkin, laid it in a diamond formation on the protruding bulge under his blue-black Assyrian beard, and tucked it fastidiously behind his collar.

"There has come to my recent attention a certain local legend," said Edward Malone, formerly of the *Gazette*, now feature writer of the *High Ordinary* magazine, a periodical furnished with a penny farthing on its shiny cover, given to devoting column inches to the follies of the rich, the enigmas of nature, experiences of crime, and the fleeting fashions of the day. "It is well known in these parts and in Cambridgeshire generally. In some instances it has been described as an ape, other times a dog. The extraordinary thing is that it is specific in location, always spotted on or near the road between West Wratting and Balsham. They call it the Shug Monkey."

Malone allowed the appellation to sink in, but Challenger volunteered no response, merely bisecting the yolk of his second egg.

"The derivation of the name is evidently from the Old English *shuck* meaning 'demon'. The most famous of many 'black dogs' in British folklore being Black Shuck or Gallytrot, said to be the size of a calf. Left his claw marks in the door of St Mary's church in Bungay, that one, if legend is to be believed."

Challenger crunched into his toast, one cheek bulging. He buttered the remaining triangle with more attention than he paid the information, but Malone went on, undaunted.

"Many people have seen it over the years. This Shug Monkey, I mean. Descriptions in the literature—by *literature* I mean newspaper cuttings—are varied. The head and body are generally said to be humanoid, but the tracks sometimes canine, the gait often upright, at other times quadrupedal. Some define it as the traditional spectral hound, 'padfoot' or *barghest* as it's sometimes termed. Other accounts much more resemble the sightings of werewolves or *woodwoses*: the age-old Wild Man of the Woods, or Hairy Man, believed to be a link between civilised humans and dangerous elf-life spirits of the forest common to most countries of Europe, though in many respects the Shug Monkey, mythologically speaking, seems to have originated with Nordic settlers. Notable characteristics seem to include the dark fur covering its body, blazing or sometimes fiery eyes, the frequent accompaniment of lights in the sky, and in more than one case, the fact that it fades away into the night like an apparition."

Challenger grunted.

"I thought you said you couldn't speak, only listen."

"That was not speaking," said Challenger. "That was an involuntary physiological reaction."

"I thought it was too good to be true." Malone threw down his notebook.

"You have summoned me for my opinion, I imagine."

"Yes. But not before I have delivered the facts."

"Facts? I have yet to hear anything of the sort. Merely hearsay and fables." The professor's enormous fingers reached for the bottle of Worcester sauce.

"That was merely the preamble, if you'll allow me to continue." Malone bristled, then remembered that this was the man known to wrestle naysayers to the ground and once broke the nose of Snodgrass of the *Times*, and he should have known by now what to expect. "What brought me here was not a selection of old wives' tales or bugaboo stories for Hallowe'en." He flipped through several tightly written pages of shorthand. "I have testimony—*first-hand* testimony—that on numerous recent occasions there have been encounters with a hairy hominid of some kind, an apparently bipedal ape-man which, unless the witnesses have indulged in a remarkable feat of collusion, point to the existence in this area of an example of the Pithecanthropus or Neanderthal branch of anthropoid primate—a cousin to early Man."

Thus Malone challenged Challenger. Yet it seemed to fall upon deaf ears. The listener remained unmoved and impassive behind his luxuriance of beard and breakfast.

"Sir, I can only believe you feign disinterest in what I have just said. Surely you realise that these descriptions are uncannily reminiscent of the lost race of ape-men we came across in Maple White Land?"

The professor grunted—this time a leonine rumble—and dabbed the corners of his lips, glaring at his companion with dark unblinking eyes as if the man had uttered some vile calumny.

Malone was perhaps forgetting that Challenger's fame after returning from the so-called Lost World he had discovered in the Amazon was very much a two-edged sword. Proof of the expedition had been lost to the skies on membranous wings, and word-of-mouth of the bizarre events at the meeting of the Zoological Institute in Queen's Hall discredited with every passing week and month, the result being that the Columbus of science and his auspicious team instead of being lauded on their return had achieved a sort of notoriety. There were those who said, even in print, that only the deluded and gullible could believe dinosaurs still roamed the earth, and knowing what he did, that he was neither a liar nor a myth-creator, made the post-expedition Challenger incorrigibly bitter. Nowadays he was a hero in some quarters, granted, but a buffoon in others. Neither was a crown he wore with pride. One newspaper responsible for a caricature of him as W.G. Grace hitting a pterodactyl egg for six had recently taken to depicting him in cartoons as the beleaguered lion of Empire, once fearsome, now toothless, his roaring days behind him. G.E.C. found this public face troublesome, in that he did not want his face public in the slightest. But G.E.C. was not just a scientist; he was also a man. And it is a rare man who lacks a modicum of vanity, a rarer man still who cares nothing of what others say of him, even if he declares otherwise.

It was in this afterglow of celebrity and disrepute that Challenger had been intrigued by Malone's handwritten request to leave London to examine a mystery the young journalist implied, in tantalising yet enigmatic terms, would fascinate him "by dint of our shared interest and experience to date".

Hence, soon after breakfast, the professor sat with all the gravitas of a local magistrate in the function room of the inn, presiding over the evidence brought before him. Evidence, in this instance, not of petty theft or drunken affray, but something of altogether more peculiar scientific interest—if true.

Mrs Ivy Pucklechurch was the first to testify, flattening her dress with chubby hands and declaring that she preferred not to sit, if it was all the same to them. She apologised off the mark for not attiring herself properly for the occasion, and Malone disabused her that this was not an occasion of any kind. In spite of these assurances, clearly she was unaccustomed to talking to the more educated classes, and somewhat intimidated by the imposing presence of a cross between a disgruntled buffalo and a colossal bullfrog.

Malone began by asking her to recount her experience, just as she had told it to him a few days previously. She said she didn't know if she could tell it *precisely* the same way. The Irishman, with a smile and a charm natural to his race, bade her do her best.

Clearing her throat, she said she had been pegging out her washing at the time—Malone informed Challenger of the *precise* time from his notebook—and, expecting her husband home from work at noon, had returned to the kitchen because she heard the kettle boiling. "A hum I heard, or thought I had. But it wasn't."

"Tell Professor Challenger about the face, if you'd be so kind." Malone turned to the older man. "I want you to hear this." Challenger raised his not insubstantial eyebrows. Such a statement by the reporter he thought self-evident, and his expression said as much. "Sorry."

"I turned from the hob to the back door to return to my sheets, when some movement caught my eye, yet when my eyes fell full on it, it was there, stock-still. For only a split seconds, mind. Then—*whoosh!* It was gone." Her right hand took flight to emphasise the fact.

"Describe it, if you please."

"Yes, sir. I can see it now. Plain as day, at the window. A man's face, if it was a man. It had the features of a man, but I'd not bet a shilling it *was* a man, honest to God I wouldn't. If you've petted a dog, a big wet wolf hound say, that was the look of it, sir, with its big muzzle and lips drawn back. And covered in hair, sir, all brown and shaggy. And when it was gone there was this stillness—a *startledness* in the air, is all I can describe it as. I confess, I had to stay and catch my breath, and waited till my old man came in, and got him to poke his nose out there before I would. And I had goosebumps over my arms like you've never seen, and that's the truth, sir."

Malone looked at Challenger and asked if he had any questions. Challenger shook his mane. The woman curtseyed and Malone escorted her to the door. Next was Cuthbert Dodds and his fiancée Peggy O'Hagan: he the local butcher's lad, she the only daughter of a recently widowed seamstress.

"We shan't keep you any longer than necessary. Thank you for coming. For the benefit of the professor, would you please recall what happened to you both on the night of the twenty-third?" As he spoke, Malone passed Challenger a copy of the local paper, guiding his attention to the headline: LOCAL COUPLE ATTACKED BY MYSTERY FIEND and in smaller letters under it: SHUG MONKEY STRIKES AGAIN.

The couple had gone for their habitual evening stroll to the church and back, to talk of the things lovers talk about when not in the earshot of family. It was a full moon that night—Malone furnished Challenger with a calendar—and the two young people decided, as the weather was mild, to walk that extra length of the lane to the end of Farthing Field, as far as the crossroads.

"Equidistant between West Wratton and Balsham," Malone remarked, for the zoologist's benefit. "The exact territory of the Shug Monkey."

Cuthbert said he had begun to joke and sing and do a little dance in the style of the music hall artistes, with his thumbs behind his lapels. Yet as he trotted backwards he saw his beloved's features change suddenly from bashful amusement to abysmal horror. Her gloved hand covered her mouth and she reeled back, evidently at the sight not of her lover, but of someone or something beside and *behind* him. Deducing this in an instant, he had spun round so quickly he almost lost his balance, in time to see something he took for a crippled deer or misshapen foal, or dog—some kind of creature—loping ("*loping* is the precise word," he said) from the seclusion of trees on one side of the lane to the dyke ditch on the other—where it immediately, in a thrash of limbs and matted fur, was lost in shadow.

Peggy shrieked and, not unnaturally, Cuthbert ran to her aid. Perhaps thirty seconds elapsed, whereupon the boy thought he should investigate the ditch into which the thing, whatever it was, had disappeared. Peggy begged him not to do so, clinging to his arm, but he prised her off and ventured to the spot, peering down into the gloom. Discerning nothing with his naked eye, he jumped down into it, but whatever had been there—whatever had *loped*—was there no longer.

Cuthbert told Malone and Challenger what he had told Peggy at the time: that he didn't know what he saw, but he saw *something*. It was brown. Black-brown. He had once seen a March hare under moonlight and that was a queer sight, with its mad eyes, as queer as he ever wanted to see. But this was no hare. This moved on two legs, and was hunched, and its arms dangled and swung, as if hoisting its body with it—that was what put him in mind of a cripple, on crutches. Malone asked Peggy if she agreed with that description, and she said she did.

Malone enquired if they were sick or ailing in any way at the time, or taking any kind of medical remedy that might contribute to causing an hallucination of any kind?

Peggy said no, then remembered that she had felt pins and needles. She'd thought it was because she'd sat reading in a broken chair earlier that evening and her leg had gone to sleep. Cuthbert said as a matter of fact he *did* feel something, too. He'd felt his hair stand straight on end, and Peggy had said afterwards his scant ginger beard had stuck out like bristles on a pig.

"That will be all for now." Malone saw, maddeningly, that Challenger had not so much as uncapped his fountain pen. "Thank you for your time. Most valuable."

"You shan't say we're mad, shall you?" said Cuthbert's fiancée as the lad took her to the door.

"Peg. The gentlemen want to explain this beast, that's what they're here for. They won't do any harm. They'll stop it, you'll see."

Malone smiled at them as they left, saying nothing in reply because he was not entirely sure that they would, or could, stop something to date as insubstantial as the words the witnesses had committed to the air.

Gomer Jenkins was last. Born of Welsh Baptist parentage, the unkempt chap had nevertheless lived in the locality all his life—though once, he said, he had travelled as far as Ely, and frankly hadn't thought it worth the fuss. Impecunious yet not entirely shabby, Jenkins was one of those specimens commonly found in hostelries and taverns throughout the land as near-permanent fixtures at the beer-pumps, commonly labelled as "A Character".

"Just left the Red Lion in Balsham, I had," the scruff declared, rolling his syllables in the drawl of the fens. "Climbed onto my bicycle, as is my wont, hoping I'd snatch a nightcap in the King's if I put a spurt on. King's Arms in West Wratting, that is. Over the street from here."

Malone looked at Challenger to see if he registered the location, again, of this uncanny creature's habitat. Again, Challenger offered no reaction, eyes half-covered by supercilious lids, as if only begrudgingly staying awake.

"Well, no sooner had I gone about twenty yards than I began to feel somebody after me. Biting at my shirttails, so to speak. Running, but no footsteps. Not as such. Just breathing. Or rather *panting*, I'd say. And it wasn't just the sound in my ears, it was the fact of the shadow cast alongside me by the light of the pub behind me.

It was—'ow can I say? All shoulders. That's it—*all shoulders. And shaking.*" He gave his hands an exaggerated trembling motion.

"Perhaps the road surface was irregular, and it was your eyeballs that were shaking," suggested Challenger with laconic dryness. "Did you deem it necessary to turn?"

"Turn? No sir. Oh, no. Not turn. I just pedalled with all my gusto. Terrible gusto I had. The gusto of ten men. I was at those pedals like nobody's business. Then before I knew it, the front wheel went askew, the handlebars slipped out of my fingers, and I went head over whatsit into a ditch. Whack! Clean out. And here's the strangest thing. The other gentleman there knows this. But when I woke up and looked round me, goodness knows how long after—minutes, hours? Bless me if I wasn't a quarter of a mile from where I fell off. On my sainted mother's life, sir. A quarter of a mile!"

"And I daresay you'll never touch a drop again," murmured Challenger to the tabletop, looking up with a not entirely sympathetic grin. "Thank you, Mr Jenkins."

"Oh, that's not all, sir." The man seemed affronted. "Not by a long chalk. Mr Malone? May I? I brought it, like you said. It's outside."

"By all means."

Whilst Jenkins was gone, Challenger's pantomime of looking at his watch was too extravagantly absurd to make Malone angry: he refused to rise to the typically childish bait, and was content to simmer until the witness returned, this time pushing a sparkling, immaculate Starley "Rover" Safety Bicycle alongside him.

"And a very fine bicycle it is too," observed a droll Challenger, stifling a yawn. "Now . . . "

"Exactly!" Gomer's eyes gleamed. "*Very* fine! Brand new, it looks, wouldn't you say? But the thing is it *isn't* brand new, sir. It's a good fifteen years old if it's a day, and covered in rust. Or *was* covered in rust—till that night I fell into the ditch. And look at it now—*not a mark on it!*"

"Well?" asked Malone after Challenger had waxed lyrical about the game pie served up in front of him. "What do you think of it all? The face at the window. The loping figure disappearing into a dyke ditch. The nocturnal pursuer of Gomer Jenkins. And, not least, the mysterious resurrection of a terminally rusty velocipede?"

"I make of it very little." Challenger gripped knife and fork in his meaty fists. "Beginning with the Welsh wizard, personally I wonder if the newspaper story about the couple's experience inspired him to concoct his own little brush with the Shug Monkey, a tale with which no doubt he will happily regale all comers for the price of a pint for years to come. Severe alcoholics have one major motivation in life, Malone—*alcohol*. Everything else, including the truth, comes second, and the broken capillaries on Jenkins's nose and cheeks attest he is of that illustrious persuasion. The summation of his story, in words that might suit a reporter like yourself? DRUNK FALLS INTO DITCH. Many a dipsomaniac has seen giant spiders in the throes of delirium tremens. This man was merely more inventive than most."

"I disagree entirely. A man suffering from delirium tremens is hardly capable enough to ride a two-wheeler."

"Well, he didn't. He fell off. I rest my case."

"I find the theory laughable."

"I find the alternative more so. And your attitude to this more than a little alarming. Why are you, a hard-nosed pressman, so headstrong on the subject?"

"Only because you are dismissing the very evidence I find compelling. What of the bicycle?"

"A brand new one. How do we know it is not? And please don't say we have the word of a habitual drunk on the matter."

"What of Mrs Pucklechurch's face at the window?"

"A tree. Branches outside. The human eye, open as it is to misinterpretation . . ."

"Tommyrot!" Malone pushed away his plate. "Why *that* face? Why *here*?"

"You said yourself it is a well-known local legend. Perpetuated no doubt from generation to generation. People talk, and imaginations run riot. Which is all the more reason for us to remain sober in the full assessment of the facts."

"Then you at least consider the possibility that there *are* facts?"

"No."

"Challenger! Really!"

"Malone. A lost world in the Amazon was preposterous enough. But in Cambridgeshire?"

"Preposterous, exactly! But it existed! We *went* there! God knows, I wish that we had not." The reporter's fingers knotted together and he pressed his thumbs to his forehead. Challenger's stubborn rejection of all he had presented made him speak from the heart, when in a more guarded moment he perhaps would not have done. "Sir, it does not say a great deal for my manhood, but perhaps a little for my honesty when I tell you I have an unassailable fear of confronting anything approaching the level of terror we faced in that accursed jungle. I know it may be thousands of miles away now, thank the Lord, but still I feel the breath of those cold-blooded gargoyles on the back of my neck. The thought of being devoured by them is ineradicable. I do not want to visit that place again, either in my body or my mind. But what if *it* is visiting *us*? And to what *purpose*?"

Challenger could see for the first time what he was foolish enough not to perceive before: that this was far more than an intellectual pursuit for Edward Malone. As a consequence he was thoughtful before he replied.

"My dear fellow, I saw bravery on that amazing plateau the equal of which I shall never behold again in my lifetime, and such a thing forges a trust I uphold as the greatest thing men can share. You did not fail the calling, dear boy, and do not think for a moment you did." Challenger saw the younger man's eyes moisten as he silently mouthed his thanks. "But you read this recent story of the Shug Monkey and were drawn here, only to hear more. Why, when confirmation is the very conclusion you most fear?"

"Because I could not pretend it does not exist." Malone looked into the older man's eyes. "And neither can you." He knew he was right and the arrow of his accusation pierced the old lion's flank. "Sir, I know you wouldn't be human if you didn't fear further ridicule after the slings and arrows you have suffered unjustly in the past. I realise that. But don't you see? If these claims are true, far from humiliating you further, they will completely *vindicate* you?"

A small but extensive growl emitted before the professor violently threw down his napkin. "Evidence!" he spat, hunching his bear-like shoulders away from the reporter. "Or this has been a wasted journey. I'm sorry, but a scientist needs evidence! G.E.C. needs *evidence!*"

Without hesitation, Malone rose to fetch both their coats. "Then it's time you met the chemist's daughter."

2. THE EMPIRE OF EMBROCATION

The bell tinkled as they entered. Behind the counter stood a man in a white coat dispensing a jar of gelid substance to a young man wiry as a pipe cleaner. "Stick a few spoonfuls in boiling water and inhale it under a towel. A lot will come out, but don't be squeamish about that. That'll be doing you good. And sleep with some smeared on your chest or under your nose. That should do the trick."

"Mr Parsons?" Malone indicated his companion as the customer moved past them to the door. "This is Professor Challenger from London. The gentleman I told you about. Is now a convenient time?"

The chemist closed the cash register with a whitening of pallor for all the world as if an undertaker had called unannounced. "Yes . . . " He coughed into his fist, standing to attention as if to ease the stress between his shoulders which heretofore had given him the appearance of a stoop. "I'm glad you're here. She has had another bad night. I have given her a powder, but she only sleeps deeply for a few hours then wakes in a dreadful panic. I swear, these nightmares are having a grip on her."

"I'm very sorry to hear that. I was hoping, with the passing of time . . . "

"They might ease? No. No, sir. It seems quite the reverse. Excuse me." Parsons edged between the two men and flipped the sign on the door to read CLOSED. "But you'll see that for yourselves. If you'll come through to the back room, I'll call her down."

"We'd me most grateful, but only if she is up to it. I mean, if she is up to talking about what happened."

"She talks of nothing else."

Challenger, entering the gloom, felt a chill and concluded it was the slight fall in temperature between the shop front, lit as it was by sunlight, and the back. He and Malone blinked as the formidable darkness was dispelled by the switching on of a naked light bulb revealing apothecary jars and boxed supplies of liniment and linctuses, J. Collis Browne's Mixture and concoctions to fight alopecia and digestive travails.

"Pol? Polly, dear? Come down, please. The men are here to talk to you."

Parsons adjusted the position of a William Morris–patterned armchair which had seen better days. "My wife normally sits here. She likes to observe the goings-on in the pharmacy whilst her husband is working, once her housework is done." He removed a ball of wool and knitting needles and brushed dust off it with the flat of his hand, gesturing for the professor to be seated, but before he could do so an upstairs door creaked and two sets of footsteps descended the wooden, unadorned staircase. Emerging from the dark, a wren-like woman beckoned her small daughter, who remained halfway up the steps, a shadow cutting across her, revealing only the hem of her petticoat and her buttoned shoes.

"Why, I do believe this is the famous Polly Parsons!" Challenger boomed, his red cheeks bunching into a seraphic smile. "Exactly as my brother described her to me. You've heard of my brother, Polly, I'm sure? His name is Santa Claus. He lives at the North Pole."

Malone covered his smile with his hand.

Timidly the little girl placed her left foot one step lower, to be joined by the right. The bulb now illuminated a teddy bear clutched tightly in her arms.

"I have his tummy, as you can see. He's slightly older than me, of course. His beard is white, whilst mine is black. Ho, ho, ho! He's very envious. But do you know? He sent me all this way to see you. He says you're a very, very, *very* well behaved little girl. Is that true?"

The reply was almost inaudible: "Yes."

"I'm very glad to hear that. Very glad indeed . . . "

One hand on the chair arm, Challenger lowered his considerable bulk to his knees, from the height of a giant to that of a child.

"You see, my dear brother Santa wants you to be very happy and very safe, and a little bird—a little *reindeer*, in fact—tells him you've become unhappy and he wants to know why. He's worried. He sent me to ask why Polly Parsons is sad. Will you tell me? So that I can tell him?"

The fearful youngster ventured to the lowest step. Then, tentatively, the floor itself. Divested of her own shadows, she showed herself to be tiny even for the six-year-old Malone had told the professor to expect.

"Is he from Santa too?" She regarded the reporter.

"Oh, certainly. He's an elf. A pixie, actually," said Challenger. "A large pixie, granted, but a pixie nonetheless."

Malone ventured a glance at Parsons but neither man said a word.

"Now that's a very fine bear. Did you get him for Christmas?"

"Don't you know?" The girl frowned. "I thought you worked at the North Pole."

"I do," said Challenger hastily. "But I forget. I'm sorry. I'm stupid."

"Bear's not stupid. He protects me."

The professor's voice softened. "When does he protect you, dear?"

"At night time, when I'm afraid the Shug Monkey might come back and eat me."

"Why do you think that?"

"Because he did try to, once. But he didn't. I ran away. I was frightened."

"I'm sure it was a very frightening thing for a little girl."

Malone was always surprised when, at times, for all his bombast and cantankerousness, his old friend could be as silent as a monk, and as patient as Job.

"I think I took his strawberries. That's why he was angry. I . . . I only took two. I was hungry. They looked so bright and red. I was sure they didn't belong to anybody, and it was such a long time since breakfast. I reached into the brambles, careful not to sting myself . . . Was I bad?"

"No you weren't bad, Polly," said Challenger. "What happened next?"

"I wanted to eat another one because the first one was so nice and juicy. I went to take it, really *really* stretching this time, and a hand came out and grabbed me and I screamed and screamed, but it didn't let go, and I pulled like this and it *did* let go. And I jumped up and ran. I didn't know what it was. I thought it was a man but I thought it was a fox because it was hairy all over and reddy-brown and horrible and smelly and—and that's when I felt . . . " Her breath caught in her throat and she buried her face in her father's white coat.

"This. This is what she felt . . . "

The chemist reached down and lifted the little girl's dress, not just to her hips, but rolling it up to her shoulders. Her back was bare and Challenger did not move. Nor did the child, except for the tremor that was visible over her unblemished skin. Unblemished, that is, but for the harsh parallel marks dragged across it which could only be the work of some violent and voracious claw.

Challenger's mouth was dry, as dry as Malone's had been when he had been subjected to the same sight days earlier, and the reporter harboured some slight satisfaction, no, *relief*, that the man was now as dumbstruck as he had been. For all his loquacious dismissal earlier, the overbearing zoologist's inability to respond now seemed a victory all too bittersweet.

"Pol, when I spoke to you before, you said you had a headache when you picked the strawberries. Is that correct?"

The little girl nodded.

"Is there anything else you want to tell us?"

She rubbed her nose and nodded again.

"He smelled of acid drops."

As she clung round her father's midriff, the chemist stroked her hair.

"What did this, sir? You're a learned man. More learned than most. More learned than me. For pity's sake tell us, for I admit I am lost. Truly I am."

"A creature." Malone crouched down and opened the span of his hand, his own fingertips aligning almost exactly with the wounds on the child's back. "A creature with five fingers." The garment fell back into place like a curtain across a particularly ghastly scene at the Grand Guignol.

"You're a brave girl, Polly Parsons." Malone saw a tear trickle down the poor girl's cheek and wiped it away with the side of his forefinger. He squeezed her shoulder gently as he rose to his feet.

"I know," she said. "But will the Shug Monkey get me?"

Mrs Parsons moved closer and kissed her daughter on the top of the head. "Nothing can get us at night time, my sweet, because God protects us, as long as we say our prayers. Isn't that right, sir?"

Malone looked back at Challenger, who was standing now, brushing sawdust from his knees. "Yes, and Santa protects us too," came the professor's reply, "if we leave him a glass of sherry and a mince pie on Christmas Eve . . . "

Malone hoped the woman was not well versed in sarcasm. Luckily the words had hardly been uttered than they all heard a rapping quickly becoming a concerted knocking at the shop door, which the proprietor attended to with speed given the urgency with which it was being executed.

The others followed him quickly from the back room, Polly's mother lifting her in her arms, Challenger and Malone surprised if not startled to recognise the face beyond the CLOSED sign as that of Mrs Harptree of the Three Horse Shoes, bursting inside with all the gasping elation of a person saved from drowning.

"Professor Challenger, thank heavens I've found you. Just had the dray. Men call. Delivery. From the. Brewery . . ."

"Good lady. Please exhale and inhale normally, or we shall never hear what you have to say because you will have expired."

The landlady took a deep breath and closed her eyes before letting it out, but, truth be told, looked no less agitated for the process.

"It has been caught. They just told me. the Shug Monkey. It's been captured at West Wratting Farm."

3. THE BRUTE CONFRONTED!

"At first I thought the evidence pointed to an escaped animal." Malone said, his gloved hands clinging to the sides of the trap as he struggled to raise his voice above the clatter of the wheels. "Perhaps from some travelling fair or circus, but there's no record of one going missing. And anyway, what animal has paws or claws the size of a man's hand?"

"First a dog," said Challenger, his dark hair whipping his face. "Then an ape. Now a man . . ."

"If it were a man I'd feel a good deal happier about facing it."

But Challenger's eyes were on the horizon, where the sun sat low, a bulbous lantern behind the haze of a dry summer. The light was fading rapidly on the road between West Wratting and Balsham. The flatness of the fens is an alien landscape to those unfamiliar with it, and to Challenger it was unfamiliar indeed. And more unfamiliar by the minute. He yearned for the security of signposts but no such reassurance was given. They had to trust implicitly in the knowledge of the wheelwright, Cobbold, whom they had commandeered for the purpose, to get them to their destination.

"You have your compass, Malone?"

"I do. It's the second time you've asked. And I still I have no idea why."

"The girl said she'd had a headache. That immediately suggested to me a change in atmospheric pressure. You recall she said her attacker smelled of acid drops. I do not think for a moment our monstrous presence was sucking confectionary. On the contrary it suggests to me the air was powerfully ionized."

"Meaning?"

"Unusual weather conditions can cause physical discomfort. Mrs Pucklechurch vowed upon a sudden calm, a stillness, and Miss O'Hagan mentioned that her fiancé's bristles stuck out on his chin, rather like the effect of a Van der Graaf generator, wouldn't you say?"

"Her body tingling with pins and needles . . ."

"Precisely. The removal of the rust from the bicycle being the clearest indication, for all the world as if these people were swamped by an electromagnetic field."

"Great Scott. If I recall correctly, several older, anecdotal offerings include the presence of a localized mist. Sometimes glowing."

"With charge. How is your compass?"

Malone consulted the instrument. "Spinning."

"Confirming my hypothesis. Many experiments have proven that static electricity in the air makes people disturbed and unsettled. These physical sensations and frightening effects, like distortions of sound and distortions of time—the humming that wasn't the kettle boiling, and Gomer Jenkins's blacking out and waking up—are all common to an influence of this sort. Caused by what? An atmospheric effect of some kind? An aberrant frontal system triggering unusual encounter experiences?"

"But, Challenger, why the *same* encounter? Why *here*?"

"And the claw marks if nothing else are real . . ."

"*It* is real."

Within minutes the sky had darkened and Malone noticed the professor's eyes had darkened too. No sooner had the pony's hooves taken to the pitted track to West Wratting Farm they passed an agricultural worker who gesticulated at them madly and ran ahead to both herald their arrival and point the way. Challenger looked back at the bruised sky crackling under thunderclouds mercifully silent yet hanging with pregnant foreboding over the county.

"Challenger . . . "

Malone's words froze as he saw the grey mist ahead of them, swathed around the farm and outbuildings, was glowing. Only as they drew nearer did the cause of the luminosity become unequivocal, as it fragmented to become torches held aloft by a clutch of figures dressed uniformly in brown suits, waistcoats and collarless shirts. Three of the four wore bowler hats and moustaches and the strange light that made the sky brighter than the land threw their shadows long on the ground.

The sting of burning leaves filled Malone's nostrils as the trap rattled to a halt. The dry bark of hawthorn and maple crackled and spat as they passed through a blue curtain of smoke. The brake squealed as it was wrenched. The wheelwright knotted the reins and dropped from his seat.

Malone and Challenger climbed off and Challenger stretched his spine as he absorbed the scene. He had thought upon arrival that the farmer and his co-workers were staring at them, but it now became apparent they were not staring *at* but *beyond* them—at the barn, inside which, in the penumbra of the bonfire and the blaze of a cow feeder full of straw, he could hear the almost intolerable racket of horses moving about, whinnying in severe displeasure. Insane hooves thrashed at the walls in a vain attempt to escape. The doors would have been shaken off their hinges in the hellish din, had they not been held in place by a plank of wood half the size of a railway sleeper.

"For pity's sake!" Malone exploded, looking at the idiotic faces before him. "Why has no-one let out the horses?"

No answer forthcoming, Challenger supplied it.

"Because if you let out the horses you also let out what is inside with them."

"Jabez Brown." A rail-thin man carrying a pitchfork had spoken.

Challenger recognised the name, furnished to them by Mrs Harptree, and took the nut-brown outstretched hand in his own.

"I thought it was a rat," said the farmer. "Scuttling in the straw of one of the stalls. It wasn't a rat, it was a hand, and with the hand an arm. I didn't wait round to see what the arm was attached to." He jerked a gnarled thumb at a mop-haired youth, more than likely his son. "Clifford and me locked it in. Then it went mad, and so did the horses."

"How long ago was this?"

"I'm damned if I can tell you. Every man Jack of us, our watches have stopped."

Malone took out his own from his pocket.

At that very moment the air was torn asunder by a cry the volume of which, the quality of which, the *ferocity* of which, somewhere between a wolf-howl and a hyena's gibber, eradicated any words on any lips.

Challenger spun to face the barn, clearly absorbed by his own flotilla of questions. *Genus? Species? Oesophagus: healthy? Epiglottis: frantic? Epidermis: hairy? Decibels: how many?*

"What in God's name . . . ?" Malone was stricken, all colour drained from his features in a way that the professor had not seen since the Amazon, and that fact alone robbed the older man's cheeks of their normally florid tincture. Had it not done so, the next occurrence would have produced the same result.

The horses became silent.

The frantic banging, whether caused by the terrified animals' thrashing limbs or the desperate attempts of the other denizen to get out, abruptly and inexplicably ceased, the sudden absence having the same appalling effect on the watchers as the sound itself had done formerly. If not more so. For its cessation meant change, and in this instance change meant . . . what?

"We are dealing with the physical realm, not the metaphysical," Challenger announced to the farmer and his labourers. "Prepare yourselves!"

Malone watched as they dispersed under barked orders to

the surrounding buildings, returning sharply within minutes with a range of implements—one a wood-axe, the boy a scythe, one arm a hook for a coil of rope being knotted into a crude lasso, and between them a net, which they strung out between them to stretch across the barn entrance. Not too far away, and certainly not too close. Jabez Brown fell to one knee and prised open a pair of metal jaws.

"No!" Challenger shook his huge head. "No traps. If we snare it, I want to snare it in one piece."

Jabez Brown laughed. "You expect us not to *hurt* it?"

"We are not beasts. And if *this* beast has scientific value, let us at least have it intact."

Malone saw from the farmer's face he could no more contemplate that concept than he could the rotation of the planets.

"Now, Malone, take your place at one end of that substantial wooden crossbar. Mr Brown, the strongest of your men at the other end. The rest of you, stand by and steady. Torches high, and nearer. We have force of numbers on our side. Don't let it get away, is that clear?"

Malone and the sturdiest fellow strode to the barn doors side by side, neither relishing the task. It took them a moment of unspoken planning to arrange themselves, each crouching with the heel of his hand under the edge of the beam. After a swift countdown it was lifted and discarded with a dull thud on the ground, whereupon the two retreated, Malone walking in reverse as the irregular weight of the barn doors allowed them to sway open.

Revealing . . .

Only a black square of unassailable darkness. A blank canvas. A cave.

An emptiness . . .

No branches soughed or creaked. No birdsong came as punctuation. The passing of the sun behind the horizon-line brought with it the hideous secrecy of night which not even an owl dared blaspheme. Only the sporadic spitting of boughs and twigs on the bonfire carried on the sultry air.

Malone backed up as far as the professor and stood beside him, fixed upon the dark, hardly able to swallow his own spittle and finding his dry eyes unable either to blink or to tear themselves away. If the horses had surged from their tethers, as the cacophony had implied, then surely they would have rushed from within, eager for freedom.

But rush they did not.

Challenger stepped closer to the building. The reporter reached out to stop him. Challenger loftily extended a hand behind and waved away the gesture.

Soon the professor himself was framed against the backdrop of nothingness, the barn doors coffin lids either side of him, easing in and out as if the edifice itself were breathing. Wood, nails, breathing, whilst a human being like Malone could not.

Challenger turned, facing both his friend and the assembled farmhands, arranged as they were in a semi-circle, sallow complexions made flickering and waxen by the torches.

"Clearly, the creature has gone."

As if in answer, an object flew in a high arc through the air from the dark behind him, something bulky and misshapen, Malone thought, even as he tried to fathom exactly what it was wheeling white-red in torn strands and spinning, lobbed over the head of the scientist, to land, crunching in shards of bone, bouncing, to come to rest in a cough of dust. He felt the flinch of the men behind him as he discerned the severed head of a horse, torn by nameless claws from the stalk of a neck, pumping gore into the soil on which it now lay, its massive boiled egg of an eye staring up at him.

Challenger swung round on his heel to look back into the barn, but a cry was going up because the rest of them could already see what he could not—that something with a crouching gait, hands brushing the ground, was already coming out of it, flying at his chest with the force of a cannonball, throwing him onto his back like a stranded whale. G.E.C. felt a crack on the back of his head and his vision became giddy and unreliable. G.E.C.'s vision was not in sharp focus as he dismissed what he saw, as he must, even as he felt the weight of its bones and flesh pinning him down and his senses assaulted by a scent of inestimable putridity. Hair, yes. Teeth, yes. Monstrous teeth in disgusting jaws. Blood-splattered face like a vision from the foulest circle of Dante's hell, red spittle coiling like barbed wire in the firelight as it reared up, huge mouth wide and ululating, a heavy wooden club with a bulbous end wielded like a battle-axe high over its head, the intent in its devil-eyes to bring the object down and smash the professor's skull to smithereens.

A shot rang out.

The club spun into space.

A bud became a rose on the creature's breast. Its simian head jerked back and, as if hooked, the entire figure was jolted away in a cartwheel of hair and limbs and teeth, then stars and the night sky above.

Challenger hoisted himself up on his elbows, but Malone was already kneeling next to him, shocked at his own impotence, but all had happened in a flash. It took two more men to help lift him to his feet and he swayed there, the Assyrian bull, gathering himself. But even in that discombobulated state, as he saw the flaming torches gathering round the awful, immobile shape now lying in the dirt—short legs, barrel chest, sloping forehead, curved skull—the professor was troubled that, for all the variety of weapons culled by the farmhands, he had not seen a single firearm.

He turned.

Into the dying light of the embers walked an instantly recognisable figure, ramrod-straight in brown mosquito-boots and a white drill suit, a .479, telescopic sight, double ejector, point-blank up to three fifty cradled on his elbow. He sported a hat worn by the gauchos of the Argentine and chewed on an unlit match: England's Glory.

Challenger smiled. As did Malone.

Never had they been happier to see their friend, Lord John Roxton.

4. AN UNSCHEDULED STOP AT DIGSWELL VIADUCT

"Ever the great white hunter, dear boy. If you want a rhino above the fireplace or a few antelope for your baronial hall, I'm your man. You can have a whole menagerie of trophies up there without so much as leaving your drawing room. If you pay the price, of course. Extraordinary our paths should cross." The sportsman tweaked the ends of his crisp moustache and stretched his long legs, settling back in the seat opposite Challenger and Malone on the train from Cambridge to London. "The commission to bag the thing came from, let's say, a rich entrepreneur of the fairground freak show variety. No questions asked. I presume he happened to read the same reports you did, young fellah-my-lad, from his lofty eyrie. Wants it stuffed and mounted for his travelling exhibition, I daresay. No accounting for taste, what? Gruesome beggar if you ask me. Not the prettiest object to walk off the ark. Still, half up front and half on delivery. Couldn't say no. It'll fund my next trip up the Zambesi."

Challenger stared out of the compartment window, massive shoulders hunched, deep in thought as Roxton chatted in his usual unflappable manner.

"What the deuce was it? Do we know? I tell you, I have seen a fair few man-eaters in India, but none like that dead abomination we've got boxed up in the goods van."

The professor's silence did not go unnoticed.

Malone was concerned. Deeply. He had seen the violence of the beast's attack, and even though his old friend had escaped unscathed but for a swollen knee, couldn't help but be worried for the after-effect. To be within a whisker of death, and such a grotesque one, was unimaginable—except he himself had imagined more than once such a fate when the plateau revisited him in dreams of elephantine lizards with fins like cocks' wattles. Such an experience could scar a man for life. And, witness to the uncharacteristic silence that had descended upon Challenger since the event, he wondered seriously if the balance of the old fellow's mind was entirely intact.

"I know what you're thinking, Challenger." Roxton puffed cigar smoke, smiling, oblivious to the reporter's thoughts. "Come, come. It's written all over your face. You never could disguise your high dudgeon. It's one of the things I always liked about you. You want that blasted chimp to grace some plinth in the Natural History Museum, don't you? To hell with my booty. Evidence of evolution's twists and turns, what? A missing link, and my missing fifty per cent."

The great scientist said nothing. Did not even turn from the window. Malone doubted severely he had been listening to a word.

"What *are* you thinking, Challenger?"

The professor wiped a small hole in the condensation in the glass and looked into his own eyes reflected there.

"We must dispose of it," he said like an automaton.

"*What?*"

"We must dispose of it. The body. The corpse. Every ounce of it. Every hair and fibre of it. As if it never existed."

"Are you insane?"

"No, I am very, very sane indeed, I assure you." Challenger turned to face the two of them.

An object sat on the seat next to him wrapped in an old horse blanket. He lowered it like a drawbridge so that one end rested on Malone's knees, then proceeded to unwrap whatever was concealed therein. What was soon revealed was the filthy club the Shug Monkey had wielded. The weapon that had nearly cut Challenger's life short. Now Malone thought the old man's marbles had been truly lost. That he was travelling with a dirty piece of wood as a memento of his recent encounter surely pointed to the man being certifiably insane.

"Please pay attention. This artefact is not wooden, as it first appears, and as I, and perhaps you, wrongly assumed." Challenger took out a ring of keys and used one of them to scratch furiously at its surface. "A rudimentary examination in my hotel room last night—clearly I had no laboratory as my disposal—told me it was, in fact, metal." He tapped it and it resounded with an appropriate chink. "I suspect a corrosion-resistant alloy, akin to that invented by Harry Brearley in Sheffield for gun barrels. Indeed I imagined the application to be warfare at first, the shape being thin and cylindrical for the most part, but not if you examine the semi-circular dial at the end where there is evidence of a slot. The dial you can just make out, here, reads MON–SAT and digit 1 and letters HR. I can also discern the letters ARK and NG and ETER. More importantly, you see the figures here? *5p, 10p, 20p, £1, £2* . . . "

"Pounds I understand but ten *p*?" remarked Malone, struggling to absorb the information. "Does it mean pence? But we abbreviate pence with a *d. Denarii.*"

"We do," said Challenger grimly, elaborating no further. "I found some hydrochloric acid—spirit of salts, as used in household cleaning extensively by Mrs Harptree, fortunately—and applied it to loosen the screws. What I found inside, with a great deal of elbow grease, is much more elucidating . . . " He took a handkerchief from his pocket and opened it in the manner of a farmer revealing a new-born chick. His hand was full of coins. But coins the like of which neither of the other two men had seen in their lives before.

"A two-pound coin." Challenger rubbed its face with his thumb.

"But there is no such thing as a two-pound coin," said Malone.

"Not yet," said Challenger, handing it to him. "Read what is on it."

"Dei. Gra. Reg. Fed. Def . . . " Malone looked at Roxton. "Elizabeth II." He stared at the crowned profile on the grubby disc between his fingers, then back at the professor. "But we've had no Elizabeth II. Only Elizabeth I. This is . . . "

"Turn it over."

"Two pounds," Malone read aloud. "2009."

Roxton snorted. "You are saying this piece of metallic junk came from 2009?"

"Not at all," said Challenger. "Look at its appearance. Mangled, distorted, it has suffered the extreme ravages of time.

Decades or hundreds of years, if not more. This object, whatever its esoteric purpose originally, is not from the year 2009 but from the ruins of the distant future."

Malone frowned. "What are you saying?"

"I am saying that, ergo, this creature in the luggage car is from the future also. I am saying this unknown hominid is not Neanderthal, not Cro-Magnon, not the Dryopithecus of Java, but the greatest hominid of all . . . *Man.*" Challenger's eyes blazed, defying the men's all-too-obvious incredulity. "And we its ancestors."

Roxton was dumbstruck.

"Impossible," whispered Malone. "No, I mean *literally* impossible."

"To today's science, yes. But tomorrow's? The evidence of the witnesses—the tingling, the glowing, the pins and needles—pointed to extraordinary geophysical forces. What if, in some way inexplicable to today's understanding, the Earth creates what I would call time geysers at certain points on the globe, where unpredictable surges throw up glimpses, sometimes phantasms, sometimes tangible beings? It could account for all manner of supra-normal events. In this case, anthropoids from the far-flung future—flung back to the here and now."

"Then I don't understand," laughed Malone. "Surely this is a more magnificent find that we could ever have imagined."

"Magnificent?" Challenger grunted. "Nothing could be further from the truth."

"I think I need this." Roxton took out a hip flask which normally accompanied him to his bothy in Scotland and gave himself a shot of single malt. He offered it to Challenger, who shook his head, but Malone partook eagerly.

The professor did not relish what he shared.

"We imagine in our ignorance that Darwin's wonderful premise means our species will improve with age, like a fine wine. That the human race will advance to become sophisticated and merciful and kind the longer we survive on this planet. This tells us the exact opposite. There will be a decline back to the brutal, the barbaric, the mindless, a slow inexorable descent to the primeval sludge. A steep and glorious rise, only to precede a catastrophic fall."

"Ye gods," breathed Roxton.

"I wish the gods, or God, had a hand in it, but they do not."

Challenger saw Malone sink, elbows on knees, and as the train trundled on with no regard to the discussion within, thought him a small boy given the news of a death in the family. He had always thought him a son in many ways, and a fine one, though never said so, and never felt it as keenly as he did now.

"That is why we must destroy the evidence," he continued. "I am convinced that, encumbered by our denials, the word of the farm employees will be discredited as the flights of fancy of inbred locals—as superstition, like all the other stories. Especially when you, Malone, write up in print what you saw as no more than, say, a malevolent crossbreed of a mastiff and a wolf hound that evaded our capture. But the *physical* evidence. That is another matter. Don't you see what would happen if the dentition were examined by experts, or a strand of hair examined under a microscope, and found not to be that of a bear or ape or dog, but unmistakably that of our own condemned and tragic species?"

Malone put his face in his hands.

"My friends. My good friends." Challenger gently placed his gigantic palm on the man's back. "Think of the consequences if this awful cadaver reaches London, or even your employer's sideshow, Roxton. The greatest scientists of the world would clamour to anatomise its organs. They would set upon its bones and teeth and blood, and find out what? What marvellous truth will we have delivered to them?" The old man's already bleak countenance clouded with the utmost disgust. "Proof that this is our fate. To be the Shug Monkey."

Roxton returned to the compartment, his shoulders hitting one side of the narrow corridor then the other as the engine took a bend, a white wall of smoke rolling past the windows thick as the clouds of Mount Olympus. He wrenched open the door and slumped into his seat, sweeping back a lock of hair that fell over his forehead. This time it was Malone who offered the hip flask, which by now was almost empty.

The whistle blew shrilly as they entered a tunnel and the malt stung Roxton's lips. He had done his job.

Challenger had feigned a heart attack as planned, a performance worthy of Drury Lane. Malone had pulled the communication cord, bringing the steam train to a long, laborious halt at the desired location, Digswell Viaduct near Welwyn Station, famously where Queen Victoria was so terrified by its height she had to be removed and conveyed by horse-drawn vehicle to the far end. This diversion suitably in place, Roxton had acted as invisibly and fleet of foot as when stalking his prey on the savannah of Africa. The guard scurried past him pink-faced in the other direction, stopping only to suck in his stomach so that they could squeeze past each other. While the poor man sought medical expertise amongst the passengers, Roxton was free to enter the goods van unopposed.

Purchased from Nimrod & Sons Funerary Services, the plain coffin with its unholy cargo, that grinning carcass, faced him. The kukri knife from his belt made short work of the straps holding it secure. He bent down and heaved it across the floor. By now Challenger was protesting mere indigestion to the doctor dragged along to examine him, playing the Royal Society card and apologising for his impetuous friend. Meanwhile, knowing time was of the essence, Roxton heaved open the doors of the car and with all his might committed the Shug Monkey to the one thousand five hundred foot drop to the River Mimram below, where it sank without trace.

"It's done," said Roxton, re-lighting his Havana in the already fuggy miasma of the compartment, remembering how he had thrown the stainless steel evidence from the future, the coin-collecting device, wrapped in its horse-blanket, after it. "Thank the Devil. It's over."

"I fear it isn't."

The voice was Malone's. His companions' expressions demanded his immediate elaboration of that statement.

Unbidden, he stood and retrieved his overnight bag from the luggage rack. Opening it, he took out a large sheaf of papers segregated by paper clips and rubber bands. The Irishman was pale as chalk. And not just from the play-acting.

"I have not told you before, but now I must. When I became interested in this mysterious entity, I did a copious amount of reading. More than was good for me, you could say. You *will* say, when you've heard this . . . " He handed Challenger a sheet of typing. "There have been other reports of the Shug Monkey in Rendlesham Forest in Suffolk." He gave Roxton a square of newsprint. "Also, a similar beast covered in hair, the so-called Man-Monkey of the Shropshire Union Canal, has been seen on numerous occasions since the late 1800s. The creeper of Evercreech in Somerset . . . Others. Many . . . "

"Hellfire," said Roxton.

"We must find them all," said Challenger, who had been gazing at the Queen's head on the burnished face of the two-pound coin before slipping it deep in his waistcoat pocket. Characteristically, he took up the gauntlet with a certainty and conviction that carried the others with him, as it always did. "At King's Cross we shall disembark, and telegraph our families and loved ones from the station. Tell them we shall not be coming home as planned, but give them no reason to suspect anything untoward. And apprise them in no sense of the truth."

The other men nodded.

"I do not need to tell you it is essential we keep from everyone, even those closest to us, the dreadful nature of the future. For, imagine, what would be the point of achieving anything in life, or sustaining hope, that most human of characteristics, if we knew absolutely that all that awaits us is a slow decline to the monstrous? Civilisation might crumble under such a weight. The realisation itself might even perpetuate what comes to pass. Let only we three suffer from the sure and certain knowledge of what will befall our kind. And give thanks that we shall long be in our graves before it does."

"Hear, hear," said Malone. "Ignorance is bliss. I say let mankind face the future with fire in his eye, not fear in his belly. If I can have a part in that, God help me, I shall do."

"You have bullets, Lord Roxton?"

"I do. And all of them at your service, professor. I can think of no higher calling."

At Oakleigh Park passengers disembarked and hurried to and fro on the platform, families carrying squalling infants, shop workers to their daily toil, perfectly shaven husbands with their dainty wives, doffing their hats with perfect manners.

"To think. All we value will be gone," said Challenger wistfully, looking out at them. "Eradicated by the steady, inevitable drive of the vicious, the vile, the basest of all instincts, the selfish. Perhaps not now. Perhaps not next week or next century, but . . . Who would have believed, my friends, that the true Lost World would be our own?"

The three men shook hands.

A hunter with a new quarry he could never hang as a trophy. A reporter with a story he could never publish. A scientist with a discovery he could never so much as whisper to the world.

"Gentlemen," said Challenger. "We have work to do."

WRONG

To my parents when I was growing up, laughable when you look back from today's perspective, job security was the Holy Grail. It didn't really matter if you had a pleasurable or rewarding life. Work wasn't *meant* to be pleasurable; it was just a means to an end. The end being going out in the car on the occasional Sunday run to Llantwit Major with a flask of piping-hot coffee, or having a week at a caravan site in Porthcawl every summer. That was their lot and they had no goals or aspirations beyond it. I did, I think, even then. Anyway the fact was I wasn't academically brilliant and there was only one subject I was even remotely good at or interested in, to their eternal dismay, no doubt, not that they ever showed it. So, not much good for anything else, with so-so A-Levels but a sliver of talent for drawing and painting, I gained a place on the Foundation Course at Newport College of Art in the early seventies, eager to learn but full of trepidation about an uncertain future.

I can't remember how we found my digs. Perhaps the art college provided a list of people who put up students: I think they must have. My father and possibly my mother—almost certainly my mother—were with me when I first met my landlady and her husband. My mum would've wanted to give the place a surreptitious once-over, and was fairly swiftly reassured that the house was as spotless as her own. I could tell she was gratified and relieved by the warm welcome we all received too: tea in a chubby pot and a plate of chocolate digestives and butter crumbles arranged in an arc like a magician's card trick. She settled back and relaxed while my dad talked about rugby. Luckily he had the ear of a fellow sport obsessive.

Mr Bisp (Percy, as I grew to know him: an old-fashioned name even then) was a short, stoutish man similar in build to my grandfather and, like my grandfather, faintly comical in appearance. Snow-white hair in a Tintin quiff when most men his age would be bald as a badger, black-rimmed glasses, bulbous W. C. Fields nose, receding chin, trousers pulled up over a potbelly to an equator just under his armpits, kept resolutely in place with a pair of fanatically taut braces. His shirt, I remember vividly, was Persil white, rolled up beyond the elbows of spindly, hairless forearms. Shoes polished within an inch of their lives, spine as rod-straight as that of a twenty-year-old, from the off he gave the impression of being a dry old stick, but as I came to know him better I could see there was always a twinkle of a smile flickering behind the grumpy exterior.

A funny little chap, he was certainly no Robert Redford, but Mrs Bisp (Enid), poor woman, was no oil painting either. On first sight I couldn't help compare her to a Goya hag—toothless, laden with deeply etched wrinkles, with a protruding jaw and rubbery lips—but she was a sweet woman whose caring nature made me immediately feel ashamed for having such a superficial reaction, and I'm sure I blushed. I was a shy teenager after all, and this was the first place I was going to live in that wasn't my home.

I was shown my bedroom. I installed a few armfuls of books, and my own twin-ring electric hob (which my parents insisted on getting me, even though I said I'd be eating at the college canteen most of the time). Mr and Mrs Bisp said I was free to cook my own food in their kitchen, use the toaster—use anything I liked, in fact, as long as I cleaned up afterwards.

I was thinking of my territory. They were thinking of theirs. I wasn't going to get in their way, and that was how they wanted it.

But it was nice. They were nice people. And my mum was happy. (On one occasion my brother, who was ten, picked up that Mrs Bisp said "muke" instead of "milk" and it became a running gag whenever any of us referred to her. Evidently she had a London accent, equally that Percy was from the Valleys, born and bred.)

As I say, Percy was quiet, but brusque. When I got home from college about seven o'clock on my first day, he said, "I expect you've got studying to do"—which immediately set out the rules in no uncertain terms. They didn't want me sitting with them all night, which was fair enough. They'd said I could use the middle room to work in, and that's where I'd set up my drawing board, so that's what I did, irrespective of whether I had *studying* or not. Sometimes I'd listen to my transistor radio, set to Radio 3, or read whatever science fiction novel I had on the go (Moorcock, William Burroughs, J. G. Ballard). As routine set in over the first few weeks, I'd get accustomed to Mrs Bisp knocking the door and asking "Tea?" Sometimes when I had nothing to do, and with the evening stretching bleakly until bedtime, I'd yearn to go and join them but thought I would intrude. It wasn't my space, and after all it was their house. Instead, as I worked, I'd hear the dim mumble through the wall of the TV set in the next room. Having said that, one or other of them would always tell me when *News at Ten* was about to begin, and I'd always watch it with them, then go to bed.

Of course it wasn't exactly imprisonment. I could have gone out with friends from college to the pub, but I didn't. I wasn't a pub kind of person. I'm still not. Besides, my closest two mates travelled home in the evening (to Usk and Cwmbran respectively) so I was a bit abandoned. There was a nice Irish girl with long hair and a springy walk who I liked very much—she blushed even more readily than I did—but if I'd have asked her to go for a drink she'd have been mortified. Not that I could ever have plucked up the courage to do so.

Percy liked his *Western Mail* but didn't engage in conversation much. As he sipped his tea—always tea, never coffee—he might remark on a topical story on TV, giving a wry smile or shake of the head, pointing at the screen with his thumb. His views were what you'd expect. I didn't volunteer mine. Maybe he tested me politically, but if he did I didn't rise to it. There again, maybe he wasn't really interested in me at all.

But he was a good sort. Sometimes I saw him going to the local shops with his string shopping bag and shopping list. I found out later he used to deliver to old dears in the area, elderly folks who couldn't get out. Didn't take any money for it. "God, no." Told me it was just something he liked to do. Said it "took him out".

One day—I think it was in the second term, because by then we were left to our own devices to get our portfolios ready and bulk out our all-important sketchbooks—a girl from 3rd Year Fine Art came to pose for life drawing. Unexpectedly, I was the only one in the room with her. She arrived on a bicycle decorated with rainbow tape, and stripped off in front of me without a glimmer of hesitation. Taking a break for a roll-up, still stark naked, she came to look at my drawing on the easel and after due consideration said it was good. She was tiny and her haircut a punkish crop. But her pubic hair was red—to be honest, I hadn't seen pubic hair before. It was richly colourful and unapologetic, totally unlike the sparse whiskers of the sixty-year-old overweight model we would become all too familiar with.

That night the sitting room door was open as I passed and Percy beckoned me to come in and sit down. He was watching *Coronation Street* and I wasn't sure from his expression if he was perplexed by it or enjoying it. "She likes this," he said. Enid's chair was unoccupied so I naturally asked where she was. "Gone to her sister's for a few days."

"Finally had enough of you, has she?" I joked.

"Aye."

He seemed quiet. "Didn't have a row, did you?"

"Row? Good God, we don't have *rows*." Percy dismissed the idea, getting up to go and make us both a cup of tea. "Two sugars?"

And so it was. I spent my spare time during the day filling my sketchbook, which was an important part of the course. We were told by our tutors we had to do at least two drawings a day, on top of our lessons and other projects such as design work, illustration, technical drawing, and such like. Consequently I took every opportunity when out and about or even sitting having a drink or chat, to draw anything that happened to be in front of me. Beer glass. Ashtray. Bus stop. Person with slip-on shoes. It didn't have to be interesting. (Mostly it wasn't interesting but you drew it anyway.) It was about training your eyes, improving your observational skills, and I must say if you compared the first scribble in a sketchbook to the last there was a marked improvement. It was remarkable, really. I always say, when people ask, that the whole discipline was like putting your eyes through a pencil sharpener.

I stayed at Mr and Mrs Bisp's from Monday night to Thursday, returning home on the train Friday night for the weekend. Not far, and only one change at Cardiff Central.

My father in those days was a bit of a control freak—he had to do everything his way, even the most banal household repairs were no-go zones for us boys, even if later in life we looked back at his DIY jobs and realised he was pretty rubbish at everything. But I think I've got a bit of that in my DNA. It would be abnormal if I didn't, but I was drastically unlike him, fundamentally. My brother and him, on the other hand, were too much alike if anything, which is why their arguments gave my mum a lot of grief. The two of them would have a shouting match and afterwards be all smiles, talking about the football results or how Cardiff City did, while my mum was left in tears. No wonder she had to see that specialist that my nan saw for her "nerves". Dad exploded on a regular basis. I think he was a man who couldn't deal in any way with the stress he was under, but lived with the pathetic and bombastic delusion he was strong-willed and in charge, which he obviously wasn't. Even as kids we could see that.

I still wonder if he envied the fact that I went on to have a job I actually loved doing, rather than one that was a necessary penance, but unsurprisingly we never had anything remotely like that conversation. Usually he'd drive me back to Newport on Sunday evening and drop me off. It was only about half an hour. Again it was probably a bit controlling rather than letting me get a train.

When I returned the following Sunday night Mrs Bisp, Enid, still wasn't in evidence, peculiarly. It was only eight o'clock but Percy said she was tired. She'd gone to bed early. I thought no more of it.

Later, sitting up in bed reading, I heard him coming up the stairs, the wood creaking under his footfalls, and passing my door to cross the landing to the main bedroom. Soon afterwards I heard his voice through the wall between us.

"How you feeling, love? Can I get you anything? Temperature, you got."

I heard the ease of bedsprings. A gentle, barely audible kiss.

I realised I hadn't taken in a word of the last page of the novel I was reading, so closed it and turned off the bedside light.

Over the following few days I detected the tang of an unpleasant odour in the air, something akin to that of a broken toilet. Hardly looking up, Percy explained it matter-of-factly as the damned drains. Said he was so used to it now he hardly noticed it. Spraying copious air freshener around my heads he described how he'd got various plumbers in over the years to try to fix the problem, but the buggers never did.

"Always gets bad after a bout of rain, it does." He said he'd run the taps in the scullery till he was blue in the face. "Didn't do any damn good." Tried bleach and whatnot. "It comes then it goes, you'll see."

The next thing I recall is arriving back one afternoon and Percy coming out of the front room to tell me a doctor had been because Mrs Bisp was ill. I said I was very sorry to hear that. He looked like he was having difficulty conveying the fact. The racing was on in the background.

"She'll be up and about soon enough. Tough old bird, Enid. Got to look after me, for one thing. Always looked after me, see."

I passed him on the stairs the next morning as I was leaving for college. He was carrying a tray with toast and jam up to her. I said I hoped she was feeling a little better. He said, "Aye." I closed the front door and walked off to some lecture on the Pre-Raphaelite Brotherhood or the importance of El Greco.

Later the same day I saw him in town having lunch in a cafe. He didn't see me. He was just stirring his coffee, sitting alone after finishing some sausage, egg and chips. He didn't look perturbed in any way, or anxious, or even thoughtful, particularly. I would say it looked like the most natural thing to do in the world, to take the weight off your feet. Then I watched him buying a bunch of flowers. Daffodils. When I came home they were in a vase in the dingy hallway, a yellow beacon against the beige wallpaper. Percy was in the front room reading his paper. I asked if they'd eaten. I could see there were no dishes on the draining board in the kitchen.

"Aye, she's got a good appetite on her, I'll say that."

He didn't look up.

Without me pressing him or even going into the room he explained that they had their main meal at lunchtime nowadays.

"Can't be doing with this 'having dinner at night time' malarkey. Recipe for indigestion, that is. Let the food go down. So that's what we do. Might have a little bit of something later, about five if we're hungry. Beans on toast or something." He shook the *Echo*. "That team, they need a good kicking. Never mind the ball."

I chuckled and nodded. Never interested in rugby, I sort of pretended I was before absenting myself into the middle room to sit at my drawing board with ink and gouache, getting back to work on the cover of a Dennis Wheatley novel, *They Used Dark Forces*, featuring a goat-headed man in an SS uniform. Once the Stephen King of his era, Wheatley was on the wane by then but his Arrow paperbacks still sold in millions. Nazis, Satanism, the occult—it was an intoxicating mix, and part of my upbringing, I suppose. I loved plunging myself into that world of good versus evil supernatural forces. I lost myself in those well-thumbed paperbacks, just as I lost myself in my artwork sometimes. The room would get imperceptibly darker and it was only when I noticed I was straining my eyes that I realised I'd better switch on the overhead light because I was sitting in darkness.

It was easy to lose track of time as the house was generally quiet and now I could only hear the TV in the next room, no voices in conversation since Percy sat in there alone, though I'd periodically hear him go up to see how Enid was. Take up a cup of tea. Bring down the empty cup later, which I'd see him rinse in the sink with a bead of Fairy liquid, his finger curling round the inside as he ran it under the hot tap.

One Wednesday afternoon there was a brisk rap on the doorknocker. I remember it was a Wednesday because that was my half-day, which explains why I was there. The two men said they were from the council. Percy looked understandably baffled. I explained I'd rung them. I said I just thought if they heard a different voice complaining they might feel they'd better do something. Percy slowly twigged it was about the sewers.

"The smell," I confirmed.

I detected a flicker of accusation. He didn't like the idea I'd done this behind his back.

One of the men said they could have a look, at least.

"Hell, aye, do what you want," Percy said, opening the door wider.

As they walked through the hallway, one sniffed the air with rodent curiosity and said he could see what we meant. Out the back yard, they lifted a manhole cover with a hook-like contraption and peered into the wet gloom below. No particular enthusiasm for exploring, though the one with the less substantial midriff eventually descended. Percy, hands in pockets, asked the older one where he was from.

"Troedyrhiw."

"Never! Where I was born, that was! Know the White Hart? My father ran that, donkey's years. Conservative Club, after."

The man looked blank and Percy looked disappointed. He started jiggling his loose change.

"Support Cardiff"?

"Not interested, to be honest with you."

The jiggling change became silent. Tea was offered, and supplied. Biscuits eaten. Those pink wafery ones, as well as the ones with jam in the middle. The men confessed they couldn't see any obvious cause of the problem.

"There you are, see." Percy turned to me as if vindicated. "Didn't believe me."

"It wasn't that I didn't believe you."

"What was it then?"

I didn't answer.

The men left and I felt bad. I went to my bedroom but I couldn't settle or concentrate. I kept thinking of the other bedroom. The one Enid was in.

Early evening I came down and said to Percy I was starving. "I'm going to get some fish and chips. D'you want some?"

"Aye, go on." He stood up and dug out his wallet to offer me money.

"Don't be daft."

He reluctantly put it away. "Pie for me. Snake and pygmy. Batter gives me heartburn terrible these days. Don't know why."

We sat at the kitchen table eating out of newspaper, the pungent scent of vinegar in the air. He hadn't asked me to get some for Enid. Now I asked if she'd like a chip or two, but Percy shook his head vigorously. "No fear! Not with the stomach she's got. Sight of it . . . " His thought trailed off in a shiver.

Later that night, I heard him talking to her in their bedroom, though I couldn't make out the exact words. Not particularly lovey-dovey. Banal, probably. The duff-duff as he plumped the pillows. The dunk-dunk as his Marks & Spencer slippers fell to the floor. The wheeze of the bed as he got into it, old springs protesting. Then the quiet settling as the light was switched off.

I didn't want to listen, but it was hard not to. Not because I thought anything untoward was going on. I was afraid of the normal, the everyday proximities between husband and wife, and the thin wall that separated us, and I was aware that it wasn't up to them to behave any differently; it was up to me. I was the usurper. I was the cuckoo in the nest. I was the one who had to try to be invisible.

I didn't think anything else. People later on said I should have. Naturally they did. They were astonished I didn't think of going to the police, but that's easy for them to say, because they think the whole situation must have been abnormal. And that's the thing. It wasn't abnormal at all.

By day I applied myself to bolstering my portfolio with life drawing and the like. To be honest, that took the majority of my attention. Requires a good deal of skill, life drawing—which is why it separates the men from the boys, as our head tutor said. You can't fake it with a flourish of the pencil or paintbrush, the line has to be right—not messy or vague but precise, bold, and confident. And only artists with outstanding talent make it look like it took no effort whatsoever. So I'd sit peering from behind my easel, trying to delineate the fatty folds of the belly of our sixty-year-old model: the purple tendrils of veins in her ankles, the sandy dapple of dried skin on her heels, the almost-yellow of cracked toenails. I'd struggle to render in charcoal the sagging pouches of her breasts, the hidden pothole of her belly button. And if I could, in a wash of watercolour, the bruise-blue ghost under the white over-garment of skin.

During her break she'd slip on a silk dressing gown and smoke a Benson & Hedges, running her fingers through her aggressively dyed pitch-black hair. We used to think she went a bit doe-eyed whenever one of our younger tutors, Prosser, supervised the lesson. As a working sculptor, Prosser sported a regulation mop of curly hair and a hedge-like, unruly beard, looking something between a mad pop star and Alan Bates in *Far From the Madding Crowd*. Sometimes the woman—whose name I forget—would sidle up quite close to him and stand swivelling on one foot coquettishly, making it cringingly obvious that she fancied him. The context of her being nude under the material of the skimpy robe suddenly made us far more uncomfortable than her being nude during the formality of the drawing class, which was strange.

By now I was used to getting home and finding Percy alone in the front room watching the TV, with the door closed or sometimes open. Occasionally I'd see a copy of the *Weekly News* or *Woman's Weekly* on the hallstand, which I knew he got for his wife with diligent regularity. I never saw him reading any magazine himself other than the *Radio Times*, which he guarded fiercely on the arm of his chair, every programme he intended to watch circled in Biro.

One night Enid's sister arrived unannounced and unexpected, the machine-gun volley of the doorknocker rousing us both. Percy was faintly alarmed. Who would be knocking the door at nine o'clock in the evening, apart from Jehovah's flaming Witnesses? But the woman on the doorstop wasted no time with pleasantries, telling him straight off the bat and in a tone lacking in warmth that she wanted to talk to her sister.

"You can't," Percy said equally curtly. "She's bad. You can talk to her when she's better, and that's that." Without asking her in, or even prolonging the niceties of conversation, he then shut the door in her face. "Bloody woman. Always trouble. Never liked her . . . "

I thought it weird that after having a door closed in your face you wouldn't knock the door a second time, but there you are. I didn't know either of these people and I didn't know their past relationship. I didn't know Enid for that matter, but I wondered to myself why she didn't shout downstairs to ask Percy what was going on. She must've heard her sister's voice after all. Mustn't she? I waited a minute standing in the hall, but I didn't hear her voice from upstairs. I thought perhaps she must be sleeping.

Thinking Percy was irritated and perhaps upset by the attempted intrusion—he'd mumbled all the way to the kitchen and back—I decided to sit down with him. I asked if he minded. He said he didn't, but he seemed disrupted under the surface. Riled, but not prepared to admit it. I suggested we gave the TV a rest for once, had a game of chess instead, or draughts.

"Aye."

So draughts it was. Percy won. Repeatedly.

"I like you," he chortled. "You can come again."

"Snakes and Ladders is my expertise," I said.

"Strip Jack Naked." A glint reflected in his glasses as he got out a pack of cards from the sideboard. "Never lost at this." He seemed to relax as the evening wore on, the games liberating him from any internal angst. We didn't talk much, if at all, then suddenly he looked up at me. "Cocoa? I got in it special. Thought . . . "

"Go on then." Watching him making it in the scullery I said: "How's Enid?"

"Mending lovely." He looked at the ceiling as he stirred. "Lovely, she is."

When we sat down again sipping our milky drinks, he became thoughtful for a long time, and instead of switching on *News at Ten* sank back in his armchair and, to my surprise, talked about their honeymoon.

He said that when they'd got married, he'd told her straight: "Don't have any ideas about doing anything on a Saturday because on Saturdays I'll either be going to a match or watching one on telly. Any other day of the week, you can do what you like." I asked if she was happy with that. He said: "Married me, didn't she?

"I booked our honeymoon at a big hotel near Swindon where Dai Jenkins at the cricket had stayed with his wife. A way that was, in them days. Swindon. One of these small cottages down by a river. Tremendous. And the weather was glorious. I'll never forget it." His eyes clouded as he allowed himself to savour the memory. "Always say to ourselves, we'll have to go back one day. See if it's the same." He rubbed one eye behind the lens with his index finger. "The old girl would love that. Love it."

I saw tears well in his eyes.

Later that night I heard his weeping—gentle, as if semi-stifled. It nevertheless woke me.

On the pretext of going to the bathroom, from the landing I saw the light on in their bedroom. Then, as if in reaction to hearing me pull the light switch cord, it was switched off.

Shortly afterwards I went home for half term, glad to get away. Like Martin Sheen in *Apocalypse Now* I always looked forward to going home, but the moment I got there I wished I could be back in Newport. I think I was at the point of feeling dislocated from my stifling and parochial past but lacking in confidence about my baby steps into the future. My old school friends had moved away or felt distant strangers who resented or envied my escape—and I didn't want to think of it as either. My dad was in work and I didn't want to get under my mother's feet, so I did a lot of walking, down the park, up the woods, and found myself, inexplicably, spending most of my time thinking about Percy.

One night in the front room after tea, and out of earshot of my family, I phoned him. He hadn't expected it to be my voice and sounded a little flustered. I said I was ringing to ask how Enid was.

I heard a pause and a sigh at the end of the phone. For a good few seconds I thought he wasn't going to say anything at all.

"Took a turn for the worst, to be honest."

"Have you called out the doctor?"

"Not . . . Not sure the doctor will do that much good, see."

I wondered what he was trying to tell me. On one level, perhaps I knew.

"Will you . . . Will you call her sister?"

"No, it'll be all right . . . "

"Her sister will know what to do," I said. "I'm sure she will."

"Aye. The thing is . . . "

"Percy. You know what to do, don't you?" I let what I'd just said sink in and waited for his reply for what seemed aeons. "Percy?" Had he heard me, or was he choosing to ignore my question because it was too loaded? Too unbearable? "Percy?"

"Aye. I know. I'm listening. What do you think I am? Dull?"

He hung up, his receiver hitting the cradle with such a bang I held my own at arm's-length.

I was concerned that I'd upset him. I'd clearly angered him. I'd crossed the line into what he thought to be private, but I had to. I'd had no choice. I couldn't envisage any other possibilities.

But I'd not intended to hurt him—far from it. Yet for all my noble intentions, his last word made my stomach turn over and I felt I'd somehow betrayed him, even though I knew I hadn't. It made me hate words and my inability to use them properly, and my cowardice in not talking to him face to face, and the geographical distance between us. And the stupid room I sat in that was kept for best, the curtains drawn to stop the sunlight from fading the carpet, in spite of the fact no bugger set foot in here except my uncle and aunt for a sherry and mince pie every Christmas Eve.

When I next returned to Newport, I found him slumped in his chair, as if the stuffing had been knocked out of him. No tie, and unshaven. I pocketed my front door key. He didn't look up.

"She's gone, son. Gone."

I didn't know what to say. I couldn't hug or even touch him. We'd barely even shaken hands when we met. Men were like that in those days. I came into the room. My throat constricted, I asked if I could help.

Percy shook his head.

I thought for some reason the burden would be lifted then, but it wasn't. I thought it might all be over, but chance would be a fine thing.

The next morning walking to art school I saw two dowdy women across the road chatting, eyeing the house pointedly.

"What are you looking at?"

They didn't answer, backs stiffening as if affronted. The blonde one unfolded her thick arms, but they refused to move, as if doing so might enact some kind of defeat. I rounded the corner without giving them the satisfaction of a second glance.

It won't come as a vast surprise to learn that soon the whole business was the gossip of the life drawing class as soon as it hit the *Echo*. Things like that don't happen in Newport without everyone talking about it and making a meal of it. And that included my fellow students.

"God alive! Can you believe this? Man slept with his dead wife for three weeks after she died. Christ Almighty . . . "

"Give us that paper."

"Good God."

"Bastard must be sick in the head."

"Don't talk about it! I don't want to think about it! It's disgusting!"

"Can you imagine the niff? Christ! What a pervert! Must've been proper mad."

Nose to her crayon sketch, the Irish girl with the long hair pronounced matter-of-factly: "He'll be damned in hell for it, that's for absolutely certain."

"Only if he's Catholic."

"Nah. Catholics love dead things."

"Shut up!"

"Tell you what though, seriously. Your dick would need a good old dose of bleach afterwards."

"Thing is, would it be squidgy and full of pus, leaking out all over you, or hard as a board with a hole in it?" Groans, pretend retching and titters. "No, no—I'm curious. Really."

"Can't see the attraction, personally."

"The attraction is you're not twenty quid down getting her drunk, mate. Sounds good to me."

"Maybe he was just randy. Any port in a storm type of effort."

Sniggers.

"Anyway, consent and all that, you can't prove she said no, can you?"

I was burning up inside and now I was incendiary. I threw down my pencil and stood up. "You're sick, you are. All of you."

"What? He's the sick one. We're just talking about it."

"Well bloody don't!" I said.

The life model was leaning against the doorjamb, blowing cigarette smoke as I squeezed past her. "Lock him up and throw away the key, I say. He's a danger to children, whoever he is." I could smell the sweat under her copious talc. Everyone knew she'd been having it off with Max Prosser, even though he was a married man with two kids. Her scarlet fingernail paint was peeling and didn't match her lipstick. She was the one who made me feel sick. Matter of fact, they all did.

I got home that night and found Percy quiet but by no means dejected. I think he was living in a self-protective bubble, and under the same circumstances I'm not sure I wouldn't do the same. I definitely wouldn't be sitting going through my press cuttings or going to the pub for a chat with the locals. That would take nerves of steel and I don't think Percy had any nerves at all at that point. His wife had been taken away from him and the slow realisation of that was bound to be difficult. Horrendously so.

I'd bought a loaf of sliced bread and said I was going to make us beans on toast for tea. Wandering in as the toaster chattered, Percy told me he'd lost his job in the shop. When he went in to do the shopping for the old dears, the owners had said they didn't want him anymore. They said they didn't want any arguments, they knew he'd been putting his hand in the till—which was a complete lie, Percy said. It was just an excuse. It was obvious why they didn't want him to come back. I volunteered to go in and talk to them but Percy frowned, pained, and said he didn't want a fuss.

"Don't you mind what people are saying about you?"

"They can say what they like. There's only person who I care about, and she's not here, God love her."

Later, when I lifted his plate of untouched beans on toast and asked if he wanted the TV on, he said no, he wasn't that interested, I could watch if I wanted to but he was going up. He was tired.

At the door he hesitated, with his back to me.

"I expect they're saying I *did* things. I didn't. I just didn't want to let go of her, that's all. I didn't want to be on my own. Forty years we'd been together. She was my first sweetheart. And my last. I just wanted one more day, see. Then I thought, another day wouldn't hurt, would it? Then I thought . . . I don't know what I thought."

The next day I wanted to go to the shop and say to their stupid faces: "He loved her. That's all he did. He *loved* her." I wanted to, but I didn't.

At the weekend I took the train home and that was where the police spoke to me. Perhaps they'd got my number from Percy, I don't know, or he'd said he had an art student as a lodger and they got the number from the college. My heart beat faster as I took the receiver from my mum. I thought they'd make me feel stupid but they didn't. I made myself feel stupid by rattling on, trying to be chatty and sound as if nothing was amiss, when everything was amiss. As soon as they'd come off the phone my mother was there, wanting to know what on earth was going on, the police ringing. I said: "Look, just shut up, Mum. It doesn't concern you, all right?"

As it was, the police didn't press charges against Percy. I'm not certain what charges they could press. It wasn't the sort of crime they'd come across every day—if it was a crime at all, technically. They told me they'd appointed a psychiatric social worker. They said some other things but I didn't take in the details. The upshot was, they didn't wish to take it any further, in terms of prosecution. They didn't consider it a wilful criminal act, or something that required the full punitive force of the law. In fact, I got the distinct impression they wanted to brush it under the carpet.

"Good. Thank you."

"He is going to need care, though," the man on the phone said. "Does he have a daughter or son?"

"No," I said. "No children. Nothing. Nobody. Enid has a sister but she and Percy don't get on. All they had was each other."

The policeman told me there'd been a post mortem to "rule out any possibility of foul play"—which was as evasive a euphemism as any I'd come across, the more I thought about it. Considering what we were discussing he was a master of sensitivity and diplomacy, finally informing me that Enid's sister was in charge of the funeral arrangements. I thought of asking why Percy didn't have a say in the ceremony, but the answer was self-explanatory: though I didn't know if Percy would see it like that. I didn't know how Percy would see the situation at all. The conversation drew to a close as the officer enquired if I had any questions.

"How did she die?"

"Fatal heart attack. In her sleep one night, from how Mr Bisp described it."

The idea of Percy describing these matters to the authorities, of him facing a dark uniform across a scrubbed wooden table in an interview room, filled me with horror. The idea of him reliving it as he recounted it in detail upset me even more. I couldn't help imagining the moment as he woke up, bleary, to find his wife's body lying next to him in bed not only uncommunicative and inert but cold to the touch.

I sat in the darkened room for a while after I'd placed down the receiver thinking about the policeman's offer to arrange "someone to talk to", which I politely refused. Straight away I rang Percy, but got the engaged tone. I knew he'd taken his phone off the hook, and that sent off a whole pile of other alarm bells in my mind, and worries about how he was coping. My dad came in and said my mum was upset and he wanted me to explain what was going on. I said I would when I felt like it.

I still hadn't told them anything by the time our car pulled up outside that small terraced house in Newport the following Sunday night to drop me off.

I had my own key and let myself in, noticing a Squezy bottle lying in what was laughingly called the front garden (a mere strip of glass and a brick wall, really) but thought nothing of it until I stepped indoors and felt my nose assaulted by the strong reek of urine. It was immediately obvious what the plastic bottle had contained and what had been squirted through the letterbox. The idea of someone doing that curdled my stomach far more than the actual smell.

A mop and bucket of water mixed with detergent stood at the foot of the stairs, but there were no lights on other than the hall light I'd switched on as I came in. By now my dad's car was on its way back to Ponty. I called out Percy's name. No answer was the stern reply, as my nan used to say.

I put my foot on the bottom step and called out a second time, "Percy?"

I went upstairs, thinking he might have fallen asleep. He was always dozing off in the early evening and often I'd find him in his armchair with his head back, mouth wide open as if catching flies. Maybe he'd lain on the bed for a nap or, as I mounted the stairs, another dread thought occurred to me—that he might have done something stupid. I even rapidly began to think it far from unlikely. My grandmother and grandfather had died within days of each other, the latter of a fall, accidental or otherwise. Nobody in my family acknowledged or even voiced out loud the possibility that, for them, being apart from each other might have been impossible to bear. That they'd wanted to share death as they shared everything in life . . . As one . . .

But no. Thankfully my worst fear quickly dissipated. The bedroom was empty. The bed that Enid had died in—and lay in for weeks—stood perfectly, immaculately made without so much as a dent in the covers. Green nylon sheets pulled taut to the corners. Eiderdown as old as the marriage folded down at one corner. Cheap, flat pillows. The scent of Imperial Leather and Pledge furniture polish in the air. The vanity mirror with Enid's hairbrush and jewellery box arranged in front of it, the small earrings and starry brooch I remember her wearing, and a half a brick lying next to it.

My inevitable question was answered by a harsh and unexpected draught making the hairs on my arms prickle, which came from a hole in the smashed window through which said object had been hurled from the street, no doubt accompanied by some choice language at the time. I shuddered.

Downstairs I found Percy's shopping basket hanging up on its hook. Next to the telephone on the hallstand he and Enid grinned at me from the framed photograph taken on their wedding day.

For the life of me I couldn't think where he could be. He wasn't out socialising and he hadn't gone to see Enid's sister. He was always here to meet me when I arrived, or surely he would have let me know in advance? Even in his perilous state of mind—

whatever state of mind that might be. But deep down I could only think that something bad had happened.

I rang the hospital. At first the receptionist said sorry but they couldn't divulge the names of patients. I said that was ridiculous. I asked her name, because if something had happened to Percy and I wasn't told, there would be hell to pay. The tone of my voice more than anything forced her to put me through to somebody else.

No, I wasn't family. He didn't have any family. I said I was Mr Bisp's lodger. I lived in his house. I wanted to know what had happened to him, please. I was told he'd had an accident. The details weren't forthcoming so I decided to curtail the phone call and get over there right away.

He'd been beaten up on the bus on the Saturday evening. I don't know where he'd been or where he was coming back from, but some yobs recognised him from his photograph in the *Western Mail* and laid into him. The nurse told me his face had impacted gravel so she supposed he'd be thrown off. I saw a shrunken, misbegotten figure propped up in the hospital bed, helpless as a child— head swollen up so much he couldn't wear his glasses (which sat on the side table), two black eyes, one of them barely a slit, the other all colours of the rainbow, bandages wrapped mummy-like round broken ribs, swellings, bruising, cuts, contusions. What the heck had they done to him? Had a boot done that to his face? Hideously I could almost make out the imprint of a sole. I tentatively approached the hiss of the oxygen tube, not wanting to wake him unduly, but he had heard me come in and turned his head fractionally, as if even that hurt.

"You've been in the wars, feller," I said, sitting in the chair beside him. "Look at you."

He reached out and took my hand. Squeezed it. Out of the corner of my eye I saw the nurse plump the pillow on the chair by the window and leave without looking at us. Perhaps she'd read the *Western Mail* too.

"See the game Saturday?" Percy croaked.

"Bloody awful," I said.

"Bloody were." Percy said.

Every evening that week before I went back to the house, I made sure I went to the hospital. Sometimes he was chatty. Sometimes he was sleeping. But I sat there anyway in case he woke up. I wanted him to know I was there. I took him some apples. I knew he liked Granny Smiths—"nice and sharp"—not them sweet red things, and not grapes—"never been a grape person". Once or twice I got a smile out of him. Once or twice.

On one occasion I took my sketchbook with me and drew him, just for something to do. Nothing special or anything. No big deal, no different from any other scribble. By now I'd heard I'd got into Lanchester Poly in Coventry (as was) to do Graphic Design starting in September, so topping up the sketchbook had just become a habit. I didn't even want to show him the finished thing, but he twiddled his fingers in the air. He took a look at it and gave a tiny hoot. "Picasso, that is." I said, "If it is, I'm a millionaire."

When I got back home to Pontypridd that Friday my mother said there'd been a phone call, the person said they'd ring back. On the Saturday evening I was told the person had rung again while I was out and this time my mum gave me the number she'd scribbled down. I recognised the code for Newport. It was Enid's sister. I geared up for an argument, not knowing what she was going to tell me, but she said she'd heard yesterday from the hospital that Percy had died. I didn't want to say anything to her so I went quiet. I didn't really want to talk to her at that point. I blanked out what she was saying for a while then I heard her say it had probably all been too much for his heart. I said, "I thought his heart was all right."

She said she'd found my name in the address book next to the phone. "This is a hell of a task, I tell you."

"I feel for you," I said sarcastically.

"Yes, well . . ."

"You don't seem sad."

"Sad? I'm livid. The things that man did. It doesn't bear thinking about. To my own sister. What was going on in his head? It was disgusting."

"You never liked him."

She grunted. "No. Is it any wonder?"

"He never liked you."

"I bet he didn't. I wish she'd never set eyes on him. My sister was a good woman. Now look at her. Look what he's done. I'll never get over this. Never."

I thought, poor you. I hung up without saying another word.

In spite of her having my phone number and address I never got information about any funeral, either that of Percy or of Enid. Maybe they buried them side by side. Maybe, on the other hand, out of some bizarre desire for post-mortem decorum, they buried them in separate plots. I have no idea. I could have gone to the cemetery in Newport and looked, but I didn't. I didn't want to be morbid like that and I felt they deserved their privacy.

I sat at home that Saturday night and didn't talk about it, though I would in time. I slumped on the settee beside my mother watching *The Generation Game* or whatever it was on the telly in the sitting room. My father was installed in the middle room listening to the sports results. They didn't say a word to each other all evening. He came out at about nine o'clock and made himself a ham sandwich with sliced bread, then went back in and shut the door.

THE MAGICIAN
KELSO DENNETT

ALL TRICKS, ALL ILLUSIONS, funnel down to a few basic misdirections, at the end of the day. The majority of it is the patter, the *spiel*, the storytelling. The gift of the gab. Taking someone on a journey, but a journey that goes somewhere they don't expect, in a way they didn't expect.

I was born in Seagate and I've lived here all my life. It's strange that people flock here for holidays, or used to, and used to have smiles on their faces and happiness in their hearts at the thought of going somewhere different. To me Seagate was never different, never fun-loving or exotic in any way, never a place to get away from it all and have a good time. It was simply my home. I suppose at times I've envied the little families I saw inside the ice cream parlour on the sea front, or sitting with their fish and chips in newspaper on the benches facing the sea. But to be honest most of the time I thought they were stupid for thinking this place was in any way special just because there were sticks of rock with its name going down the middle. It certainly wasn't special to me. It was a dump.

The fun fair I remember being seedy ever since my childhood is derelict now, segregated by a massive chain-link fence and guard dogs, its name—*Wonderland*—nothing but a sick joke. The only people who have 'fun' there are the pill-heads and drug dealers whose scooters whine around the Esplanade from mini-roundabout to mini-roundabout touting their wares. Up on Cliffe Road a whole run of grand Victorian-era hotels lie abandoned, semi-restored by property developers who inevitably ran out of cash.

Sometimes you see a light on inside one at night time and wonder if it's a solitary owner living under a bare light bulb eating beans on toast, or a bunch of junkie squatters shoving needles in their veins. This is the image of the resort now, not candy floss and deck chairs, but inflatable li-los flapping in a bitter wind outside beachside shops that get more money from selling lottery tickets.

When they announced a big, new, posh art gallery was going to be built at the old fish market near the harbour, a lot of London people argued it would bring much-needed prosperity to the town. Predictably, the locals didn't want it. In fact they gathered hundreds of signatures on a petition about the loss of a car park where old ladies came in coaches to buy cups of tea and go home again. But that was typical. Seagaters have no interest in the outside world. They just want to keep all the things that made a crappy 1950s seaside resort crappy, even though it's dying on its feet.

Anyway, the art gallery happened, with a bistro-style cafe offering Mediterranean stuffed peppers and risottos of the day. Meanwhile, two streets away on the High Street, the most artistic thing you were likely to see was a wino coughing his guts up outside an amusement arcade or pound shop.

Sorry for not having a rose-tinted view of the great British seaside town, but I'm not the Tourist Information Centre. I live here. And I've spent all my life listening to people telling me I'm lucky—I'm not.

I guess when I heard that Kelso Dennett was coming, I thought that might change.

And it did.

I work in a hotel, though I don't have any professional qualifications. When my grandmother died, my dad had enough money to give up teaching, which he hated, and invest in a hotel, the White Hill—two AA stars, fuck knows how—on one of the narrow streets off Quayne Square leading steeply down to the sea. That's where I was born and that's my day job, setting the tables for breakfast and dinner. Serving hard, crusty rolls with watery, microwaved soup so hot it gives you mouth blisters. My father's made a profession of being pleased with himself. What he has to be smug about I have no idea. What is he? The owner of a shitty hotel in a shitty little town, and there he is, sounding the gong to call people down for dinner like it's the Ritz? What a loser. Still, he's happy running his little empire, and I've seen that gleam in his eye when he tells people he's fully booked. Power, that's all that is. It's pathetic, but in the present economic meltdown, in this armpit of the universe, there's precious little to give you any feeling of power over anything.

The power to change. To make things better. It's always seemed almost impossible. Yet there was one person in the world who was regularly telling us that *anything* was possible. That 'the impossible' was just a mindset to be overcome.

And suddenly, according to the *Advertiser*, he was coming to Seagate—to perform his most outrageous stunt ever.

Everyone knew that Kelso Dennett was a Seagate boy. Or, more accurately, from the Links—which, I remember from my childhood, was known as the rough part of town, synonymous with the poor part. You didn't want to mix with boys from the Links, my mum used to say. They were always kids who used to smoke in the street, and that said it all. To her mind, anyway.

It was also well known that the TV star's return to his home town was being touted as something of a gesture of thanks to the residents. Though the fact he said he was looking forward to it either meant he had lived in blissful ignorance of how much the place had gone tits-up (to put it mildly) or that the sentiment was complete PR bullshit to get the locals on side. After all, he had a reputation as a master manipulator. He was hardly going to rubbish the place. He was too much of a canny operator for that. He wouldn't have done it in Seagate if there wasn't something in it for him. As everyone who watched his television shows knew, there was always more than meets the eye. That was the attraction. That, and the prospect of real physical or mental harm.

Within days of the official announcement, the production company took out ads looking for runners. No prior experience necessary, but good local knowledge a bonus. I reckoned I was in with a chance, and my dad could find a temporary replacement or get stuffed, so I applied and got an interview. The form I had to fill in was about thirty pages long.

"Nick Ambler." My name.

"28." My age.

"Single." My status.

The girl with the razor-sharp marmalade fringe asked if I had a relationship.

"Sort of. A girlfriend. But only sort of." She asked her name and I said Cyd, spelt that way. "After Cyd Charisse. The dancer? *Singing in the Rain* and shit?"

She nodded in a vacant, prosperous kind of way and see-sawed her expensive roll-point pen as she asked the all-important question about local knowledge.

"I have that." I shrugged. "I've lived here all my life."

"Then you're perfect." She brightened, nodding again. "Nice town."

I thought, *You haven't lived here.*

She showed a lot of teeth but was pleasant enough, though the guy next to her, black guy—I mean *really* black, like ink—didn't say a word. But they must've liked me, because later, in The Bear, I got a text saying I'd got it.

The teaser ads were already going out between programmes, so it was no secret this was going to be a *Kelso Dennett Special*, as they called them now. This one, leaving very little to the imagination, and full of succinct, if dubious, promise, was called *Buried Alive*. (No prizes for guessing its central premise.) The magician was planning to be buried in a wooden coffin six feet under on the beach at Seagate—his most daring stunt to date—with no means of escape or communication, and no access to food or drink for the entire period. He would be sealed in the casket and that would be it, until they dug him up forty days and forty nights later.

As soon as they'd heard about it, certain corners of the media were, predictably, incendiary with outrage. It was shocking, yes. Audacious, yes. Mad, yes. But, frankly, you'd hardly expect anything less. Pushing boundaries—not only physical boundaries, but boundaries of what was acceptable as popular entertainment—was this guy's stock-in-trade. 'Going too far' had rapidly become his business model.

Previous 'specials,' which had involved apparent decapitation, invisibility, and even a poltergeist haunting, always caused controversy. It was almost part of the Kelso Dennett 'brand'—but now there was a new element, the element not just of jeopardy, or of harm, but of death.

From the moment it was announced there was a great deal of conjecture as to whether what he was attempting to do, and survive, was even medically possible. Was consummate showman Kelso Dennett really simply tarting up weary old illusions in new clothes (always the accusation), or genuinely (as he claimed in this case) forcing his physiological and psychological endurance to the absolute limit? It was, of course, impossible to tell.

Certainly, as a TV viewer, it was always hard to know exactly what methods he was using to achieve his mindboggling effects. You definitely couldn't trust what he *said* he was doing. His sometimes wild, irrelevant gestures or pseudoscientific preambles may be just that—irrelevant. And just because he said he wasn't using stooges, did that really mean he wasn't? His previous compulsive extravaganzas had relied on not just trickery but the use of techniques such as hypnosis and suggestibility—or did they? The paranormal waffle might just be window dressing for a gag no more complex than Chase the Lady or Tommy Cooper's bottle/glass routine.

Was the poor guy who thought he'd been in a time machine, or the couple who were convinced a serial killer was hunting them down, actually in on the joke all along? You always sensed that your eyes, and ears, were on the wrong thing—which was exactly where Kelso Dennett wanted them.

My job was to keep an eye on the assembled crowds standing at the rail on the Promenade—to keep them at bay. 'At bay' is probably too strong a phrase. But I had a Hi-Viz vest and a walkie-talkie which kept me in direct contact with the third assistant director in case some of the locals wanted to get a closer look at the set before the team wanted them to. I watched them setting up a white tent on the beach above the high-tide mark. The crew were busy in their various capacities, but I had little idea what most of them did. There seemed to be a lot of quilted windbreakers, a lot of pointing, a lot of coffee in polystyrene cups, and a lot of talk.

The production company, for their own convenience, were putting me up in the hotel where they were based. I told my dad my shifts would be weird so wouldn't be back to lay breakfast or wait at tables for dinner, and I squared it with Cyd I might not be around much too. In view of what happened, that was just as well, on my part. You might even think it was forward planning. It wasn't. I wasn't planning anything. All I was planning was earning some money.

I watched them digging the grave with a JCB. It wasn't like digging into soil, and the sand was dry, but eventually they managed to get a fairly good, rectangular hole without the walls crumbling or it filling with water. For some reason the police were in attendance, and so were the fire brigade. Possibly to do with Health and Safety. Probably to do with just seeing themselves on TV. We were going live at 10.00 p.m. and everything was stressed to the hilt.

On the far side of the beach I saw somebody talking to the man who did the donkey rides. Whether they were asking him to get into shot or get out of shot I couldn't tell. In the end he just stood there.

The crane shot went up beside me so that the crowd, which had now increased to several hundreds, if not thousands, on the Promenade and down the length of the pier, could see a high angle view of themselves on the big screens erected on the beach.

A second camera panned along the route of a hearse down the High Street. Security men parted the throng to allow it to drive down a slipway to a flat bed of concrete normally kept clear for use by the lifeboat crew and ambulances. Five undertakers got out and I was surprised to see that they weren't actors but the family firm that had operated in town for as long as I could remember—adding a macabre dimension of authenticity. Four acted as pallbearers, sliding a pale teak coffin from the back, hoisting it to their shoulders and following the fifth with complete solemnity towards the grave.

The dignity of the enactment seemed to make people forget they were watching an entertainment programme and the strangely reverential silence that fell continued as the undertakers lowered the coffin onto a rustling purple tarpaulin laid flat beside the grave, then stood aside with their heads bowed. The sense of anticipation was electric.

Similarly followed by street cameras, a black Mercedes with tinted windows glided through town and descended the slipway. A chauffeur opened the back door and Kelso Dennett stepped out—fashionably mixed race, distinctive shaved head. Small. Tiny. I hadn't seen him in the flesh before, but it was weird. I've heard people famous from TV have a presence when you meet them in real life, a kind of vivid familiarity because we feel we know them, we're intimate with them, I don't know, or maybe it was the makeup or the lighting—but he seemed to glow. His skin seemed literally golden against the black, zippered tracksuit one of the tabloids later said gave the proceedings a "dark Olympics" vibe. Anyway, the crowd went mental. If I didn't have a job to do, I think I might've gone mental too.

Calmly taking a microphone from a production assistant, he thanked everyone for coming and said in a high, surprisingly boyish voice he'd do his utmost to reward them for their faith and their patience. He faltered a little, very slightly giving away his nerves (unless that was part of the act), finishing by saying he got "succour and strength from their love and their prayers." He almost made it sound like a prayer itself.

Then, according to the voice-over, he was off into the graveside Winnebago "to mentally prepare for the greatest challenge of his magical career."

While he did, and while forensic experts from the Royal Navy and RAF examined the coffin inside and out, a pre-prepared VT about the Victorian fear of premature burial played to the gathered fans, with an obligatory nod to Edgar Allan Poe. It quoted from a hundred-year-old article in the *British Medical Journal* about human hibernation, in which it was said Russian peasants in the Pskov Governance survived famine "since time immemorial" by sleeping for half the year in a condition they called *lotska*, while James Braid (father of hypnotherapy) wrote in his 1850 book *Observations of Trance* that he had seen, in the presence of the English Governor Sir Claude Wade, an Indian fakir buried alive for several months before being exhumed in full health and consciousness. More recent findings came from a 1998 paper in *Physiology* which described a yogi going into a state of "deep bodily rest and lowered metabolism" with "no ill effects of tachycardia or hyperpnea" for ten hours. Another study, on a sixty-year-old adept named Satyamurti, recorded that he emerged from confinement in a sealed underground pit after eight days in a state of Samadhi, or deep meditation, during which time electrocardiogram results showed his heart rate fell below the "measurably sensitivity of the recording instruments."

Kelso Dennett, in ten-foot-high close-up, then gave chapter and verse on the techniques perfected by such mystics and gurus to cut down their bodily activity to the frighteningly bare minimum. The essence of hatha yoga, he said, is the maximization of physical health as the necessary basis for self-realisation—the purification and strengthening of the body as the means to effectively channel powerful but subtle forces (*prana*)—in this case, to slow the processes down to an extremely low rate, and so achieve a state of physiological suspension. "But this terminology and classification is multi-layered and elusive—not easily open to standard observation and measurement. The concepts are far from being embraced into mainstream biology and science. Some might say that makes them *primitive* or *superstitious*, but turning it the other way round, maybe science has got a lot to learn." A tiny light reflected in his dark irises. "My hope is to replicate these physical states—to hover on the very brink between life and death—and test them to the ultimate limit of what is humanly possible. I have prepared for this event not just for months, but for years. Perhaps even my whole life. Now I believe I am ready to successfully attempt it. But do the experts?"

As we were about to be told, clearly not.

The medical professionals interviewed were unanimous that the enterprise was foolhardy to the point of insane recklessness. As if to confirm this, we saw footage of Kelso Dennett training for long periods in a sensory-deprivation tank—but only for as long as *eleven* days, after which he sounded the alarm and was lifted out, gasping, dripping, shielding his eyes from the camera light. This time there would be no alarm button. No microphone. Nothing. For *forty* days.

The coffin having been pronounced tamper-free, a disembodied voice asked the crowd to remain absolutely quiet when the star emerged from the trailer so as not to disturb his intense level of concentration. The murmuring drained to a complete hush. He emerged barefoot and stripped to the waist, distinctive sleeve of tattoos up his left arm, pentagram on his right shoulder, astrological symbols inked all over his back, pure muscle, but wiry, a runner's physique, wearing only a pair of black Lycra shorts.

A woman wearing a fur coat, tight jeans, thigh-length boots, and shades threw her arms round him, and he kissed her. I saw she didn't want to let go of his hand. It looked as though she genuinely didn't want him to go through with it. She seemed upset but trying to control it. He hugged her and held her by the shoulders for a moment and looked into her eyes and she obediently backed away, tucking lariats of blonde hair behind her ears.

Everyone knew who she was. His wife, Annabelle Fox—most famous from a fish fingers commercial when she was five years old. Not done much since, other than date famous boyfriends, rock stars, or actors, from what I could tell.

We waited patiently in the freezing wind as the supervising medical team fitted him up to their biofeedback machines, attaching electrodes wired to their contraptions, the EEG and ECG. Immediately, flickering wavy lines appeared on the big screens and we could hear the magician's amplified heartbeat coming from the gigantic speakers. We were told it was forty beats per minute. A normal basal heart rate is between sixty and a hundred. Under sixty is called bradycardia and can be dangerous, but it's not unusual for an athlete to show a normal rate as low as forty—and Kelso Dennett was certainly as fit as an athlete.

He put his hands together over his chest in an attitude of prayer and gave a miniscule nod to the crowd, Hindu fashion. He climbed into the coffin and lay flat as the undertakers screwed the lid back into place.

The crowd remained silent and still as the pallbearers lowered it into the bespoke grave. Sand was first piled in by a bulldozer, then flattened by spades—an irrationally or perhaps rationally disturbing experience for those of us watching, resembling as it did some laboriously drawn-out execution in some far-off barbaric fundamentalist dictatorship. Later on some bright spark had the theory that there was an escape hatch to a fully fitted underground apartment kitted with plentiful food and drink, though how a "fully fitted apartment" could have been constructed under the beach of a popular English holiday resort without anybody noticing is anybody's guess.

Barely seconds after the spot was marked by a wooden cross, the magician's face appeared back on the massive screens, showing us in a pre-recorded message that he had written something down and put it in a sealed envelope, handed to the mayor of Seagate to place in a safe deposit box in a bank of his choice.

Close-up. "This envelope contains something vitally important—but it must only be revealed when the coffin has been removed from the grave after forty days and forty nights. Not before." Finally, and movingly, he said he believed he could perform the superhuman task he has set for himself, but fate might have other plans—and that if he failed, he wanted his family to know that he loved them very much. "And Annabelle, what can I say? You are my rock, my sun, my moon. I will see you in forty days and forty nights, my darling, or I will see you in the afterlife. God bless you all."

The end credits rolled—no music—as the camera tracked back from the grave, cross-fading to the ECG.

The woman with wind-tossed hair watched. Eyes behind sunglasses. Her cheeks white. Her lipstick red.

That night, when the crowds had dispersed and the production crew had drinks and canapés on the beach to celebrate, she left early. It must've been quite an ordeal for her, so I wasn't that surprised. It must've been a strange sort of thing to celebrate, if you were her. I watched her cross the beach alone, leaving the penumbra of the television lights, her husband's heart still pulsing with an even monotony in the air. When I went back to the hotel, there was no sign of her.

The next morning the cross was at an angle. Messages had been left there. Flowers, predictably. I guess security let them through the cordon. A trail of thin wires led from the grave to the trailer where the scientists had their equipment. The bass throb of the magician's heart was still beating loud from the speakers. It had become slower over the first twenty-four hours, imperceptibly at first, the number in the corner of the screen flashing thirty beats per minute—technically well into bradycardia. Near it I saw Annabelle Fox drinking one of the coffees in polystyrene cups. She was surrounded by members of the production team, but she looked terribly alone.

Eventually I plucked up the courage to sit next to her in the hotel bar, because nobody else did. She didn't know my name, but knew I was one of the runners. I'd brought her those coffees enough times. She said she thought she needed coffee right now.

"I love his shows." I ignored the fact she was tipsy. "What a great man."

She laughed. "Nothing is what it seems." She could see I didn't know why she'd said that, so changed the subject. Or did she? "You know, people talk about *charisma*, but they don't really know what charisma means. Charisma is power. The power to make the other person, the weaker person, to do exactly what you want."

"Is it?"

"Look at Aleister Crowley. You've heard of Aleister Crowley? Frater Perdurabo. Ipsissimus. Master Therion." I tried not to look blank. "Magick with a K. The Great Beast 666. Crowley wasn't particularly attractive. Pretty fucking far from it. He was a repulsive, pot-bellied old goat—but he was *charismatic* in spades." Her eyelids were heavy. "He'd say to a friend, 'Watch this.' And he'd follow a person down the street, make them faint to the floor by just *willing* them to. Just by staring at the back of their head. That's *real* magic. Through Crowley—through Thelema. Tantric rituals . . . Sex magic . . . " She looked at me lopsidedly. "My husband is really, *really* interested in sex." Then she held me with a steady gaze, rolling ice cubes in her glass. "You're interested in sex, right?"

"Yes," I said without thinking.

She rose and swayed and pronounced the need to go to bed. My room was on the same floor as hers and I said I was tired too. By the time we got out of the lift I wasn't sure what I'd heard or why I'd heard it.

"Do you want to come in for a"—she paused before the last word—"chat? I was going to say 'drink', but I think I've had more than enough of that."

Immediately I was through the door she started to undress and so did I. The bedside lights were on and neither of us switched them off. I told her I'd never felt so hard before. She laughed and pressed me down on my back, and knelt beside me and slipped a Durex over me with her fingertips. I came almost immediately but she kept me erect, a smile on her face the whole time. We switched positions and I felt her cold hands stroking my lower back then gripping hard as I drove in. She covered her mouth so that nobody could hear, but I snatched her hand away and held her lips with mine until we ran out of breath.

Afterwards I lay inside her and said I wanted to lie that way all night. She laughed like it was a childish but nice thing to imagine. Her skin burned against mine, but her hands and feet were like ice from a day on the beach. The soft thrum of his heartbeat touched the windowpanes as we lay in each other's arms.

She said she didn't like hotel rooms. They made her a bit crazy. I grinned, saying you can do crazy things in hotel rooms. She said Kelso liked the anonymity. The fact nobody could tell anything about you because a hotel room contained none of your belongings. None of your history.

"He doesn't like people knowing things about him. He's a bit paranoid like that. He's worried about the *paparazzi*, yes. It's enough to make anyone think they're being watched, bugged, hacked. It's a terrible feeling. But it's more than the press, to him. They're not the enemy anymore. *Everybody's* the enemy. *I'm* the enemy. He likes me to stay indoors as much as possible, or know exactly where I am every second of the day."

"Why?"

"He thinks I might give away his secrets."

"What secrets?"

"All kinds."

She went and crouched at the mini bar, a sprig of damp pubic hair visible in the gap between her buttocks. She returned with shorts of whisky emptied into teacups from the hospitality tray.

"When we were on honeymoon in Rome we woke up one morning and the bells were chiming in St Peter's Square. We'd asked for breakfast to be delivered to our room, and pastries and coffee arrived piping hot. He got up, stark naked, and put crumbs on the windowsill. I asked him what he was doing. He said he could control which bird would peck it up. I giggled, but he said he meant it. He came back and sat cross-legged on the bed next to me. I waited for seconds, minutes. Then he smiled at me and clicked his fingers and right at that moment—that *exact* moment, a bird landed and started eating up the crumbs."

"What first attracted you to millionaire Kelso Dennett?" I ran kisses up her arm.

She smiled. "Maybe his—manual dexterity . . . " She took my hand and placed it over her private parts, guiding my middle finger towards her clitoris.

"Obviously he likes to be in control."

"That's what magic is. The ultimate control of the external world."

"Well," I said. "He can't control you now."

I arched over to kiss her on the lips, but she stiffened.

"I think you should go." She held my face in her hands. "I'm enjoying this too much."

"So am I."

"I mean it."

She got off the bed and put her dressing gown on, pointlessly, not moving as she watched me dress.

"What's your name again?"

"Nick."

"Nick, this never happened."

"Pff. Gone," I whispered before closing the door.

My own room was significantly colder than hers, so I turned up the thermostat. My mind was racing. I knew I wouldn't sleep so I put on the bedside light to read, but the bulb was dead. I switched it off and on again, mystified, because it hadn't been dead earlier.

I saw Kelso's wife again at breakfast but she didn't acknowledge me with so much as a glance. I also saw her later in the catering wagon—a converted double-decker bus. I wanted to sit with her, in fact I had a fantasy of touching her up under the table, or her touching me up—but that was impossible. There was no way any of these people could find out what had happened between us. What was I thinking? That she would call a meeting? Announce it from the rooftops?

I looked at the rota. I stood at my allotted station, by the coin-operated telescope overlooking the sweep of the bay.

The grave had almost lost any delineation against the rest of the sand. You wouldn't have known where it was, if not for the circle of footsteps around the small cross, the fence of plastic ribbon attached to iron rods, the trailer containing the equipment, and of course the video projection screens and tall, angled spotlights, the kind you often pass on motorways when they have road works at night.

People gathered occasionally in small groups, pointing or taking snapshots or videos with their camcorders. Then they'd move on, or linger, sometimes not moving or speaking. Typical British holidaymakers with their anorak hoods up, peering around like meerkats, not wondering for a second about the metaphysics of life and death, wondering where to go to get a two-course lunch for under a tenner.

As well as the channel's news programme, which gave it a minute slot every day, there were teams from most of the terrestrial and cable networks, a few from America—where Kelso was big—and Japan, where he was even bigger. Then there was the locked-off CCTV cam pointed at the grave itself, uploading to the Internet on a dedicated website, buriedalive.co.uk, where you could watch 24/7. The fact there was very little to watch was irrelevant. It was already going viral on Twitter, with endless comments and retweets—"OMG loving @buriedalive"; "KD completenutterorgenius?"; "Cant watch 2 spookie"; "Diggin the Kels"—the numbers exceeding even the broadcasters' high expectations. It was quickly obvious that this wasn't just 'event' television; it was a national event, period.

The tall lights came on as the sunlight faded. The slippery rocks where Dad and I used to catch crabs reflected a shiny glow. The men in Hi-Viz vests protected the twelve-foot cordon around the grave, but they let through a little girl in a sky-blue parka and matching wellies who stuck her little windmill in the ground next to the flowers before running back to her mum and dad.

When my shift was over I went to the hotel bar. Kelso's wife wasn't there. I waited. She didn't appear.

I went to my room. Drifting to sleep, I started to hear scratching, like a small animal trapped in the cavity wall behind the headboard. A bird but bigger than a bird. Perhaps a squirrel. Wings or paws scurried as if desperate to escape. I was annoyed because I knew it would keep me awake. Obviously something had fallen down the chimney and got trapped—then I heard a sudden bang, like a door slamming, and it stopped completely.

I pulled on my jeans and went out into the corridor. Nobody else was out there. Surely the person in the next room must've heard it too? I raised a fist to knock on the room next to me, but I could hear the TV on. They were listening to the live coverage of

Buried Alive. I looked down the corridor to the far end. For some reason I expected Kelso's wife to be standing there, but she wasn't.

The next day I saw her overlooking the beach. I went up to her and leaned on the rail beside her. I wondered if she felt guilty and might move away, but she didn't. It was almost as if I wasn't there. Her eyes were fixed on the circus—by which I mean, her husband's grave.

"It's getting to people," I said. "Anticipation."

"That's what it's all about." She took a deep drag on her cigarette. I wondered if it warmed her. "Will people lose interest, d'you think?"

"They adore him. Look at the viewing figures."

"Things can change."

"Can they?"

"Have you read the newspapers today?"

"They can't get enough of him."

She exhaled a short, sharp breath. "You know what the papers are like. They build people up and up, then they like to knock them down. He's a cash cow right now, yes. But they could turn against him without batting a fucking eyelid." She sucked the cigarette like an addict.

"Are you afraid?"

"For him? Yes, of course. Always. But he knows what he's doing. He *always* knows what he's doing, don't worry. He plans it to the nth degree. You have no idea. He leaves nothing to chance, my husband the magician. He knows everything, absolutely everything that can happen, and will happen."

"That's what I mean. Does that scare you, ever?"

"What do you think?"

She crushed dead ash on the balustrade and brushed it off into the wind, her hair flickering and lashing like the torn shreds of a flag. I heard a rasping voice in my walkie-talkie and switched it off.

"The woman from *Hello* magazine is waiting to do an interview. She says she waited all day yesterday, with her photographer. The office are hassling me to hassle you, but if you don't want to do it, don't do it. Fuck them. I'll tell them you're not feeling well."

"Thank you."

Over the next few days I decided not to intrude into her space. In my spare hours I slept or when I couldn't sleep I watched old DVDs of Kelso Dennett's magic shows: *Bamboozler* and *Scaremongering* and *MindF****. You probably remember them all. I know I do. The man who wakes up to find all the doors and windows of his house have been bricked in. The girl made to think she can bend spoons. Even more astonishingly, the guy who wakes up in what he thinks is the past, thirty years ago, and meets *himself* as a child, having been hypnotised to think a lookalike boy actor was literally him.

This one set the tone for the outrageously ambitious and controversial 'specials' to come, some of the greatest 'did you see?' TV moments of all time. *Abduction*—inducing a UFO abduction experience. *Guillotine*—inviting an audience who believes in the death penalty to witness a beheading. *Invisible*—making a young woman think she is invisible for a day. *Sleepwalkers*—getting a dozen people to sleepwalk at exactly the same time, on the same night—making them climb onto roofs across the London skyline—a stunning image caught by a helicopter camera as the sun came up. In the minds of many it was the culmination of the use of technology and sense of 'event' that had become Kelso Dennett's hallmark.

Then there was the infamous Easter special, *Crucifixion*. Not hard to see why Christian groups were immediately up in arms. Badgered by the press, the magician explained he simply wanted to find out whether the experience was as truly transcendental as some claimed. No slight to any religion intended. Nevertheless, lobby groups found a loophole in the broadcaster's charter and the transmission was cancelled. It was rumoured that he went to the Philippines anyway, going through with the ritual without the presence of cameras. However there *were* cameras at Heathrow on his return, to film him—as I saw now—getting off the plane, hobbling, and with bandages round his hands.

I paused the picture as the phone rang. It was Annabelle's voice asking me to come to her room. I left the DVD in the player and went. She was already naked and her first kiss as she captured me in it tasted strongly of white wine. She almost gnawed off my lips, tore out my tongue. I wanted to do it the same way as before but she had different ideas and got onto the bed on all fours.

As we lay afterwards in our salty sweat, I asked her how she'd got the long, puckered scar I'd felt across her shoulder blade. She said her mother always told the story that when she was born she shot out so quickly she hit the bedpost.

"Unlikely."

"All right then. My father said I was an angel come down to earth. And that's where they had to cut off my wings so that nobody would notice. You prefer my father's version?"

"What about the other wing?"

She laughed and kissed my bare chest. I thought I could hear my own heart beating, but it wasn't. She didn't need to say anything.

I sat up and pulled on my socks and underpants. The sliding door of the closet was half open. Beyond my bisected reflection I could see a row of Kelso Dennett's suits on hangers, all black, all identical. Black patent leather shoes arranged perfectly on the floor.

"Nick? Stay."

On sentry duty, I looked down at the grave, a mandala-type geometry incised around it by a myriad of footprints, now. The print place in Church Street had the enterprising thought of printing *Buried Alive* T-shirts and were doing a roaring trade from a stall next to the fishing boats and cockle vendor. Groupies descended, some booking into B&Bs for the whole forty days. Others—the vultures of the tabloids, for instance—seemed to be hovering in morbid expectation, eager for him to fail, to die. I thought about him dying too. I thought about him lying in complete darkness in that coffin under the sand and not coming out. I thought about that a lot.

When I passed a camera crew one day, a female student from Israel was saying, "People are tweeting he's dead, but he isn't. That's just evil. He's not dead. He wouldn't leave us like that. He'll come back, I know he will."

On day twelve I asked permission to take Annabelle away from the set. I said I thought she needed it, and they bought that. They gave me petty cash to get a hire car. We drove somewhere, only about twenty miles away, but a nice place with a spa, and stayed overnight. We swam in the heated swimming pool. Booked two rooms but slept in one. Didn't even set foot outside the door one day. Made love ridiculously, non-stop. I called room service and ordered more champagne.

"Are you paying for this? You can't afford this."

I told her it was all on the production company's dime. Her expression changed completely. I crawled across the bed towards her, said it didn't matter, did it? "So what?"

She prowled the room for her smokes, then said she'd like to drive back to Seagate after lunch.

I said, "Fine."

We didn't converse over the food. Picking at her salad, she was dived on by some spotty lad from the local rag who asked her about the rumours her husband is dead, that the television company knew it and were covering it up. Annabelle seemed to tighten and wither, covering her face with her hands. I told the moron to get out and get lost, following him through to reception to make sure he did. Outside I caught another guy taking photos through the dining room window with a hefty lens. The two of them stood back and stared me out, like cornered rats, afraid of nothing.

Cunts. That explained it. I'd had a weird feeling all day. I'd sensed somebody watching us at the poolside while we swam. I'd thought I saw somebody, backlit by the sun, but when I'd wiped the water from my eyes they were gone. Like I say, that explained it.

We drove back in silence. When we were five minutes from the hotel, Annabelle placed her hand on my thigh, resting it there.

That evening I couldn't stand the laughter and music in the bar. I stood overlooking the beach, listening to the sombre toll of his heartbeat coming from the speakers, seeing the iridescent green lines of the projected ECG. Thirty people or more were gathered down there with candles, though whether they were Christians praying for his wellbeing or avid fans I couldn't tell. Were they proper visitors at all, or was it prearranged? You couldn't take anything at face value anymore. What was genuine public reaction and what was part of the shtick? The channel was after ratings, but they were legally culpable too, weren't they? Wasn't there some kind of professional duty of care? Could they be sued if he *didn't* come out alive? And if something went disastrously wrong, wouldn't they do everything they could to bluff it out, play for time—just like the reporter was saying?

Children were playing hopscotch on the sand near the giraffe lights and generator. I shivered at the unbidden fantasy that the trucks would move away, the electrics and machinery towed off, and he'd be left down there through lack of interest, a victim of the viewing public's fickle apathy. I shivered because I found myself almost willing it to happen.

"He's strong." Annabelle's voice, right behind me. "You have no idea how strong. He'll never let down his public. Never. They made him who he is. He'll never forget that. Never."

I held out my hand. Pale as paper, she took it. Pressed her lips against mine. When she stepped back she must've seen my eyes flicker.

"Nobody can see us."

"I know." I turned up my jacket collar and we walked to somewhere out of the icy wind, the little gift shop by the turnstile to the pier that sold fishing bait and postcards.

My teeth were chattering. "What are we going to tell him?"

"When?"

"When? When he comes out. What do you think I mean?"

"We tell him nothing, of course. Why would we?" She looked at me like I was the stupidest, most naïve idiot in the world. "Oh, Nick . . . "

"Don't be a fucking bitch, all right?" I turned my back to her.

"Well, what are *you* going to do? Tell your girlfriend?"

"Yes."

"No you're not."

"I *will*. I'm prepared to."

"To do what? Throw away what you've got?"

I barked a laugh. "Got? What have I 'got'? I've got nothing. You're kidding. This place? This life? In this dump? It means fuck-all to me."

"You don't mean that."

"I fucking do. And don't act as though all this is bollocks, what we've been doing together for the last twelve days, because I know—"

"Oh, grow up! You've had good sex. I've had good sex. I'm not saying I haven't enjoyed—"

"Oh, thanks a fucking—"

"I just don't want to take away—"

"You're not taking away *anything*!" I turned on her. I'd had enough. "For fuck's sake, you're *bringing*. Bringing me everything I've ever wanted! Christ. I've never felt so . . . "

"What?"

I choked back the word, then thought, fuck it. "So . . . *alive*."

Her eyes filled up and her lip curled. "Go. Go."

I knew I wouldn't be invited to her hotel room that night. I thought I may even have blown it completely. I sat in my room and sobbed. I felt like doing a Keith Moon and tearing the room apart, disgusted with myself that I was so fucking well brought up I'd never do anything that would embarrass my parents. I thought, fuck my parents! I looked down at the ghost-written biography of Kelso Dennett I'd thrown at the wall. It had fallen open at a photograph taken in India. He was fire walking. Everybody was grinning. He was taking Annabelle by the hand. She was doing it with him, stepping barefoot onto the coals, but she looked frightened to death.

 I heard a rap at the door. She took me by the hand and led me down to the beach. She found a secluded spot out of sight of the men in Hi-Viz jackets, under the shadow of the lip of the Promenade, not far from the concrete slipway. She knelt on the sand and took me into her mouth. The mixture of hot and cold was explosive. I almost passed out in a shuddering fit. My fingers ran through her hair, which was the colour of seaweed in the spill of artificial lighting. I yelped, "No." I said, "No." I was facing the grave and she wasn't. I turned my cheek to the wall and shut my eyes.

At the twenty-day mark, I thought things would settle into a routine as far as the stunt was concerned, but I couldn't have been more wrong. The tension, far from easing off, was ratcheting up unimaginably. Everyone could feel it, and the callous metronome of those insidiously slow heartbeats—fifteen beats per minute now—did nothing to calm anybody's nerves.

 I was getting blinding headaches. Maybe it was because I was existing on Red Bull to pep me up through a whiskey hangover most of the time, or maybe the pressure of lying to Cyd was getting to me. I was flying off the handle and giving excuses why I couldn't sleep at her grotty one-bedroom flat, cuddled up on stinking nylon sheets. I blamed it on the job, but the truth was I couldn't stand the sight of her anymore with her M&S cardigan and lank, boring hair. I'd say I was going for a walk, but I wasn't going for a walk, I was going to her. To Annabelle Fox from the fish fingers commercial I used to watch when I was seven years old.

"Did he really spend months at a Tibetan monastery?"

"No. Not months. Years." She was sitting up, twisted in crisp white sheets in our post-coital sheen. "See, what people don't understand is his body doesn't matter to him. It's just an instrument. The mind is what matters. That's how he got into tattoos and scarification and body modification. Medicine men who put needles through their cheeks and don't feel a thing. It's all about physical extremities, pain, distress, fear—whatever—anything to remove you from your sense of self, your sense of mortality."

"I'd have thought his mortality would be all too important to him, down there in the dark, alone."

She looked at her own reflection. "That's because you're not him."

"Good."

She didn't turn to me. "It *is* good."

We fucked again, deliciously, freer now, and while I was in the bathroom disposing of my used Durex I heard the sound of a glass smashing. I shouted but Annabelle didn't answer. When I came back into the bedroom she said it was an accident, she'd dropped it. Although she was in bed and the glass was over on the coffee table.

I didn't say anything, but I had a strange feeling that what she told me wasn't the truth.

Later that night I woke up in the dark of the room. It must've been four or five in the morning, but really I had no idea. It scared me that my heart was drumming in my chest. It was inside my ears and it made me think of the heartbeat coming from the speakers down on the beach. At the same time I had a definite, overwhelming sense of a presence. Of someone in the room. Luckily my eyes had opened because if I'd had to open them I wouldn't have.

A spill of intense yellow came from the bathroom—one of us must've left the light on. Illuminated by it stood a figure. A man standing there, arms hanging at his side, simply looking at me. Looking down at the bed. It was Kelso Dennett, dressed exactly as he was when he stepped into the coffin. Naked to the waist, Lycra pants, sleeve of tattoos, pentagram, shaved head.

I switched on bedside light.

"Wha . . . ?" Annabelle rubbed her eyes, contorting against her pillow. "Nick? Jesus . . . " I was blinking too, inevitably—the sudden brightness flooding my vision, a complete searing whiteout. "What the hell?"

But by the time my eyes had got accustomed to the glare, there was nothing to tell her, because there was nobody there. "Fuck. Nightmare. Really bad. Shit. Sorry. Sorry." I kissed her. "Sorry. It's gone. Gone . . . "

But it didn't go.

It didn't go at all.

The next night I sensed him in the room again. In the exact same place, like a replay. Like the image from the DVD. Except this time I didn't turn and face him, and this time I could feel him walking slowly towards the bed.

I didn't open my eyes.

He stayed there for several minutes, but it seemed like hours. Perhaps it *was* hours. I have no idea.

And I thought: *How long has he been there? How many times before and I haven't noticed?* And I tried to close my eyes even tighter, and shut out the sound of his beating heart, but it only seemed to get louder.

The days come, and the nights, and I haven't told Annabelle what

I saw standing by the bathroom door, not that I'm sure what I saw, or even if I saw it. When you think about what you did yesterday, it's like a dream, isn't it? If somebody told you it didn't happen, or it happened differently, you wouldn't be able to contradict them, would you? All you could say is—well, what *would* you say? I don't know.

I don't know what to say to her. I don't know whether to ask her to come to my room instead of me going to hers, or whether that will even make any difference. Why should it?

Now, I hardly sleep anyway because I can't bear the thought of waking in the middle of that night with that feeling of panic in my chest. I can't bear it because I know who will be there, looking down at me.

Jesus Christ. Jesus Christ . . .

Twenty-nine days now. Thirty tomorrow . . .

I count them like a prison sentence. With my unblinking eyes fixed on it, the digital clock at the bedside moves past midnight. I can hear her gentle breathing inches away from my back. I feel the aura of another warm body next to me. I cling to her the way a child clings to its mother, and she strokes my hair.

She has no idea what is inside my head. She has no idea what is in the room. Now it's my secret.

It's all about *my* secret now.

Day thirty-six . . .

The headaches are worse than ever. I need to go to the doctor. The doctor has to give me something for this. It's not normal. It just isn't.

And I know the viewing public is getting excited, but I'm starting to spend all my waking hours thinking what they are going to find when they dig down and bring up his coffin. My stomach knots on a regular basis. Is he going to be dead? Is that his last, greatest trick, after all? The great almighty fuck-you? Then, at other times, I become absolutely certain that when they dig him up, the coffin will be empty.

I'm not sure which of the two eventualities terrifies me the most.

Which is why I dare not sleep anymore. I can go four nights without sleep, can't I?

Just four nights. Of course I can. I'll make sure I can.

Then it will all be over.

I dare not close my eyes. Because shutting them means opening them—and opening them . . . what the *fuck* will I see?

BBC News (UK)
BAFFLING TV "STUNT" ENDS IN HORROR: MYSTERY OF MAGICIAN'S "FINAL TRICK"
Thursday 11 April 2013 12.44 BST

DNA tests are expected to confirm that the body found under Seagate beach yesterday—buried in a coffin as part of a stunt by an acclaimed television illusionist—is that of local man Nick Ambler.

Mr Ambler, 28, was the son of hotel proprietor Stuart Ambler and his wife Corinne, and had been working on the production as a runner.

Detectives have said they want as a priority to interview TV magician Kelso Dennett, whose present whereabouts are unknown. They are also urgently seeking his wife, actress Annabelle Fox, to help them with their inquiries.

Famous for controversial and sometimes blasphemous stunts, the showman had returned to his home town claiming, in typically audacious fashion, that he would survive being buried alive for forty days and forty nights. It was only when the coffin was exhumed yesterday that the body of the dead man was discovered.

A spokesperson for Kent Police said: "Initial findings indicate that the young man had been in the coffin for the entire forty days. Scratches on the inside of the lid, together with broken fingernails, indicate a desperate and no doubt prolonged and agonising attempt to escape."

Last night, in the glare of the news cameras, the visibly shaken Mayor of Seagate opened the sealed envelope entrusted to him by Kelso Dennett before he stepped into the coffin forty days earlier. It contained a single sheet of paper, folded once, on which was written just two words in block capitals—the name of the deceased.

NEWSPAPER HEART

A ROCKET WHOOSHED AND POP-POPPED somewhere in the night. Iris Gadney's heart jumped. She hated this time of year. It always crept up on her, and her biology reacted before her brain did. It was funny like that. She should know by now, but she never did. It was always unexpected, the knotting in her stomach that came with the smell of sulphur in the air. What was in fireworks anyway? Gunpowder, she imagined. She didn't really know. She could ask her husband. He taught Chemistry after all. He'd know. But she didn't want to. She didn't care. She just wanted November the fifth to come and go and everything to return to normal. That's all she ever wanted—normality.

Des hadn't so much as twitched at the noise. In fact hadn't moved from behind the *Daily Express* for at least twenty minutes, but she knew better than to try to winkle him out of his shell into conversation. When he came home from work he was like one of those deep-sea divers who have to go into a decompression chamber. He was never himself—whatever 'himself' was—until he'd gone through the sports results, always reading the paper backwards, as if world events like the Vietnam War and the famine in Biafra, the latest pronouncement by Prime Minister Ted Heath ('Ted *Teeth*' as Des called him) or the army firing rubber bullets in Northern Ireland, were of far less importance than men kicking a ball around—which, to him, they probably were.

She went into the tiny scullery at the back of the house, and was halfway through making tea, buttering sliced bread for some corned beef and Branston sandwiches, when she heard the familiar ding-dong (*Avon calling!*) of the doorbell.

"Who's that?"

"I don't know, do I?" Iris lowered her voice to a sarcastic murmur as she wiped her hands on a tea towel and strode past the expanse of newspaper. "I expect it's for me. I expect it's Blue Boy from *The High Chaparral* . . ."

By the time she got to the front door Kelvin had already opened it and her mood instantly lightened because he was facing another eight-year-old, Gareth Powell (she knew his mam Gloria, only by sight, mind). It hadn't happened much before—a friend coming to call. It hadn't happened *ever* before.

"Mam!" Her son looked over his shoulder at her with eager eyes under the scissor-line of his fringe. "Gareth wants me to go out to play. He says a whole pile of boys are up the quarry making a bonfire!"

"Well you can forget that for a start," Des said from the sitting room before she could answer. "There's probably a load of yobs from the Sec Mod up there, and I'm damned if I'm running you to hospital because some headcase does something bloody daft."

"They're only collecting wood," Kelvin bleated.

"You're telling me they're not going to be messing round with sparklers? And matches? And *bangers*? 'Course they are—and little nippers like you are the ones that get picked on. When I was in school a lad called Truscott got a jackie jumper put in the hood of his duffel coat. We never saw him again after that."

"Gareth, love. Why don't you come inside and play?" Iris offered, ever the peacemaker. "You can go in the middle room."

Kelvin frowned hard. "He *wants* to go up the *quarry*!"

"Yes, well, *you're* not—and that's final," his father called, shirtsleeves rolled up, tie still on. "If he wants to go, he can go on his own."

Kelvin swivelled his head back to his friend, who was already looking sheepish and backing away as if frightened. Perhaps his dad didn't talk to him the way Kelvin's dad talked to Kelvin.

"Gareth?" Iris said.

The boy didn't meet Kelvin's eyes and his cheeks reddened as he faded into the shadows beyond the glow of the porch light.

"I—I'll see you in school tomorr—"

The word was broken by a crackling rasp in the sky and splutter of magenta, the explosion above spilling arrows of sodium yellow. Iris's heart sank and he was gone.

"Hey. Children's hour is on." She pressed the door shut. Kelvin was already climbing the stairs, head downcast. "Tea's ready in a minute."

"I'm not *hungry*."

"Don't be ridiculous. You got to eat. Get down here. *Now*." The slight lift in his dad's voice was more than enough to get Kelvin to do as he was told. "I'm not in the mood for it, all right?"

———

The corned beef and pickle sandwiches were eaten in silence. Kelvin had a face that looked like it was chewing cardboard, and that annoyed his father, who glowered. "Having a meal together is important. He can see his friends in school."

"Lots of things are important, Des," Iris said quietly. "Lots of things."

"Please may I leave the table?"

Kelvin's mother told him of course he could. His father told him not to slam the door. Both adults listened to his small footsteps on the stairs.

"He needs to watch that. The face on him." Des drank the last of his tea and replaced the cup in its saucer.

"He's only a kid. God help him, whatever he does he can't please you."

"Maybe he can't," Des said. "I never pleased *my* dad."

"That's no reason to take it out on him."

"Let's just pack it in there, can we? Christ . . . " Des ran his fingers through his flat Brylcreem-slick of hair.

"If it's work, don't take it out on him. That's all I'm saying. It's not his fault you don't get on with the new Head. It's not his fault you're taking on extra duties to try to impress her, things you—"

"It's not work," Des cut in.

And she knew it wasn't. She also knew he wouldn't talk about what it was. How the hell could he talk about it when he couldn't even look her in the eyes? In the beginning she'd wanted to say something, and sometimes she tried, but all she got was a stone wall, and no tears. Never any tears. The tears were all hers. And if he'd let go—just once—she might have thought they were sharing something. But he never did. Never could. And it made her feel like a cow, bringing this badness into his life every time she opened her mouth and every time she walked through the door. Sometimes she wanted to ask him if he wanted her gone. And she *would* go, except deep down she knew he needed her to cling to, like a drowning man needed driftwood. Not a particularly nice or wonderful piece of driftwood, just something that was better than nothing to keep him afloat.

He caught her wrist as she gathered the plates. "Hey. I love you."

"Well, love *him* too, occasionally."

"I can't help it."

"Yes, you can," Iris said firmly, managing to avoid her voice cracking. "If I can, you can."

Kelvin was monosyllabic over his cornflakes, and Des seemed to want to match him for sullenness, as if two could play at that game. Iris, as ever, was piggy in the middle, relieved to have the house to herself as Des drove off up to Porth in time for assembly and Kelvin left to trudge his weary way down to the primary school in Tyfica Road. By himself, of course. Always by himself.

A lonely little figure—but perhaps he wasn't lonely at all. Still, it gave her a little stab in the heart every morning as she waved him goodbye. She always told herself he'd probably meet some mates on the way and chat and have a lark around, as boys do. But *what* mates? He never talked about any. Or he'd talk about one, and the next week they wouldn't be friends anymore. She remembered the awful perils of her own playground life: finding a best friend one minute who turned into a horrible enemy the next. A bit like marriage. God, did she really think that?

At dinnertime Des stayed in Porth and got something from the school canteen—silly driving all the way home to barely have time to bolt his food—but Kelvin came back, and this was a time she looked forward to. They could talk about stupid things. Different things. But today Kelvin didn't seem to want to talk at all.

She asked him what was wrong. At first he didn't want to say. She asked if it was about his dad. He said no. What was it, then? "Come on. Tell me. I'm your mam."

"I don't know. I just saw these boys on the way home, and they had a sledge, just a box with wheels on, but it had this guy in it and it had a . . . one of those . . . waistcoat things and a sheriff's badge pinned on it, and a face with a beard stuck on, and a floppy hat—and it looked *brilliant*."

She shrugged. "Well, we can make one of those."

"Can we?" His eyes looked like they'd pop out.

"'Course we can. Don't be daft. It's easy."

"Dad won't like it, though."

"'Course he will. He did it himself when he was your age. Everyone did. Come on. He's staying in school to do some marking tonight, so we'll start it now and do the rest before he gets home." Before she'd finished the sentence her son was out of his chair, baked beans on toast abandoned. She smiled. For some reason she felt almost as excited as he did.

They chose the clothes together. Iris suggested that old, baggy pair of trousers Des wore when he was decorating. They'd seen better days and were only fit for the bin. Then there was that red polo-neck jumper that *had* been put out with the rubbish, shrunk in the wash and too tight for her husband's burgeoning potbelly—she salvaged that from amongst the potato peel and tin cans. It smelled of tomato soup and earth, but Kelvin said it was great, and he was the boss. He snatched it off her and she couldn't admonish him. It was fabulous to see him enthusiastic about something, lost as if in a quest for treasure as they raided bedroom drawers for a pair of old grey football socks and some woollen gloves that were a Christmas present from an auntie in Aberdare: white, with green holly leaves on the back.

They laid out all the items on the carpet in the sitting room. Even the rough shape of the trousers, socks, gloves, and sweater had the immediate semblance of a person, although an extremely flat one—this was shortly about to change. Iris switched on the transistor radio. They sang along to the recent number one, "In the Summertime" by Mungo Jerry. Kelvin was grinning from ear to ear. Iris dumped a mound of old newspapers, which had been gathering beside the fireplace, and both of them started scrunching up the pages of newsprint into balls, stuffing them deep into trouser legs Iris had knotted at the ankles with string. In no time the lower limbs began to thicken lumpily, rolled-up paper filling in the hips, groin and pelvis.

"Don't do any more till I get home," Kelvin said breathlessly as he left for school, but Iris couldn't resist finishing the task she'd begun. Sewing box open beside her, she stitched the bottom of the poloneck to the waistline of the trousers, after which she bit off the loose thread with her teeth. Alone in the house now, looking down at the semi-deflated-looking body draped across her lap, she felt ridiculously like a surgeon repairing some wound. Repairing a life. Not building, but resurrecting. Silly . . .

She abandoned it for the ironing, not even looking into the room for the rest of the afternoon. She didn't know why. But when Kelvin burst in his feet didn't touch the ground. He skidded on his knees onto the sitting room carpet and he was instantly shoving more screwed-up pages of the classified ads from the *Western*

Mail—births, marriages, deaths—into the cavity of the pullover. She chuckled as he stuffed it into the open neck, watching the torso fill as if with bone and tissue. The arms were tied at the wrists and soon sported white woolly gloves with flappy, insubstantial fingers like the teats of uninflated balloons. They worked to "Tears of a Clown" by Smokey Robinson and the Miracles, "Back Home by the England World Cup Squad" and "The Wonder of You" by Elvis Presley—a song Kelvin said was for old people but his mam said she liked it because it was romantic. She knelt on the floor with him and sewed the football socks, now bulked out with paper like the rest, onto the knotted stumps of the ankles.

"I know!" An idea galvanised Kelvin and he vanished upstairs, reappearing with a shiny, frog-green anorak that hung in his wardrobe even though he'd grown out of it a long time ago. Together they dressed the guy in it, sliding one arm then the other into the sleeves. It lolled between them, feeling as though it should be heavy but light as a feather. Kelvin stood back, admiring his handiwork. "He looks good, doesn't he? I think he looks the *best*."

His mam smiled. "Needs a head, though, don't you think?" The hood gaped like a feeble mouth. "What are we going to use?"

"We'll find something."

"Hang on. Where are you going?" He'd already hoisted the guy in his arms and was shuffling to the door en route to his bedroom. "Don't you want to show your father?"

Kelvin whispered, "Not yet." He put his finger to his lips as he heard the back door open and close. And when, over tea, Des detected the whiff of secrecy between them and asked what the two of them had been up to, both of them said, almost in unison: "Nothing."

Friday was the day Iris got her meat and veg from Ponty Market and, as often as not, if her timing coincided, went to Tyfica Road to collect Kelvin from school at home time. Children were already drifting out of the school gates in twos and threes, chatting and playing boisterously or blowing pink spheres of bubble gum, yet her heart ached a little bit to see her own son walking alone, idly scuffing his feet along the pavement, the strap of his school bag pulling his jumper half off his shoulder.

"Look!" He suddenly piped up as he saw her, running up, thrusting a punctured Adidas football in her face—the black and white patterned type they'd used that year for the World Cup in Mexico. Seeing her perplexed expression he swiftly added, almost too excited to get the words out: "For his *head!*"

Des remarked that the lad had lost his appetite and found a horse's. Kelvin had scoffed his fish fingers in record time, asked if he could leave the table, and was gone in a flash.

"He's got ants in his pants."

"That's boys for you."

"What does he do up there?"

"I think he's got a hobby." Iris didn't like lying and knew she wasn't good at it. She watched her husband get up from the table, turn over the cushions on the settee, delve through the magazine rack. "What are you after?"

"Last week's *Echo*."

"I chucked it out, I expect."

"Thanks. I hadn't read that."

"Sorry. How was I to know?"

"Bloody hell. I better move quick round here or *I'll* get thrown out."

"That's true."

She kissed him on the cheek, sat down, and turned up the telly. Gordon Honeycombe was reading the ITV news and she pretended to watch, but she was thinking about the guy upstairs, with his Adidas football head, which she'd sewed into place on the throat of its scarlet polo-neck, sitting cross-legged on her son's bed, Kelvin watching her raptly, chin on his fists, before her husband got home.

As she made the bed she stepped on a human hand and jumped back with a shrill yelp. Quietening her heart with the flat of her hand she looked down at the white Christmas glove at the end of a misshapen arm sheathed in anorak green.

Hell!

Annoyed, she poked it with her toe, but each time it fell back into place so she bent down to shove it back under the bed where the rest of the effigy was hidden. Now on her knees, she couldn't avoid seeing its bulbous chest packed with paper sinews sandwiched between the carpet and the bedsprings. In the dark it looked like a body wedged in a coffin. She didn't look at it for long, and stood up. It was Saturday so Des had gone to Cardiff with his cronies to see a match. Cardiff City were playing Hull F.C. at Ninian Park and they always went to a pub first to get the 'atmosphere' with other supporters over cheap pies and Brains bitter. Kelvin had nipped out to spend his pocket money, but when she heard the front door slam— that making her jump too—she knew he'd returned.

"What's that?" she said, meeting him on the landing. He was carrying a brown paper bag. He walked straight past her.

"Come and see."

By the time she'd entered the bedroom again he was hauling the guy out from its hiding place, and slung it, football-head nodding and jerking, onto the bed.

"I bought it from Gould's," Kelvin said, meaning the newsagent's round the corner from the Army Recruitment Office, opposite the Muni. It was where he bought his *Beezer*, *Dandy*, *Spider Man* comics, and Marvel Classics like *20,000 Leagues under the Sea*. But this wasn't any of those. This was a plastic mask with an elastic loop at the back. A shiny, pink mask of the face of a baby, with a ginger curl in the centre of its forehead and holes for pupils.

"Why that one?" Her thought came out in a breath. She heard it like it was said by somebody else, trying to blink but fixated on watching him place it over the blank football head. "Why not Guy Fawkes, love? I mean—the traditional one, with a pointed beard?"

"I don't know." Kelvin shrugged, his back to her. "I just saw it and I thought it would suit him. Come on. I want to show you something else." He jumped up, taking her by the hand, the guy trailing under his other arm. "I got it from the dump."

At the bottom of the stairs was a pushchair, filthy and scuffed, but otherwise fairly intact.

"His car. His chariot," Kelvin said, hoisting the guy and plonking it into the seat. The baby face tilted to one side and he adjusted it, punching it gently into position, tucking in one stray, poking-out arm.

"Does he like it?" she found herself saying, just to say something. Just to fill the air.

"He doesn't *like* it—he *loves* it!"

And—silly—she didn't remember much else except the squeak and squeal of the wobbly wheels as he manipulated the pushchair towards the open door. She didn't remember—silly thing—what he said, just that he was going out and she was still standing on the stairs and she remembered telling him, hand splayed on the wallpaper, not to be long and that she was going to have a (breath) lie down . . . Just a (breath) little lie down for five minutes . . .

The door banged and she woke in fear. Her first thought was that Kelvin had just left, but why was she lying on the settee, and why was the room in darkness? Why wasn't the light on? Why was it dark outside and why weren't the curtains drawn? She looked at her watch and saw to her shock it was half past seven. She shot to her feet, but the blood drained from her head instantly and she had to steady herself on the back of a dining chair.

"What the bloody hell's going on?" Des filled the room,

flicking the light on, blinding her. When she could see again she saw him marching in Kelvin like some condemned prisoner, the kid clutching the guy to him in a tight and resilient embrace with his father's meaty hands clamped on his shoulders.

"I don't know. I fell asleep. I told him not to be out long. Where was he?"

"Where *was* he? I'll tell you where he was. Down the bloody precinct! Out begging!" Her husband's eyes were ablaze. She'd never seen him so angry. Never so close to being out of control, and that frightened her, but instinct to protect her son overwhelmed it.

"Des. It's a *game*, for God's sake—they all do it."

"Yes, the layabouts! Those boys with no hope. The *poor* kids. Boozing and smoking fags because they've got nothing better to do. From Berw Road and up the Common. Educationally subnormal, the lot of them!" He tossed a sheet of cardboard emblazoned in black block capitals with the words PENNY FOR THE GUY onto the settee where she'd been curled up asleep moments before. He gestured at it, gasping for words, as if its very existence were a massive personal insult. "Is *that* what I'm working for, all the hours God sends, and your mother's slaving away at home for? Is it? For you to go out there and show us up? Well, *is it?*" Kelvin was staring at his shoes, his shoulders hunched, and Iris felt sorry for him, in fact she wanted to hug him, but dared not. "You know who was in the car with me? Elwyn, Dick, Ike Jones—my *friends*. The people I work with. What do you imagine they were thinking, eh?" Kelvin didn't have an answer, or didn't feel inclined to give one. "I'll tell you what they were thinking. That I can't look after my own son, and there he is out on the street like a bloody ragamuffin asking people for money because he doesn't get given enough at home! Like his parents are bloody *depriving*—"

"Des—"

"It's not *begging*," Kelvin muttered, showing a scowl now. "*Everybody* does it."

"Yes, well *you*'re not everybody!" Des heard his son mumble something. "What was that?"

"Nothing."

"Nothing. Good job it's nothing. It *better* be nothing, I tell you!" Des turned away, exasperated beyond his power of expression, walking back and forth in the miniscule sitting room like a bear in a cage. "I'm . . . I'm ashamed of you!" He snatched up the cardboard sign and threw it onto the open fire.

"Oh for God's sake!" Iris cried out, crouching quickly and retrieving it before it fully caught light. "I tell you what you should be ashamed of: the fact your son was afraid to tell you about this because he knew you'd blow a flamin' gasket!" She thrust the flimsy sign, only slightly charred, towards Kelvin, a gritty whiff of coal smoke stinging her nostrils. The boy held it tightly to his chest and backed away. Pulling out the sheet of cardboard made the glowing embers of the coal fire reignite with crackling vigour. But this was as nothing compared to the inferno Iris saw in her husband's dry and unblinking eyes as the realisation sank in.

"You *knew* about this?" His voice thinned like his lips in disbelief.

"Yes. Of course I did. I helped him, if you must know. What's wrong with that? All the kid wants to do is go out and enjoy himself with his friends."

Des laughed. "What 'friends'? He hasn't *got* any friends."

"Well we all know whose fault that is, don't we? You're like a bloody big kid yourself."

"And you're not? Making a doll for him? What's that supposed to do for him, eh? A big bloody doll. That's what it is, isn't it? Why don't you buy him a Barbie while you're at it?"

"Oh, go and boil your head. I'm sick of this. I'm sick of you and your . . . "

Iris stopped as she saw past Des that the ribbed glass door to the hallway was ajar, and beyond it the pushchair from the dump was parked, but there was no sign of the guy and no sign of Kelvin. She hurried past Des, shoving him out of her way, and stood at the foot of the stairs in time for them both to hear the slamming of Kelvin's bedroom door.

"Now look what you've done."

"Me?"

"Yes you." Iris returned to the room, shook an Embassy from her packet and lit it with trembling hands. "All he was doing was going out playing because you don't let him. What the hell is he supposed to do?"

Des pinched the bridge of his nose with his fingertips. "I don't care. I really don't."

"No, you care more about John Toshack than you care about that boy up there. Well you'd better. And bloody fast too, I'm telling you. Or do you want him to grow up hating you?" He looked daggers at her for that. "Or does what your beloved cronies down the club think count for more than what I think?"

"Christ, I can't do anything for doing wrong, can I?"

"No. Poor you." Iris was too angry to back down. She wasn't having it. She'd had enough. And it was ridiculous. She took a long drag on the cigarette and blew smoke. The *ratatat* of a firework stuttered a few streets away, followed by the distinctive *skree* of a rocket. "Go and talk to him."

"Let him stay up there. A clip round the ear, he wants. He needs to be taught a—"

"Go and talk to him. *Now.*"

Bap bap bap! something went in the sky before fluttering and sparkling earthwards.

He could see she was upset, and more because of that than that he was in the wrong (he *wasn't* in the wrong—*bloody hell . . .*) he went upstairs, unbuttoning his Mac and draping it over the banister before ascending. Iris watched his hand, rendered pink by the cold night air, gliding up the wooden rail until his creaking footsteps reached the landing.

Her hair felt brittle and she tore through it with her hairbrush. The skin on her face felt tight, her throat felt constricted as if half strangled, her skull blocked and salty, all the usual symptoms after she'd been weeping or felt it was imminent. She still didn't feel fully awake and hoped that the scene that had just happened was a dream, but it wasn't, and she wanted to wish it away, and she couldn't. Wishes didn't work. She of all people knew that.

Brushing her hair didn't do the trick. She needed to give herself a wash and headed upstairs to the bathroom, squeezing past the semi-rusted pushchair, the PENNY FOR THE GUY sign dumped in its seat at a skewed angle, and went up and give her cheeks a cold swill at the sink.

As she passed Kelvin's bedroom on her way back down, she couldn't help listening at the door. The man's voice was soft and sympathetic. Loving, even. It didn't sound like her husband at all. It sounded almost like the person he used to be. Almost.

"See, I say these things because I care about you, that's all. I get angry because I just want you to be safe and sound. I do it for your own good, see. What you got to remember is, not all people are dangerous, but some are, and when you're out on your own you don't know who's who, do you?"

She wished with all her heart she could see Kelvin's little face and know how he was reacting, whether he was nodding or just listening, snuggled down in his bed under the eiderdown, but she couldn't. After a moment of silence, Des spoke again:

"Hey. You done a good job, you and your mam."

"Me, mostly."

Iris smiled. Swallowed the lump in her throat.

"Don't!" Kelvin gasped suddenly, bursting into panic. "Don't move him!"

"OK, OK, OK . . . Cool head . . . Here you are . . ."

"He wants to stay here and sleep next to me."

"Orright, orright, niblo . . . Let me tuck you in, then . . ." Her husband's voice grew faint as she padded downstairs, not wanting to reveal she was standing outside, earwigging the conversation. "You're a funny 'apeth." Fading away, her son replied that he wasn't. He wasn't any kind of 'apeth.

She switched on the TV. When it had warmed up it showed Mary Hopkins as a guest on *The Rolf Harris Show* on BBC1. Her trilling, virginal style of folk singing grated with Iris, in spite of her being Welsh and a discovery of Tom Jones—Ponty boy himself, bit of a boyo by all accounts, and without doubt the town's only claim to fame. She wasn't a big fan of the bearded Aussie either with his fair dinkum, Down Under cheeriness. It always seemed entertainers were desperate to create happiness, but when the programme was switched off, where was the happiness then?

Presently Des came in, Schools Rugby tie loosened, easing the glass door shut after him, and sat in the armchair that was vacant—not the settee, which was always where she sat. Peculiar the habits you got set in. He sat in the glow of the screen. By the time she was crushing out a new cigarette in the ashtray she knew she had to speak, because she could hold it in no longer.

"Did you see the mask he bought?"

Des nodded, or flinched, she wasn't sure which. "Grotesque bloody thing."

"Why couldn't he get a Guy Fawkes mask like all the other kids?"

"Who knows what goes through that lad's mind, honest to God. I give up. He can do what he likes."

"You don't mean that."

"I don't know what I mean." Des rose from the chair as if the act was a gigantic effort. His pallor was grey. He looked exhausted. Emotionally drained. Even to talk, talk normally—to her—was clearly too much for him to bear. "I'm going to bed."

Touch me. Touch me, she thought. *Kiss me.*

But he couldn't. How could he?

Do I smell of blood? she thought, in the empty room, eyes fixed blindly on the television programme. *Is that it? Do I, still?*

On Sunday morning when Iris opened his bedroom door she found Kelvin with a snakes and ladders board laid out between himself and the guy, moving one of the counters up a ladder. When she asked if he wanted to come down the park for a walk, he shot a look at the guy—for all the world, she'd swear, as if deferring for an answer. None being forthcoming, he scuttled over and whispered via a cupped hand to the side of its earless head.

"He doesn't want to stay in on a nice day like this, does he?" Iris said, persuasively, realising that her attempt to get her son to abandon the thing for a few hours was misguided.

Kelvin sat back on his heels. "Is Dad coming?"

"Not today. He's got some DIY to do." She didn't elaborate on what they'd actually said to each other: her trying to persuade Des that getting out the putty to re-glaze a window in the scullery was not exactly a priority, Des insisting it was a job he'd put off for months, and that was what Sundays were for. *If you say so*, being her final, curt reply as she got her coat.

She helped the boy put on his shoes at the bottom of the stairs, the guy with its plastic smile perched a few steps behind him, as if sitting pillion. Observing through its holes for eyes. Watching her as she double-knotted the laces.

Kelvin rearranged the guy's scarf, plumping the pillow in the pushchair behind its spineless back, evidently wanting the thing to be seen at its best.

"He likes sunshine."

"Good."

At the bottom of Mill Street they crossed the bridge over the Taff into Ynysangharad Park, the black water of the river below stark testimony to the industry of the Rhondda Valleys. As they passed the tennis courts—deserted at this time of year—she watched Kelvin run ahead with the pushchair at speed, with the intent of creating a thrill either for himself or, strangely, its immobile occupant, a figure that never looked straight or comfortable in its *chariot* but awkward, ill-fitting, with an aspect of frozen entrapment reminiscent of a physically impaired child. It struck her horribly that, from a distance, a passer-by might take them for a family—especially the way Kelvin would regularly pause to tuck in a blanket around the thing's bulbous, paper-filled legs, and whisper to it in a way that . . . No, it didn't disturb her at all. Why should it? It was just play, and it was healthy for children to play, and use their imaginations. She just wanted to switch off her own.

The sticks of dead rockets lay on the tarmac, having fallen from the sky the night before. Their cardboard carcasses lay semi-charred and redundant—the spark of excitement they'd delivered now just a memory.

Iris buttoned her coat against the wind and stuck to their customary route past the cricket pavilion and band stand, inside which a small vortex of yellow leaves did a pirouette, and Iris paused to sit on a bench near the playground next to the mini-golf where Kelvin usually played on the slide and swings. She indulged in her last Embassy in the packet and opened the *Woman's Weekly* from her bag, but after a few minutes the words, "Penny for the guy . . . Penny for the guy . . . " made her look up.

To her dismay she saw that, far from playing with the other children, Kelvin was standing with the pushchair at the gates to the playground, delivering his repetitive litany to every adult who entered. He didn't seem unduly bothered by their disinterest and his mantra continued undiminished. This upset Iris more and more, as she saw the perplexed and then bemused looks on peoples' faces quickly turning into expressions of unease and pity as they hurried their own children in the opposite direction.

"Penny for the guy . . . Penny for the guy . . . "

Iris hurried over and took Kelvin's hand. "Come on. Let's go home, love. It's getting a bit cold and I need to get a cooked dinner on for your father . . . "

Heading towards the bus stop they passed Woolworths, its window resplendent with a vast display of Brock's fireworks boxes, gaudy and brash, and a cardboard cut-out Guy Fawkes in an Elizabethan ruff and tall hat, holding a sparkler like a magic wand. Kelvin gazed at the arrangement with what she first thought was wonder, but then saw was more of a worried puzzlement, and from being chatty all afternoon the boy became suddenly silent.

On the bus she tried to lighten the mood—*her* mood, if nothing else—by unwrapping a tube of fruit pastilles and offering him one.

"I don't like black ones," Kelvin said. "But he does. He *loves* them." He took a sweet between his thumb and forefinger and pressed it into the mask's mouth, then turned to his mother and popped an orange one into his own, grinning broadly.

Iris was looking at the little boy and his guy, side by side next to her in the back seat of the bus when the stout, greasy-haired conductor arrived, ticket machine thrusting from his midriff.

"One adult and two halves, please," she said.

Kelvin's grin spread into a laugh, and Iris smiled too, before she saw an elderly woman with the face of a boxer dog who'd been kicked up the bum by Sonny Liston was giving them a look like they were insane, or beneath contempt, or both.

"What are you staring at?" Iris said, and the old woman turned her considerable chin—or rather, chins—in the other direction.

Kelvin was still chuckling at this as the bus changed to a lower gear halfway up the hill, taking the wide, hairpin curve from Graigwen Place into Pencerrig Street. But Iris was glad he didn't see what she saw, and what made her own smile fade very quickly. From the side window and then the back window, she got a passing glimpse up the rocky path leading to the quarry, where a large wigwam-like structure was taking form out of assorted planks of wood, fallen branches, sawn-down tree trunks, and pieces of discarded furniture. Even now a man dumped more wood on it from the boot of his car, and was dwarfed by the structure. It must've been fifteen foot high already, if not twenty. And to Iris—she didn't know why, or rather she *did* know why—resembled nothing so much as a funeral pyre.

Still in his pyjamas, Kelvin brought down the guy and sat it on the settee while they all had breakfast. Des and Iris looked at each other but neither said a word. Kelvin was humming happily, his bare feet dangling under the table as he spread Marmite on his toast. Finishing first, Des picked up his car keys for the Anglia and said he was off. Iris didn't expect him to kiss her, and he didn't.

"You'd better run up and get dressed if you're not going to be late," she told her son. "Hang on. Aren't you going to take him back to your room?"

"No." Kelvin shot a glance at the guy. "He wants to stay down here today. He wants to keep you company."

Iris stared at the plate in front of her, not wanting to look at the dummy in case the dummy was looking at her, and rubbed her bare arms before faking a smile through clenched teeth. "That's nice." Then calling, "Don't forget to brush your teeth!" Then, in the silence, tried to address the remains of her toast but wasn't hungry and pushed it away. It was scorched. Black. She hated that. Bread tasting like coal, because coal tasted like death. Her grandfather had worked down the mine all his life and that's what he smelt like, however much carbolic he used to wash it off him.

Ten minutes later, when Kelvin came back down in his smart school clothes—corduroy trousers, V-neck, parka—she was sick of looking everywhere but at the thing half-sitting, half-lying on the settee. With a freshly lit cigarette in her hand, she said:

"I'm not sure this is a good idea, love."

"Why?"

"I don't know what to do with him, that's all."

"Just make him feel at home. Just give him anything he wants."

"What does he want, though?"

"He might want the radio on."

Iris hid a laugh in a sigh. "Oh, I see. OK. What kind of music does he like?"

"Any kind."

The front door banged and the house was hers. Whether she liked it or not. She looked for the Senior Service ashtray—relic of The Collier's—and found it.

She switched on the transistor and it played "Yellow River" by Tony Christie and, by the time she'd finished the washing up, "All Kinds of Everything" by Dana. Drying the last teacup, she looked round the corner of the kitchen into the sitting room to see the settee side-on, and the guy hadn't moved. Of course it hadn't. How could it *move*?

She spent half an hour in the kitchen, tidying what needed to be tidied and wiping down the Fablon surfaces and the hob of the oven, when she realised abruptly she was lingering there because she didn't want to go back into the sitting room, which was pathetic and silly. As an act of defiance, to her own nonsensical fear if nothing else, she strode back through, not even looking at the horrible object—though one of its socks brushed against her calf—and went into the hall to get the Hoover out from under the stairs. She shut the door behind her, but couldn't help seeing the vague, rippled shape of the occupant of the settee through the semi-opaque glass. As she moved her head from side to side it almost gave the illusion it was . . .

She carried the vacuum cleaner up to the landing and gave all three bedrooms a good going-over. She didn't enjoy housework, but she was house proud—got that from her mother, never a speck of dust on anything—and she was a good worker, and soon lost herself in the mindlessness of the task. By the time she came back downstairs an hour later she'd forgotten the guy and when she saw it gave a start.

Bugger!

Left tilted at an angle, the gnomish creation had now slumped on its side and gave every appearance of snoozing, impossibly, behind its plastic grin.

Annoyed at her overreaction, Iris grabbed it and dropped it unceremoniously on the carpet, leaving it a discarded and distorted sack while she vacuumed the upholstery, after which she sat it back in position, puffing the scatter cushions around it.

The machine droned and sucked. Afterwards she stood breathless with the spout of the appliance in her hand. The mask was looking at her like she was stupid. Like it knew something she didn't.

Sod you, she thought.

She desperately wanted a smoke. She poked the 'off' button with her toe and went to get the packet of Embassy from the mantelpiece, but it wasn't there. It wasn't on the stool next to her armchair either, which was always where she put it. It wasn't in the kitchen and it wasn't on the small table next to the telephone. She scanned the room, turning in a circle twice, but her eyes only fell on the inscrutable guy with its boneless neck and hollow fingers in its freshly puffed-up throne.

"What have you done with my cigarettes?"

She didn't mean it literally, of course. She was just voicing her frustration at not finding them. But she found herself saying it again, out loud:

"What have you done with my cigarettes?"

It was mute. It had no lips. It had no voice.

She knew it didn't.

But when she made herself a mid-morning cup of coffee she didn't have it in the sitting room, she took it in the front room, the posh room, and drank it in the quiet away from the radio there, without opening the curtains.

When Kelvin came home he burst past her as if she didn't exist, went straight into the sitting room, and emerged almost immediately with the guy, his arm hooked round its midriff, trailing it with him as he hurried upstairs, its baggy limbs flailing. The bedroom door slammed. It would have been nice for him to say hello or to tell her about his day in school, but that was fine if that was the way he wanted it. She went back to her ironing.

At five to five she gave him a shout to tell him *Blue Peter* had started. There was no reply. She called again, louder, from the foot of the stairs but heard nothing but a solemn and disinterested, "OK."

Twenty-odd minutes later the show finished with the usual chirpy goodbyes from Val Singleton, John Noakes, and Peter Purves and its distinctive hornpipe theme music—but Kelvin still hadn't come down. Iris went upstairs to see what was so important to keep him from one of his favourite programmes.

As she approached the bedroom door, hand raised aloft to rap it with her knuckles, she frowned and froze. Could she hear not one but *two* voices coming from inside? Two children. Two boys in conversation, laughing and joking. One of them her son, yes . . . and the *other*?

She lowered her hand and twisted the door handle.

The scene that confronted her was an unremarkable one, yet not one that gave her any sense of relief: Kelvin sitting cross-legged on the bed with a comic open on his lap, the guy next to him, shoulder pressed against the wallpaper, mask askew on its round football head, arm twisted in a rubbery, inhuman curve. Kelvin looked at her as if interrupted mid-sentence.

"Sorry," Iris said, feeling foolish. The TV was on downstairs and the other voice must've come from that. Mustn't it? "I . . . thought you had a mate in here."

"I do." Kelvin smiled.

It took her a moment to realise what he meant. When he grasped the guy's hollow Christmas-gloved hand in his, a damp chill dispersed in the bowl of her pelvis.

"Come downstairs." She stiffened, trying not to let the feeling intensify. "I don't like you spending all this time in your room."

"I do."

"Well I don't. Do as you're told." She found a firmness in her voice that didn't come naturally. "And put your friend out in the shed, please. He doesn't belong indoors."

"Who says?"

"*I'm* saying, and I'm your mam."

"I don't have to do what you say."

"Oh, don't you?"

"No. And neither does he."

"I'm not arguing, Kelvin. You can either do it now or you can talk to your father when he gets in. I'm not kidding." She said nothing more, ignored the fact he threw the comic onto the floor, and went back downstairs to let him stew.

She sat and watched the BBC news with Kenneth Kendall as her son put the back door on the snib and hauled the guy out into the yard to the garden shed in the corner with the peg holding closed the latch. Feeling sorry for him now, she went to the kitchen, made him a glass of orange squash, brought it in, and put it on the table with a couple of chocolate digestives, but when she turned she saw him standing, still clutching the guy to his side.

"He doesn't like it in there. It's too dark and smelly. It smells of paint. It's horrible."

"I don't care," Iris said. "He'll like it in there when he gets used to it. He wants a home of his own."

"No he doesn't. He *said* he doesn't. It's too cold. He likes it in here. In *our* home."

"Kelvin, I said no." She was utterly powerless as he dragged the guy past her and back upstairs. "I said *No!*" But she knew he wasn't listening, wasn't even hearing. She didn't go up, and for the rest of the evening he didn't come down.

Later, while Des was doing his marking in the middle room, she watched *Steptoe & Son* and couldn't concentrate at all. Albert had broken Harold's prize Ming vase and the audience on the laughter track was finding it hilarious, but it was all Iris could do to stop bursting into floods of tears.

It was Tuesday morning and she had some thinking to do, not something she was ever told she was good at. She didn't have a degree like her husband. The most she'd learned in school was how to sit up straight, and couldn't wait to leave that place, even if it meant working behind the bar in her father's pub, The Collier's, till her brother rolled in with a silly sod he'd met on National Service who pulled faces and acted the goat when she played "The Blue Danube" at the piano. Didn't think she'd go on and marry him. Not in a million years. Neither did his mother, who didn't approve and thought he could do better than a publican's daughter, and made that plain on more than one occasion. She wished she could speak to him now, about her fears—her daft ideas he'd probably call them—but how could she do that when she couldn't even talk to him about the chemistry of fireworks?

Instead she made herself a pot of tea and gradually let it warm her insides and the mug warm her hands. She wondered what a doctor might say about Kelvin and his new obsession with the object he had created. That there was no harm in it? That it was just like his collecting Mexico '70 coins? That it was just a phase he was going through? But what *sort* of phase, and why? She remembered herself as a ten-year-old having a sudden hankering to play with the teddy bear she'd adored when she was two or three, really wanting it back in her life, and asking her mother to find it in one of the tea chests in the attic. Had she wanted it to replace something missing? She couldn't remember. Did she just want it because it was somebody she loved, and she imagined loved her back?

She knew Des thought she wrapped the boy in cotton wool, that she was too much of a blinking softie half the time. Maybe men in general think a child should be told what's what. Do this, don't do that. Maybe it's about rules for them. *Their* rules, that is. But what about happiness? Did happiness ever come into it? She just wanted her son to be happy, and he wasn't. He couldn't be. Not when his best friend was a . . .

Then it struck her, what should've been blindingly obvious all along.

That if Kelvin had a real, proper friend there was a possibility he wouldn't need his make-believe one anymore.

"Kelvin," she said at dinnertime as he ate his sausages and beans. "Why don't you ask your friend Gareth to come over for tea tonight?" Kelvin stopped chewing. "I'll phone his mother and make sure it's all right with her, but I'm sure it will be. You can show off your guy. I'm sure he'll be impressed." She didn't get an immediate answer, and Kelvin buried himself back in his dinner.

"And *he*'ll enjoy it too," he said, looking over at the pile of clothes stitched into a human shape. "*He* hasn't got any friends either, see. Just me."

"Exactly," she said, wiping the drip of tomato sauce off his chin with her finger.

She phoned Gloria Powell while he ate his thin brick of Walls ice cream, then accompanied him to school, stopping off on the way back at Graigwen Stores to stock up with what she needed for tea. Jaffa cakes seemed a necessity, and she got a tin of salmon for sandwiches (it was a special occasion after all; *she* felt it was). Oh, and some individually wrapped Cadbury's Swiss rolls, as well as bottles of white pop, Tizer, and dandelion and burdock, just in case. It was a hike back home, but she found she had a spring in her step and didn't stop to catch her breath till she reached Jeff Beech's sweet shop, lightheaded, round the corner from her house in Highfield Terrace.

As it happened, Gareth said he'd like a cup of tea, please—he always had tea at teatime; didn't they? Iris said they didn't, not always. Or rather, she and Kelvin's dad had tea, but Kelvin didn't, he preferred squash. It already seemed a difficult conversation and she wondered why she was getting so flustered, given she was talking to an eight-year-old. The way he sniffed suspiciously at the salmon sandwich also didn't greatly enamour him to her. She said they could go upstairs and play with Kelvin's Scalextric if they liked, or Monopoly. Gareth said he always beat his sister at Monopoly. Kelvin said he didn't like Monopoly anyway, he liked draughts best. Gareth sniggered, repeating the word derisively and said his father was teaching him chess. He asked Kelvin what his dad was teaching him.

"Anyway Gareth," Iris said. "What are you doing on November the fifth? Going up the quarry to the big bonfire?"

Gareth shook his head. "My dad gets a box of fireworks and lights them in the back yard. I'm allowed to hand them to him, but he lights them."

"Quite right too. Light the blue touchpaper and stand well back!" Iris laughed, hoping the boys might laugh too, but they didn't see what was so funny. "I hope you keep your cats and dogs indoors."

"My mam and my sisters have to watch through the window. They always put their fingers in their ears. Dad says this year I can light a rocket."

Kelvin had left the table and now plonked himself down next to the guy on the settee. Frowning hard, he entwined its arm round his. "*He* wants to watch TV."

"What do you want to do, Gareth?"

Gareth shrugged.

"Well, you go and sit down and watch TV with Kelvin, and I'll get some cake and biscuits. How's that?"

Out in the kitchen she folded paper serviettes and arranged the mini-rolls on two small plates. A sense of satisfaction sank in as she heard nothing from the other room but the twinkly 'Gallery' music from *Vision On*, played when they showed the drawings and paintings sent in by its child viewers. The boys were quiet. They were getting on, thank goodness, she thought. She'd been right. It was *working* . . . Then the spell was broken, the apparent calm torn asunder by a lilting, innocuous rhyme.

"Remember, remember, the—"

"*No!*"

"Fifth of—"

"*Shut up!*"

"—vember. Gunpowder, treason and—"

"*Don't! Don't do that!*"

"—reason why gunpowder treason should *ever* be—"

"*Don't! DON'T HURT HIM!*" This turning into a shriek. From her son.

Iris couldn't get into the sitting room quick enough. "What the heck is going on in . . . ?"

Three small figures sprawled, entangled on the cushions of the settee, limbs for a moment indistinguishable. Kelvin was wrestling the guy away from Gareth, who in turn seemed to be making pincer-like gestures at the effigy's polo-neck with crablike hands.

Kelvin tugged the guy's head towards him protectively and flung a foot out at the other boy, aimed at his face. Luckily this was countered by a swing of the arm, while Gareth's other arm swiped the guy with a karate chop in the middle of the chest, caving in the torso with a massive dent and bending it double. Kelvin emitted an even more ear-piercing shriek.

Iris caught his free hand. "Now! Stop it! Both of you!"

"He was pinching him!"

"I don't care what he was doing. You don't kick someone. Is that clear?"

"But he was—"

"I don't *care*! Is that *clear*?"

Kelvin scowled at his mother, eyebrows lowered, eyes black as coal. She was frightened by what she saw there—perhaps because she saw herself, her hatred of herself, or her husband's—but just as quickly the moment was snapped in half.

"*Owww-ah!*" This time the cry came from Gareth Powell, who was rolling around, knees in the air, one hand pressed into his armpit, then shot to his feet, tears springing to his eyes as he hopped up and down. "He bit me! The pigging thing *bit* me!" The boy held out his finger and the scratch across it welled with a ruby pearl of blood. Acting automatically, Iris held it in her hand and the boy continued sobbing pitifully—it made her think of the little baby he once must've been rather than the superior little prig he was now. She hastily took out her handkerchief and started dabbing, but it kept on bleeding. Damn, it wasn't just a scratch, it was a cut. A bloody deep one. How the *hell* had . . . ?

She wrapped his finger in her hankie as she looked over at Kelvin, whose arms were wrapped round the guy, hugging it, rocking it slightly as if to comfort it after the unprovoked attack it had suffered at the hands of a stranger. Iris instantly saw that the safety pin that held the anorak in place over the guy's chest was undone.

"It's all right, love. It's just a nick. Just a flesh wound, like they say in the pictures, eh? Nothing serious. It was just the safety pin caught you, that's all, look . . . "

"It wasn't!" Gareth bleated, snot dribbling from his nose, his eyes reddening slits. "I didn't *touch* the safety pin! I wasn't anywhere *near* it! I didn't do *anything*!"

"All right, get upstairs you." Iris pointed Kelvin to the stairs and he shambled away with hunched shoulders, the wobbly-legged torso trailing after him by one inelegant sausage arm, one flaccid glove.

Gareth said he wanted to go home, and kept saying it throughout the process of Iris putting an Elastoplast on his wound—which wasn't that shocking, certainly not shocking enough for the hysteria it engendered. She then realised that Gareth wanted to go home not because he was hurting or in pain, but because he was terrified. He was terrified of staying there any longer, and the thing he was terrified of was upstairs.

Des walked in and asked what was going on. Iris said she was taking Gareth home, she'd explain when she got back, and she did.

"Hell," he said, swilling a Scotch behind his teeth. He never drank spirits. Never drank at all, really. The bottles only came out at Christmas, and she'd never seen him tight. "This—this, whatever it is—attachment he's got, don't you think it's embarrassing enough without advertising it? Seriously?"

"I just wanted . . . " She rubbed the back of her neck.

"Well, great. Well done. Tomorrow it'll be all over the school. You know what children are like. He'll be a laughing stock. None of the other kids will touch him with a barge pole."

"It's a phase," she said, trying to convince herself.

"What if it isn't, Iris? What if it doesn't go away or get put right? What then?" He wanted his wife to answer but she didn't. Couldn't. "What do we do? Do we take him to a doctor?"

"No. I don't know." She held her head in her hands. "We just have to act like it's normal."

"It's *not* normal though, is it, eh?" A distant fire engine whined. Bangs and splutters adorned the air, more plentiful now than even the night before. "*Is* it?"

At breakfast they sat in thorny silence over their plates as Kelvin chattered about how much blood was in the average human body, that the heart pumped it round and round, that's why we had redness in our cheeks, and other organs did other things, like the kidneys that got rid of things the body didn't need, but sometimes the things the body didn't need stayed in the body and got worse.

"How did you find out that?" Iris asked wearily. "From school?"

"No," said Kelvin with a mouthful of Frosties (*They're Grrrrrreat!*). "*He* told me."

The guy occupied one of the straight-backed dining chairs at the table, semi-deflated and lolling, its mask tilted, giving the illusion it was staring at the bowl of Coco Pops in front of it. Kelvin reached over and lifted a spoonful to its smiling slit of a mouth.

"For God's sake . . . " Her husband left his seat.

"Quiet," Iris said. "He's only playing."

"And I'm only on my way to work." Des struggled into the arms of his gabardine Mac. She followed him to the kitchen, stopped him opening the back door. "This has gone beyond a joke," he whispered, fear and desperation as well as rage in his eyes. "That kid needs to see a bloody psychiatrist." She let the door open wide for him to go.

The bowl of Coco Pops was empty when she returned.

"Don't get upset," Kelvin was saying to the guy, tugging its sleeve. "You're one of the family. He loves you really. He just doesn't know how to show it."

The boy looked round at his mother. His lips twitched, but failed to resolve into a smile.

On the way back from shopping that day, Iris chose not to walk her usual route past the police bungalows and up the hill. Instead she decided to go the other way, up Graigwen Place, the way the bus went, then took the shortcut by foot round by the quarry. The bonfire had grown, and she wondered how, since nobody was in evidence. What made a person build a thing like this for enjoyment? Was it just children? Obviously not. Part of a fence had been added, as well as a broken ladder, and even a couple of doors—*doors!*—and a good number of large branches, of uneven lengths and thicknesses, some as hefty as telegraph poles, propped and crisscrossed, tepee fashion. She stood looking at it when a banger landed near her feet. It cracked, making her jump, then banged again two or three times, flitting around her before phut-ting out. She called out bitterly, telling someone they were stupid. Nobody replied, and she could hear only an aeroplane crossing the sky. She walked away rapidly. Whatever fool had done it was hiding, or was gone.

"God, what's wrong, love?"

Kelvin stumbled past her, flailing arms, red cheeks wet. His school bag hit the floor. He started to climb the staircase on all fours, then collapsed with his face buried in crossed arms.

"What's happened?" Iris went and placed the flat of her hand on his back, rubbing it in circles, feeling his tiny chest rising and falling in awful shudders—it almost made her well into tears herself. "Love? Tell me. Please. Tell your mam. She'll make it better."

He turned on her, viciously. "*How*? How will you make it *better*? You *can't!*"

"Well tell me what it is, love, please. I can't do anything if I don't know, can I? Come downstairs and I'll get you a nice glass of—"

"I don't want a glass of *anything!*" His voice cracked, throat already raw and swollen. "I just want . . . " The sentence disintegrated into sobs, and Iris could do nothing but tear off her apron, lie there on the stairs on top of him and wrap her arms around him, tight, whether he wished her to or not, whether he struggled or not, and let him wail until he could speak. His little body shook in the embrace of her. She felt the warmth of him, the salt-streaming helplessness of him and tried to absorb him and rid him of it, but she could not. And the cruelty was he didn't even want her, and pushed her off him, and clung to the banister rods instead, too much the man, not letting his mother see him cry, poor baby. Not wanting her. But *she* wanted. She wanted so much.

"They . . . They said it's *tomorrow* . . . "

"What's tomorrow, love?"

"Bonfire Night! November the fifth!" He was incensed at her ignorance. "The boys in school said I'll have to burn him. I won't have to burn him, will I?"

"What boys?"

"Gareth! Everybody!"

"You don't want to listen to Gareth Powell . . . "

"It's *true* though, isn't it? The teacher said. We had a whole lesson about it. That's when they started laughing at me!"

"Oh, sweetheart . . . " She ruffled his hair and kissed him through his pullover. "It's November the fifth. It's OK. It's what everybody does. It's a celebration . . . "

"Why?"

"Years and years ago Guy Fawkes was a man who stored up barrels of gunpowder in the cellars under Parliament and was waiting there to light the fuse, but he got caught."

"But why do we have to *burn* him?"

"I don't know. I suppose we have bonfires and fireworks to give thanks he didn't succeed. Our politicians weren't blown sky high—so we burn our own poor old Guy Fawkeses instead."

"Yes, but we don't *have* to, do we? Why does he have to *die?* It's not fair!"

"It's doesn't matter. It's only a silly bunch of old clothes, love. He's not a human being. He's not alive."

Kelvin turned and began screaming into her face. "*You're* not alive! *He* is! I *know* he is—but you're not! You don't care about him! You don't *love* him! But *I* do!"

With that he ran up to his bedroom, where she found him, face down in the pillow, next to the guy, which was lying on its back staring up at the ceiling, still bouncing very slightly from the weight that had just landed on the bed. To Iris it looked almost as if its head was moving from side to side. She sat on the bed next to her son and touched his body again. Couldn't bear not doing.

"Kelvin. Kelvin, love . . . "

He turned his head the other way, facing the guy and not her.

"We don't have to go to a bonfire," she said. "We don't have to go to a big firework display. Your dad can just light a few—"

"Stop it! Don't *talk* about it!"

"What? Firework night?"

"Shut up! Don't say those words! You're upsetting him!" Kelvin threw one arm across the guy's chest, tugging it closer to him and lowering his voice to a hush. "It's all right. Don't worry. I'm here. I know you're scared but nobody's going to hurt you. I won't let them."

"Kelvin, it's November the fifth and—"

"*Don't!* Don't mention it again!" He glared at her. "How would you like it? To be stuck on a pile of sticks and set *fire* to? It's horrible!" His head spun to the guy. "Nobody's going to burn you, I promise."

"Kelv, you have to burn him, lovely . . . "

"*Why?* Why should I? I don't want to. I'm not going to! There's no law against it. He's mine! I'm going to keep him, just like he is. You can't make me!"

A voice behind her said: "Nobody's going to make you do anything, son."

Iris turned and saw her husband standing at the bedroom door.

She struck a match and lit up, grateful to have the house to herself again. *Almost* to herself. Herself except for . . . *it.*

Des had told Kelvin to get his football togs on, sharpish; they were going to be late for the match if he didn't get his skates on. His voice had been uncharacteristically mellow, soft—not even rising to accuse his son of having forgotten the extracurricular game. Iris's first instinct had been to think something was wrong. She's expected Kelvin to resist, say he didn't want to go, but he didn't. He sat up, rubbing his eyes with the heels of his hands, probably not wanting his father to see the state he was in. *Come on. Shake a leg, buttie. You don't want to let the rest of the team down. They're waiting for you.* Kelvin had stripped to his underpants. She'd left the room, feeling redundant as Des helped him lace up his heavy, studded boots. *Atta boy . . .* Then she'd called out, wishing him good luck, then heard *'Bye, mam!* Though it was not Kelvin who'd called back but her husband. A second later Kelvin's face appeared round the sitting room door, but he had no need to voice his anxiety. She'd already anticipated it:

"I'll look after him. You go and enjoy yourself."

She'd have liked a kiss on the cheek but that hadn't been forthcoming. She was a bad person now, in his eyes. She couldn't help that. Just hoped he'd return in a better mood, and that they could have a *cwtch* watching telly like they used to. Wished that more than anything.

Now, smoking as she bent to poke a lacklustre fire into life, then pulling a guard in front of it, she wondered how much of the conversation upstairs Des had heard. She'd known what he was doing—he was clever, with his degree and everything, after all—distracting the boy with something physical to get his mind away from the damned guy for five minutes. That much was obvious. But what did he think of *her*? Did she think she was being panicky? Shrill? A bit mad? Had she said the right things? Hell, why was she frightened of what he thought? *She* wasn't the problem after all, was she? And when her husband had opened and closed the front door he must've let the night air in, because she got that smell of sulphur again, rank and noxious in her throat.

From her chair Iris looked at the ceiling above her, picturing beyond the swirls of Artex her son's bedroom and its twisted, cuckoo occupant.

I'll look after him.

She wouldn't. She wouldn't go up there. Bugger that. She didn't want to, and didn't have to. She'd sit here and read her magazine by the fire and watch *Nationwide* and whatever else was on until they got home, and then it would be over with. They'd be a family again and she'd make supper on trays, or maybe Dad would get fish and chips from up the Graig, and that would be that.

Which was fine until she needed to go for a wee, and for once she wished she could go outside to the back toilet, but Des had converted it into an extension of the kitchen for the washing machine and tumble drier.

She literally crossed her legs. Then she thought: *This is damn silly. I'm not afraid of it. What the bloody hell is it I've got to be afraid of? It's not even made of anything. It's nothing.*

With determination she shot out of her armchair and went upstairs, switching the landing light on and for some reason making her footfalls heavy, as if somebody might be listening, and wanting them to be aware she was coming.

She stiffly walked past her son's bedroom door to the bathroom at the end of the landing, once inside locking the door after her, even though she was the only one in the house. Sheer habit, she told herself, that was all.

She sat on the toilet seat but nothing came. Her bladder was empty. She felt desperately weary again, drained from seeing Kelvin so upset earlier, she supposed. As his mother she couldn't stop herself being affected by what affected him. It was part of what being a mother was. A kind of symbiosis you were never free of. If they suffered, you suffered. There was no getting away from it.

She stood up and pulled the chain even though she hadn't

gone, staring at the swirling water and remembering the terrible day she'd seen blood staining the white of the pan.

She heard footsteps on the stairs. Light. Far too light for a grown man. More like a pet, but they had no pets. And not walking so much as scuttling.

"Kelvin?"

She zipped up her slacks and opened the bathroom door.

The landing was empty. Kelvin's bedroom door shut. Of course it was.

She was being stupid. It was probably the kids next door. The terrible twins. They were always running up and down stairs, causing a riot. That was it. Yes. Definitely. What else?

She went back, washed her hands at the sink with the brick of Imperial Leather, dried them with the towel, then tugged the ring-pull to switch off the bathroom light.

Downstairs she walked into the sitting room and saw the guy slumped on the settee in the glow of the TV set, for all the world as if watching it, stunted legs sticking out with socks dangling at the end of them, fat arms hanging limp at its sides, gloves bunched up, non-fingers at inconceivable angles.

Iris's hand clamped over her mouth.

Her first thought was that she had misremembered earlier— that was it, that must be it—and that Kelvin must've brought down the guy before he'd left for the match with his father. But she'd been sitting in the room only minutes earlier *and it wasn't there*! Surely that was true—wasn't it?

She laughed. She didn't decide to, she just did. It just began to happen. And she didn't even know what she was laughing at, but she couldn't stop.

Minutes later she ran out of breath, and went to the front room and raided the drinks on the hostess trolley and poured herself a gin and tonic, and when she'd drank it, poured a second one.

The guy was still there when she returned. It hadn't moved. That was one thing, at least—*it hadn't moved*. She wondered if she sat there long enough it would, while she was looking straight at it. But no, of course not—it was too clever for that. Cleverer than her, anyway. She knew where it got that from, its brains . . .

She switched the TV off, because she hadn't switched it on. She was positive she hadn't. And she sat cross-legged on the floor with her back to the screen, because that's where the guy's face was pointing.

"You're treating this like your house," she said to it bluntly, pleased that she was managing to disguise her emotions. "Well it isn't. It never was and it never will be." She sipped her drink and tried to discern what, in its cheap plastic smile, it was thinking. Or was it just mocking her? Mocking all of them? "What do you want with us?" Her eyes narrowed. "What do you want with *him*?"

Even as she said it, she knew the guy, in his cunning, would not reply.

When the wanderers returned she was in her bedroom, curled up but not asleep, as far away from the guy as possible. Coming down when she heard the door slam, she asked how the team had done, whether he'd scored, but nobody told her. She crossed Kelvin on the stairs, his white shorts muddied and his knees scuffed. Down in the sitting room she found Des lifting the guy by one shoulder. "I better take this upstairs. Or he'll go nuts." Iris tightened the belt of her dressing gown as he—*they*—passed.

By the time Kelvin had had his bath, *Tom and Jerry* had finished and *Star Trek* was on, but the boy didn't come down to watch it, though he never missed an episode. He loved it. But tonight he wanted to be with the guy, Des reported. Because the thing had *missed him*, Des said.

"Didn't you tell him he had to?"

"You're forgetting who the boss is in this house."

"Who?"

"Well it's not bloody me."

At nine o'clock, just as *Special Branch* starring that actor with the thick lips started, Des took up a hot water bottle and put Kelvin to bed because Iris said she was still in the doghouse for some unknown reason. When he returned back down he was carrying the guy like a sack from its scrawny neck.

"I know. I know. You go and talk to him if you want to. He said it wants to sit with us and get to know us, apparently, so we'll 'grow to love' it."

"I don't *want* to love it," Iris said through gritted teeth. She didn't even want to look at it either.

"That's his . . . his logic, I don't know. I didn't know what to bloody say."

"You could've said, 'Go to sleep.' And don't put it on my nice clean . . . Christ, put it over *there*." She pointed to one of the dining chairs over by the closed curtains, between the phone table and the TV set. Blowing air unhappily, he dumped it there, where it hung, boneless, baby mask snug in the receptacle of its hood.

Sniffing at his sleeves with repugnance, Des sank into the armchair at an angle to his wife's, also facing *Special Branch*. "I can smell it on my clothes . . . " Soon it was clear to both of them that neither were paying a great deal of attention to what the programme was about, though their eyes were fixed on it.

"Today . . . I was in the bathroom . . . " Iris shuddered, faltering. "Des?"

"What? I'm listening."

She shook her head, deciding she didn't want to go into details. "I . . . I just don't like having it in the house. I hate it."

Des grunted. "And I don't?"

"But to him it's like . . . I don't know . . . "

"Probably full of maggots from that pushchair, for a start . . . Goodness knows what diseases . . . Spreading its germs . . . " He plucked the *Express* from the footstool and opened it wide, arms stretched.

"Some sort of a . . . friend . . . a . . . " Again, she floundered.

"Stinking out the house . . . "

"Des, I can't bear it . . . "

"You don't have to bear it," he said, eyes scanning the sports results. "Not for much longer. Roll on tomorrow and we'll be shot of the thing."

"Don't say that." Iris was aghast. "Don't even *think* that, for God's sake! We can't. He *loves* it. We can't be that cruel."

"We have to. For his own good. We have no choice."

"You said nobody was going to make him do anything. You said that to him a couple of hours ago."

"I know. I lied."

"He won't let you. You know that. He won't let him go."

"He'll have to," Des said. "He's got to grow up."

"Why?"

"Because we all have to."

Iris started to cry, and perhaps she wanted him to come over and put his arms round her and hold her tight, or perhaps she wanted him to fall to his knees and cup her hands in his, or wipe her tears away with his thumbs in a gentle and caring gesture. But what happened was, he sighed and folded up his newspaper, dropped it into his lap and turned to her with tight lips, dry eyes, and an expression of intense irritation.

"What can I do? What do you want me to do? Tell me." When she didn't, he said, "Breathe. You know what the doctor said. Breathe." And she wished and prayed that his eyes weren't so dry and his lips weren't so tight and he would just tell her everything would be all right, but she knew he couldn't. He got up and turned down the volume on the telly, but that only made the chemistry of fireworks louder. "Tell me what you're thinking."

"You know . . . " she began. "You know how, when he was younger, Kelvin would have a nosebleed every so often, and it was weird—he didn't know it, but we did. It would always be at my time of the month. Like clockwork. I'd start to bleed, and the next thing, he'd be saying . . . "

"Iris . . . "

"No, like he was in tune with me. Like he was part of me, still. And if he's part of me, does he know what . . . ?"

"Stop."

"It was my body. I mean, did he feel . . . ?"

"*Stop it!*"

Now Des was on his knees in front of her, not kissing her and not holding her, but gripping her wrists. She feared he would shake her. Strike her, even. But his grip became feeble, impotence turning to sudden alarm in his eyes.

"Why the hell are we *whispering*?" But they both knew the reason.

The reason was behind him, slumped half-on, half-off the dining chair like the imitation of a husk of a corpse at a wake, long arm dangling, chin sunk into the crater of its chest.

Remember, remember . . . Dread wasn't a word she thought about very often but dread was the only word that would do. As soon as she woke she couldn't wait for the day to be over. *The fifth of November* . . . The old feelings flooded back. She couldn't stop them. She didn't dress, and asked Des to make the boy his breakfast, please. *Gunpowder treason and plot* . . . Alone in the double bed, she turned over into the pillow but was unable to drift back to sleep. She had a splitting headache pounding against her skull, a real humdinger. Not even a shower and two aspirins from the medicine cabinet did anything to shift it. *I see no reason why gunpowder treason* . . .

Hearing Des leave in the car, she shambled downstairs in her dressing gown and slippers to make a cup of tea. Maybe that would do the trick. Kelvin sat on the settee looking pale. She looked at her watch. She'd expected him to be halfway to school by now. He gave a few unconvincing little coughs into his fist.

"I don't feel well."

"You're going to school. I don't care what day it is." She tugged open the curtains, tied them back with the cords. The sky was like dirty dishwater.

"I've got a temperature."

"You think I don't know what you're playing at, young man? That's enough of that malarkey." She held out his school bag to him.

"I have to stay here with him. I have to protect him."

"Please, love. Not now. You're being silly." She rubbed her forehead. It was as sore and agonising as if she'd prodded a wound.

"I'm *not* being silly! People want to hurt him. People want to *burn* him!"

"Nobody's going to do anything. Nobody's going to get in here, are they? *I'm* here."

"But I don't want to leave him all alone—because he's scared, really scared!" Now her son's voice was going through her and she couldn't stand it. She certainly wasn't up to a full-volume row with a forceful and stubborn eight-year-old.

She crouched down, took his hand in hers and kissed it. "Sweetheart, I know he's been a really good friend, but . . . "

"But he's *not* a friend. He's not *just* a friend. You *know* that!"

Her heart flipped. Her throat tightened. What did he mean? *You know that?*

"All right." She let go of his soft flesh and stood up quickly. "Just this once, all right? You haven't got me round your little finger. Don't think that for one minute. I'll phone the school and say you're feeling poorly." No sooner were the words out than he got up and threw his arms round her hips, pressing his cheek to her tummy. She held in her breath, arms aloft, until he let go.

Moments later she could hear his voice as he reached his bedroom: "She said you can stay! She said you can stay forever and ever!" She saw herself shudder in the mirror over the mantelpiece.

Blap-ap-ap!

Rockets were going up early. She couldn't tell where, probably over Maes-y-Coed. The windows protected her from the occasional and unpredictable bursts—going off like some small-scale civil war—as she rang the secretary in the primary school office, saying her son had a cold and wouldn't be in today. When the secretary sounded sympathetic and said she hoped Kelvin felt better soon, Iris felt guilty and hung up abruptly, then regretted it. Goodness knows what impression it gave, but she felt under a lot of strain and she didn't want long conversations with people. Not today, of all days. Even that simple task had been an enormous strain—OK, it shouldn't have been, but it was.

Not long afterwards, Des rang, which he never did. Between lessons.

"How did he get off?"

Iris thought of lying, but didn't have the strength. "He wouldn't go." Des didn't sound as if this was totally unexpected, but it's hard to tell on the telephone exactly what somebody is thinking. Perhaps he was thinking it was her fault—being soft again. "It's only one day," she said. "What does it matter?"

"I'll see you at five-ish," he said. "I'll come straight home."

"You don't need to."

"I do."

Mid-morning she wanted to get a tin of Heinz cream of tomato soup for Kelvin's dinner. But the truth was she wanted to get out of the house. She was rattling in it and it was jangling her nerves. As she walked downhill to the shop in the burnt, already pungent, nitrogenous air, she wondered how the bonfire up the quarry was doing, whether it had enlarged, swelled, whether it was gathering bulk even now for the festivities that would kick off come nightfall when grown-ups and their offspring alike gathered to celebrate. Celebrate what? Celebrate death. She wished the air was clean and fresh and reviving but it wasn't.

"Penny for the guy?"

Two munchkin sentinels stood outside the Spar. One wore a mask of Frankenstein's monster in lurid green and the other, a girl in pigtails, the more traditional bearded Guy Fawkes. Their construction, which sported a 'Dai' cap and cricket pullover, wasn't nearly as impressive as her son's—its face merely a child's crayon drawing wrapped onto a cardboard box with Sellotape. Iris ignored their biscuit tin of coins as she went inside, and ignored them again as she came out.

"Penny for the guy? Penny for the guy, please, missus?"

The words screamed round the inside of her head with the repetitiveness of a stunt motorcyclist on the Wall of Death. Halfway up the hill she saw a four-year-old child in a pink duffel coat and woolly hat sitting on a wall. The little girl made shapes in the air with a lit sparkler, mesmerised by its intensity. The man and woman in charge of it smiled and Iris smiled back, but didn't pause. Kept her head down. She didn't know them, and didn't want to.

Before she reached her door and took out her key from her purse, she was rubbing drips of water from her cheeks brought on by the cold air, the blighted air, thinking:

He would have been four years old by now.
Four years old, to the day.

She couldn't hear anything from upstairs and she didn't want to go upstairs so she called Kelvin down, and he took his soup up on a tray with some sliced bread. The Grand Canyon of the afternoon widened ahead of her, as did the silence. She switched on the wireless. It was playing "Love Grows" by Edison Lighthouse. She made a cup of coffee and thought of the children with snotty faces and shoddy clothes—who should've been in school, not out playing truant—and the lumpen figures with twisted limbs at their feet.

Penny for the guy? Penny for the guy?

The coffee made her more jittery still. One hand on the newel post, she called upstairs.

"How is he?"

"Fine. I'm trying to keep his mind off it."

"Can I get you anything?"

"No, thanks. Oh, wait a minute. I'll ask him." Pause. "He says no, thanks very much."

Iris closed the door of the sitting room after her. She looked at the clock above the fireplace and wondered how she could fill the next couple of hours. She tried to read, but a flashing fizz in the sky would make her head jerk upright, or the sound of little padding footsteps across the bedroom floor above.

Penny for . . .
Penny for them . . .

Her mouth felt parchment-dry and she fetched herself a glass of water from the kitchen tap. She hated water. Never liked the taste of it—people always laughed when she said that—but she drank it nonetheless.

I see no reason . . .
No reason . . .

Des arrived ten minutes later than he'd predicted, holding up a large box of fireworks, the bright colours carnivalesque in the dull room. Horrified, Iris jumped up, snatched it off him, and hid it in the sideboard, out of sight, slamming the drawer as if it were some illicit and disgusting contraband.

"I thought . . ."

"Really? You could've fooled me." She rubbed the goosebumps on her bare arms. "Don't you realise anything?"

"I thought he could watch from his bedroom window . . ."

Iris shook her head, eyes squeezed into squints of irritation. She bent forward and hooked her fingers into her hair.

Des looked down at the packet of sparklers in his hand, discarding it onto the table with a sigh. Then sat with his knees apart and his elbows on them, wiping the anguish from his face.

To her, the air in the room felt acrid, bitter, sour—perhaps she'd brought it in with her, but those were its ingredients. The stuff that contributed to the burning she felt inside. The chemistry that was her.

"My dad used to hammer a nail to the door of the shed for a Catherine Wheel, every year without fail." Her husband spoke, but she didn't even know if the words were for her. "I can see him lighting it, taking charge, standing back, all of us willing the little glow of light to burst into life. But it always just fizzled into nothing, spun round once or twice, and went out. We all expected something so great and it never bloody worked."

She stared at the blank television screen. She could say nothing. Her throat felt scorched.

"I talked to the Head today. I told her the problem." *You didn't talk to me*, Iris thought, listening. *You didn't talk to me.* "She was very understanding, as a matter of fact. She wasn't the cow I thought she'd be, looking down her nose at me. She said we could get in a child psychologist." Iris didn't hear *child*, she just heard *psychologist*. She heard *get a psychologist*, just like she'd heard it four years ago, when the problem was her. "They know what they're doing, she said. She was very sympathetic, actually. I was pleasantly surprised."

"Bully for you," Iris said, without looking at him.

The silence hurt. He went into the middle room to smoke one of his Hamlet cigars and listen to the news. When he came back twenty minutes later he said:

"I'll call him for his tea."

"Leave him," she said. "He'll shout if he wants anything. If you want something, make it. There's ham and there's sliced bread." She didn't move as he walked past her, other than lift the cigarette to her lips.

Shall never be forgot . . .

Be forgot . . .

Des returned to the middle room while she watched *Top of the Pops*, the sexually provocative but, to her, faintly ridiculous Pan's People gyrating to the hardly ribald White Plains song "My Baby Loves Lovin'". A sparkly green glow saturated the room and, peering between the curtains, she could make out the fronds of a Silver Fountain in the yard next door. Something red corkscrewed across the black sky, blooming into machine-gun arcs of lavender and puce. With another boom, copper-blue and orange rain mushroomed and fell.

The blasting gust of a Roman candle accompanied her pouring Kelvin's hot water bottle. The music had turned to Jethro Tull's "Living in the Past" as she went upstairs.

The guy was in his arms. Her son was fast asleep. Iris tugged it slightly but he woke immediately, whining and hugging it back to him.

"I'm only putting it to one side, love. He'll be here when you wake up. You don't want it in bed with you, do you?"

"Yes. I do. I *have* to."

His head sank back into the pillow. His lids were heavy. He had trouble keeping his eyes open, poor mite.

"Don't worry. It'll all be over tomorrow."

"Did you hear that?" he said to the baby mask, the football-head secreted in the sheath of its green anorak hood. "Tomorrow you'll be safe. She wouldn't lie to you." He struggled to keep his eyes open, drifting between sleep and wakefulness. Grasped one empty glove with urgency. "She knows you're special. She made you, silly. She doesn't want you to die. She wants you to live."

That feeling, that old feeling, that stab of acid in the churning ice bucket of her stomach, came again and she thought she might faint. Her hand pressed against it.

"Go to sleep, love."

"Don't let anything happen to him, mam, will you?"

"I know."

"Promise?"

"I promise." Iris switched off the bedside light, put last year's *Doctor Who* annual with Patrick Troughton and Jamie and a Cyberman on the cover back on the shelf. She leant over and kissed him, as she always did. His cheek was blisteringly warm, almost pulsating.

"You have to kiss him good night too."

She wanted to say no, but she knew he would insist. Her stomach loosened. She felt hollow. She felt outside herself, looking in. Not part of herself at all. She bent down, already feeling the tension in her back rebelling against it, and pressed her mouth to the inert plastic.

———

Before entering the sitting room she wiped her mouth as if she had tasted something abhorrent. She'd pinched her lips together with her fingers as soon as she'd shut the bedroom door, but still her stomach jerked, wanting to void itself of something revolting, some intrusion, some infestation. She took several deep breaths, telling herself to pull herself together. That was all behind her now—the pain, the worthlessness, the drifting, disembodied *other*-ness that had possessed her for too long. She remembered being organised, being meticulous. Knowing something was wrong and going to her GP with a well-thought-out list:

> *Can't sleep (but always feeling tired)*
> *No appetite*
> *Aches and pains*
> *Feeling of heaviness*
> *Headaches*
> *Anger*
> *Don't want to go out / see people*
> *Can't be bothered to do things I used to enjoy*
> *Sex (difficulties)*
> *Grief*

The doctor looked down the list and showed her what was written at the bottom—the word *Grief*. He said, There's your answer right there. That was the cause of all the other things. And she mustn't put a time limit on it. Everybody's different. Not everyone has the same reaction or behaves the same, or gets over things the same way. There was no way of predicting it, but the one thing she shouldn't do is punish herself about it. Time is a great healer, he said. But sometimes it isn't. It just isn't.

She sat with Des watching *Play for Today*. It was called *Angels Are So Few* and it was by somebody called Dennis Potter, who Des knew of but she didn't (she didn't pay attention to things like that), but it had that actor in it she liked, Tom Bell, from that film *The L-Shaped Room*—one of those ones who had a surly sort of charisma and was strong and handsome but didn't feel the need to smile a lot to make you like him. Hypnotised slightly by his face swimming in and out of shot, she realised she hadn't been following the story at all. It could have been *Sooty and Sweep* for all she was concerned.

"Do it," she said halfway through.

Des looked at her.

"Do it," she repeated. Elaboration was unnecessary.

He went into the hall and took his Mac from the hook. Pulled his leather gloves from the pockets.

Iris listened not to Tom Bell in his television play, but the sound from the landing as Des crept into her son's bedroom, easing open the door.

She was alternately holding her breath and sucking at her cigarette, a combination that quickly made her feel light-headed. The picture on the TV screen became blurred and wishy-washy, the words gobbledegook.

Seconds later she heard his footfall on the stairs again.

She got up and stood by the door into the hall, one hand on the jamb, cigarette smoke rising, holding back behind an imaginary line as if present at an accident where her inexperience in what was needed might be a hindrance.

Des descended the stairs—the guy's fat, misshapen sleeves and green hood dangling down his back. The thing was slung over his right shoulder in a fireman's lift. His right hand held it in place where Iris had stitched the polo-neck to his old, paint-stained decorating trousers. His left hand reached to open the front door—and she knew her task was to close the Chubb quietly after him so the sound wouldn't rouse the boy. The sound from the TV set was garbled: its shimmer a nebulous flicker back-lighting her.

He left carrying his unnatural cargo without turning. As she closed the front door she saw them dissolve into the night as he walked to the garden gate and the path to Llwynmadoc Street...

And *after* she closed the door, now standing with her back pressed to it—did she see a slight *wiggling* of those arms, or was it caused by the natural sway of her husband's motion? Did she see what was—no, silly, ridiculous—empty white Christmas gloves *beating* on his back in tiny fists? Little malformed hands *clawing* at the material of his Mac? A manic dwarf *struggling* in the flashing-then-dead strobe light of an exploding rocket?

How many fires were burning? How many children cheering in wonder, wrapped against the cold of night? She buried what she saw—*imagined* she saw?—in other thoughts, *any* thoughts. Turned up the TV, but the cacophony outdoors only seemed to cut through even more violently.

Remember, remember...

But she *did* remember. There was no need to demand it. She remembered that November four years ago when they had another child. One that died. She remembered the fuzzy, crackling Tom Bell voice of the consultant, telling her of the abnormality they'd detected. She remembered him telling them that it wouldn't live after it was born. That they'd have to induce labour. She remembered asking him not to use that word. Please. Please don't...

Never be forgot...

Never. Never. Never.

Des returned as the Big Ben chimes of *News at Ten* tolled their sonorous knell. Alastair Burnet and Reginald Bosanquet talked as he lowered himself into his armchair, brown leather-gloved hands resting on the white arm covers. He sat staring at the screen with blank eyes.

"Did you see it burn?"

"Yes."

"*Did* you?"

"*Yes*. Iris. I watched it *burn*. What more do you want me to say?" He made it sound as though he'd been made to do something unwillingly, and despicable. Then he softened, realising that had upset her and it wasn't fair. "There were others," he told her, "other guys already on fire. I threw our one in. High as I could, into the middle where the flames were biggest. A shout went up. I don't know who was doing the shouting. It buckled, went up. The mask started melting. Football head caved in. Gloves evaporated into ash. Something gave way behind and it fell into the centre, alight all over. Then some bangers went off. Kids were running round waving sparklers like they were Zorro. Mostyn Edwards and his boys were there. They said hello. They asked where Kelvin was. They asked where you were. I walked away. I didn't say hello back." He rubbed his eyes. They must have been stinging from the smoke. They were red-rimmed. "Yes, I watched it burn."

Iris stood up and switched the television off. In the silence she took his gloved hands in hers and kissed them. But in the silence also they could now discern Kelvin's gentle sobbing from upstairs.

Des moved to get up. "Oh, no . . . " If he'd woken, then he knew.

"I'll go," said Iris. She didn't relish the prospect, but somehow felt it was a responsibility that fell on her own shoulders. She would know how to break it to him. She would find the words. And she would be there for him to hold, to hug, or to hate, as she would always be.

She was halfway up the stairs when the doorbell unexpectedly rang. (*Ding-dong—Avon calling!*) She turned round but could see only darkness beyond the glass panels.

Des was already on his way. "I'll get it." He flipped the light switch for her, illuminating the stair carpet. "It's probably Elwyn."

"Offer him a cup of tea."

As she reached the landing, the door opened below and let the night in. She felt the cold on her back and the rancid tang of sulphur ushered in vivid memories as if it were yesterday, but of course it wasn't yesterday—it was today, November the fifth, when the nurses told them her and Des should hold their dead baby. That they'd regret it if they didn't see how *beautiful* he was. And he *was* beautiful. So *very* beautiful in her arms—and in his father's. Such a pretty face, a gorgeous, perfect face—but no head . . . no *head* at all . . .

She heard voices downstairs but not what they said. If it was Elwyn it was bound to be about rugby, so she wasn't that interested.

As she entered Kelvin's bedroom the opening door cast a wedge of light. Her son's crying clawed at her deep inside, as it always did. That's why she had to be the one to make it better.

The landing light was on, but she didn't want to startle him by switching on the bedroom light too. Consequently, while the side of the room behind her was lit, the bed itself was slathered in gloom. She could just about make out the staring eyes of Jon Pertwee in a magician-like pose as the new *Doctor Who* on an old *Radio Times* cover Sellotaped above the bed head.

Her foot touched something not the texture of the carpet.

She looked down.

The latest issue of *TV21* was pinned down under her slipper.

She picked it up and placed it aside, next to the Airfix Lancaster bomber he and his father had made together in meticulous wonder.

To her relief she could see that the guy was gone. Its absence finally confirmed, only the slightest indentation remaining in the blanket where it had lain. Kelvin lay flat on his back under the sheets, head sunk in the pillow, wearing the baby mask with the orange curl on the forehead.

She gasped. Then laughed.

"Oh, Kelvin, you monkey! That's a horrible trick to play on your mam, that is. You gave me a heart attack!"

But wait a minute—wasn't the *guy* wearing the mask? Didn't she see it when it was hanging over her husband's shoulder? No, because it was hanging face down. That was it. The mask must've fallen off as Des . . .

No sooner had she dismissed that worry than something perturbed her far more. Why wasn't her son answering, now that his prank had had the desired effect? Why was he still *sobbing*? In fact, why was he sobbing *at all*?

She moved towards the bed.

No, ta—we won't sit down, sir, all the same . . . The voices downstairs, though real, sounded as disembodied as those on the TV. *It's about your son, sir* . . . The man had more of a Welsh accent than her husband's, and was older. She pictured him with grey, bristly hair. *I'm afraid there's been a tragic accident* . . . She thought he must be talking about something else, not her, not us, not . . . *Doctor there with his family—too late to do anything* . . . *Children climb inside bonfires, see—do it for dares or whatnot* . . . *Must have got trapped* . . . *Fire was roaring, no-one could stop it* . . . *Members of the public started screaming, saw his face, his arms waving—trouble was, the more he waved, the more he fanned the flames.* Her pulse was leaping, belting through her body, thudding in her chest. *Mr Edwards—I believe you know Mr Edwards?—tried to call you back, but you were walking away* . . . *He said you probably couldn't hear because of all the fireworks going off* . . .

"Kelvin?"

Iris reached the bed. The smell filled her nostrils: earth, ash, rot, blood, sulphur, decay . . .

"Kelvin?"

She stood staring down at the child with the mask on, no longer able to tell whether the sobbing was coming from behind it or from the grown man downstairs. The lost, last sky rocked with rockets, thunderous in her head, spiked and buckled by the wounds of gunpowder.

She reached down to take away the mask, because what was a mask if not a face with no head? And she did so not only with dread but with incalculable longing. The two things fought in her violently in that moment as her fingertips touched plastic. And when she saw what was behind, something made of bone and fire closed around her heart, crushing it as if it were no more than a ball of paper.

STORY NOTES

CELEBRITY FRANKENSTEIN

Esteemed Texan editor Danel Olsen asked me for something for *Exotic Gothic 4*, a new volume of his anthologies of stories set anywhere but the traditional European gothic locations. The title and idea came first, the voice and story quickly followed. It seemed to me that almost every UK television series at the time had the prefix *Celebrity* (*Celebrity Shark Bait* being the most ludicrous, and most disappointing, example). Clearly, no procedure or abuse was too intrusive, private, or extreme to merit attention from programme-makers hungry for ratings. Equally, a lust for fame and body image perfection has long since become the Holy Grail in culture as we seem to be inundated with spectacles of celebrity suffering, via meltdowns, miscarriages, surgery, sectioning, and ultimately death. Elvis, Britney, Michael Jackson, Tom Cruise, and every *X-Factor* and *American Idol* winner was in my mind when I was writing this. Though I'm using Mary Shelley too. Someone who, ironically, knew a little about fame in her own lifetime. (Though never had her own chat show.)

BLESS

When Willie Miekle, after the death of a close relative, announced that he wanted to edit a charity anthology on the theme of cancer, many writers, like me, saw it as a worthwhile cause. However it had an erratic on-off gestation and, though the book later came to pass, in the interim I'd sold my own contribution to *Crimewave*. Subject-wise, I decided I did not want to focus so much on the disease itself, or death even, but its aftermath, grief—and specifically, grief gone wrong. I'd had an idea in the back on my mind: merely one scene in a supermarket. A woman abducts a child, imagining her own dead daughter has come back to her. In the writing of it, though, her voice became curiously more chilling as it got more amusing in its banality. And I found the juxtaposition of the everyday and the metaphysical quite exciting, albeit only in Esmée's deluded mind.

A WHISPER TO A GREY

The legendary BBC *Ghost Story for Christmas* series was a massive influence not only on my love of genre fiction but also directly on my career as a writer, both of short stories and TV drama. In my previous collections you may have met my "Amateur Supernaturalist"—an English "psychical investigator" named Venables, created knowingly in the tradition of M. R. James's terrified scholars. (He was first called "Ogilvy": my first job having been as a copywriter for advertising agency Ogilvy Benson & Mather in London, then I realized "Ogilvy" was a character in H. G. Wells's *War of the Worlds*, so I stole our chairman's name—"Venables.") His occasional narratives are dotted mostly through issues of *All Hallows*, the journal of the Ghost Story Society, courtesy of Barbara Roden and her husband Christopher. This one was actually the first in the series, written many moons ago, which you will realise when I tell you it was originally called "The Horse Whisperer"—long before that other pesky writer stole that title.

THE ARSE-LICKER

This one came about because Mark West asked me to contribute to a seventies-themed horror anthology called *Anatomy of Death: In Five Sleazy Lessons*. Sleazy horror isn't really my bag, so I was thinking of giving him an Amicus-type story, much more my cup of tea. But somehow I thought I was short-changing him and the word "sleazy" became something of a challenge. Then I thought of an idea simultaneously repellent and hilarious (to me). I was pleased, because it was an Amicus-style "poetic justice" tale, but done in a way Amicus would have been utterly appalled by. One reviewer said it reminded him of Chuck Palahniuk at his most outrageous. I'll take that as the greatest possible compliment.

THE PETER LORRE FAN CLUB

A request came from the redoubtable Johnny Mains to come up with a horror story on the theme of clubs or societies. For some reason this title occurred to me quite quickly, but I had no idea what to do with it. Censorship and the repression of ideas is something I care about deeply, and, hearing of such things as extremists in Mali breaking the hands of guitar-players, and the activities of the Taliban elsewhere, I wondered how a person would react to having their most beloved art form forbidden. How would I react? How far would I go? I remembered my school friends and me as adolescent film buffs and how we had later gone on our separate paths—then wondered, in a different era, how different those paths might have been. I'd long ago read *Kiss of the Spider Woman* and the dialogue form seemed right here. The other big influence, especially on the ending, was Elem Klimov's masterpiece of war and horror, *Come and See*. And because we discussed that film in some detail, and because he will get it, this story is for Adam Nevill. (Note: I've edited it a little for this reprint: I couldn't resist tinkering. Sorry!)

CERTAIN FACES

My aim in this novella was to explore the question: can we be culpable by inaction? Can the lack of empathy of artistic endeavour make us remote from common humanity, and what is the cost of that? My thanks go to the wonderful portrait painter Jennifer McRae for her time and talent when I wrote this story. Her anecdote while I posed for her got me thinking—but the characters within are entirely fictional and any resemblance . . . (etc., etc.). This was originally to be the first part of a novel or television series (or film), comprising three (or five?) separate stories all about the same missing teenager (based, tragically, on a true missing-person mystery that happened near the town where I live). My series proposal was called *Love Like a Murder* because Alfred Hitchcock always said you should film a murder like a love scene, and a love scene like a murder. (This story was written a while ago, with such anachronisms as smoking in a public place, but I decided not to update it. Instead I ask the reader to consider it a "period piece".)

WITH ALL MY LOVE ALWAYS ALWAYS FOREVER XXX

This is a piece of flash fiction (with a deliberately Robert Shearman–esque title) that I wrote for Michael Wilson's "This Is Horror" website. Michael wanted something in the lead-up to Christmas 2012, and out of the blue I thought of the Fleet services we always stopped at on the way to my daughter's place for the holidays and the way carloads of gifts are left unattended. I'd also had an idea for ages of an antique mechanical necklace—made by the Borgias to dispose of their enemies, perhaps?—but didn't know what to do with it. The two things gelled, and for all its brevity, I was pleased with the result.

MATILDA OF THE NIGHT

I like stories about sound. About tape recorders. I love Francis Ford Coppola's film *The Conversation*. And ghost stories have always been part of a "telling" tradition. I was very much taken with this idea of a folklorist gathering oral tales when, many years ago, I was researching Welsh mythology for a putative TV series called *Welsh Tales of Terror*, to be made by the BBC drama department in Cardiff. The story developed under the watchful eye of Karl Francis and Ceri Meyrick, producer and script editor respectively, but the series sadly never got underway, probably due to disinterest from London. I returned to the storyline when Paul Finch asked me to consider contributing to his uncannily similarly named anthology *Tales of Terror of Wales*. Revisiting it afresh, I found myself more interested in the protagonist's interior life: Ivan Rees seemed to be a modern version of those bachelor scholars of M. R. James I mentioned earlier. And the more I wrote, the more it seemed his encounter with the "Gwrach-y-Rhybin" was waiting for him all along. Rather like death itself is, for all of us.

THE SHUG MONKEY

While growing up I was captivated by the Sherlock Holmes stories, of course, but also enjoyed enormously Conan Doyle's other less famous characters, like the comically inept Brigadier Gerard, and the brilliant but rambunctious Professor Challenger of *Lost World* fame. Canadian editors Jeff Campbell and Charles Prepolec, taking R&R from their Holmesian *Gaslight* series, said they wanted to do a Challenger anthology for a change, and I was immediately on the case, rubbing my hands with glee in search of cryptozoology. My start point was the "Shug Monkey" of the title, a genuine Cambridgeshire legend (many thanks to Oliver Jackson for local knowledge), but I knew I wanted it to be more than that. I fooled around with Challenger meeting another professor, Bernard Quatermass, as a young boy, but that felt a bit "cute". Then I realised the clue was in another of Nigel Kneale's works—the formidable *Abominable Snowman* movie with its eerie and humane conclusion. The secret was the Shug Monkey itself: not a throwback to the past, but from the future. I was particularly pleased with the final sentiment that the real "Lost World" was Challenger's (and Doyle's).

WRONG

This was directly inspired by something that happened in my home town a few years ago, a story as bizarre as it was sad—though without the outcome portrayed in my story. The way prurient gossip surrounds this kind of thing, and the attendant moral outrage, made me think it was the core of an unusual story, but I didn't know how to tell it, quite honestly, until I combined it with my memories of student life. The two things seemed to coalesce and make it work, I hope. The editor, Mark Morris (who accepted it for *The 2nd Spectral Book of Horror Stories*) said that "it wasn't really horror, but it was"—which was exactly as intended.

THE MAGICIAN KELSO DENNETT

My good mate Paul Finch said he wanted stories for an anthology called *Terror Tales of the Seaside*, the latest in his series for Gray Friar Press. Was I interested? I didn't know. But that's normal. The first image I had, not unnaturally, was of digging with bucket and spade. Of children burying adults in the sand. Very much of my childhood, but very much of Poe. Being buried alive. But it had to be more than that, didn't it? A stunt. OK.

A magician. Yes. Derren Brown. David Blaine. A TV transmission of a trick, yes—or was it a miracle? But if it was to be like a Derren Brown stunt, it would have to have a Derren Brown punch line. Halfway through writing, it suddenly occurred to me with a genuine chill what that had to be. In the end I didn't have all the answers. Kelso Dennett had outsmarted even me. And the story became about the unknown, and the unknowable—about magic and mystery itself (with a little bit of Margate, Hastings, and memories of childhood holidays in Weston-super-Mare thrown in).

NEWSPAPER HEART

I was absolutely delighted to be on the shortlist of writers asked by Mark Morris to contribute to his passion project—*The Spectral Book of Horror Stories*, something of a homage to the Pan and Fontana volumes we all grew up with. I immediately knew the idea I wanted to deliver, and thought it would appeal to Mark because it had echoes of the kind of stories that were in the Van Thals. It also had echoes of my novella *Whitstable*, which I know Mark liked very much. But most of all it is a story I've wanted to tell for a long time because, amazingly, it is based pretty much on fact. When my brother was about eight he made a Guy Fawkes effigy and got attached to it. *Very* attached. Propped up in the sitting room—just like in my story—it spooked my mother when she did the housework. And my recollection is that, as November 5th got closer, my brother didn't want it to be burned on the bonfire. That, happily, is where any resemblance to real life ends. Though, while the parents' tragic backstory is entirely my own invention, Kelvin's mum and dad are somewhat based on my mum and dad (a science teacher), and the setting is my childhood home—the exact house in Highfield Terrace, Pontypridd where my mother still lives, in every detail. I found I couldn't write it any other way.

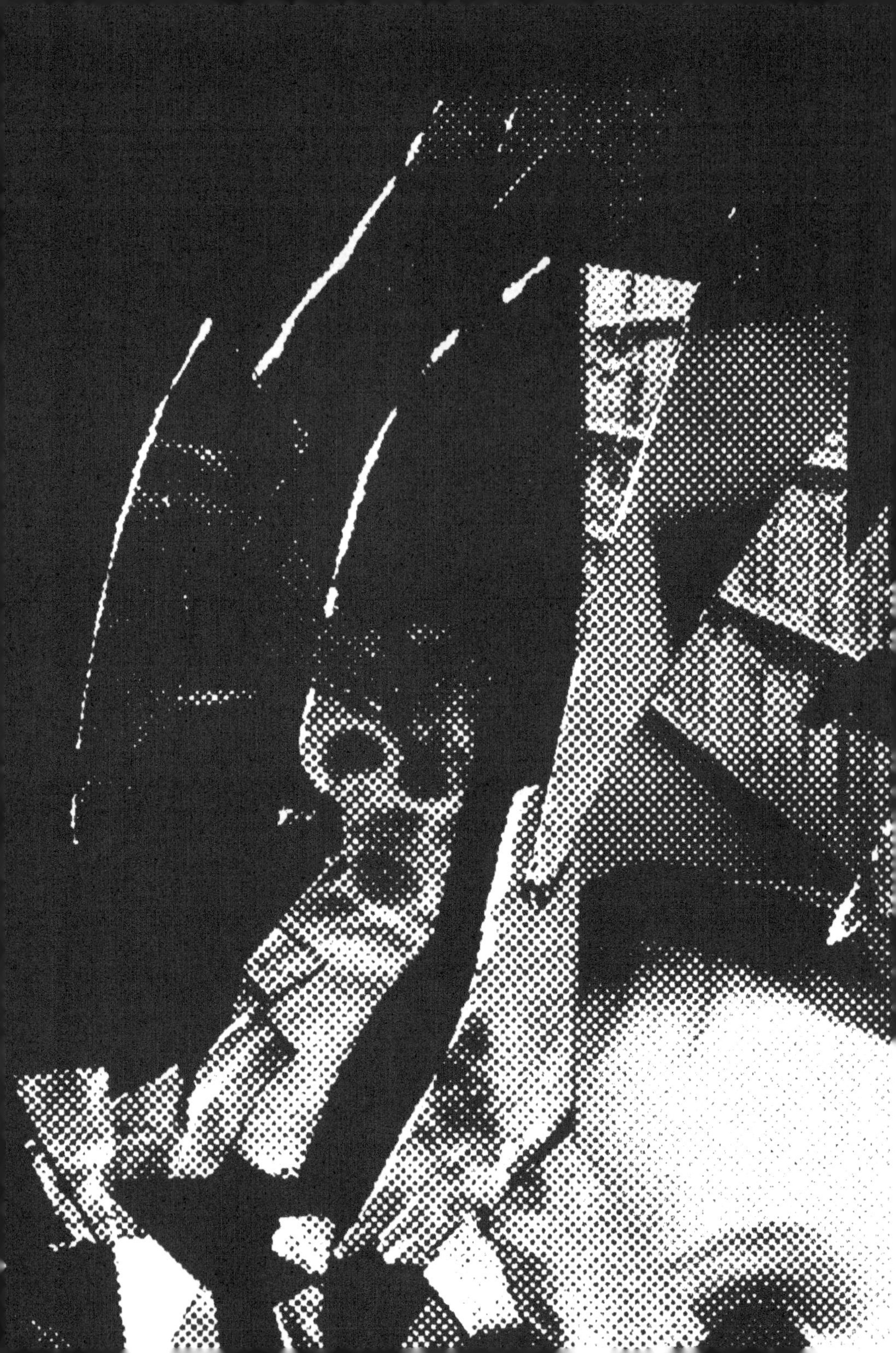

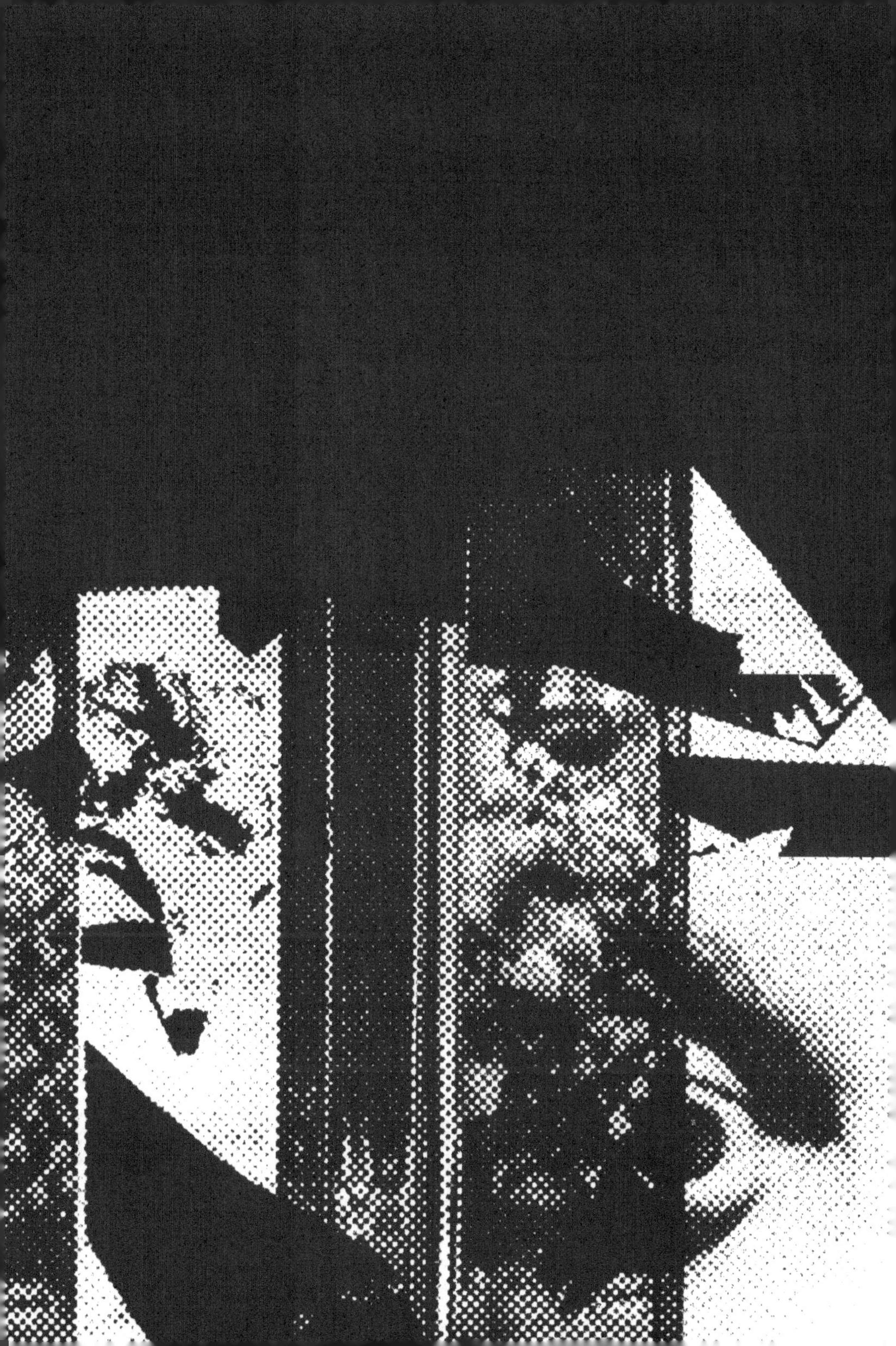

STEPHEN VOLK is the BAFTA-winning creator of the notorious BBCTV "Hallowe'en hoax" *Ghostwatch* and the acclaimed drama series *Afterlife*. His screenplays include *The Awakening*, Ken Russell's *Gothic*, *The Guardian* (co-written with director William Friedkin), and ITV's recent mini-series based on Phil Rickman's *Midwinter of the Spirit*. His stories have been selected for *Year's Best Fantasy and Horror*, *Mammoth Book of Best New Horror*, *Best British Mysteries*, and *Best British Horror*, he has been a Bram Stoker and Shirley Jackson Award finalist, and is the author of two previous collections, *Dark Corners* and *Monsters in the Heart*, which won the British Fantasy Award in 2014.

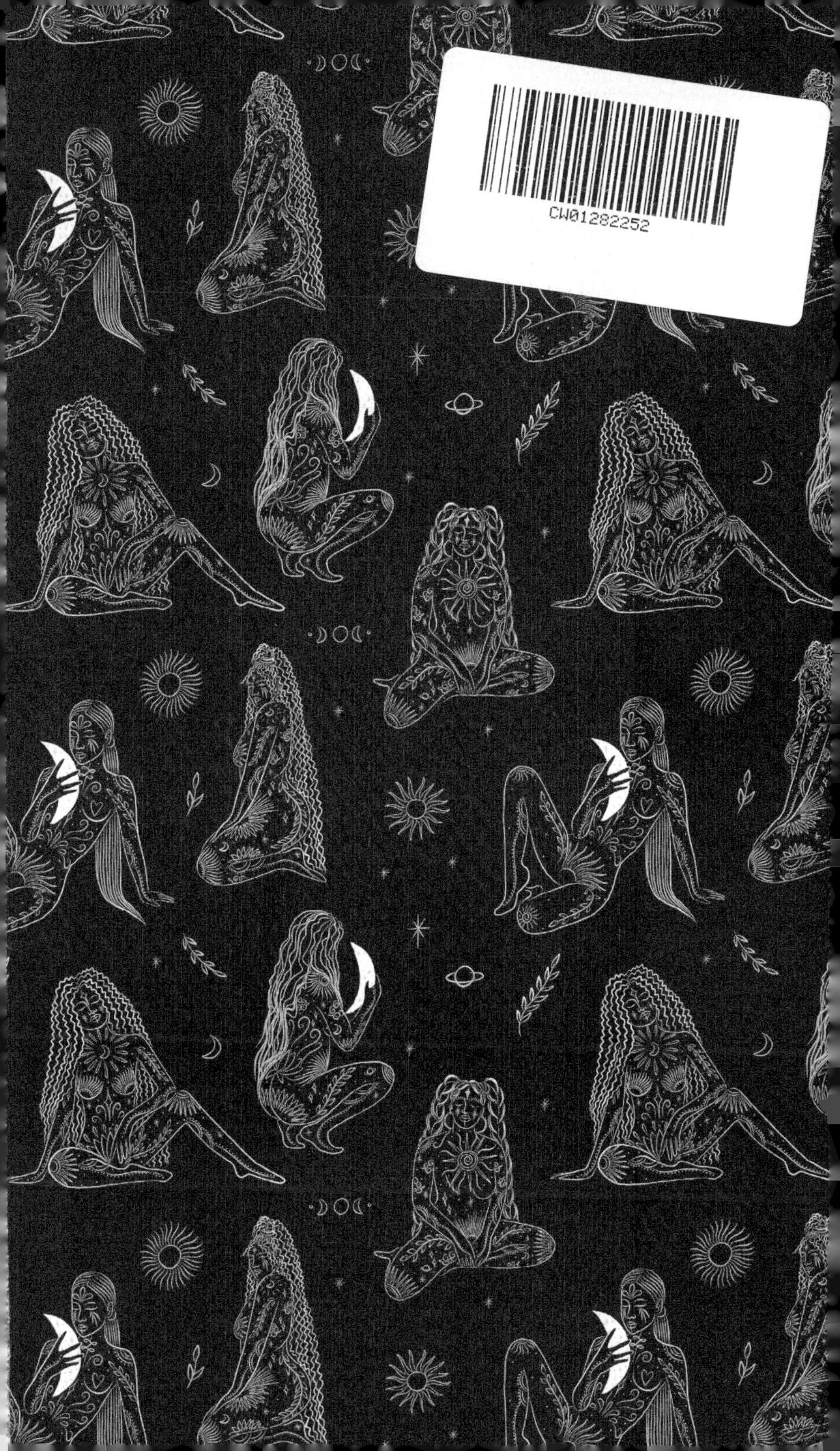

The Little Book of Quotes for Goddesses

For my all of my beautiful friends

Never forget your worth

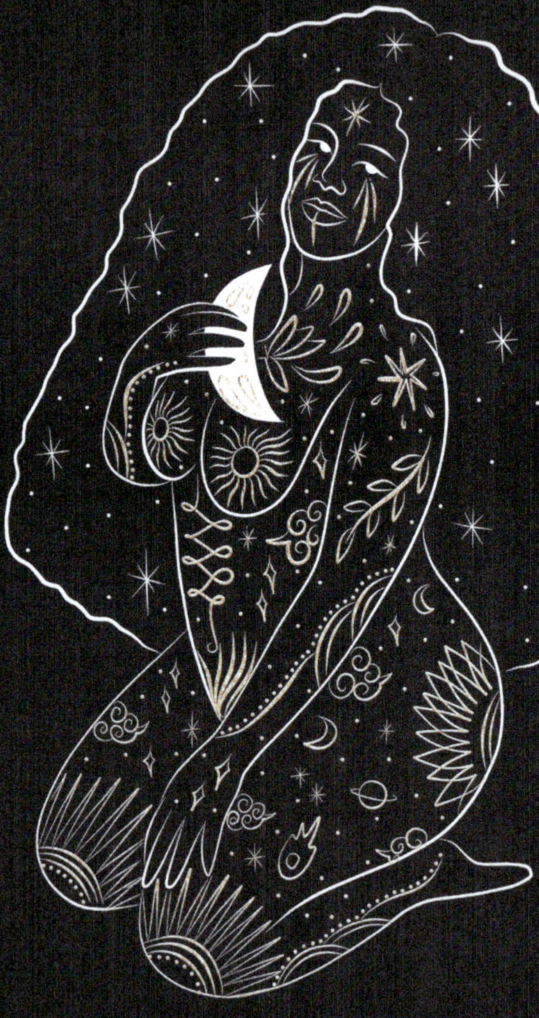

The Goddess does not rule the world; She is the world.

Starhawk

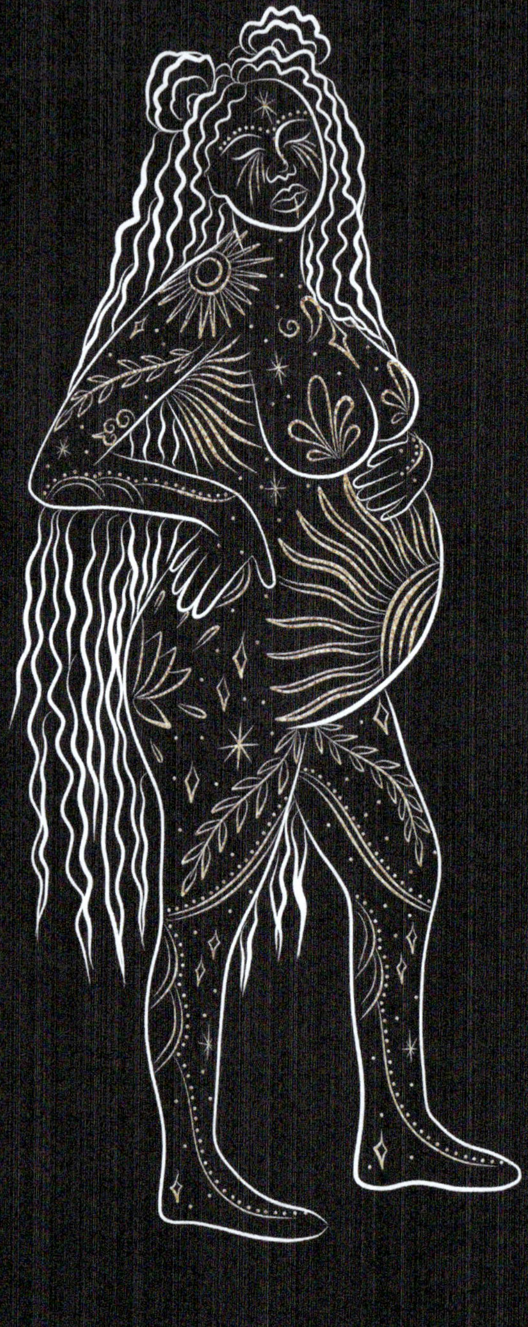

Who is she?
She is your power, your feminine source. Big Mama. The Goddess.
The great mystery.
The web- weaver

Lucy H. Pearce

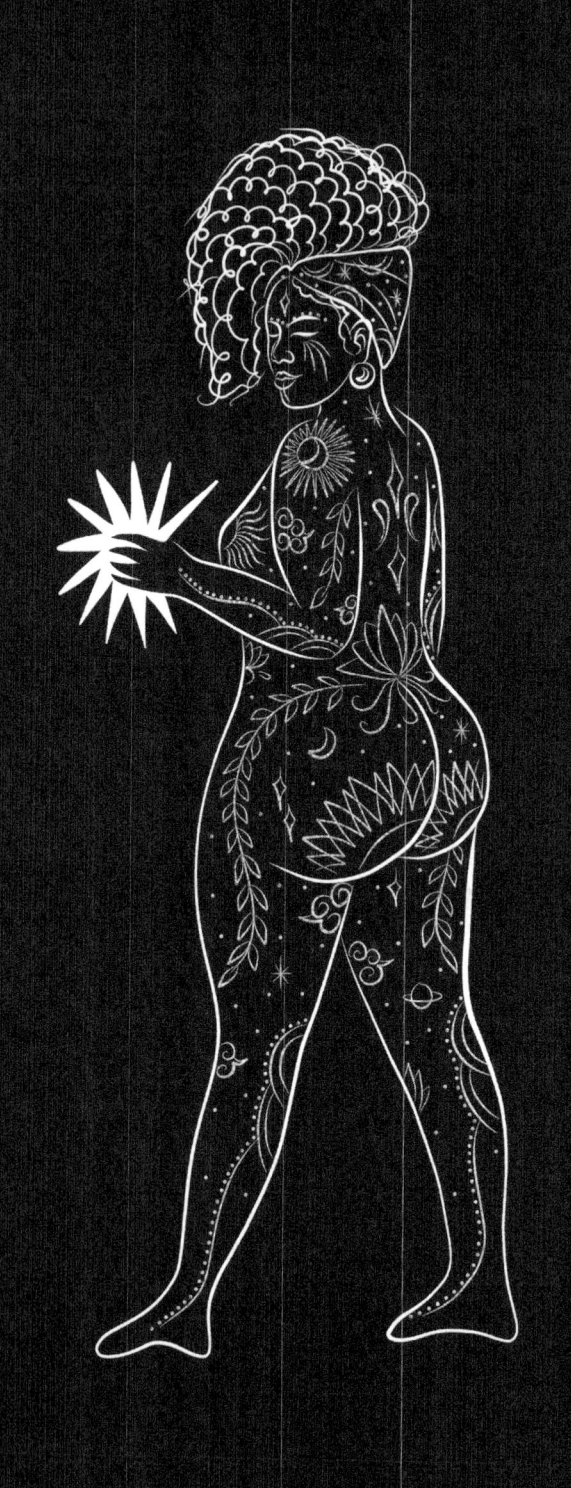

> I have called on the Goddess and found her within myself.

Marion Zimmer Bradley

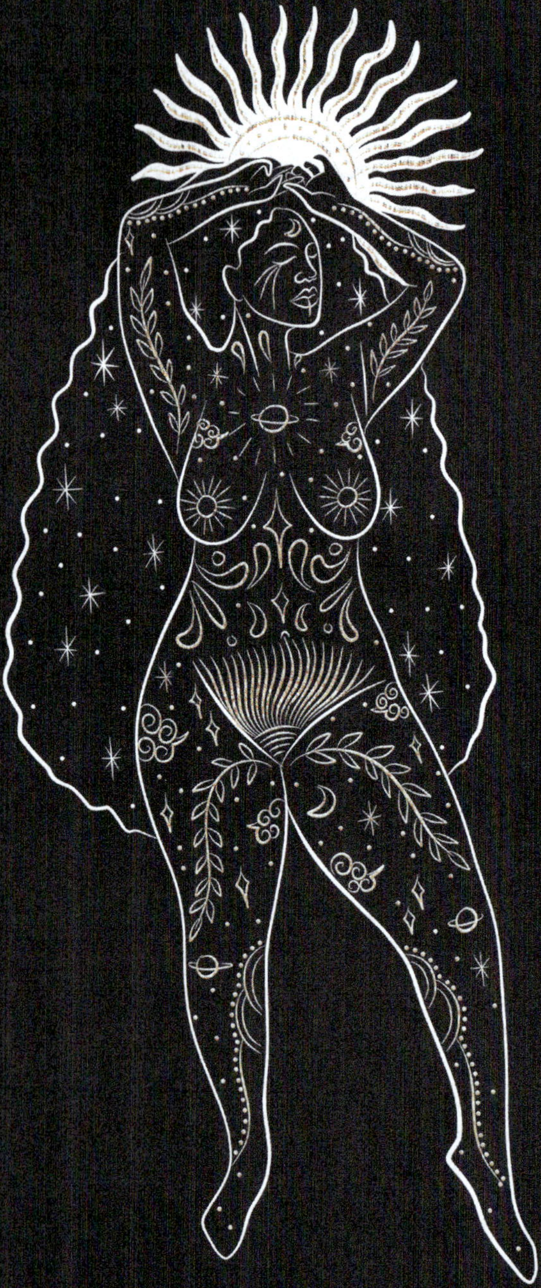

I am the blue-lidded daughter of Sunset;
I am the naked brilliance of the voluptuous night-sky.

Aleister Crowley

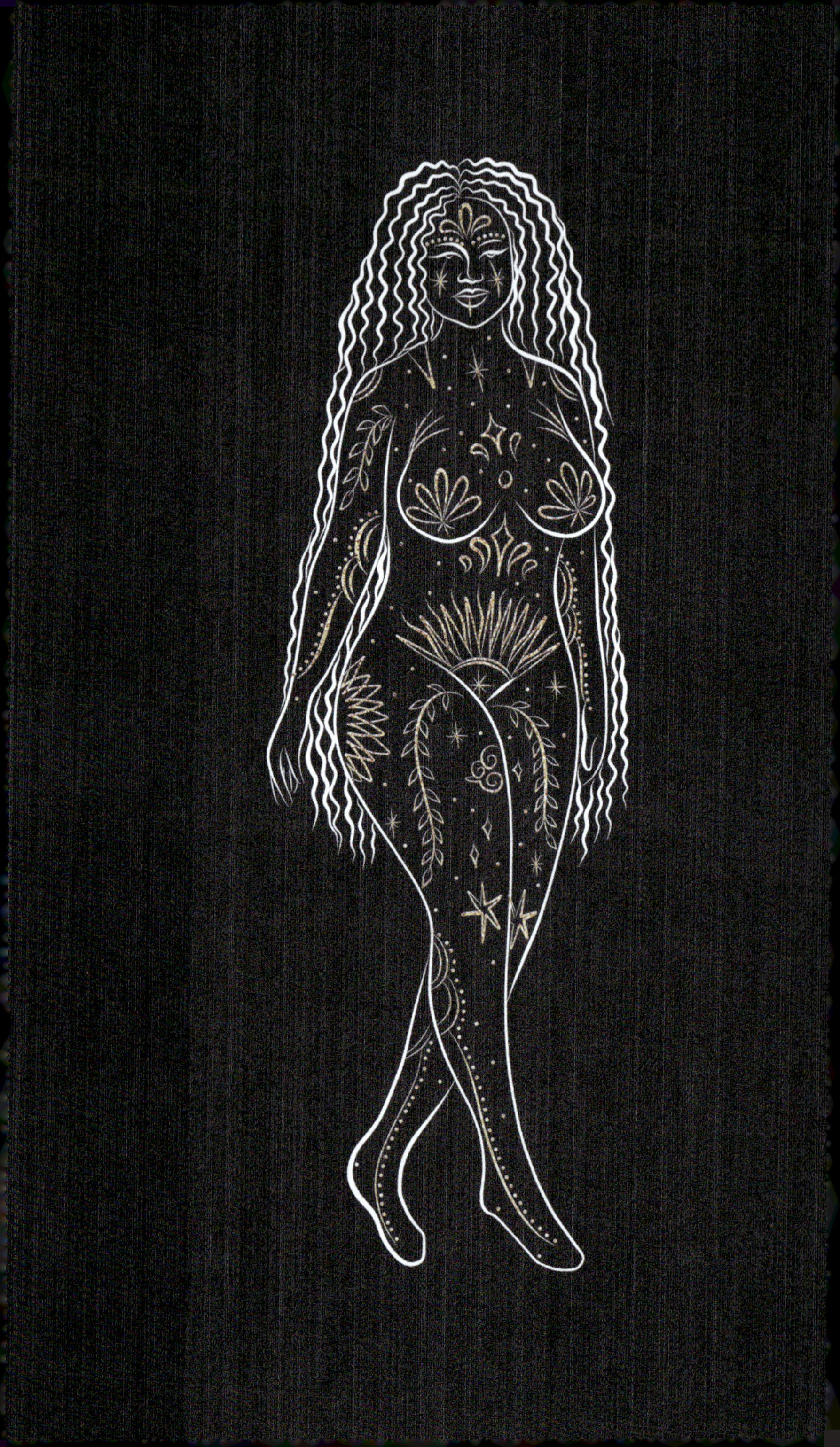

In the end, Goddess is just a word. It simply means the divine in female form.

Sue Monk Kidd

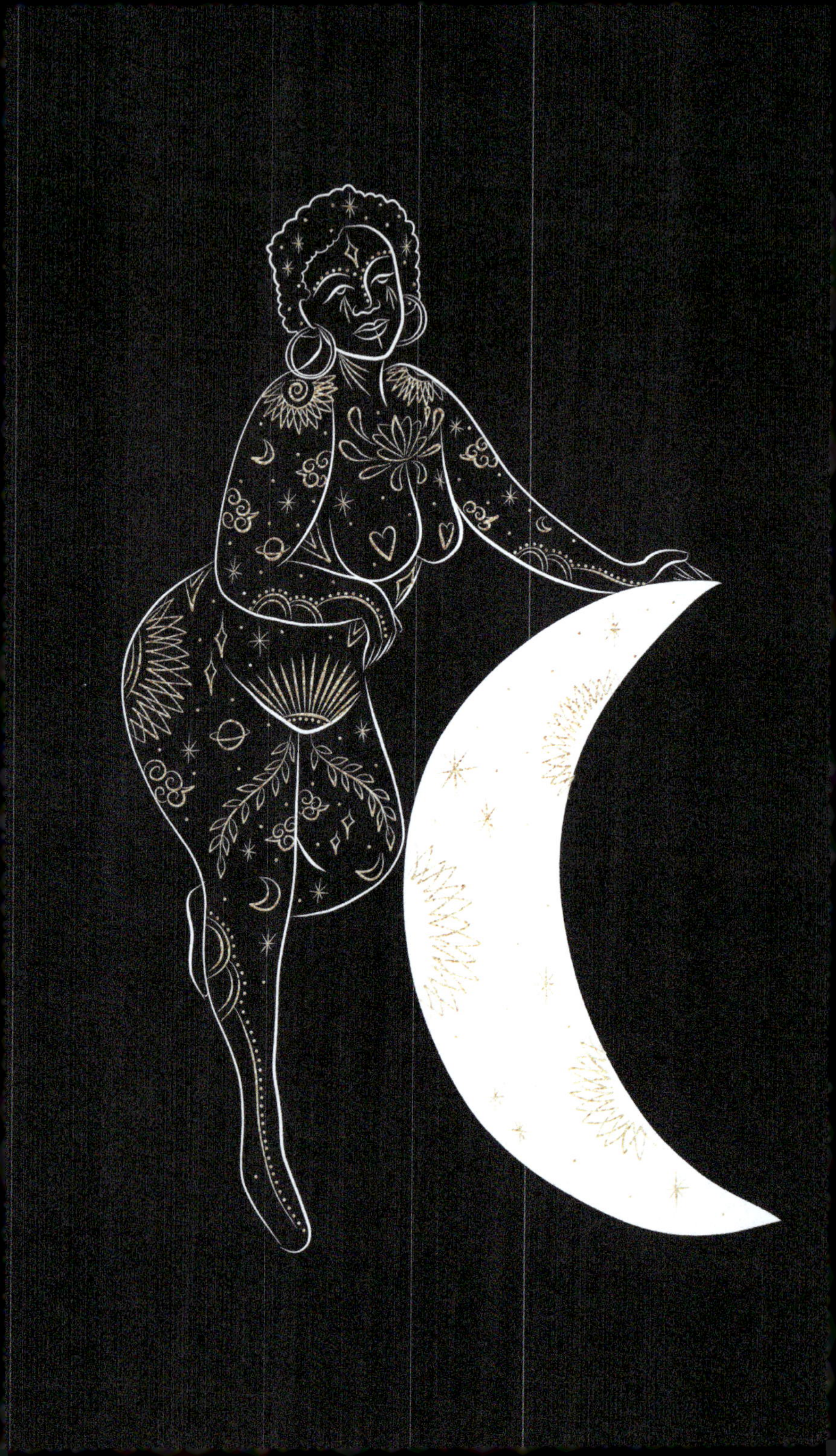

> You think I'm not a goddess? Try me. This is a torch song. Touch me and you'll burn.
>
> — Margaret Atwood

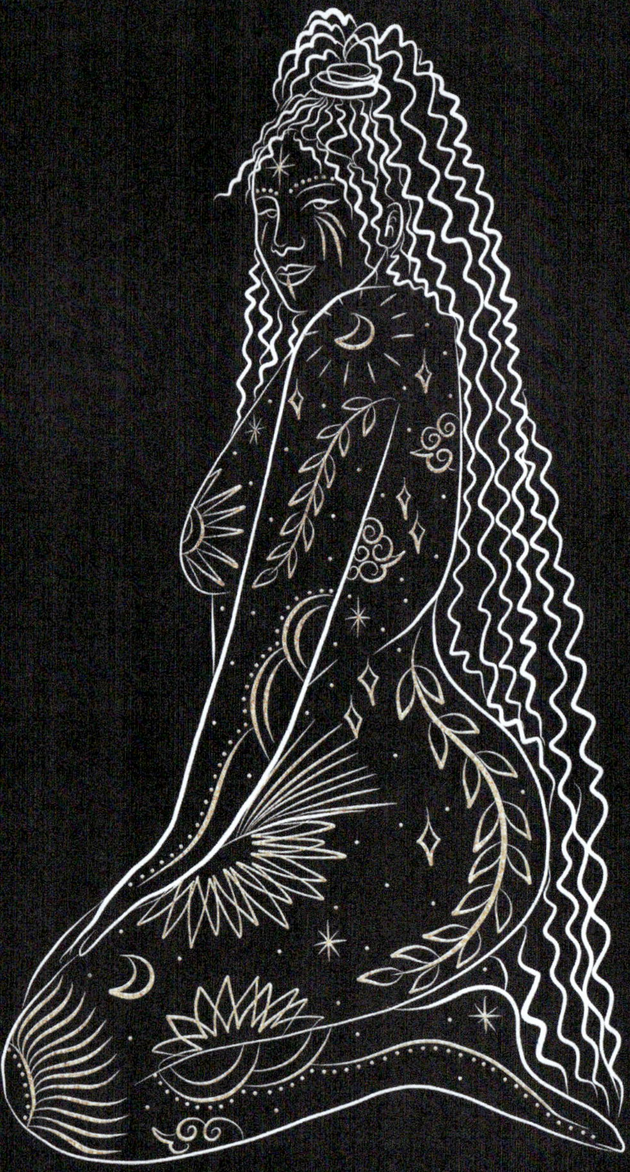

A queen keeps a court that is spoken about. A goddess keeps a court that is never forgotten.

Nalani Singh

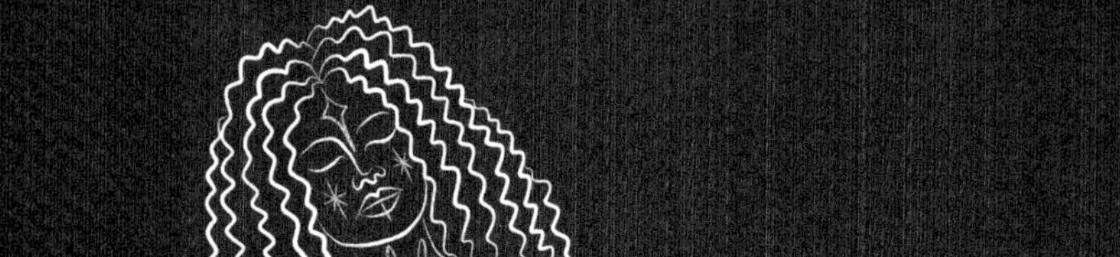

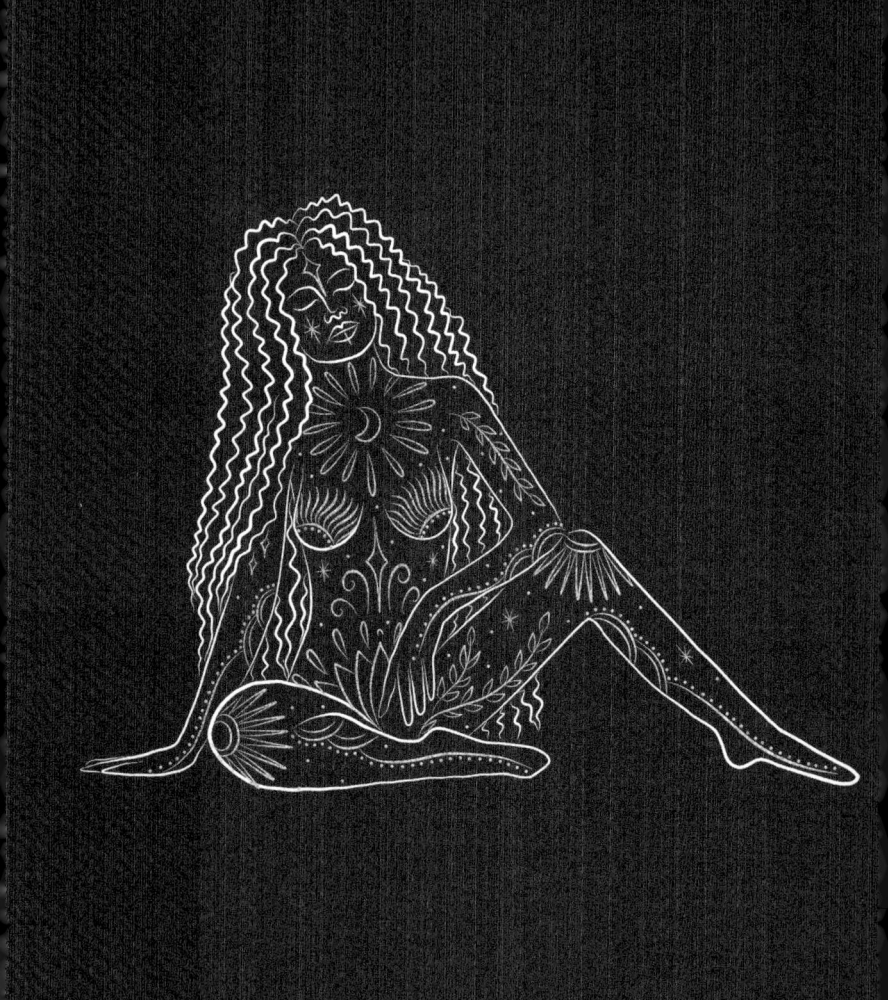

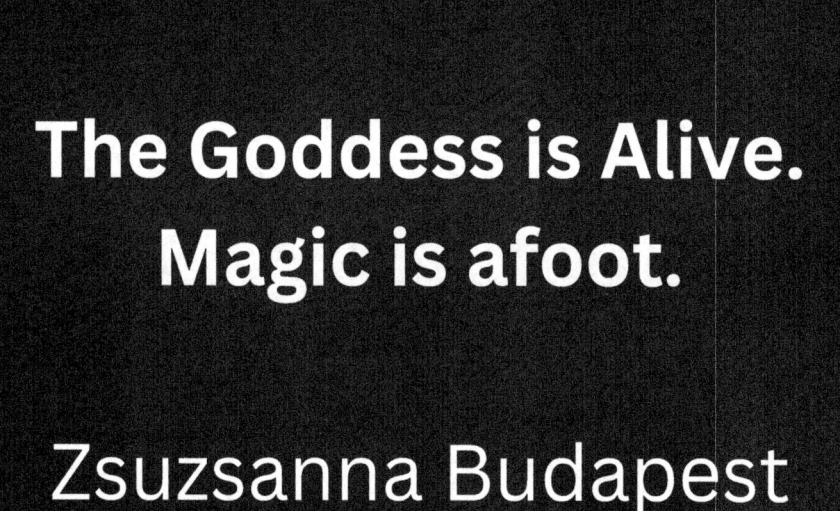

**The Goddess is Alive.
Magic is afoot.**

Zsuzsanna Budapest

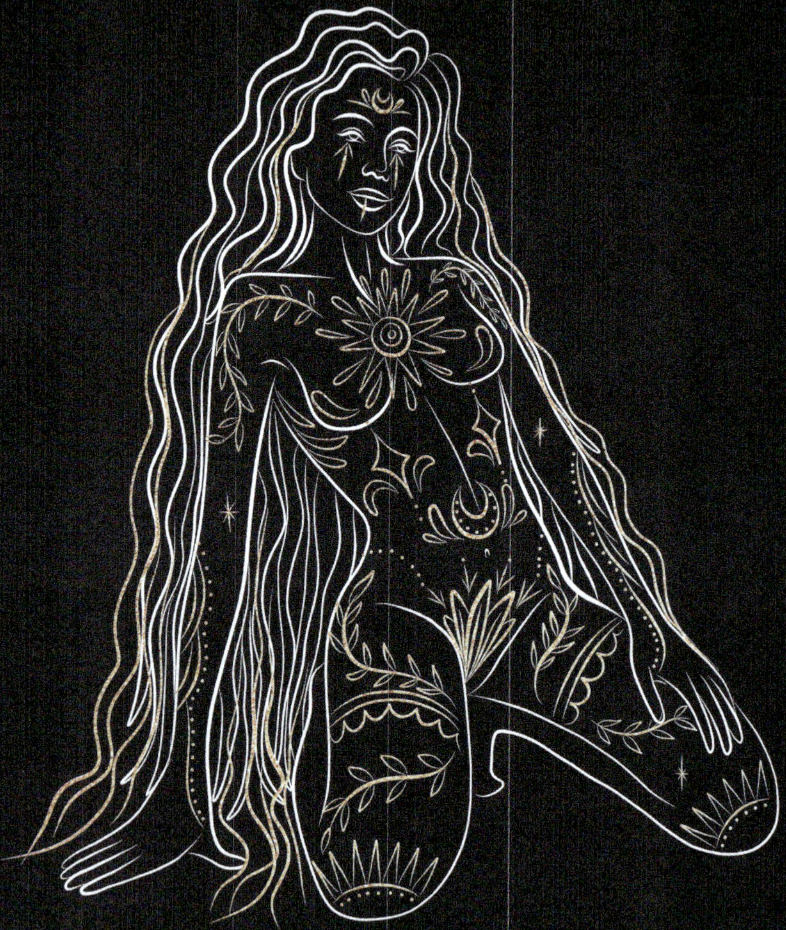

The goddess has never been lost. It is just that some of us have forgotten how to find her.

Patricia Monaghan

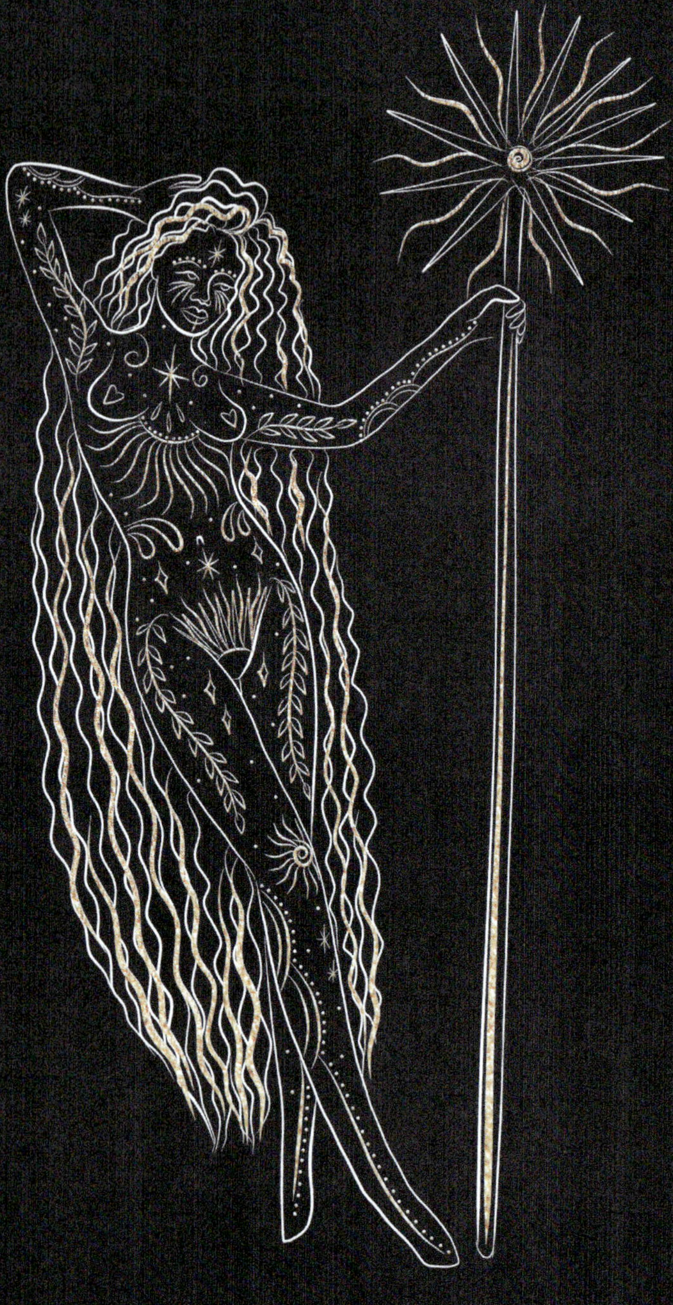

The feminine is more powerful than the masculine, the soft is more powerful than the hard, the water is more powerful than the rock.

Rajneesh

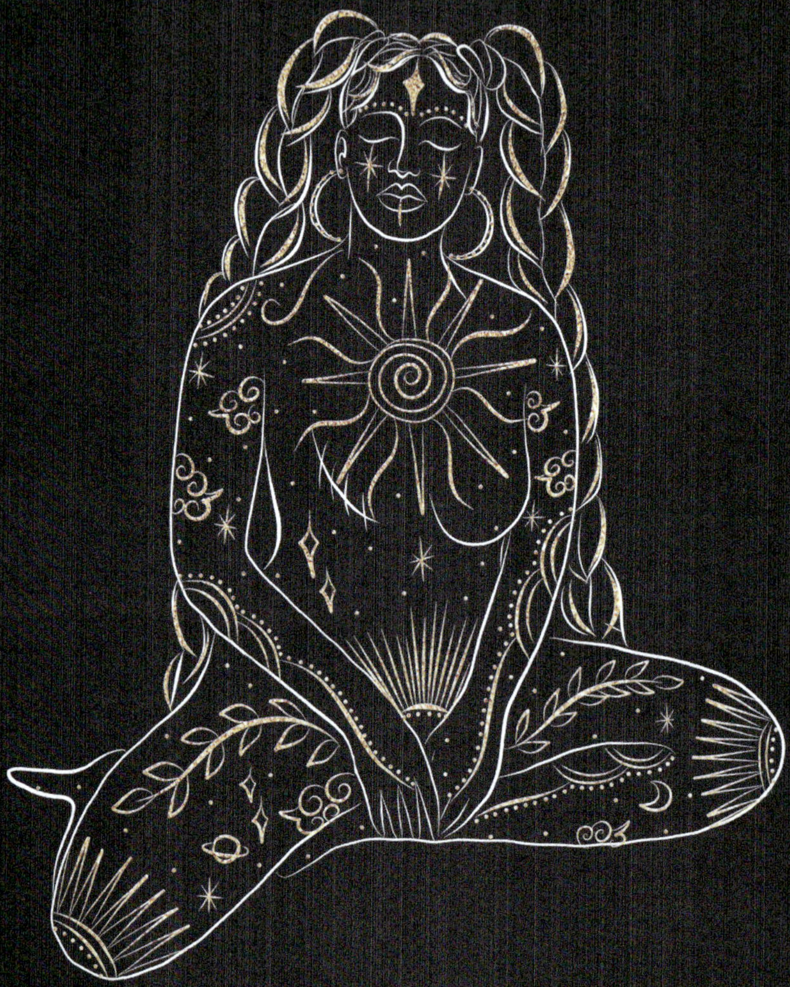

God may be in the details, but the goddess is in the questions. Once we begin to ask them, there's no turning back.

Gloria Steinem

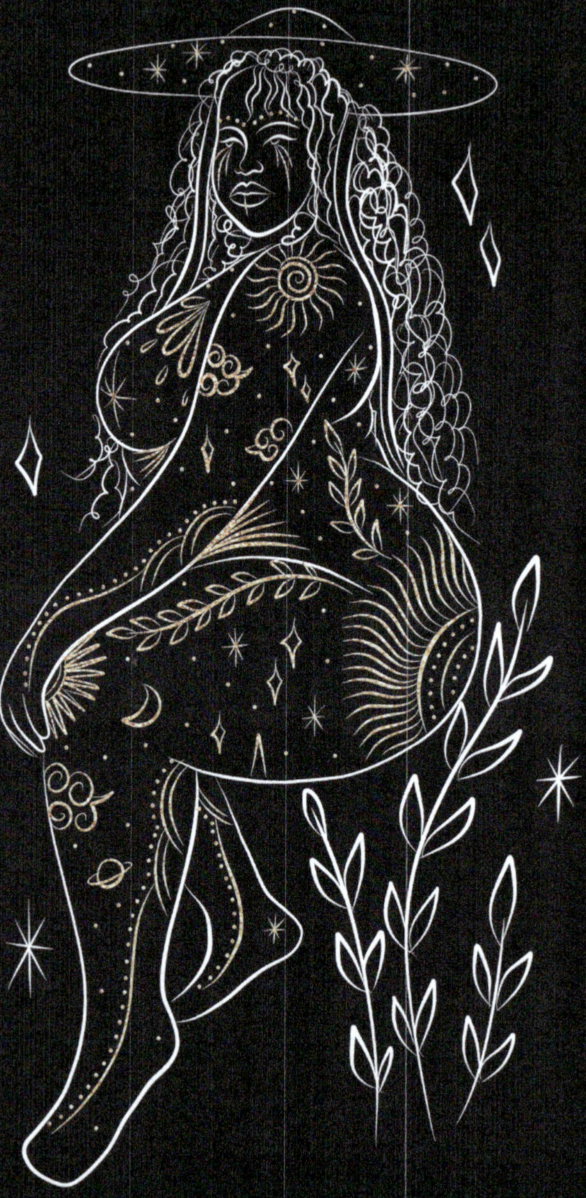

All acts of love and pleasure are my rituals.

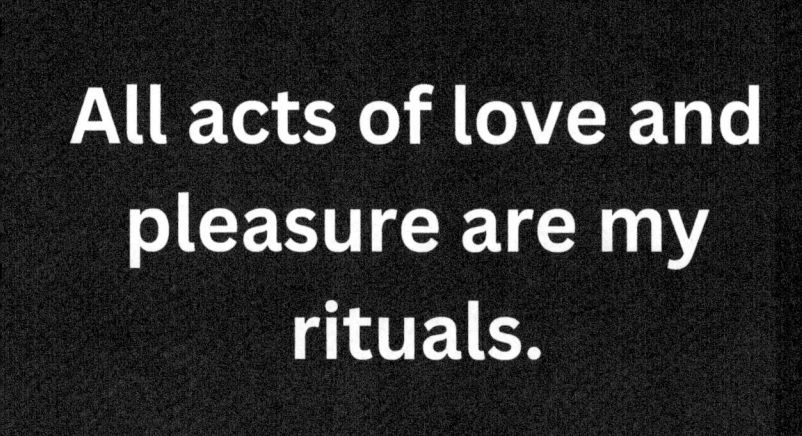

Doreen Valiente

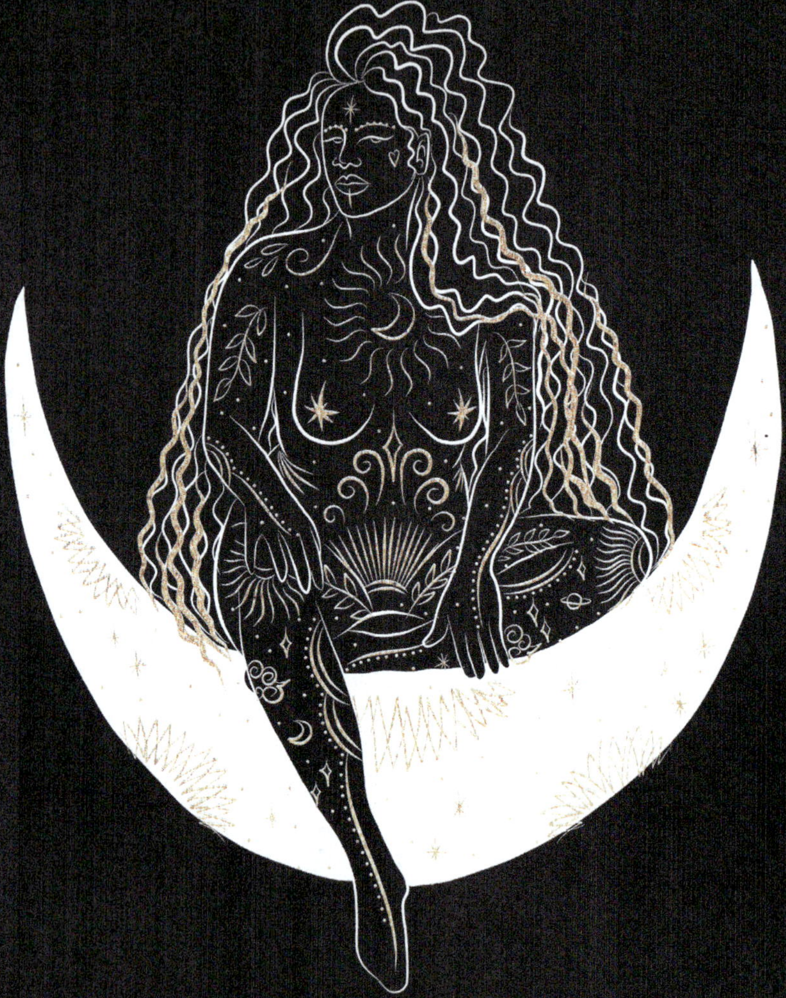

The simplest and most basic meaning of the symbol of the Goddess is the acknowledgment of the legitimacy of female power as a beneficent and independent power.

Carol P. Christ

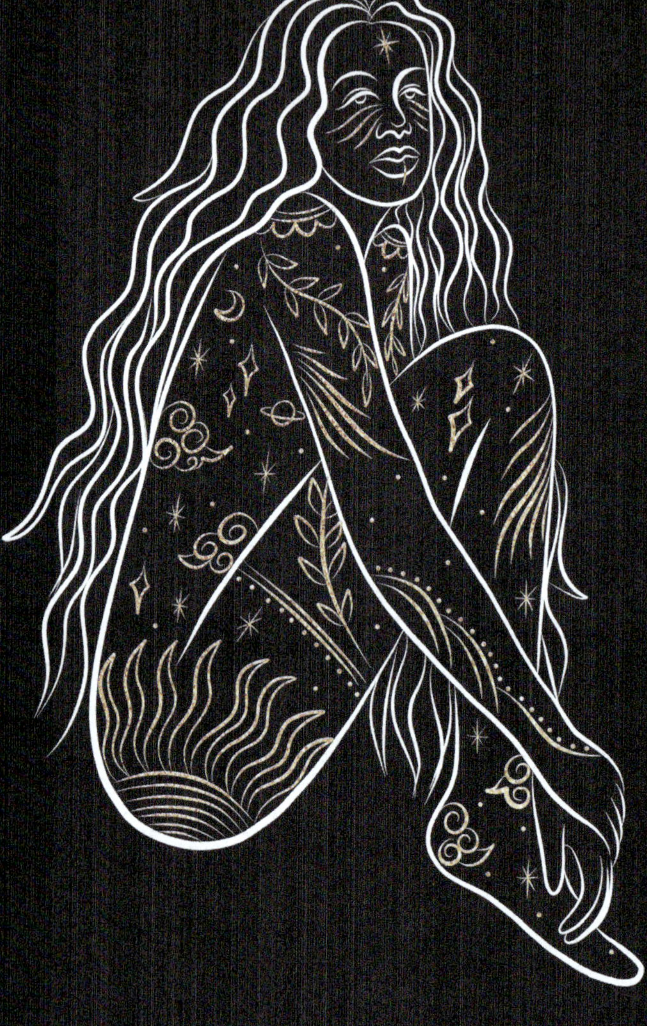

The Goddess does not shower her gifts on those who reject them.

Marion Zimmer Bradley

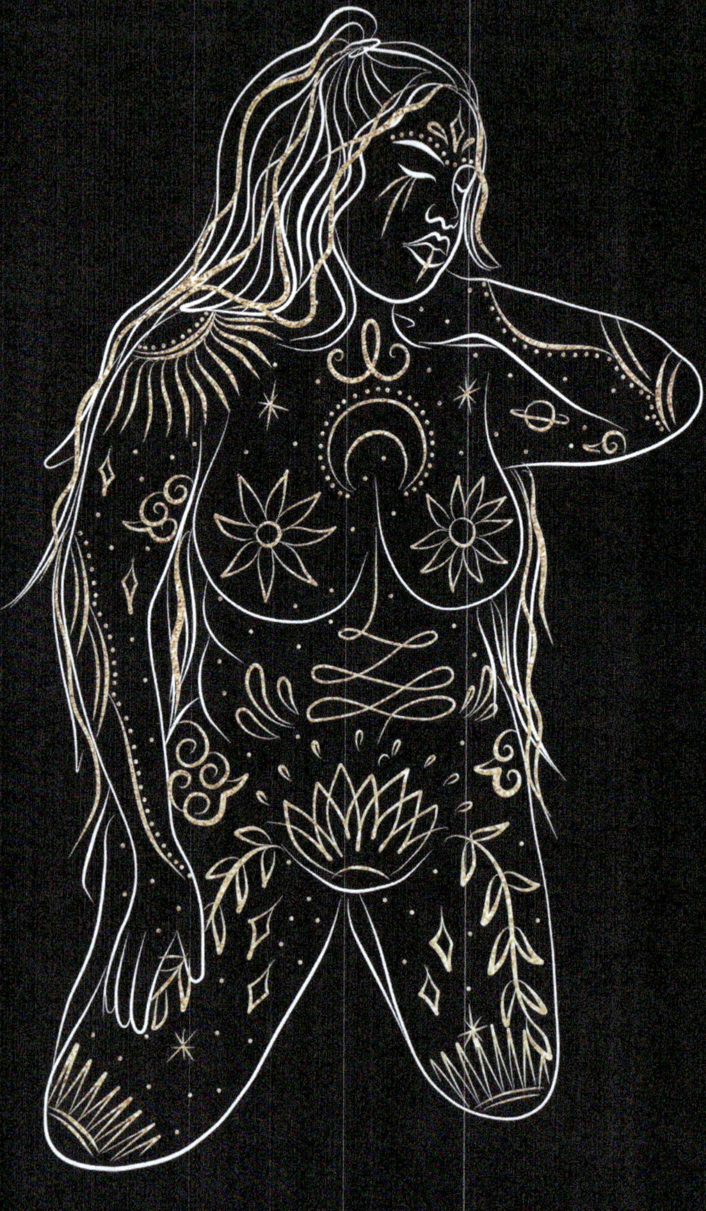

Anytime you feel love for anything, be it stone, tree, lover, or child, you are touched by the Goddess's magick.

Cate Tiernan

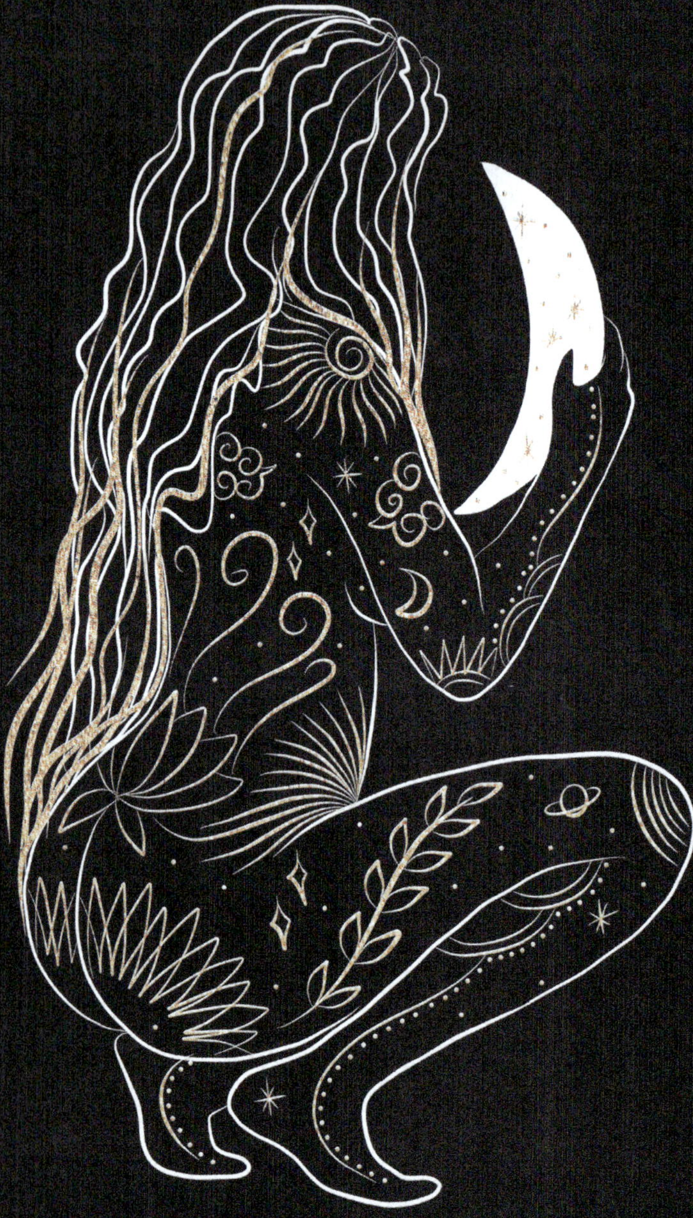

Violence cannot destroy the body of the Goddess, for Her body is the world itself.

Rachel Pollack

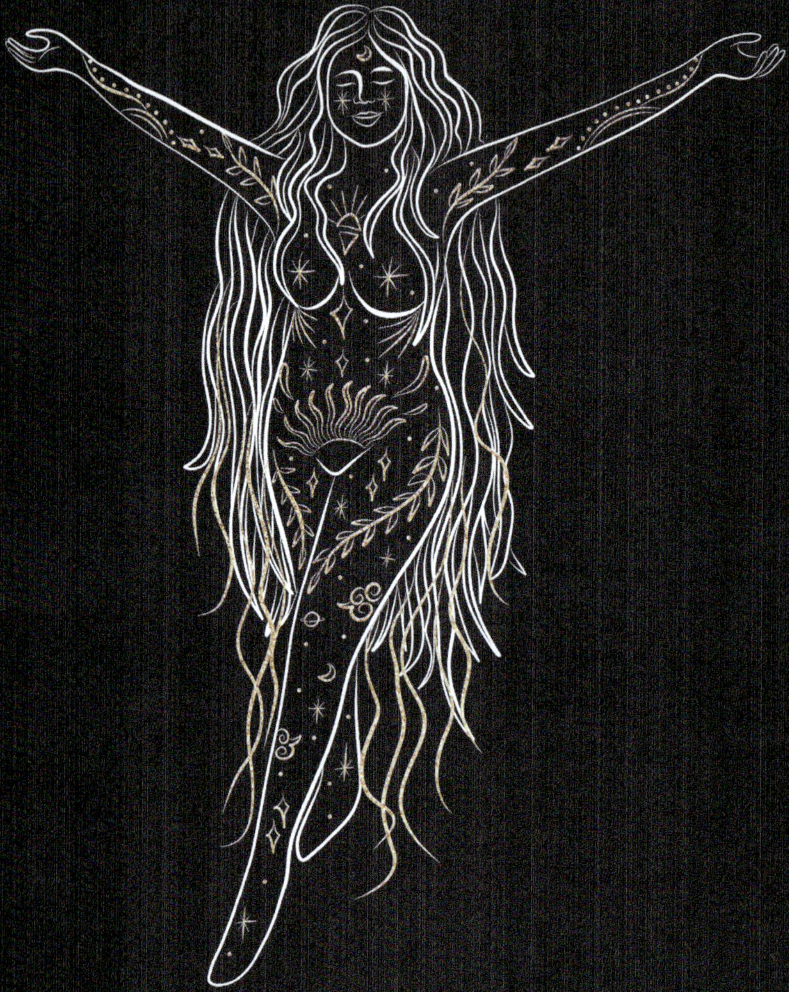

I vow to interpret every experience as a direct healing of the Goddess with my soul.

Rob Brezsny

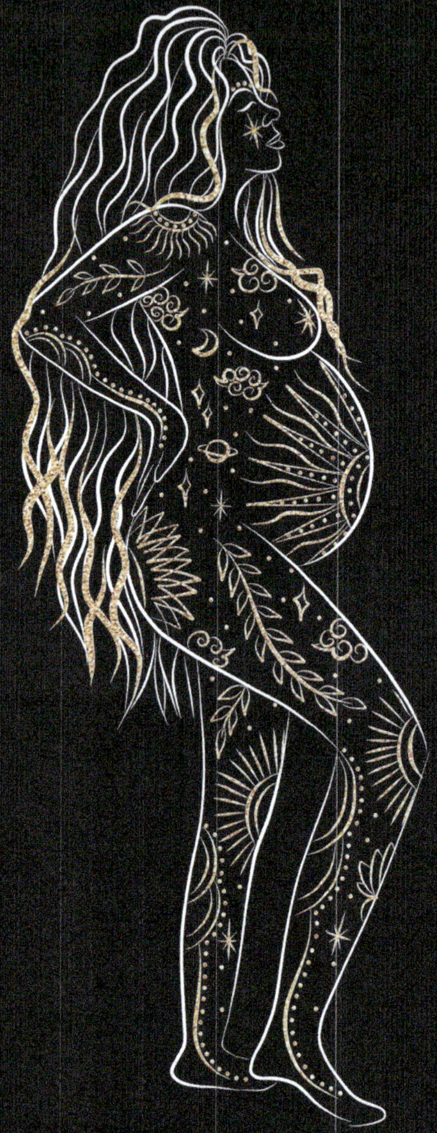

Goddesses can be both fierce and beautiful, just like nature itself.

Nitin Namdeo

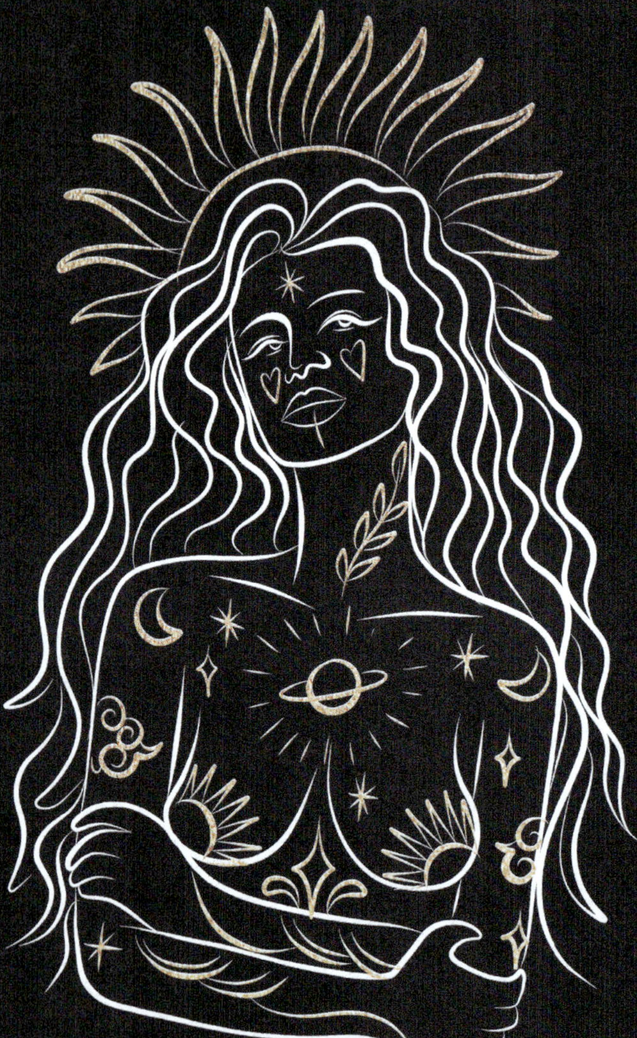

Inside every woman there is a Goddess.
Do not mistake the exterior for the interior.

Jennifer Beals

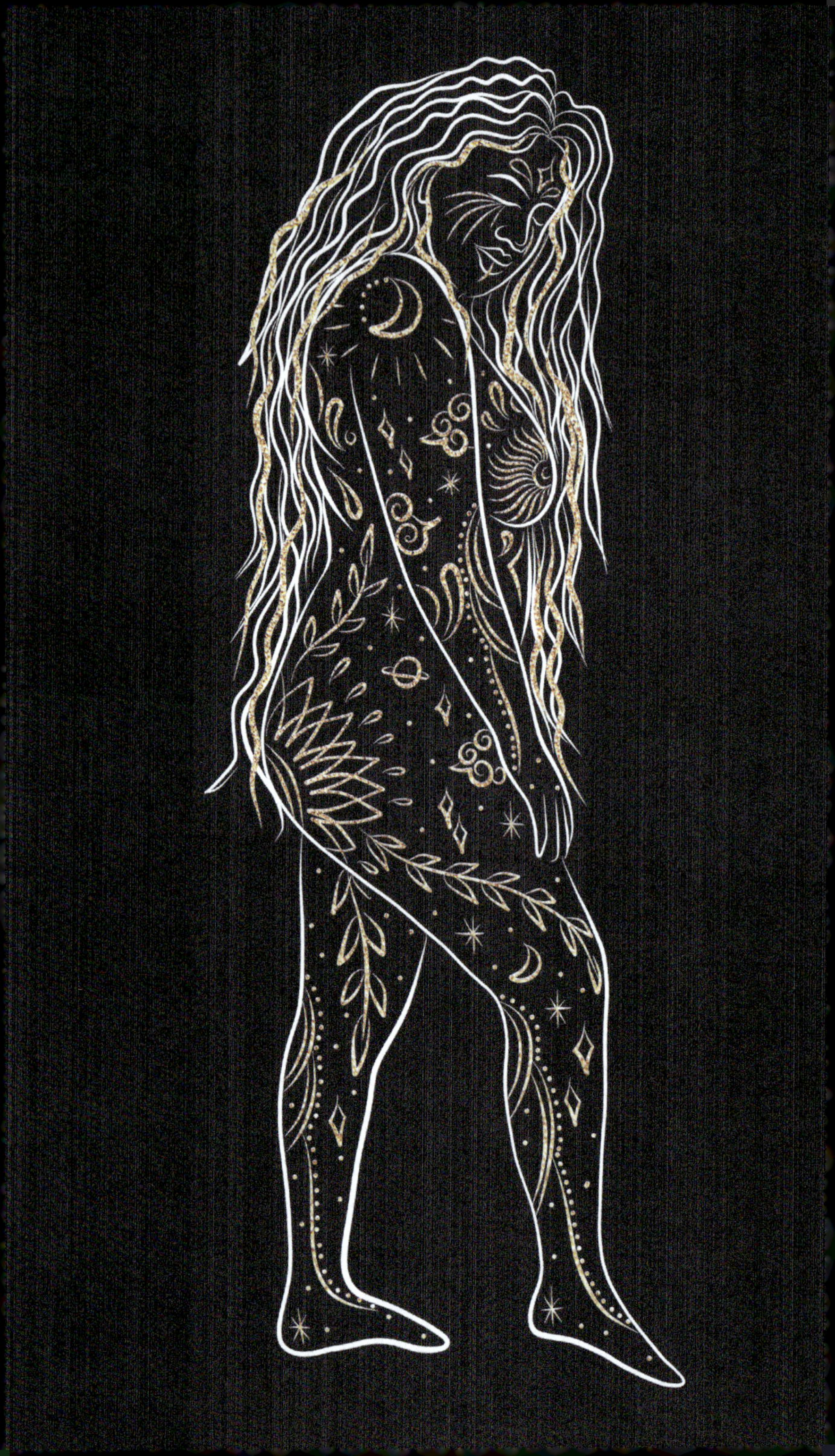

The Goddess is not just the female version of God. She represents a different concept.

Merlin Stone

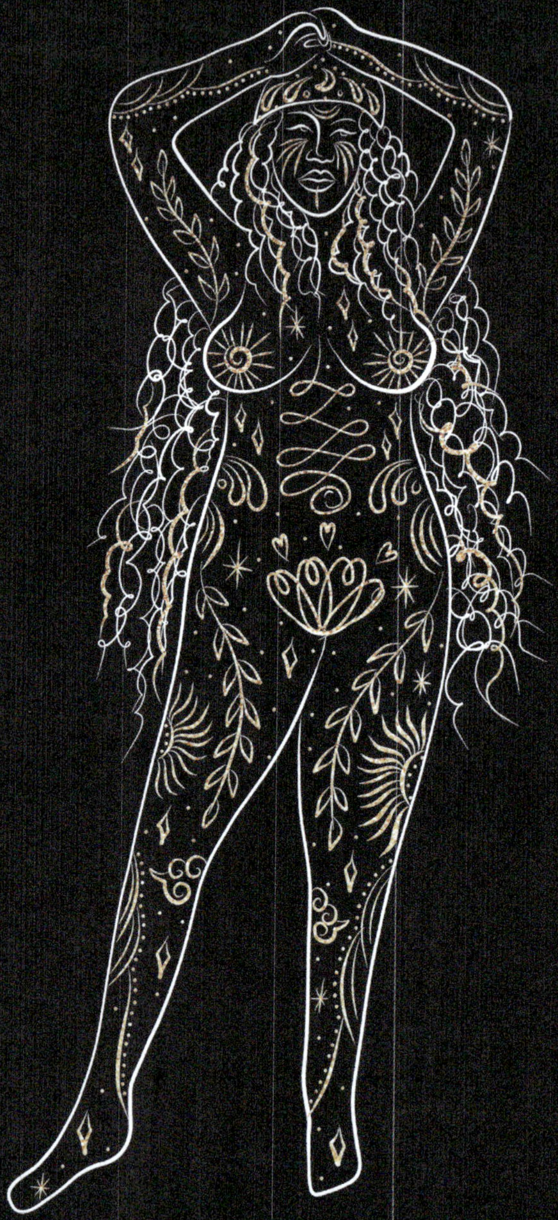

Philosophy is a goddess, whose head indeed is in heaven, but whose feet are upon earth; she attempts more than she accomplishes, and promises more than she performs.

Charles Caleb Colton

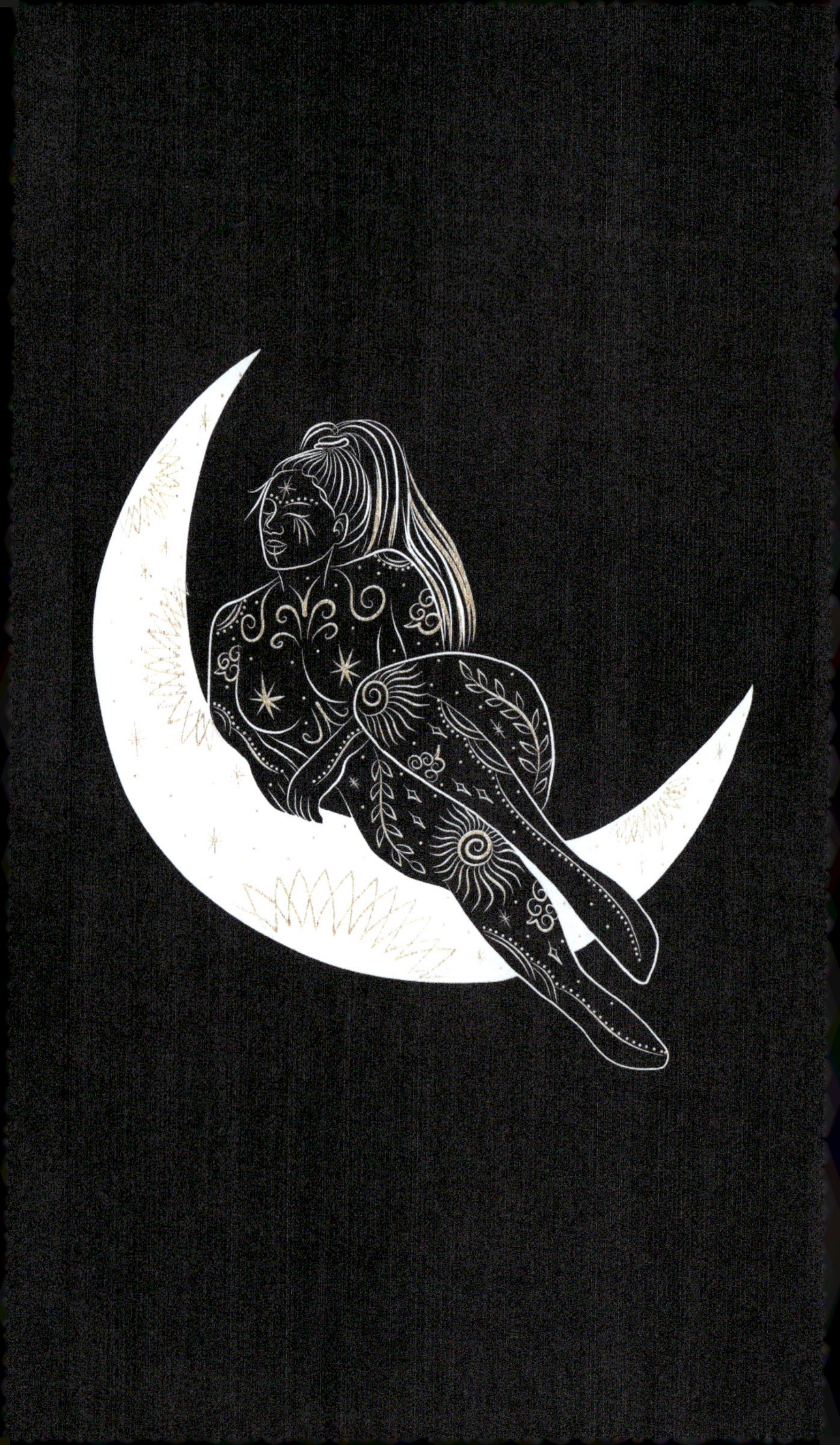

Goddesses never die. They slip in and out of the world's cities, in and out of our dreams, century after century, answering to different names, dressed differently, perhaps even disguised, perhaps idle and unemployed, their official altars abandoned, their temples feared or simply forgotten.

Phyllis Chesler

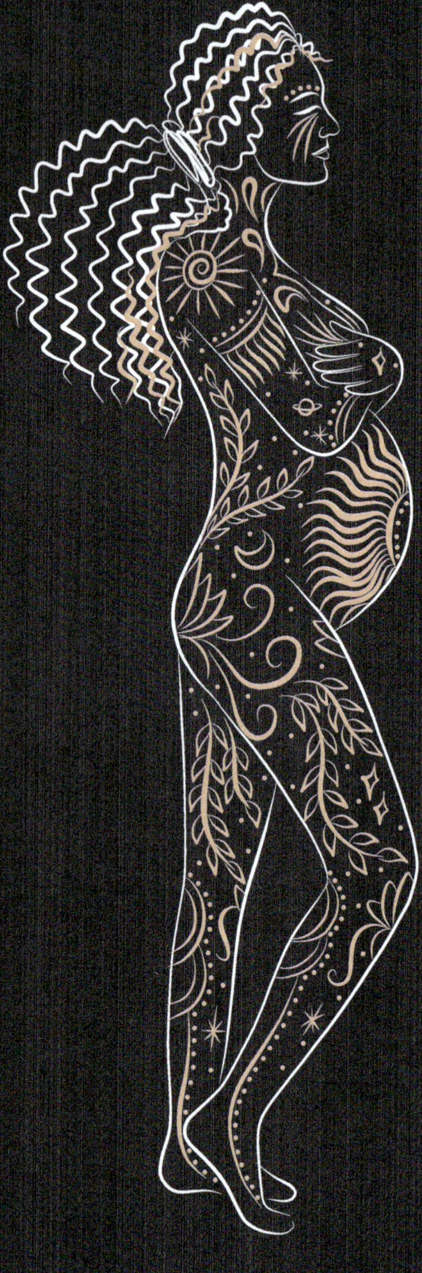

Mermaids don't lose sleep over the opinion of shrimp.

Mermaid, Peter Pan

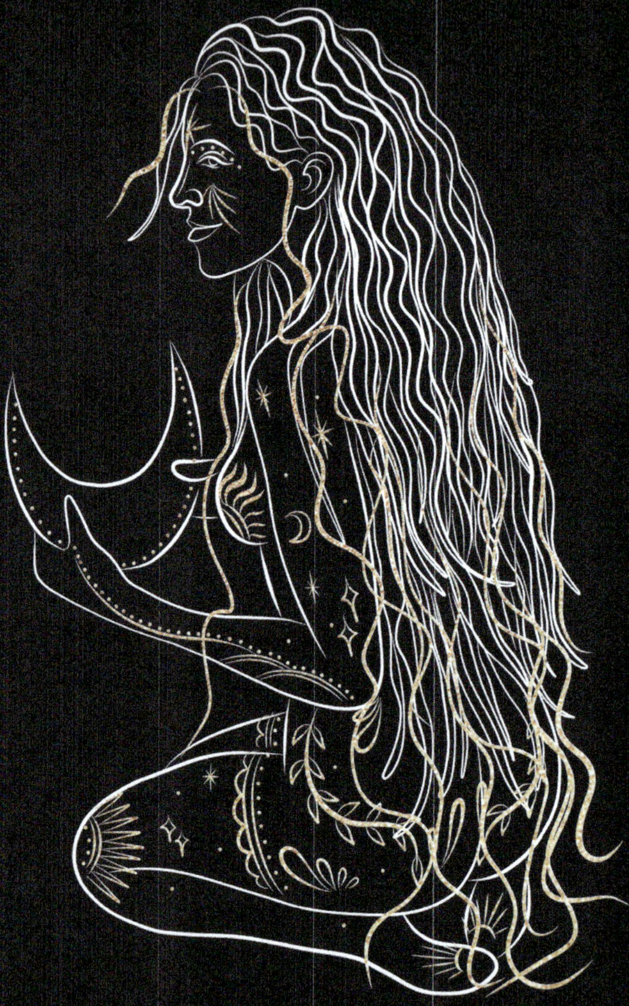

The world needs strong women. Women who will lift and build others, who will love and be loved, women who live bravely, both tender and fierce, women of indomitable will.

Amy Tenney

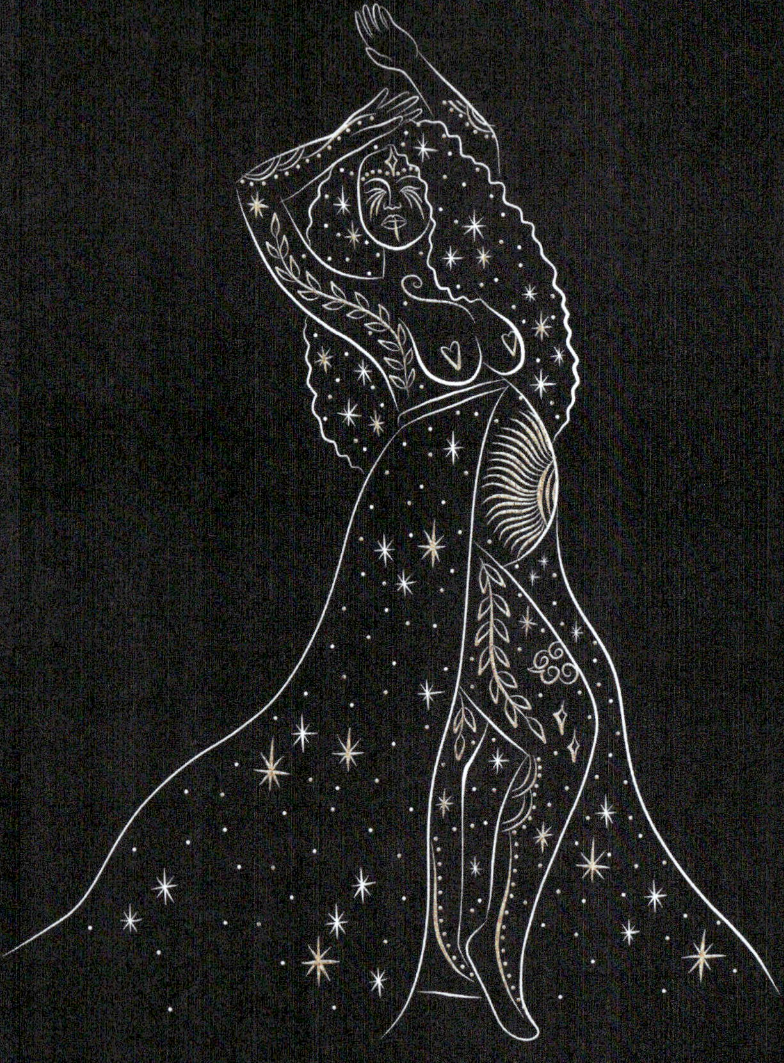

A woman is the full circle. Within her is the power to create, nurture and transform.

Diane Mariechild

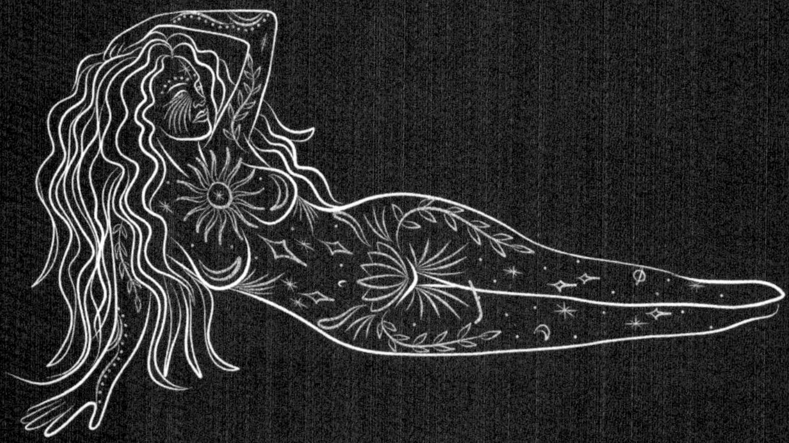

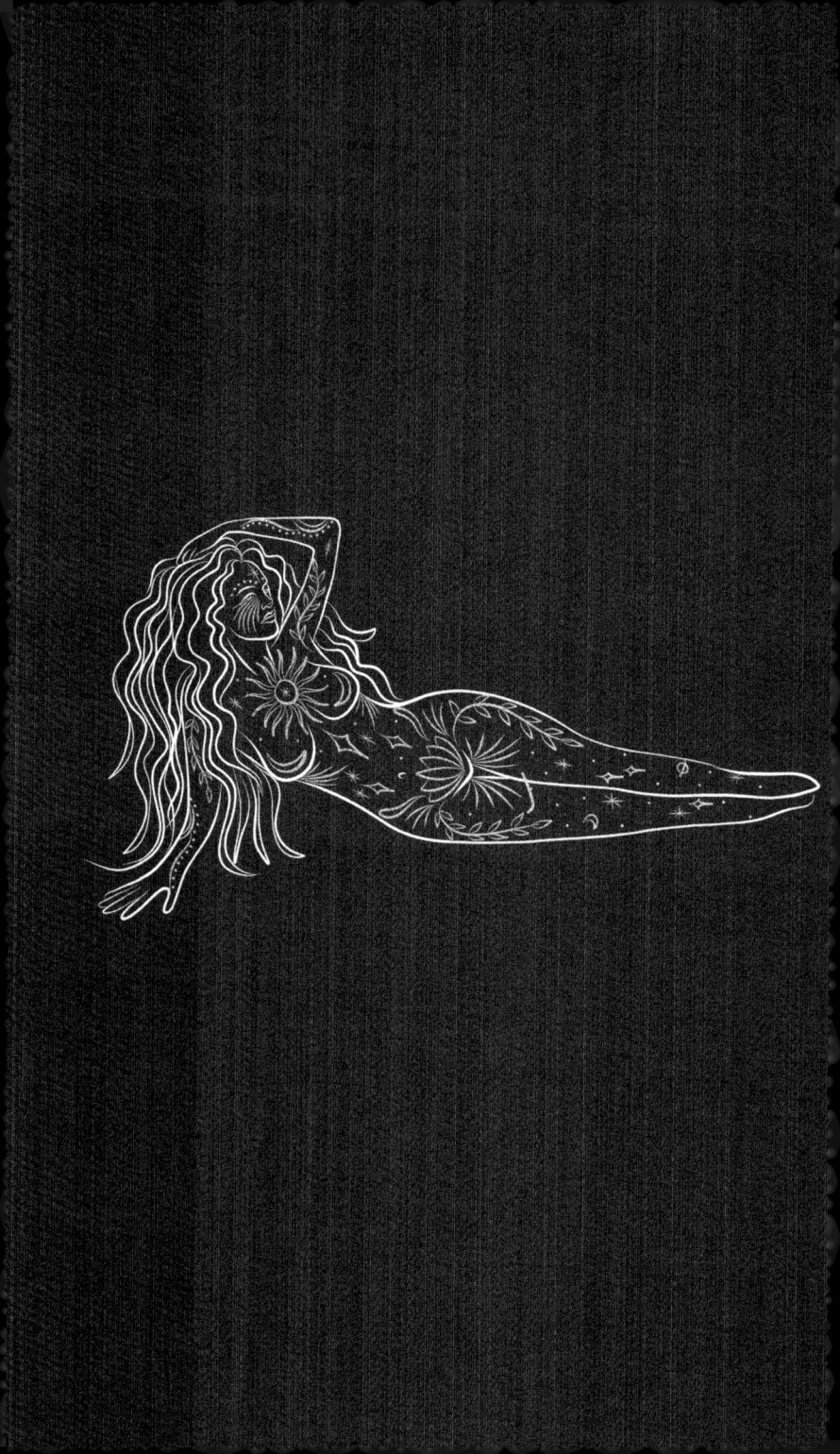

A strong woman is a woman determined to do something others are determined not be done.

Marge Piercy

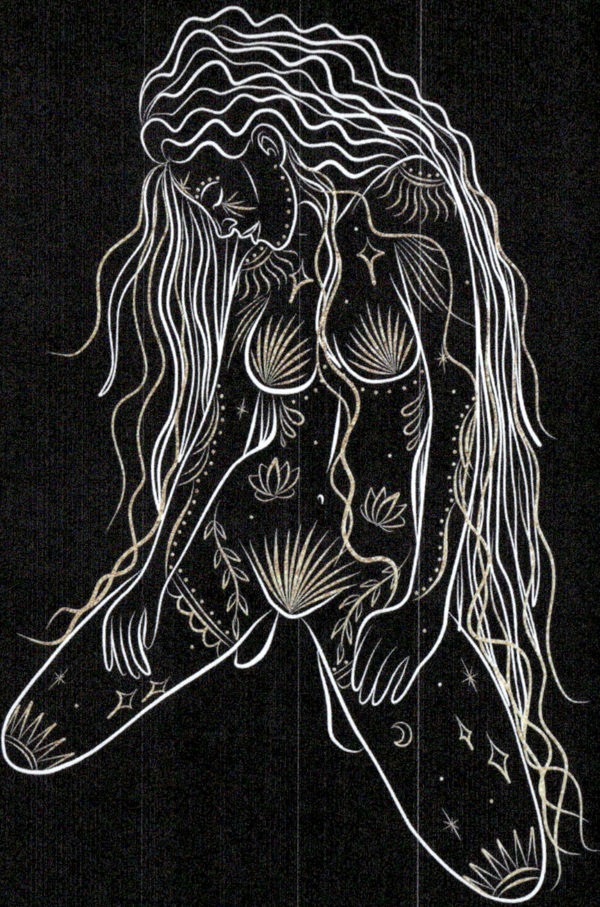

She is a wild, tangled forest with temples and treasures concealed within.

John Mark Green

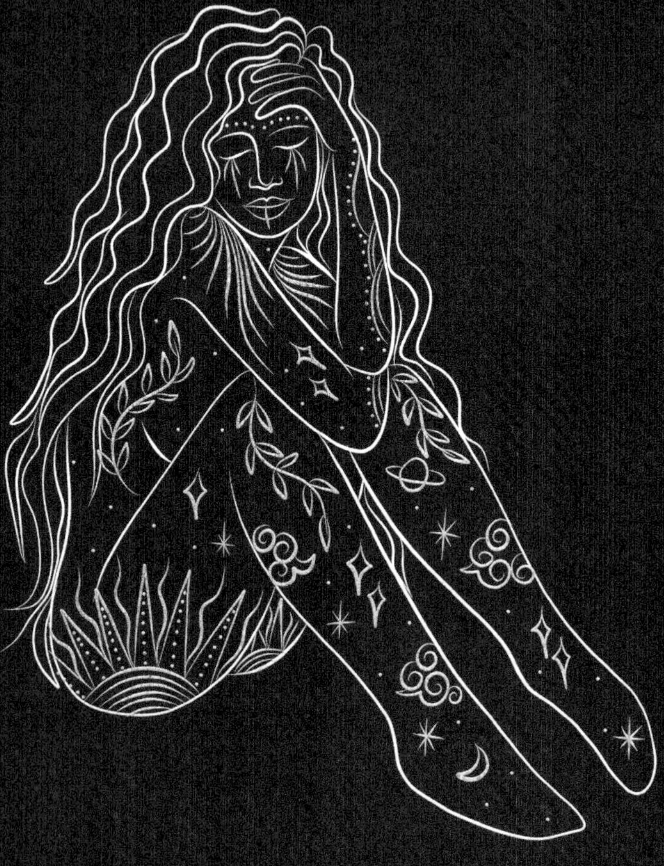

if there is a God, God is a woman.

Erin O'Riordan

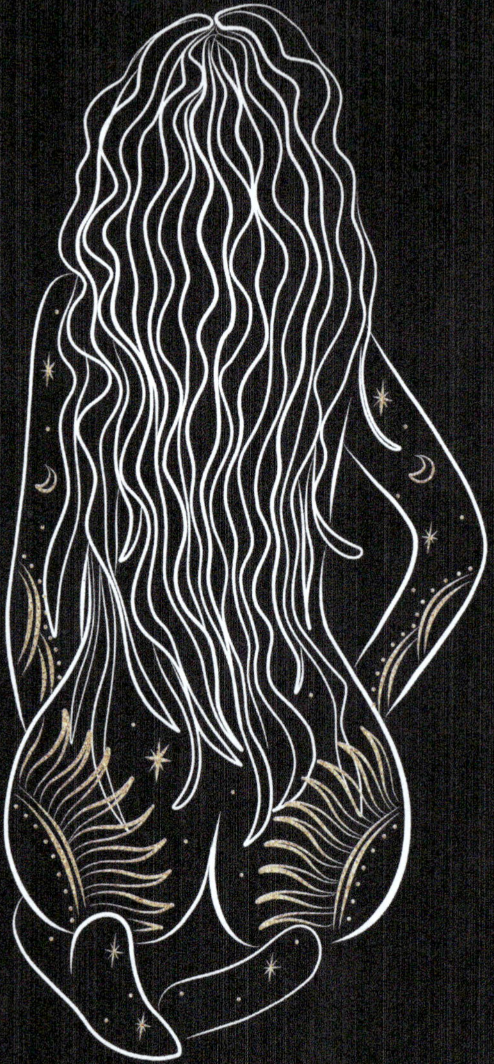

In celebrating the Divine feminine, you will know the true beauty of life.

Sadhguru

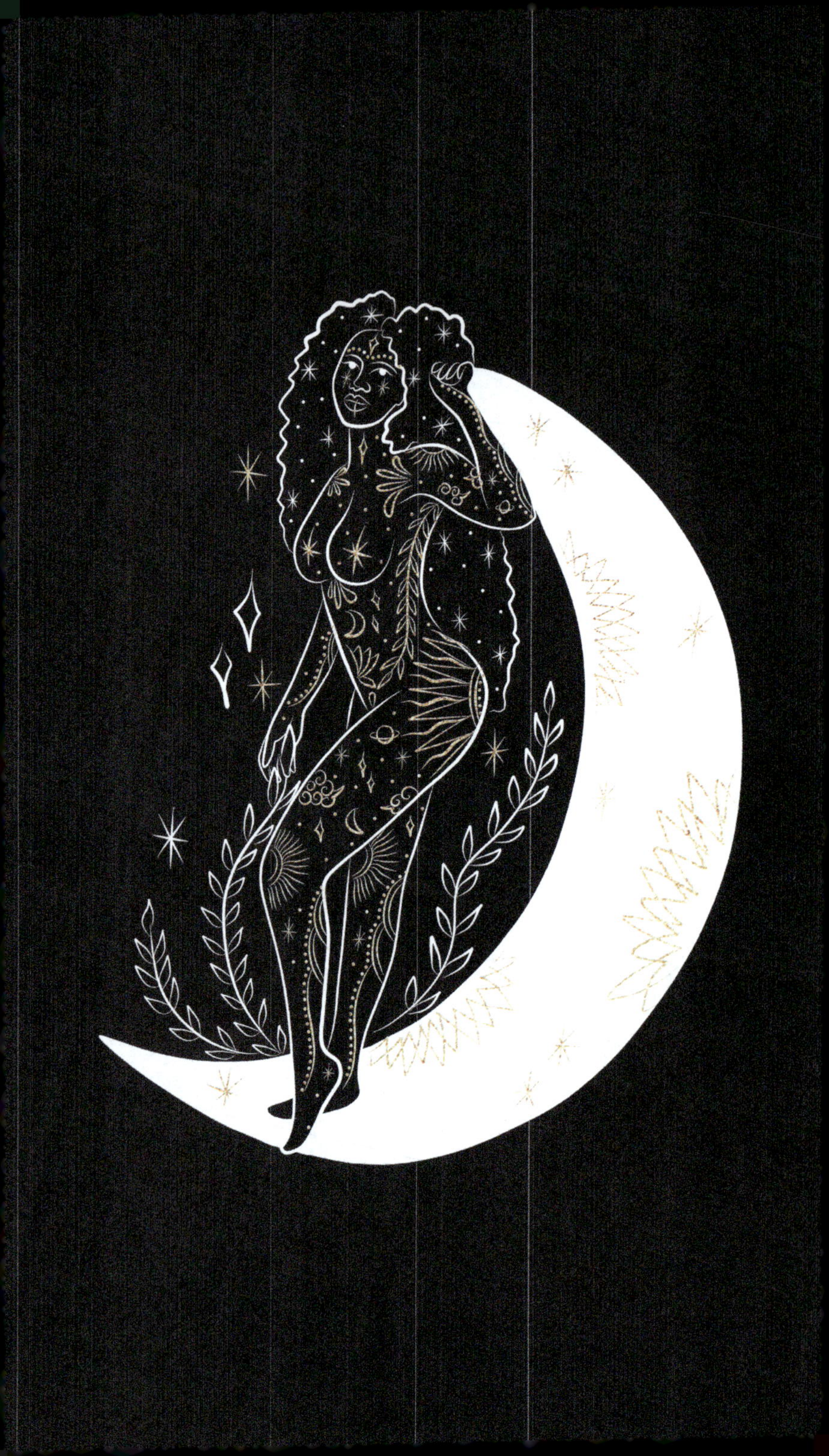

When you feel you are being moved by the creative spirit, you are in fact being moved by the divine feminine.

Teri Degler

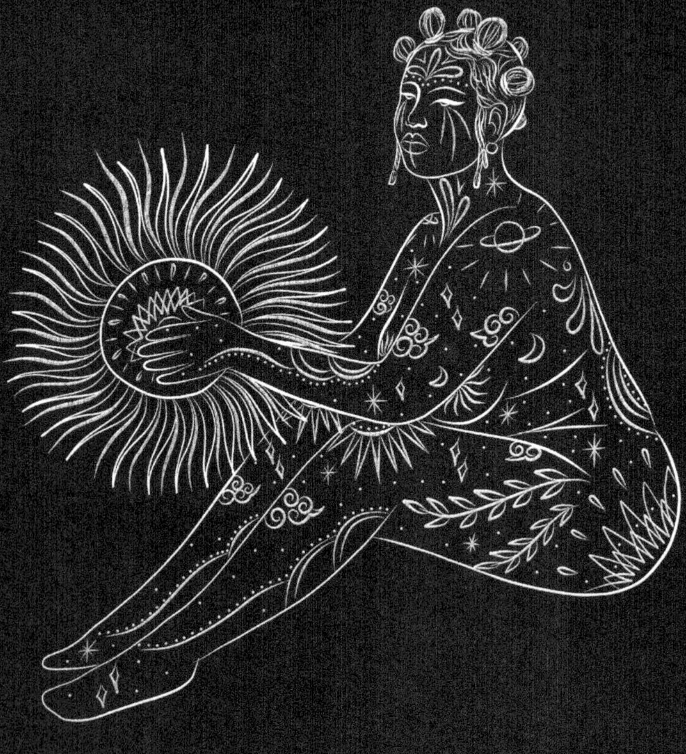

She unleashed her inner goddess and became the woman her soul knew she could be.

Michelle Schafer

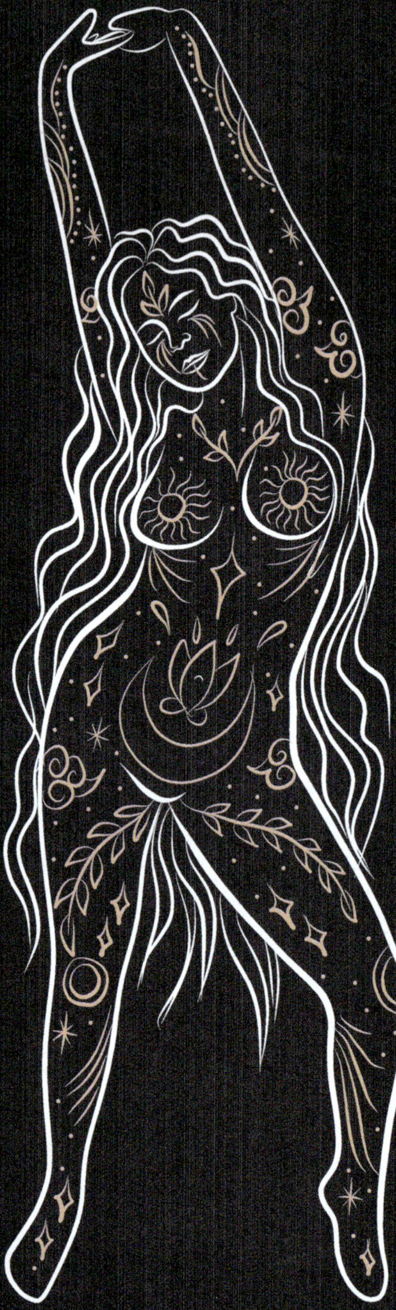

The feminine are the portals to forgotten knowledge. To ancient energy, medicine, creation and recalibrating the soul back to it's original source self. Before being human got in the way.

Nikki Rowe

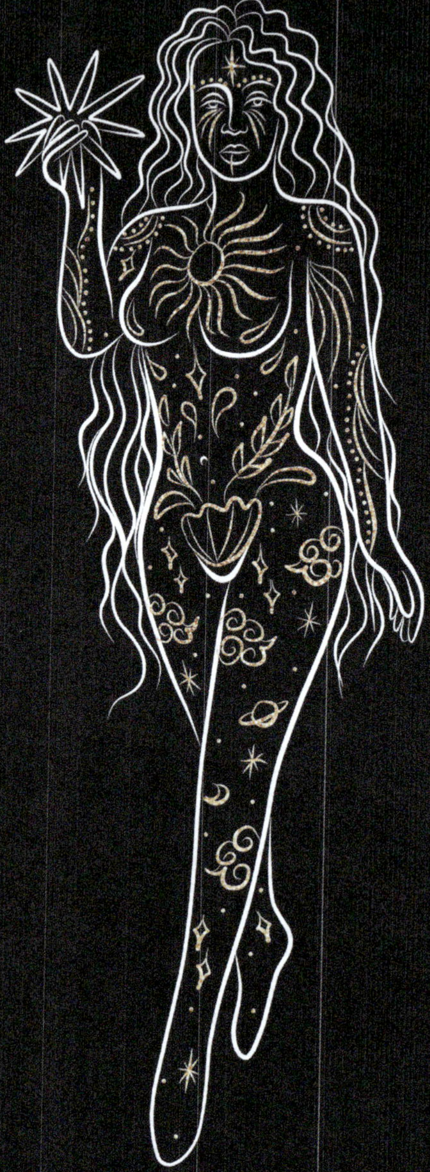

You are a wild priestess with a courageous divine feminine heart and the spirit of wise ancients within.
Never let them tame you.
Stay free.

Ara

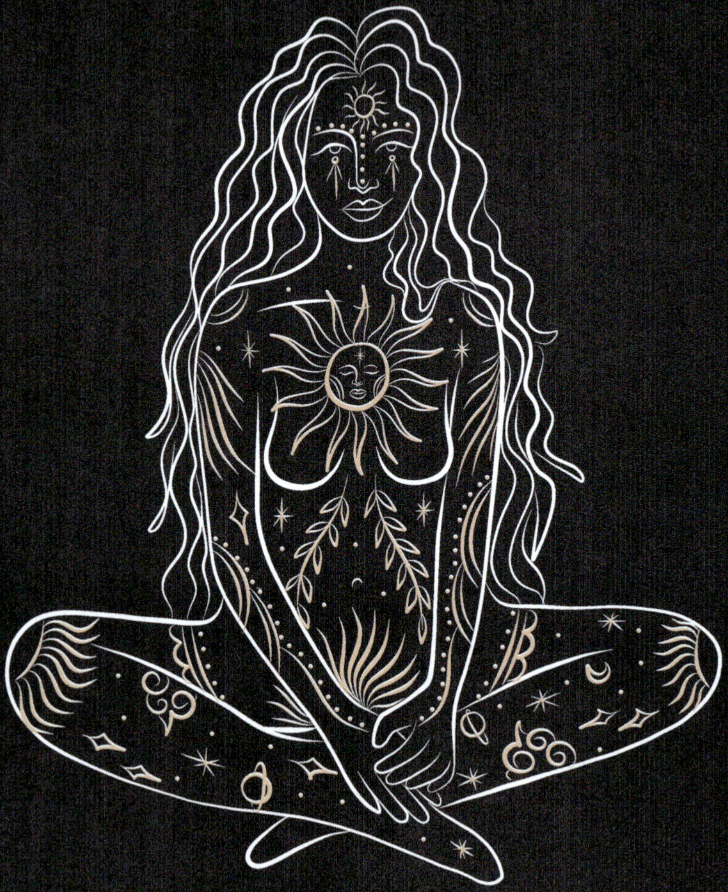

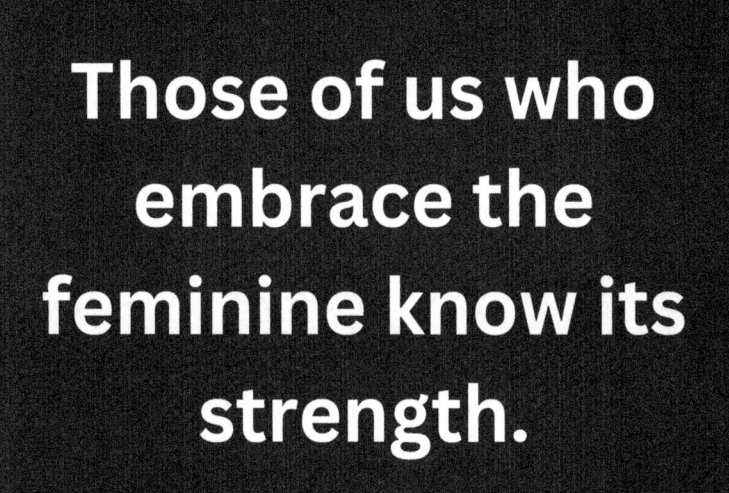

Those of us who embrace the feminine know its strength.

Betty Cornwell

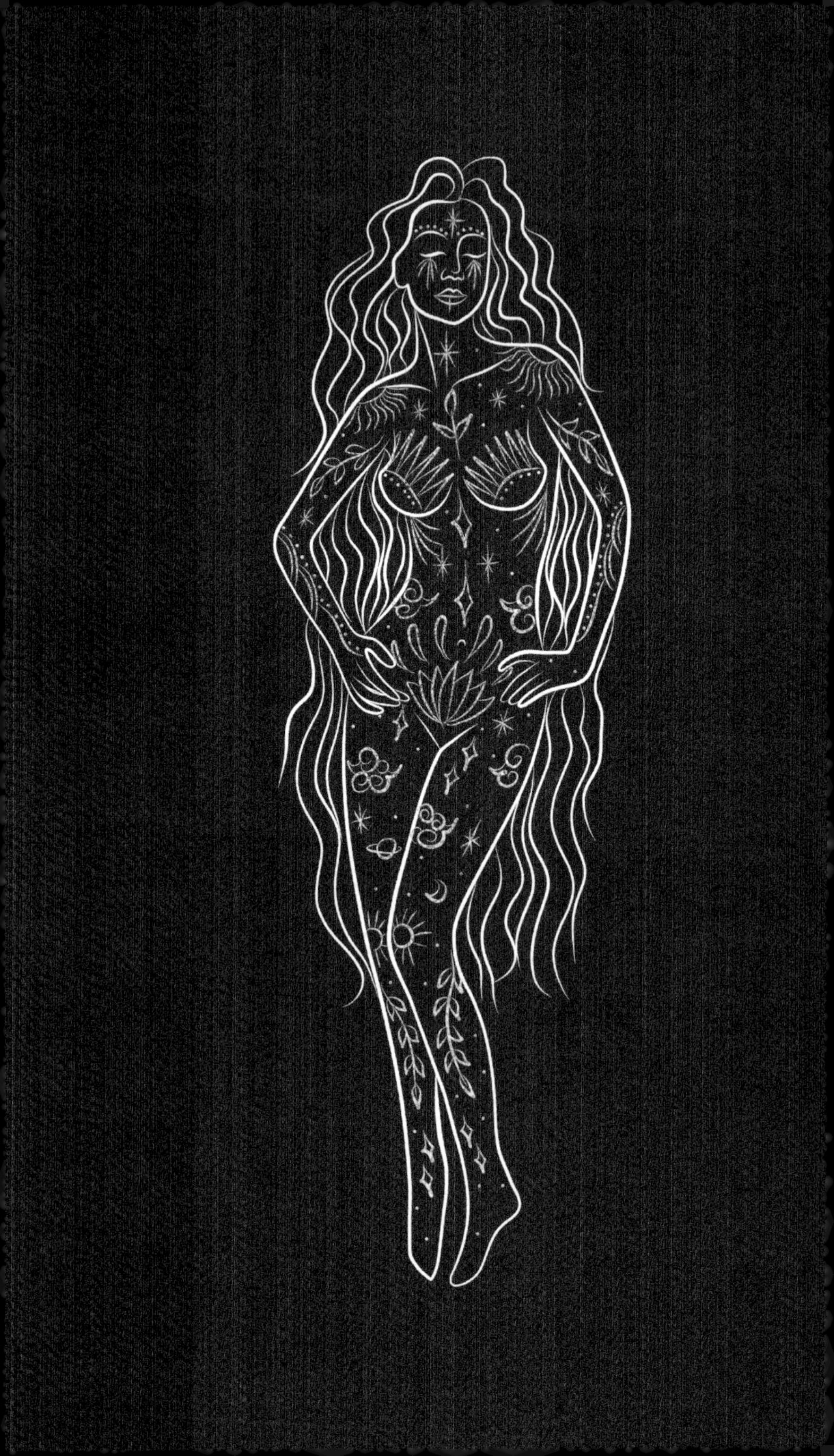

All women are goddesses, and it's just a matter of letting that goddess-power shine – and if you don't try to be the biggest and baddest damn goddess you can be, you are selling yourself short.

Kimora Lee Simmons

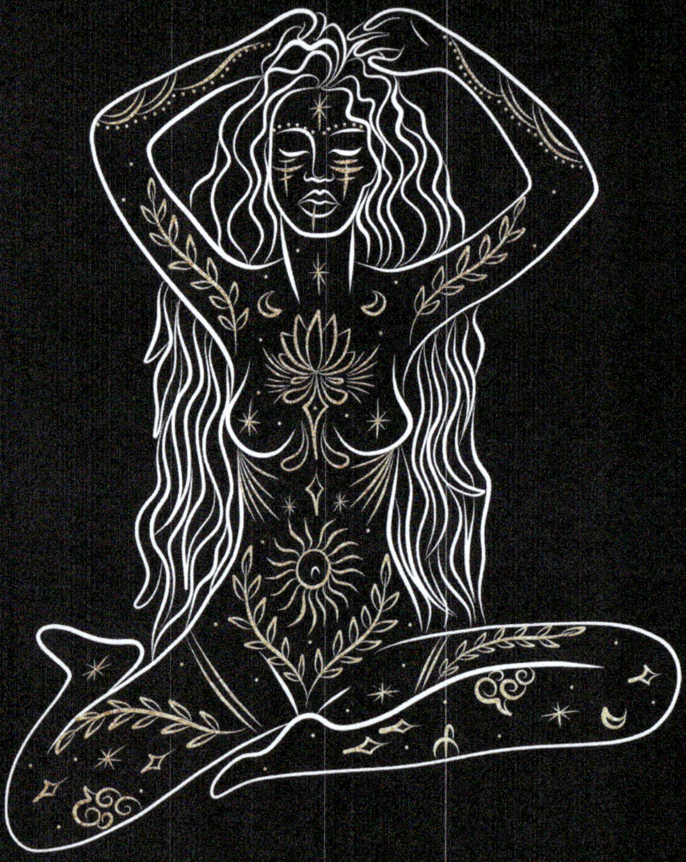

Find the goddess inside yourself instead of looking for the god in someone else.

Francesca Lia Block

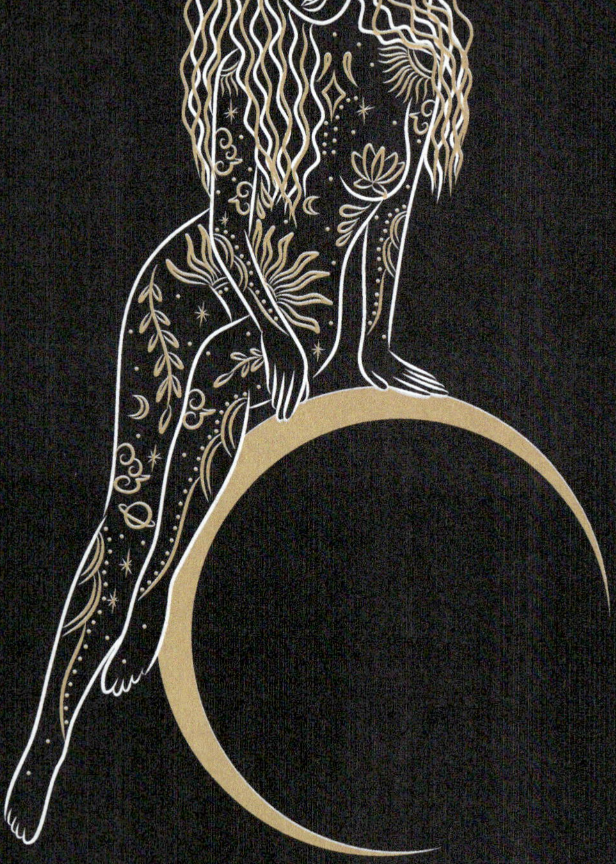

Goddesses have their own way of seeing things. They see the beauty in the ordinary and sparkle in the darkness.

Nitin Namdeo

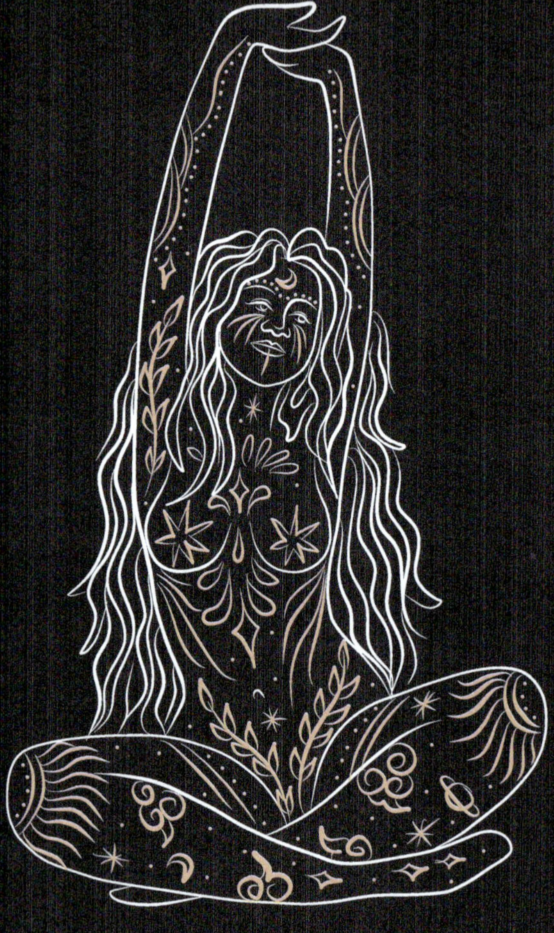

> Goddess is the deep Source of creating integrity and the Self-affirming be-ing of women.
>
> Mary Daly

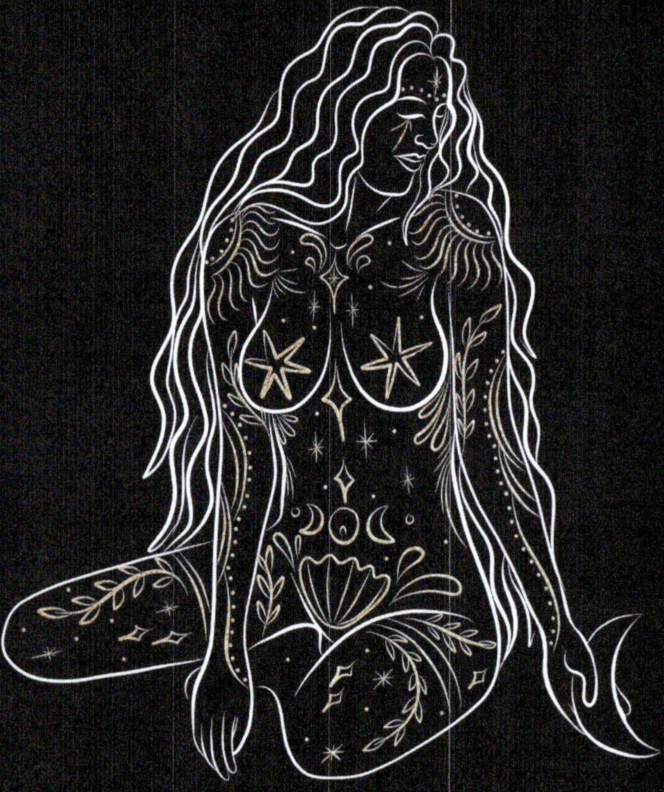

A goddess is a woman who emerges from deep within herself and towers, unafraid.

Victoria Moran

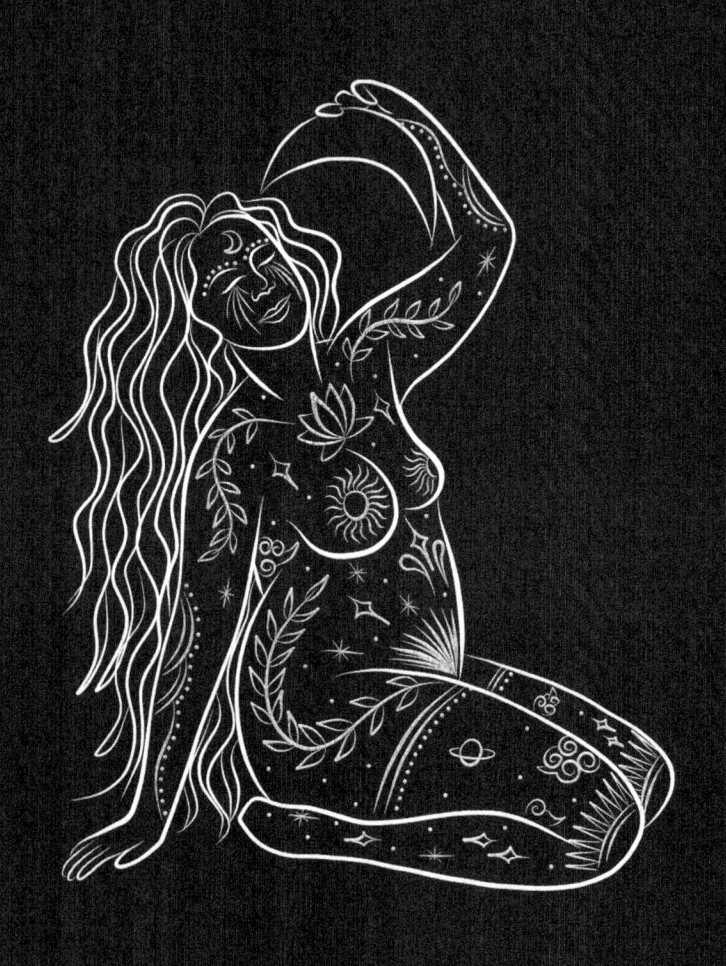

Not everyone will notice the way you shine, but you will shine all the same in beautiful, natural ways.

Morgan Harper Nichols

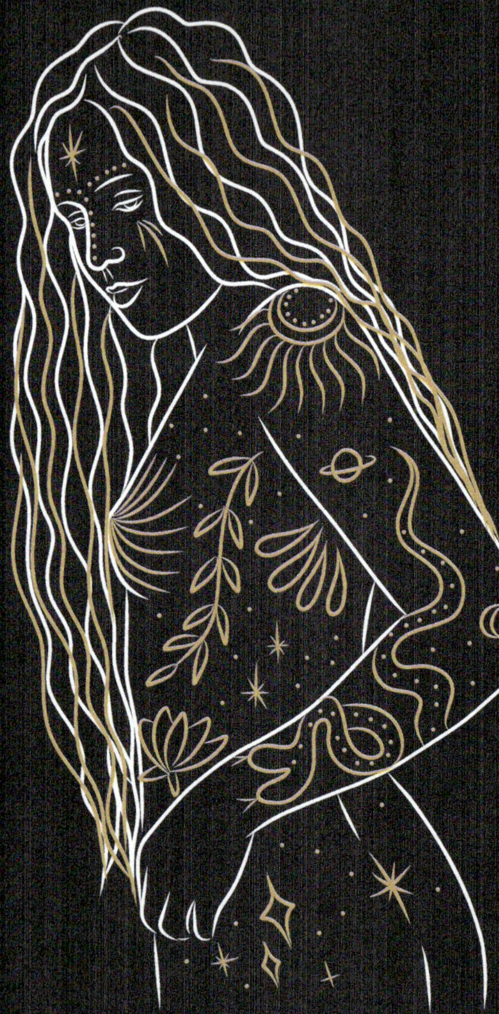

> I am not eccentric. It's just that I am more alive than most people. I am an unpopular electric eel set in a pond of catfish.
>
> — Edith Sitwell

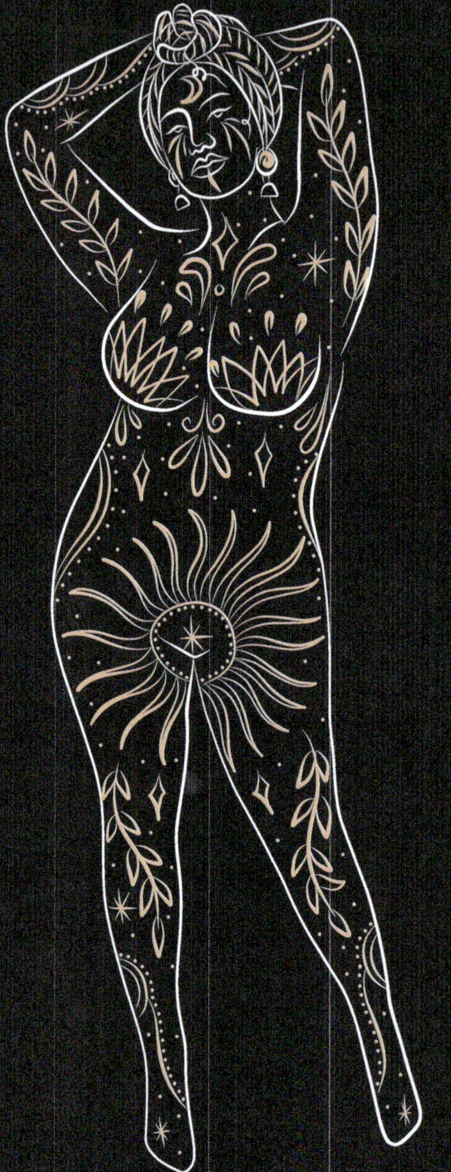

One woman is a tiny divine spark in a timeless sisterhood tapestry collective; All of us are Wild Women.

Jan Porter

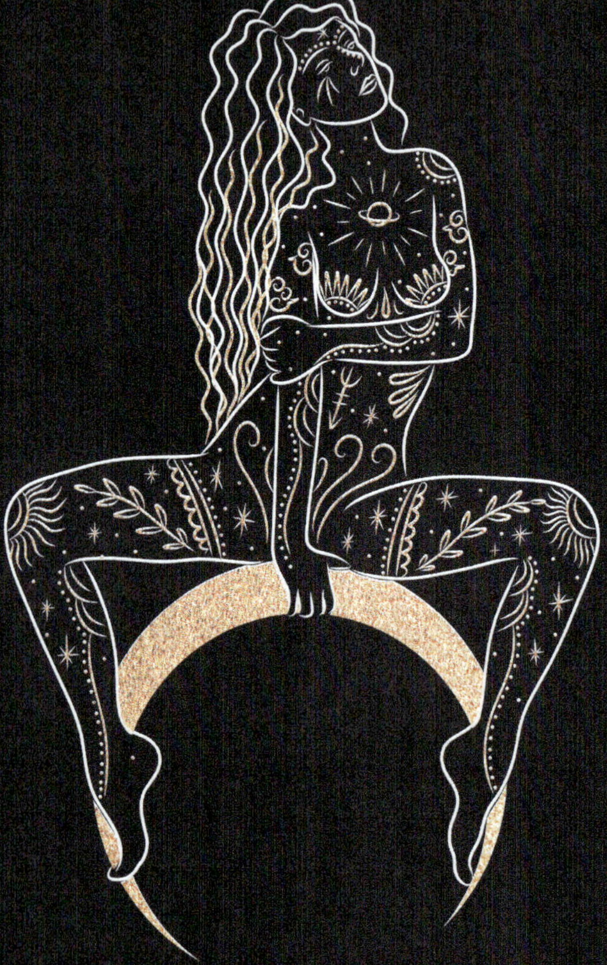

Never filter your soul to suit a mould.

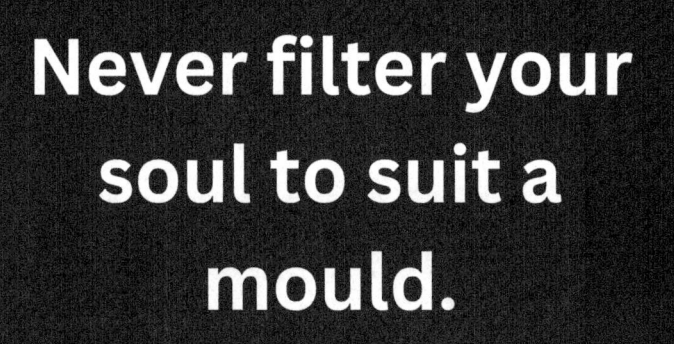

Nikki Rowe

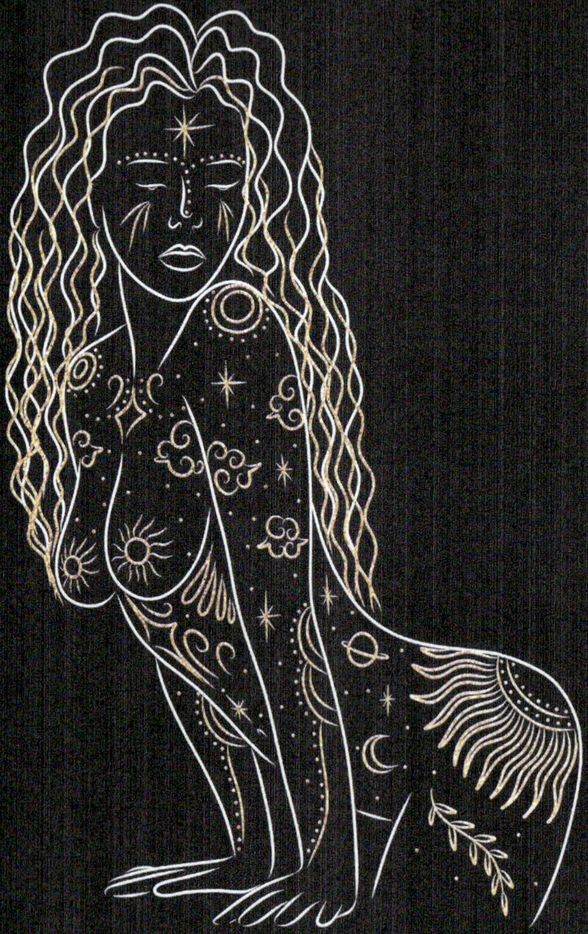

Life is not about waiting for the storms to pass. It's about learning how to dance in the rain.

Vivian Greene

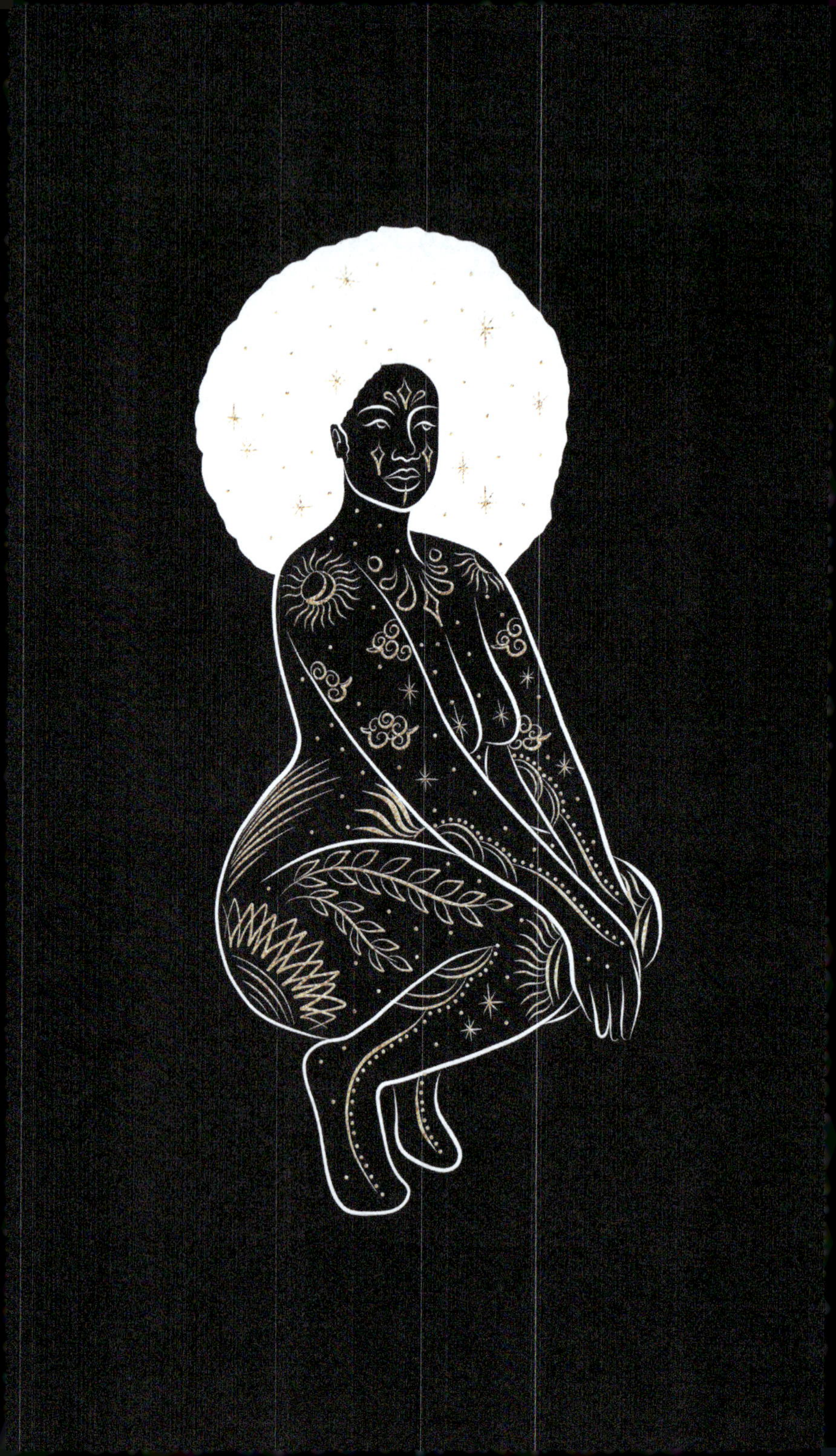

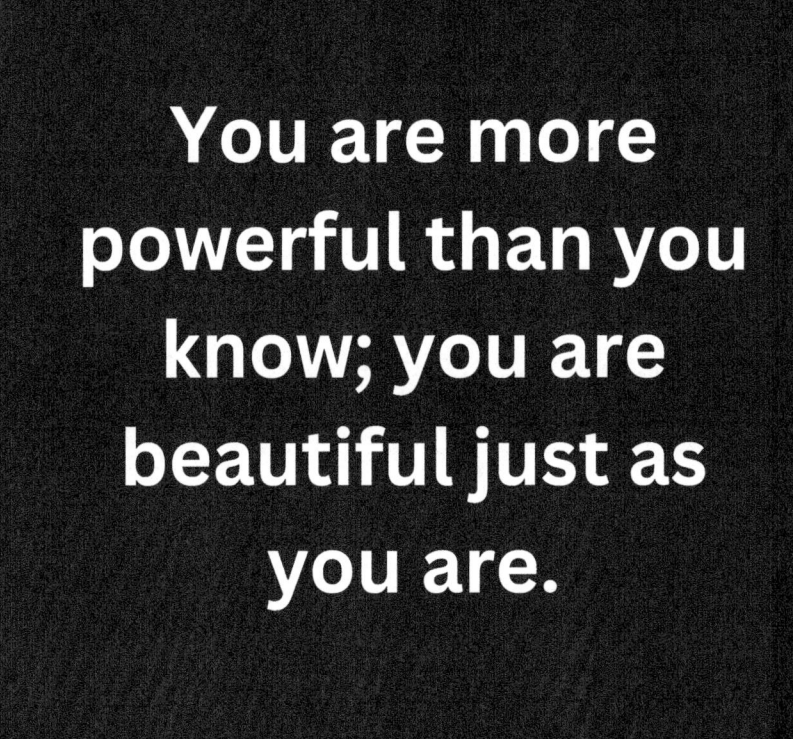

You are more powerful than you know; you are beautiful just as you are.

Melissa Etheridge

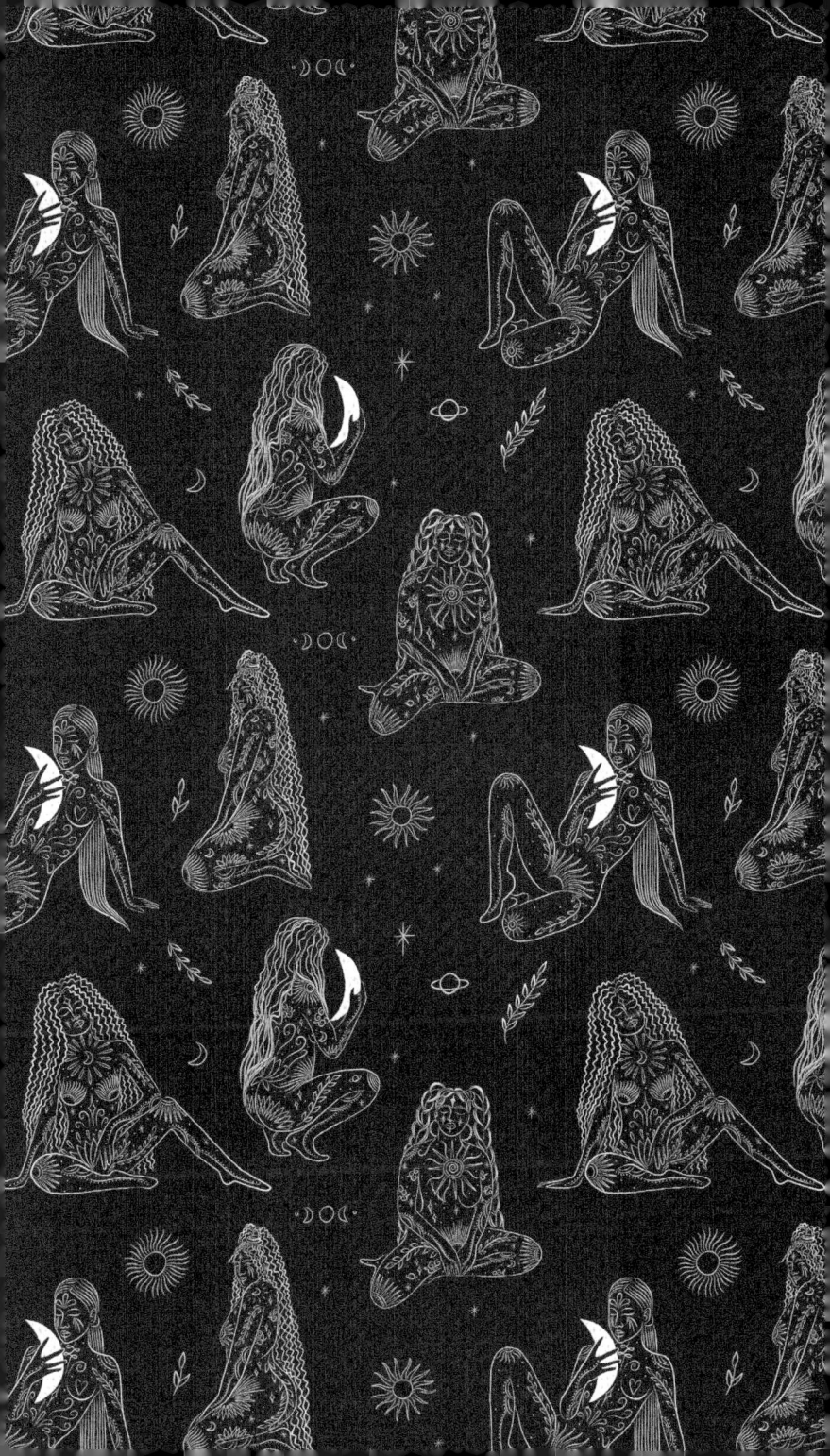